ALSO BY BRIGID PASULKA

A Long, Long Time Ago and Essentially True

The Sun and Other Stars

Brigid Pasulka

Simon & Schuster

New York   London   Toronto   Sydney   New Delhi

90

Simon & Schuster
1230 Avenue of the Americas
New York, NY 10020

First Simon & Schuster hardcover edition February 2014

SIMON & SCHUSTER and colophon are registered trademarks of Simon & Schuster, Inc.

For information about special discounts for bulk purchases, please contact Simon & Schuster Special Sales at 1-866-506-1949 or business@simonandschuster.com.

The Simon & Schuster Speakers Bureau can bring authors to your live event. For more information or to book an event, contact the Simon & Schuster Speakers Bureau at 1-866-248-3049 or visit our website at www.simonspeakers.com.

Interior designed by Ruth Lee-Mui
Endpapers drawn by Charlene Floreani

Manufactured in the United States of America

10   9   8   7   6   5   4   3   2   1

Library of Congress Cataloging-in-Publication Data

Pasulka, Brigid.
The sun and other stars / Brigid Pasulka.
p. cm.
1. Self-realization—Fiction. 2. Loss (Psychology)—Fiction. 3. Italy—Fiction.
4. Soccer stories. I. Title.
PS3616.A866S86 2013
813'.6—dc23   2012030403

ISBN 978-1-4516-6711-0
ISBN 978-1-4516-6713-4 (ebook)

For Kang and Kodos

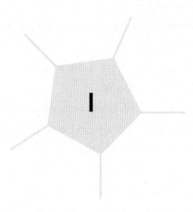

I

*I*n the beginning, God created the Azzurri and the Earth.

Or at least that's how Papà used to start the story.

1982. The genesis of all order in the universe, the Alpha with no Omega in sight, the Tigris-and-Euphrates, the Watson-come-here of all years.

Anno Domination.

And if you're sitting there scratching your head, trying to figure out what the cazzo happened in 1982, you must've been either living under a rock or in America—one and the same when it comes to calcio. And that would not be calcio to you, or even football, but "soccer," or as most people here say it when they're trying to speak English, SO-chair, with a little roll on the *r* and a couple of kilograms of reverence in their voices.

Don't get me wrong. I've got nothing against people who live under rocks, play sports where the clock stops, or otherwise escape, deny, and ignore reality. Believe me, if I could, I'd hide myself under a nice, big rock by the sea, order in a week's worth of pizza, and shut off my phone. But that is impossibile here, or in-cazz-ibile, as my friend Fede likes to say, because the only way he can expand his vocabulary is by wedging vulgar words into it. In-cazz-ibile to escape, deny, or ignore this fottuto town, this attractive, charming, concentric circle of hell smack in the middle of Liguria, which has conspired to peck at me with a thousand idiotic conversations a day and bury me one obligation at a time.

But. Before the victory of entropy, before the descent into hell, before the Brazilians dominated every calcio field whether it was theirs or not, before the French pilfered the 1998 World Cup one suspicious call at a time, before the *shame* of the 2000 Euro Championships (this is still Papà telling the story), there was 1982—a small, glimmering miracle of a year that flared like a match before burning the cazzo out of the fingers that held it. Because not only did the Azzurri win the World Cup that year, the planets also aligned to allow a college art history major from California to meet a butcher's son from Liguria in the nosebleed seats of Estadio Balaídos in Vigo, Spain, during the first round, a union sanctioned by FIFA and witnessed and consecrated by tens of thousands of half-sober fans.

And this is where Mamma used to interrupt Papà and break into the story, at the point when she found herself sitting in the row right behind Papà and his friends. Mamma was with some Scottish guys who were staying at the same hostel as she was, and one of them was trying to hit on her. This, of course, annoyed Papà to no end because for Papà, every match is sacred, but talking while the great Dino Zoff was wiping his nose, much less defending against a corner kick, was the equivalent of telling a joke during the consecration. So as much as he tried to block it out, by the second half, the constant flirting, even though it was going on in English— especially because it was going on in English—had really started to squeeze his coils. If they'd been Italian, there would've been a simple "Non rompere le palle, tu aborto di puttana," accompanied by the appropriate hand gestures, and there may have been some additional shouting and mumbling under the breath, but the matter would have been more or less closed. In this case, however, Papà had to think of the correct insult in English, which up to that point he'd passed in school only thanks to his best friend, Silvio, and the Hand of God (which, for those of you who call it soccer and not calcio, is a sharp allusion to an Argentinean soccer player named Maradona that I will not go into right now). Suffice it to say that Papà's English was terrible, and every time they told us the story, I could practically hear the scolding voice of Charon, the English and classics professor for generations of San Benedettons, and the smack of his ruler ringing in my head.

"And what are you going to do when you need to speak English someday and Silvio is not there to help you?" Charon would always ask Papà.

Which was a ridiculous question because besides Papà's honeymoon, he and Silvio have never passed a day of their lives when they didn't see each other. And that day at Estadio Balaídos, Silvio was in fact sitting right next to Papà, and Papà consulted with him several times before finally turning around and saying to the Scottish guy, "Do not take my balls with your chat, you abortion of prostitute."

"Break!" Silvio hissed.

"What?"

"Do not *break* my balls."

"Do not break my balls with your chat, you abortion of prostitute," Papà repeated to the Scottish guy, but with less conviction than the first time because by then, he'd gotten a glimpse of Mamma, tanned and smiling and twenty years old, the lines at the corners of her eyes swooping skyward from years of squinting into the California sun. Which is how I like to think of her now.

Anyway, Mamma, the Scottish guys, and Papà's friends immediately started laughing at Papà's English, and nearly set off an international incident when they were shushed by the Spaniards in the row in front of them, who were shushed by the Peruvians in front of them, who were shushed by the Cameroonese or Cameroonians or whatever in front of them, who were shushed by the Poles in front of them. In the end, Papà's entire section was so distracted, they ended up missing the Azzurri's goal completely, and the Italian fans had no choice but to blame themselves for lack of focus when the Cameroonians scored the equalizer.

You'd think this would squeeze Papà's coils even more. But after that first glimpse of Mamma, Papà—to everyone's great surprise—ceased to care about the match, the Scottish guys, Dino Zoff, and everyone else in the world. Instead, he pushed Silvio to negotiate a truce between the two rows and a celebratory drink after the match, and he spent the rest of the evening trying to impress Mamma with his English and his ability to hold his liquor, only to be carried back to the beach at midnight, blathering past participles.

Drink. Drank. Drunk.

When he woke up the next morning, Papà thought he would never see Mamma again, but when he turned out his pockets, he found a small scrap of a receipt with the name of her hostel scribbled on it. He and Silvio spent hours walking up and down the streets of Vigo looking for it, and more hours waiting for her to come back that night. But it was worth it, because Silvio somehow helped Papà convince Mamma to spend the rest of the week camping out on the beach with them, cooking meals over an open fire and hitching to Barcelona and Madrid once the matches moved there.

How they managed to communicate at first is one of the divine mysteries of the universe. Silvio says their conversations sounded like the traffic circles in Naples, with cheating-schoolboy English, phrasebook Italian, California Spanish, and bad charades all weaving and blaring and cutting each other off. When there was a pause, it was almost always punctuated by "Te lo spiegherò domani," or "I will explain it to you tomorrow." Or next week. Or next month, depending on how complicated the subject was. When Mamma took Papà to see *Guernica*, newly installed at the Prado, and tried to explain Picasso and the fascists, the murder of the innocents, and the splintered planes, it was such a mess, she had to tell him she would explain it to him next year. And by the time Dino Zoff hoisted the cup for the Azzurri, Mamma and Papà knew there *would* be a next year. Because Mamma had indeed taken Papà's palle with her chatting, along with everything else he ever had or wanted.

When Luca and I were very little, we would demand to hear The Story of 1982 at least once a week instead of Pinocchio or Chupacabra or old Brady Bunch episodes. If we pressed them, they would keep going and tell us about the winter after that, when Mamma quit her college in California and started working as a maid in a ski lodge in Piedmont, and Papà would visit her on her day off every week using various, borrowed rides: the shop Ape one week, Silvio's Turbo Spyder or Nonno's 2CV the next. One week,

Papà could only arrange a Vespa, and he made it as far as Cortemilia before a sympathetic truck driver took pity on his 150cc engine trying to buzz its way up the mountains, loaded the Vespa and Papà into his truck, and drove them the rest of the way.

When we didn't have school the next day, we could convince them to tell us about the following spring, when Papà managed to find Mamma a job in the hills above San Benedetto, preparing vacation homes for absent Germans, and how, by Christmas, she was already taping paper snowflakes to the window of the shop, married to Papà, estranged from her parents, and pregnant with Luca and me.

Mamma especially loved telling the story, her hands swooping in the air, free like gulls, her homemade bracelets jangling on her tanned wrists. She was like a magpie the way she collected everything in her life on her wrists—a charm bracelet with all of her swim team pins since she was five, an uneven string of shells I made for her in asilo, a length of turquoise fishing net from the beach they camped on in Spain. Mamma was also very good at impersonations, and she would do all the characters in the scene— the Scottish guys and their accents, Papà answering back in English, and Silvio hissing corrections at him.

Papà would interrupt and tell his version, and they would laugh and talk over each other, weaving the story together with the language they had created during those first weeks in Spain, the language our friends used to make fun of and Charon had christened "La Lingua Bastarda," but that was only because he was jealous that Luca and I spoke better English than him.

"Better English than *he*." Mamma had a good impersonation of Charon, too, which she would reprise every time he gave it to our nerves at school. "Hhhhhonestly, Etto, a-what are you a-going to do-a when you need to speak-a English e don't-a have your mamma to help-a you?"

And Luca and I would have tears in our eyes we were laughing so hard, Luca's magic calcio feet kicking the table legs, my voice hitting the falsetto octave that is the enemy of every mid-pubescent boy in the world.

"You shouldn't talk about their professors like that, Maddy," Papà would say sternly, the white, untanned lines between his eyebrows disappearing into the creases. "Professors are to be respected."

But Mamma was already bent from laughing and could only manage to wave him away.

That was probably the thing I loved most about Mamma. She didn't live by shoulds and shouldn'ts, and she didn't try to paper over the world with fake rules. No, if there were any rules Mamma lived by, it was the natural order of the universe—food chains and tides, the brushstrokes in paintings, the armature of birds and buildings, and the psychology of why people do what they do. And if there was one single rule she lived by, it was "Puro vivere." Simply, to live. And even that one, she ended up breaking in the end.

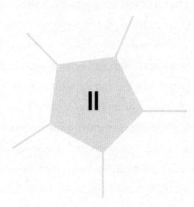

II

Martina keeps the Missing poster of Mamma in the front window of her bar. It's yellowed from the sun and rippled from the damp of the sea, turning Mamma into a shimmering mirage, an angel in a wetsuit, her hair slicked behind her ears, her face backlit and glowing.

Tomorrow it will be exactly a year—two since Luca's accident—and while everyone else has moved on, for me it feels like two dark shadows stalking behind me. Wherever I go, they follow. Whatever I do, they're there. I can't hide from them or outrun them. It's only when I flick my head to have a good look that they disappear, like someone playing a trick.

"You're late," Mino growls as soon as I open the door to Martina's. He's hovering in his usual spot, keeping track of everyone who comes and goes. "It's almost the half."

"Ciao, Mino."

"Your degenerate friends are standing over there in front of the windows."

"Thanks."

I slip in next to Fede and try to follow the ball on the flat-screen.

"Ehi. About time, Etto," Fede says. He puts me in a headlock and gives my hair a rub, his eyes still riveted to the screen.

The bar is filled with smoke, noise, hot air, and the stink of humanity, everyone oriented around the flat-screen like zombie yogis doing a sun salutation. Sky Sport, the true magnetic north. Calcio, the one true religion. At least if you ask anyone else in this country. If you ask me, it's Kabuki for Europeans. One big, six-continent, multi-billion-euro charade, all so people can pretend the reason their lives are shit is because someone won a match or didn't. It's even worse here than in other places. In the big cities, at least people actually have lives between the matches, and there are only two teams to root for. In Turin, you are either for Torino or Juventus; in Milan, for Inter or Milan; in Rome, for Roma or Lazio. And depending on your allegiances, once a week you either sip imported beers with your university friends or put on your brass knuckles and your best Mussolini scowl and turn whichever bar into a smoldering wreckage. Maybe even shed some blood depending on who gives the order and how thick their chin is. Anyway, it only lasts a few hours, and you're done for the week.

But here in San Benedetto? The matches are the only thing happening, and thanks to cheap satellite TV, a steady stream of migrants from the south, and our GPS coordinates in the middle of fottuto nowhere, everyone is for a different team: Roma, Lazio, Inter, Milan, Torino, Juve, Genoa, Sampdoria, Fiorentina, Bologna, Bari, Palermo, Napoli, Parma, Udinese, the scarves hanging like a line of dirty laundry across the top shelf behind the bar. All day Saturday and Sunday and sometimes Wednesday, there's a constant babble of matches at Martina's, of coaches giving postgame eulogies, young guys in ten-thousand-euro suits and wet hair droning on about teamwork, and women who could be showgirls straining the buttons of their shirts as they make predictions about the World Cup in Germany next year.

"What's the score?" I ask. Not because I care, but because once in a while you have to fake interest in calcio or risk being called a finocchio. A fairy.

Fede keeps his eyes on the screen, tapping his words out like a telegraph. "One–nothing. Venezia. Yuri Fil. Injured and off. Ankle. Something."

Yuri Fil is Papà's favorite player, a thirty-two-year-old, two-footed

Ukrainian striker who split the first ten years of his career between Kiev, Glasgow, and Tottenham, wherever that is, and who was traded to Genoa only at the beginning of this season. I look over at Papà, who's sitting at the bar between Silvio and Nonno, all three of them looking stricken. Nonno only comes down the hill for the big matches, and this is definitely one of them, the kind they put all the cardiologists on call for. It's the thirty-eighth and final week of the season. All the teams' fates for next year have been sealed except for Genoa. And since Genoa is only a hundred kilometers away, guys like Papà and Silvio and Nonno, the poor saps who grew up without cable channels and twenty-four-hour calcio coverage, the ones who were born here, who will die here, who will come back and haunt the place, they are all for Genoa—the Griffins—who have not had a prayer of moving up to Serie A in at least a decade.

Until tonight.

If only they can win this one match.

The clock ticks toward the half, Genoa still losing, Yuri Fil out for good. On the flat-screen, the stadium is all colors, chants, songs, and flares, banners waving and smoke rising from the stands, but in the bar, it's silent, white despair coating every face. The usual clever banter, the tactical analysis, even the vulgar and personal insults against the referees, some of them containing the only glimmers of our national creativity since the Renaissance—all of that is over. No one dares to speak for fear of rupturing the collective concentration.

Finally, just before the half ends, the announcer's voice rises, and grunts and gutturals leap up from the crowd.

"Oh!"

"Sì!"

"Euh!"

And then:

"Gooooooooooooooooooooooolllllllllllllll!!! Gol! Gol! Gol! Gol! Gol! Gol! Gol! Goooooooooooooooooooooooooool!!!!!!"

The room explodes. I duck out of the way of Fede, who's bear-hugging everyone he can get his paws on. Grown men jump up and down, screaming like Japanese schoolgirls, slapping fives over my head.

"Gooooooooooooooooooooooooooooooooooool!!!!!!!!!!!!!!!!!!!!!!!"

The dance-party music pumps through the flat-screen, shaking the walls, the deafening roar rising and falling again and again as they show the replay.

"Gol! Gol! Gol! Gol! Gol! Gol! Gol! Goooooooooooooool! Gol! Gol! Gol! Gol! Gol! Gol! Gol! Goooooooooooooooool!!!!!!!!!!!!!"

Finally, after ten or fifteen replays, the commercials come on, and Martina turns the volume down. The room fills with chatter and relief, and Fede defaults into scanning for girls, his eyes in constant motion since puberty. You've got to admire his persistence. I've given up. I look over toward the bar. Papà, Nonno, and Silvio have their heads together in a heated discussion, and Martina gives me a little wave from behind the tap. She raises her eyebrows at me and mimes eating, and I gesture over my shoulder to tell her I already ate. Luca and I used to have this when we were young, before he went off to the academy. We could hold a conversation clear across the room with the smallest twitches of our faces and hands.

"Etto. Oosten to Etto. Etto, come in please. It is Ooston."

"It's 'Houston,' Fede. *H.* Hhhhouston. Learn English."

"Fine," Fede says. "Hhhhouston. Whatever. Who's that girl in the denim jacket over there?"

"That's Sima's little sister, you pedophile."

"That's my little sister, you pedophile," Sima repeats without looking up from her phone. The usual group is here tonight—Sima, Claudia and Casella, Bocca—everyone except Aristone, who's still off at university.

"Really. How old is she now?"

"Thirteen."

"Thirteen! Cazzo! If that were my sister I'd lock her up!"

"Why? You're the only vampire she needs protection from."

"Yeah, you're the only vampire, Fede."

"That's not true."

"Yes it is."

Now, I don't like to make a habit of defending Fede, because everyone knows that's a slippery slope, but Fede is far from the only vampire in San Benedetto. And while right now, I don't feel like telling you the whole tragic history of desperate men in our region, I will say it's mostly a supply-side problem, and if I can be bothered, I'll tell you all about it later, along with the Maradona Hand of God story if you haven't already googled that by now.

"What about that one, then, the one in the black leather coat?"

"That's a trans, Fede."

"A what?"

"A trans . . . you know, a girl with a surprise."

"In-cazz-ibile."

"It's true."

"That is one hundred percent woman."

"Fifty percent, maybe . . ."

"No . . ."

"Yes. It's Alessandro-Alessandra-Whatever. Works over at the Hotel Paradiso. He-she-whatever has been taking the hormones for two years now."

"I guess they're working," Fede says. "Who's that one, then?"

"Which one?"

"That one, in the black pants. The one whose culo is practically singing my name."

"That's Forese's cousin. She's going into the novitiate."

"The what?"

"She's going to be a *nun*, Fede."

"She is not. Whoever saw a nun with a culo like that?"

"Deficiente. They don't cut off body parts when you join."

"They might as well."

I look over to the bar again, and this time, I catch Signora Semirami staring straight at me. She gives me her pathetic two-second blink that's supposed to be seductive, I think, like fifteen minutes with her would be granting my every fottuto wish.

"Hey, Etto," Bocca says. "Remember that little man from Naples that Professoressa Gazzolo used to tell us about in biology class?"

"With the tail?"

"Yeah, what do they call that again?"

"Vestigial."

"Yeah, a vestigial culo, that's what she has."

"Whatever," Fede says. "I'm sure whatever can be nunned can be un-nunned."

"Fede, you're a pig."

"Oink."

"Fede, did you just oink?" Sima's thumbs are twitching against her phone, her face tilted toward the soft, blue light, Madonna-and-Child-style. The only time I ever see Sima smile is into her phone, and the only time any of us ever hear from her is when she SMS-es us. When she's actually with us, she's SMS-ing her university friends in Genoa. I think she thinks she's keeping up with the conversation, but her timing is always a half second off.

Fede puts on a serious face. "I was just telling them how my cousin got attacked by a wild boar. He made it to the hospital, but . . ." He hangs his head.

Sima looks up. "That's terrible!"

We all laugh.

"What?"

"Never mind."

The second half starts, and a reverent hush drops over the bar. Another forty-five minutes and it will all be over. Well, maybe not *over*, because calcio is never, ever, *really* over, but at least it's the end of the regular season, a break until the Champions League and the Coppa UEFA start up again, an annual air pocket that the ten stations, the fifty calcio shows, and the thousands of commentators and journalists try to fill with cycling, Formula One, and the leftover scraps of the calcio season that they have to exaggerate to make them sound important—wild speculations about transfers, praise heaped on the teams who experienced "salvation" and shame on the ones who were demoted, eulogies of the washed-up players sent to America, and endless superlatives about the Juve dynasty, who won the Scudetto yet again this year.

I can't take any more calcio this season. Not even another forty-five minutes.

"I'll be right back," I say.

"Bring me another beer, eh?"

"Get it yourself."

I walk around the scattered tables, trying not to look at Signora Semirami as I pass.

"Ciao, Etto." I can feel her eyes molesting me as I walk past the bar and the computer alcove, back through the kitchen, and into the bathroom. I pull the accordion door shut, lock the latch, and sit down on the seat, but I can still hear Signora Semirami's cackling laugh as clear as if she were in here with me. I put my hands over my ears and press hard. Mamma showed us this trick. It sounds exactly like being underwater. I used to do it all the time—cover my ears, close my eyes, and dream of diving to the bottom of the sea, of disappearing as completely as Mr. Mxyzptlk when Superman makes him say his name backward and he gets sent back to Zrfff.

Etto. Etto. Etto. Otte. Otte. Otte.

Then I remember.

I open the cabinet behind the toilet. Martina keeps her inventory here. I pull a bottle of vodka out, break the seal, and take a drink.

Cheers, Mamma. Cin-cin, Luca.

The bar erupts again. Another goal for Genoa. 2–1. Everyone is screaming and hugging, and jumping up and down. I slip out of the bathroom and walk right out the door. And you know what? No one notices. Not Papà or Fede or Martina or Signora Semirami. Not even Mino.

"Gooooooooooooooooooooooooooooooooooooooooooooooooooooooool!!!!!!!!"

The door of the bar closes behind me, the heat and noise immediately replaced by the salty sea air and the polite murmurs of the tourists taking their after-dinner walks along the sea. It's mostly Germans in June—one giant, pale, scrawny-legged, poorly tipping flock, arriving every year like the transumanza of the sheep from the Alps to the plains. The families from Milan will start coming thick and fast in July, bloating our little town of five thousand to something like fifty thousand by Ferragosto, then draining again like a burst blister come September. If you live here long enough, though, you learn to ignore the tourists, to walk past them like the benches and the palm trees. So even though the passeggiata is packed to the railing with people tonight, they ignore me and I ignore them, and it's almost as good as being alone.

Venezia comes back and scores another goal. 2–2. I can hear the wailing and moaning from the open windows, and the quieter yelps of pain coming from the waiters and bartenders huddled around small screens along the passeggiata.

I look back toward Martina's, but nobody's coming after me. I take another drink and look in the other direction, down the stone-and-metal curve of the passeggiata that follows the natural arc of the beach below. In the distance, I pick out the security gates of our shop and the darkened shutters of our apartment above. I could go home and wait for Papà. I could sit on the sofa and let him turn on the light, look at my face and peruse Luca's features buried somewhere between the skin and bone. I could, without a single word, ruin the whole night for him, snap him out of his glorious fandom and remind him of his awful reality—that instead of a championship calcio player for a son, instead of a woman he loved, he's left with me.

A woman walks by, and out of the corner of my eye, she looks exactly like Mamma. I watch her pass. From the back she has the same broad shoulders and sloppy ponytail, but the laugh and the walk are all wrong. This is something they don't tell you when someone dies, that a few times a month, at least for a second or two, you'll swear you see them, and whenever it happens, you'll feel the need to ballast your mind with all the sanity you have in order to keep yourself from tipping into crazy.

I take another drink and look up at the curved wall of terraces, cupping San Benedetto like a giant's hand. The sun is setting behind them, flattening into a disk like an Ufo, and I imagine it crushing a flock of sheep somewhere in the valleys, some half-wit shepherd crawling out from under it, toothless and resolute that he has seen God. I lean back into the railing and listen to the shush of the waves behind me, the metronome that has kept time my entire life. The darkness will come quickly now, any life left in the land breaking apart and scattering into stars.

I head to the back of town, where the crowds drop away and the sound of clanking dishes becomes a distant tinkling. I pass the playground of our old asilo and cross the railroad bridge to the hill. Twenty steps up the incline, I'm already huffing and puffing, cursing and sweating, my thighs working against the hill. Vaffanculo, gravity. Vaffanculo, stony path. Vaffanculo, weakling legs and shallow lungs. The shadows spread into darkness, and the streetlights blink on.

I stop at Via Partigiani and set the bottle on the flat rock the nonne use as a bench to wait for rides. I sit down and light a cigarette. Vaffanculo, American tobacco companies and your crack marketing teams. I exhale and look through the cloud of smoke to the town, the buildings and cars shrunk to Lego size. There's another round of shouting from the villas around me, echoing across the hill. Another goal. Genoa takes the lead, 3–2. Cheers, Griffins. Salute. You have made Papà proud, not an easy feat.

I hold the bottle of vodka up to the light and swirl it around. It shimmers a little, an entire world of winds and currents inside a bottle, and I start to imagine the people who must populate it, sloshing around, holding on for dear life. I take another drink, stamp out my cigarette, and keep moving, higher and higher, through the tunnel of foliage. The pavement gives way to cobblestones, and finally a dirt mule track, studded with rocks that have been washed down and embedded by the spring torrents. I can feel my breath squeezing in and out, my heart flopping against my rib cage like a dying moth, and I imagine flipping a switch and opening a panel of gills all the way up my side. The mule track closes in on me, and I scrape my hands along the rough walls, combing the weeds that grow out of the cracks between the stones.

> Midway upon the journey of our life
>   I found myself in a dark wilderness,
>   for I had wandered from the straight and true.
>   How hard a thing it is to tell about,
>   that wilderness so savage, dense, and harsh,
>   even to think of it renews my fear!

It comes into my head, light and bubbly like a nursery rhyme. The first week of liceo, Charon tried to scare us by making us memorize the entire first canto. Casella and I stayed up all night, high on espresso, singing it to different songs to make ourselves remember. First the national anthem, then a stupid Lùnapop song that I won't even try to remember the title of because I don't want to get it stuck in my fottuto head. Then that bella-ciao-bella-ciao-bella-ciao-ciao-ciao song.

Shit. Now that's in my head.

I keep walking. I catch a whiff of an unearthly stink, and I know I'm close to Mino's house. The last thing I need right now is to wake up his stupid attack dog di merda. I try to creep by slowly and quietly, but a set of small yellow eyes appears in the path ahead. I freeze, and so do they.

"Go away!" I whisper.

It's a cat, and through the darkness, I can hear it digging in, hissing and spitting at me.

"Go on. Shoo! Go!"

She gives a rolling yowl, filled with all the desperation of the world, a heat that will never be relieved. You will not get through here, she hisses at me, not if I have anything to say about it. No chance. Turn around and go back. And she punctuates it with another yowl.

"Come on, you fottuto cat. Move! Go! Via! Shoo!" I whisper.

I pull a weed from the wall and throw it at the eyes of the cat. The dirt explodes off the roots, and the cat screams, its lean body leaping away into the ether. Mino's stupid attack dog di merda wakes instantly and starts barking its head off. I throw a clod of dirt at him, too, and I can hear him smacking his lips as he eats it. I throw another one in the same direction, and he's finally quiet. I hurry up the last stretch of the mule track, feel for a gap in the wall of cypresses, and push my way onto the field. It's dark now, and the faint outline of the vegetation takes shape around me.

I take another drink and wait a minute for my eyes to adjust. This is the only flat spot above town large enough for even a three-quarter-sized calcio field, but nobody but me really comes up here anymore. The grass is so long, it could wrap itself around my ankles, and I stumble and high-knee my way toward the goal, the shadow of the old liceo looming behind a second row of cypresses. I haven't been inside in three years, but that's a story for another time, and after I tell you about the Hand of God and the Great Woman Famine, I will tell you that one, too. I reach into my pocket for my phone and shine the light on the ground, cutting a narrow swath through the grass until it finds the headstone. Luca's photo smirks back at me from the laminated frame, his face scrubbed, his uniform ironed, his cleats immaculate.

"Ciao, stronzo. Happy anniversary. Tomorrow, eh?"

I'm not sure exactly how Papà convinced Mamma to bury Luca in the goal. *Convinced* is probably not the right word. After Luca died, Mamma was just a husk, and maybe all he did was plow her under. All I remember was that there was a lot of crying (Mamma) and yelling (Papà).

"I coached him in chickadees on that field! He scored his first goal on that field! He will be buried on that field!" And he had Silvio make a strong recommendation to Gubbio, the mayor, who signed a piece of paper that said Papà could be leased the field for one euro per annum plus responsibility for the maintenance.

But even after that, nobody believed it would actually happen. I mean, being the mayor is all well and good, and Gubbio can sign whatever piece of paper he wants, but there's nothing like a bunch of old women with loosened tongues and long memories to maintain order in a society, and everybody knows things in San Benedetto are ultimately approved or vetoed by the nonne. I think maybe that's why everyone sat back, because they expected the nonne to step in, but in the end, they only crossed themselves and called Papà matto for it. Crazy. Behind his shoulders and not even to his face.

I sit down next to Luca's headstone. I comb my fingers through the grass and tease apart the knots. I'm supposed to be the one mowing it, and maybe it's just my guilt, but I can practically hear it growing and proliferating in real time around me, the roots sucking up the water, the chloroplasts filled to bursting, the cells madly dividing. A testament to life, and yet tall enough to bury me. I pick up the calcio ball Papà left here two years ago instead of flowers. It's soft and damp, and I roll it between my hands.

"Genoa's leading," I tell Luca. "Three to two, but Yuri Fil left the match early. Something about his ankle. Then again, you probably know that already, don't you?"

I lie down and let myself sink beneath the surface of the grass. For a while after Luca's accident, I'd try to get him to talk to me. I'd look over at his empty bed on the other side of the room and complain to him about Papà or tell him how depressed Mamma was. Because that's what Father Marco and everybody else kept saying to me: now he'll be watching over you, blah, blah, blah, you've got another angel praying for you in heaven, blah, blah, blah. Whatever. I'd wait for him to answer, give him plenty of time, but there was nothing. Niente. Only a rushing sound around my ears. I guess in heaven they have better things to do than worry about us—making out with cherubim or playing Quidditch or whatever you do when you don't have to lug your body around anymore.

The shouts of the end of the match rise up from the villas on the hill.

"I guess they won, eh? Papà must be happy." I sit up and take another drink, then pour a generous shot where Luca's feet must be. Magic feet, they called them. He was perfectly two-footed, and over the years he'd learned a litany of feints so the defenders could never tell which foot he was going to use until the ball was already past the keeper. He had his first tryout when he was twelve, went away to the academy in Milan at fifteen, and worked his way up the junior leagues. At his funeral, the assistant coach they sent said they were going to call him up to the first team in the fall, though he could have just been saying that. I wonder if Papà watched the match tonight thinking about Luca running back and forth across the flat-screen.

I get up and walk over to the edge of the terrace. People are pouring out onto the streets now, chanting and cheering, cars honking and air horns blasting. Someone is shooting fireworks off the end of the molo, and the car headlights respond, blinking in some fottuto Morse code I've somehow never learned. Nonno's got the 2CV down there, and it honks like a dying goose. He actually won it from a French guy back in 1960-something after the Italians beat the French in a match that was so important, evidently people were betting their cars on it. I don't know what color it was originally, but Nonno painted the front blue and red—Genoa colors—with a yellow griffin spread across the hood. The back half of the car is painted in red, white, and green, with "VIVA L'ITALIA!" scrawled across the rear window. Below it, on the flat of the trunk, he put a skull and crossbones with the words "AND DEATH TO FRANCE!"

I take another drink, and the bottle feels light, the vodka plinking against the sides as the tide pulls in and out of my mouth. I lean forward, looking over the edge of the next terrace into the darkness, and I can feel all the gravity of the earth pulling at me, as if at any moment I could drop into the abyss. And I don't believe in supernatural stuff—really, I don't—but all of a sudden I feel a shot of cold air hit me from behind, as cold as the air from the walk-in at the shop. I jerk my head around and look up at the shadow of Signora Malaspina's massive villa rising several terraces above. It was built in the sixties by her ex-husband, a Hollywood movie director, and every third tile on the roof is actually a little mirror. During the day, it sparkles like a piercing set into the brow of the hill—discreet, but enough to change the whole face of it. Now, it's dark except for one light in one window.

I take another drink and keep staring at it. After about a minute, the light in the window blinks out, and the next window lights up. And the next, and the next. Seven of them, like a band of lights on a spaceship. The last one holds steady for a minute or more before there's another flash of light, this time on the rooftop veranda, hovering over the whole villa. It stays on longer than the others, maybe five minutes, and there's something about it that makes the hairs on my neck stand up. I start thinking about the possibility of aliens landing on top of Signora Malaspina's villa, and my mind drifts to the comic Casella and I started the summer we were twelve. That one was called *Manna.* Pieces of bread mysteriously dropped from the sky, and when people ate it, it turned out to contain alien life-forms, which expanded in their stomachs like those seahorse sponges, eventually taking over their bodies and then their thoughts. Trust me, if we'd been able to finish it, it would have been bigger than *E.T.* Two sequels, kids' carnival costumes, alien-shaped breakfast cereal, the works.

The entire villa goes dark again, and there's a great boom of fireworks from the pier. I turn toward the sea in time to see the red and blue flashes of man-made lightning, the embers like stars sinking toward the horizon, the cheers fading in the distance as I stand up and start back down the hill.

III

*E*very morning I hear a sound in my subconscious just before the alarm goes off. It can be anything—a gunshot, an old-fashioned phone ringing, someone laughing, a door slamming. Maybe it's just a coincidence, or maybe it's my mind trying to distract me and delay the moment that always comes—the moment when I realize they're both gone.

On Tuesday morning, I wake up to a great crash of thunder, but when I listen for the rain, there are only the voices of my neighbors floating up from the vico, and Jimmy's truck idling in the alley. I go to the top of the stairs that separate my bedroom from the rest of our apartment like the crow's nest on a pirate ship.

"Papà?" I call down.

Nothing.

I pull on a pair of Luca's jeans and go downstairs. Right after Mamma died, Martina came in and helped Papà clear out all her things, and Nicola Nicolini offered to redecorate our entire apartment for free. Restart from the top and all that. I think Papà must have planted him upright in the middle of the living room and said, "Make it look like no family ever lived here." There are no photos and no clutter. Only clean surfaces, squared corners, tasteful shades of tan and brown, and a few carefully chosen, perfectly quirky accessories, none of which have anything to do with us.

I get the rubber envelope of small bills and coins from the top drawer of the credenza and go down to the alley. Jimmy is sitting on the bumper, having a smoke.

"Ciao, Jimmy."

"Ciao."

I've known Jimmy since he was a kid in the passenger seat keeping his papà company on deliveries, but I don't really know that much about him. I know their farm is somewhere north of Turin and that he plays a lot of video games, but that's about it. I'm not even sure what his real name is. I don't think it's Giacomo or anything close to Jimmy, but Jimmy's all he's ever answered to.

"Sorry to make you wait, Jimmy."

He shrugs. "Not like I have anything better to do."

I open the back door while Jimmy reaches into the cab and kills the engine. After Luca died, Papà added an alarm to our apartment and floodgates and two extra locks to the shop. Not cheap floodgates, either, but top-of-the-line like they have in Venice, as if somebody had kidnapped Luca or washed him away in the middle of the night and might come back for the rest of us.

Jimmy and I slide the calf carcass off the plastic and carry it into the walk-in. It's a big one, and I bang my hands against the door frame. Shit.

"So did you see the match on Sunday?" Jimmy asks.

"Part of it."

"People must have been out of their heads here."

"Yeah."

"Your papà, especially."

"I don't think he's slept since Sunday."

Jimmy laughs and changes the subject to video games. It's all he ever talks about. I picture his room back on the farm as a floating mangrove of cords, screens, consoles, and hand controllers. He tells me about an advance download he got of FIFA 2006, then starts taking me through the plotline of this crazy Japanese one where all the monsters have made-up English names like Tramplefrost and Curlybeard, Swinetooth and Dragonsnout, and all I can say is, "Ah . . . sì, sì," like the old men, by which of course I mean, "Jimmy, you're such a loser. Why don't you get a life?"

We get the calf and the side of beef hung up and bring in the chickens, new roosters, rabbits, and non-EU-sanctified eggs some neighbor of his sells us. By the time we're finished, we're both sweating, and Jimmy stands next to the grinding counter, runs his hand through his hair, and looks at his shoes like he wants to say something deep. He got the same look both times we reopened the shop after the funerals, and I wonder if by chance he remembered that yesterday was the anniversary.

"Until next week, then," I say, to save him the awkwardness.

He looks up at me, startled. "Yeah . . . next week."

He goes out the back, and I smell the smoke of another cigarette before the diesel engine rumbles alive. It's still only seven fifteen, so I leave the fluorescents off and work by the light of the front window. I turn on the television in back and flip it to one of the morning shows just for the noise. We keep it in the corner of the grinding counter with a white pillowcase over it to protect it from the grist and splatter, but I usually leave the pillowcase on just so I don't have to look at the news anchor on Rai Uno and her botched Botox job that makes her look like she won the SuperEnalotto. Instead of her this morning, though, there's the voice of the homelier one—the real news correspondent they save for serious stories—talking on and on about Sunday's Genoa-Venezia match. That's all everybody talked about all day yesterday, and probably all they'll talk about for the rest of the fottuto summer. Serie A, blah, blah, blah. Who cares?

Next door, Chicca rolls up her security gate in one yank, and it sounds like thunder. I put on my apron, wash my hands, and start setting up the banco. If I ever get my eyes gouged out, I can probably set up the banco blind without even smudging the glass. I get the trays from the back for the chicken, the rabbit, and the shish kebabs. The rest goes right on the marble. Meat, splat, card in front of it. Ossibuchi, punta di petto, spezzatino, tacchino, spalla, polpa magra, polpa mista, reale, braciole, lonza, carré con osso. Splat, splat, splat, splat. Then the cold cuts in their own case: Parma ham, salame, prosciutto cotto and crudo, mortadella, and coppa. Papà is a perfectionist, so I must account for every quarter kilo on the inventory and make sure that every surface is as immaculate as the Virgin.

The first knock of the morning plinks against the window, the start of the procession of nonne on their way to Mass. Nonne, nonne, nonne, and more nonne. This is what sociologists call the aging of Europe, and Liguria's demographics are the most top-heavy of them all, crammed full of nonne, nobody stupid or naive enough to bring more babies into this world. They clutch each other's arms, crossing the front windows so slowly, you can see the gossip gathering in clouds above their heads. If I ever get that wrinkled and infirm, I think I'll spare everyone and just stay home, but the nonne take to the streets every morning without fail. After all, they're in training. They must have strong backs to prop up the 80 percent of us who have stopped hedging our bets with God. They must develop stamina to withstand the barrage of hip-hop music and American movies, and military discipline to protect themselves and their grandchildren against the Muslims and their bombs, even though if you ask me, it's the Buddhists and their ninja levitation shit we should really be worried about.

Kneel.

Sit.

Stand.

Kneel.

Sit.

Stand.

Uno.

Due.

Hup!

And as the world crumbles around them despite their aerobics, they must have the patience to say the 777 trillion rosaries necessary to pray the hundreds of billions of fallen souls out of purgatory.

"Ciao," the nonne mouth as they pass by the window.

"Ciao," I mouth back. I have to wave to each and every one of them every single day or they will talk about me on the church steps and complain to Papà that my hair is too long to be serving food. Mamma used to be friends with all of them, but they never talk about her anymore. After Luca died, it was like a soft fog creeping in, gradually obliterating him from the stories people told, but after Mamma, it was like a door slamming shut. Sure, there were the respectable visits right after, when everyone would come and pat our hands and drop off plates of food, but even then, they always came in pairs and hurried away spooked, like if they looked Death or Suffering or Heartache directly in the eye, it might be contagious. This is another thing you will discover if you lose someone close to you—if you ever want to go out in public again, you'll have to learn how to treat your grief like a goiter or a great big boil. You'll have to learn how to camouflage it and tuck it away so as not to scare the living.

"Ciao," another group of nonne mouth through the window.

"Ciao." I put on my fake smile.

When I'm finished setting up the banco, I have a good twenty minutes left, so I get a pair of scissors and tear a sheet of paper off the roll. I pull out the stool and sit in front of the ghost television. The anchorwoman with the botched Botox job is back, babbling on and on about somebody bombing the cazzo out of something somewhere, which is apparently not serious news anymore.

"Deficiente," I hiss at her shadow, shifting and darkening through the pillowcase.

I decide to do the new German pope today. I cut out the tall hat and the cape, poking the scissors into the middle of each and cutting out crosses like superhero logos. I string the chicken in the case so it stands up on its legs, then wrap the cape around its chicken shoulders, balance the hat on top, and tuck a skewer into its wing. If I had more time, I would soak and bend the skewer into a shepherd's crook or take some red plastic wrap and make those Prada shoes. Maybe even give him a paper Sancho Panza to keep him company, the way he's been riding around in the popemobile for the past two months, shaking his staff at windmills and calling Europe back to the faith.

Good luck with that.

I clean up the scraps of paper and snap off the television, cutting the anchor off midsentence. I go out onto the passeggiata and light a cigarette. The sky is clear and the sea a deep blue, painted especially for the tourists.

"Ciao, Etto." Chicca is dragging her display racks outside, the sand buckets and crab nets wobbling and banging together.

"Ciao, Chicca."

"Some match on Sunday, eh?"

"Yeah. Some match."

"I saw your papà this morning on his way to Martina's. He looks like he hasn't slept in two days."

"I know. Genoa in Serie A. It's like Christmas for him."

Across the passeggiata at Bagni Liguria, Franco and Mimmo are already outside in their swimsuits and bare feet, sweeping the boardwalks clean and unlocking the cabanas. They're the same age as Papà, both from the south, both perennially half clothed and almost preternaturally calm and kind. They say Franco's father was a mafia kingpin in Napoli, and his house growing up was decorated in frescoes and leafed in gold. They say he renounced his father's life and hitchhiked to San Benedetto with only the clothes on his back. But he never tells any stories from before he came here, as if this is where his real life started. Franco waves to me across the passeggiata.

"Ehi, Etto." His dog lifts his head from his paws and looks me up and down.

"Ciao, Franco."

"Just saw your papà this morning. He said to remind you about the band saw blade."

Shit. Papà has been bugging me about it for a week. I stamp out my cigarette. "Chicca, could you . . . ?"

She waves me on. I jog over to Casella and his papà's shop in my apron, dodging through the pedestrian traffic. The door's open even though the sign says Closed.

"Anyone here?" I call to the back of the shop. I edge through the tall, narrow shelves to the counter, the trays of nuts and bolts rattling as I pass.

"Etto, is that you?" Casella calls, a faraway echo.

"Yes."

"One minute."

Eventually he appears in a T-shirt and a pair of cargo shorts, his hair tied back, thick like a mop. Claudia likes it that way. Claudia, Claudia, Claudia. Casella and I used to be best friends before Claudia, as close as Papà and Silvio. When we were in liceo, they would call us Troll I and Troll 2, like those dolls you rub between your hands until their hair stands up like a flame, mine burned orangish-brown by the sun, Casella's bleached white-hot.

"Sorry," he says. "I was in the back room trying to make some space."

Casella says "sorry" all the time now. Claudia's conditioned him. It's become a blanket apology for his existence, an evolutionary adaptation that he will pass on to his children. Like sea anemones curl up or sharks attack when they see blood, his children will say "sorry." His grandchildren. Their children. And that's how his lineage will manage to survive—obediently and apologetically. He balances on one foot and reaches behind the counter.

"The blade, right?" he says. "Your papà called yesterday." He hands me the blade, folded over on itself and pinched with a thick rubber band.

"Thanks."

He stares at me, and I stare back at him.

"How's your papà?" he asks.

"Fine. You know, still wetting himself over Genoa."

"Aren't they all. And your nonna?"

"You know, the same. No worse. Your parents?"

He shrugs. "They're fine. They're in Friuli this week."

"Visiting your aunt?"

"Uh-huh."

This is the curse of the drifting friendship, to be close enough to know all the people and details in each other's lives, but not close enough to really care. I wonder how many more times in our lives we will have this bullshit conversation instead of talking about why we only have bullshit conversations anymore.

"Lots of tourists already, eh?"

"Yesterday was pretty busy."

"Just wait until Ferragosto."

"I know, eh?"

He glances back at the storeroom door.

"I better go," I say.

"Yeah," he says. "Two minutes to eight."

"Thanks for the blade."

"No problem. You coming by Camilla's tonight?"

"We'll see."

I jog back. Chicca is still outside, watching as a pair of German grandparents and their charge paw over the inflatable turtles and crocodiles leaning against the wall. It's hard to believe that sixty years ago they were clicking around our streets in jackboots, cocking weapons in the faces of our grandparents. Sometimes I want to stop one of them and ask, whatever happened to the dream of a pasteurized and homogenized gene pool? Whatever happened to the government awards for reproducing humorless Aryans at factory capacity? The single cruelty they are capable of these days is bringing only children into the world, their one aspiration to be inoffensive and organized, their only Blitzkrieg to come here for the same three weeks of vacation every year, stay in the same rental apartments, and sit on the same bagni under the same umbrellas, generation after generation after generation in limbo, until the four horsemen of the apocalypse politely ask them to pack up and go home.

"Thanks, Chicca."

"No problem."

I put the band saw blade on the grinding counter, come up front, and slip behind the banco. The rest of the day is predictable. First a steady stream of German mothers buying sausages and cold cuts for their efficiency kitchens. Then the nonne on their way back from church. Then the local mothers and children, trying to beat back the endless summer boredom with routine. Regina Salveggio was in our class at the liceo until she dropped out to marry Beppe, and her kids bang through the front door and run straight for the calf's head, pressing their grubby little hands and faces against the glass.

"Moo-ooo," the boy brat says, and the girl brat follows.

"Moo-ooo."

Regina laughs. "They're so curious about everything at this age. They're like little sponges. I hope they'll turn out to be as smart as their father."

"You mean Beppe?"

"Of course I mean Beppe." She laughs like it's a joke. "I'll tell him you said that, Etto."

"Well, it looks like they're already bilingual."

"Moo-ooo. Moo-ooo," the little brats continue, practically French-kissing the glass, as if the fottuto calf is suddenly going to start carrying his end of the conversation. "Moo-ooo . . ."

"Oh, you're so funny, Etto."

"So what will it be, Regina?" I ask. "Two hundred grams of prosciutto?"

"Yes, and four chicken breasts, no bone, no skin."

No bone, no skin. Not much of a happy homemaker, are you, Regina? I wrap it up and write it down in the notebook we keep under the register.

"Do you want to carry the package, tesoro?" Regina asks the girl brat. The boy brat whispers something in her ear, and the girl brat lets out a yelp.

"Antonio Riccardo, what did you say to your sister?"

But instead of backing down, the boy brat extends his arm, pointing it at my crotch. "I said, *that's* the man who chopped the cow's head off," and the girl hides behind Regina's legs and peeks out at me in fear.

I give her a friendly little smile and a wave, and I crouch down to her level. Her eyes widen. "Actually, your brother is wrong," I say. "The cows arrive on a truck already dead, and then I chop the carcasses into little bits!"

The boy brat laughs, swinging his arm around and around. The girl brat's mouth gapes open slightly, silent for a moment before letting out the wail of an ambulance.

"Thanks a lot, Etto," Regina says, snatching the package from me and scooping up the howling girl in the other arm. "I'll call you at four in the morning when she wakes up with a nightmare."

"No problem, Regina. Anytime. Tell Beppe I said ciao."

The rest of the morning is busy, and all the conversations blend together.

"Take off the skin."

"Beautiful day, isn't it?"

"Slice it thin, please."

"He always was a cheapskate, though."

"Three . . . no, four."

"She'll never get married."

"They haven't talked to each other since the fifties."

"Well, you know, she wasn't at Mass this morning."

The bachelors are always the last to come in, just before the afternoon break. Nicola Nicolini orders two fillets and has me trim some of the meat off to make them into perfect circles.

"New girlfriend, eh, Nicola?"

He turns red and pretends to be searching inside his purse, man bag, whatever, mumbling that they are both for him, and something about being an eternal bachelor, blah, blah, blah, and we should come next door for dinner sometime. One of these days, I'm going to put him out of his misery and tell him that everyone knows he's gay. That doesn't he realize he lives on the other side of our fottuto wall, and besides, we have the ever-vigilant nonne to alert us and everyone else in San Benedetto whenever he brings a man home?

"Have you heard about the Genoa-Venezia scandal?" he asks, as if talking about calcio is going to camouflage the flames.

"Let me guess . . . steroids?"

"Match fixing."

"What's new?"

There's been a scandal every couple of years now for as long as I can remember—match fixing, steroids, horse tranquilizers, cocaine smuggling, fake passports to dodge the foreign-player quotas, Rolexes magically appearing on every referee's wrist. It's the same old story every time. It'll be analyzed and overanalyzed for a couple of weeks in the media—especially if it's not Berlusconi's team—until finally the players involved will appear, heads hanging, making the obligatory and televised act of contrition and asking for absolution from the fans. When they're ready to move on, the media will cauterize the whole thing by giving it a nickname, and then everyone will forget about it until the next scandal breaks, when they'll get excited by the gushing blood all over again.

"I don't know, Etto," Nicola Nicolini continues. "It looks pretty bad this time. They've been at it all morning over at Martina's."

"Let me guess. My papà's leading the charge."

"He looked like he was about to lose his straps."

Figures. I'm sure he'll use it as an excuse not to come into the shop at all today. In the past two years, we've created an entire branch of science out of living together but not living together, like if we circulate in some provisional reality, the permanent one doesn't have a chance to harden into place. Like if we aren't in the same room together, we can still pretend nothing is missing, and we don't see the gaps we've been cursed to illuminate for each other.

He finally appears ten minutes before close, out of breath, clutching his precious *Gazzetta dello Sport*.

"Have you heard the news?" he pants.

"Ciao, Papà."

"Yes, yes. Ciao, ciao. Have you heard?"

Papà looks almost the same as he did twenty-five years ago. Still the same sturdy torso, the same heavy hands and thick crew cut he had in his photos from military service and our team pictures when he coached us in chickadees. Only in the past two years has it been shot through with gray—small, silver wounds at his temples and in the back of his head.

"The scandal?"

"The mistaken scandal. The only real scandal is that they are tarnishing the image of Yuri Fil. Can you believe they are trying to blame him for match fixing and conspiracy now? Because he left the field with a bum ankle! Incredible!"

"Well, how do you know he wasn't in on it?"

My father gasps. "How do I know he wasn't in on it? Maradona!" This is the strongest word Papà ever uses, both a blessing and a curse, same as the man himself was. "No, he did not do it! Yuri Fil is an innocent man! I would bet my life on it! They are only using him as a scapegoat or for some other scheme!"

He throws up his hands in exasperation, and the *Gazzetta dello Sport* falls to the floor, a pink spot on the clean, white linoleum. He bends over to pick it up, and when he comes up, his face is red, like someone has turned off a spigot in his neck. He tucks the paper under his arm and stares at me with his bulging eyes, shaking his head, as if he can't believe we're related.

"How do I know?" he says again. "Really, Etto . . ."

Luca would never have blasphemed Yuri Fil. If Luca was here—not that Papà would've ever allowed him to waste a minute behind the banco—but if Luca was still alive, they would've stood around for hours, dissecting the entire affair, taking turns at proving Yuri Fil's innocence in a hundred different ways.

Papà squints at the glass and pokes a finger at the plastic sack keeping cold in the back of the case. "Who's that for?"

"Pia."

"Make sure she pays cash."

"She always does."

"Good. I'm not subsidizing that stronzo of a husband of hers. And what's this?" Papà stabs another finger at the glass.

"Those are shish kebabs."

"Not those. *This.*"

"It's a tribute to the new pope. I thought the Germans and the nonne would like it."

"Take it out."

"But, Papà . . ."

"It's disrespectful. Take it out. Your bisnonno and your nonno and I did not build a dignified business in order for you to turn it into a joke." He gestures to the portraits on the wall behind him, as if that gives him a majority. "And while you're at it, take those shish kebabs out of there and redo them. It looks like they were made by the home for the blind. Honestly!"

"But I was just about to close up."

"Redo them. And how many times do I have to tell you to put on a hairnet?"

Let me be clear. I am *never* putting on a fottuto hairnet, and Papà *knows* that I am never putting on a fottuto hairnet. He's just using it as leverage so I will fix the shish kebabs and let him run his mouth. He's shouting from the back now, launching into his speech about the nobility of the profession, the butcher as the guardian of morals in the community, and the fact that an entire line of French kings descended from a butcher. Pretty soon he will be on to how my bisnonno arrived in this town eighty years ago with only his leather roll of knives.

"Are you listening to me, Etto?"

"Yes, Papà. I'm listening."

I clip the paper hat and cape off the chicken pope and slip the skewer out of its wing, but just to show him that he is not the master of me, I leave the chicken suspended, upright and naked in the case. Papà reappears in the front with the crate of dirty laundry, the newspaper balanced on top.

"I mean it, Etto. Either a hairnet or a haircut. I tell you this every week. And you need to get that field mowed. This weekend. Gubbio says it looks as if it's been completely abandoned."

"Gubbio's exaggerating."

"Would you just do it without complaining for once, Etto? Maradona, you're twenty-two! I shouldn't have to tell you everything. Your brother was living away from home at fifteen."

Papà rarely invokes my brother, and once it slips out of his mouth, he disappears as quickly as he can.

"Right, and look how that turned out," I say, once the door is safely closed behind him.

Nonno and my bisnonno both scowl at me from their portraits on the wall.

"I know, I know. I'm a bad son. What's new?"

I used to think about leaving all this, maybe living on my own or even moving to the city. When Mamma's sister was here to visit that one time, before she got bogged down with her six kids, she and Mamma talked about me and Luca maybe spending a year in America once we graduated from liceo. There were even a few years when Casella and I talked about enrolling in the animation institute in Milan. But if you live here your whole life, you grow up hearing a steady chatter of people who talk about leaving, who sketch out their big dreams with too many words and sculpt their plans out of the air with grand, sweeping gestures. A few even manage to pack a suitcase and shake the sand of San Benedetto off their feet for a few years. But one way or the other, they always come back, and over the years, I guess that's inoculated me from becoming another big talker in a long line.

I lock up and cross the passeggiata to Bagni Liguria, shielding my eyes from the sun. Mimmo is manning the entrance hut. It's not July yet, so there are still a few tags left on the board behind him, a few empty chaises and umbrellas in the grid.

He looks up from his book. "Delivery?"

"Ciacco called it in."

Mimmo takes the bag from me and trots off to find Ciacco while I stay on the boardwalk and survey the beach. The sun is out in full force, the white sails of the boats poking up out of the waves like shark teeth. There are a few people treading water, their heads floating in the sea. The rest are lying facedown on their chaises, backs burned, arms and feet dangling off the edge in some sort of medieval torture. I hate the bagni. I never go.

Mimmo hovers over one of the chaises in the front row, and Ciacco squirms until he finally raises himself to a sitting position, the rolls of fat rearranging themselves as he digs into the purse hanging around his neck.

"Ehi. Ciao, Etto." Franco appears in front of the showers with a bucket of crabs and a gaggle of little kids following him around like he's the magic piper. We used to collect crabs when we were little, too. We'd leave those poor little suckers sloshing around in a thin soup of sand and water until Franco made us dump them back into the sea so they wouldn't die.

"Ciao, Franco."

"What brings you here? Delivery?"

"For Ciacco."

"You should put on your suit. Go for a little swim."

"Thanks, but I have a delivery up in the hills."

"Who?"

"Pia."

He shakes his head the way everyone does when Pia's name is

mentioned. "Ah . . . sì, sì," he says, by which he means, what a shame, what a shame. "You want me to let Fede know you're here?"

"That's okay, he looks busy."

Franco laughs. "As usual."

Fede's on the shore, his tanned back shaped like an arrow pointing to his culo, just in case you missed it in those tight trunks. He's ankle deep in the surf, flirting with three blond girls, as Bocca leans down from the lifeguard chair, poised to catch the crumbs if they happen to fall from Fede's table. I hold up two fingers and squish Bocca between them. Poser . . . squish. Fede . . . squish. Blond girls . . . squish, squish, squish. When Luca was around on breaks from the academy, Fede at least had some competition, but now he's out there completely unchecked, roaming the savannah like on Animal Planet, and all you can do is turn your head at the last second.

"Hey, thanks, Etto!" Ciacco is holding up one of the sandwiches and waving at me from his chaise, his stomach doubled up. "Extra meat. Just the way I like them!"

Ciacco's voice is faint against the waves, but it's loud enough to get Fede's attention, and Fede spins around and starts waving at me, his whole arm sweeping into an arc as if he's stranded on some fottuto island.

"Ehi! Etto!" he calls. "Come here!"

I shake my head. "I'm not translating for you, deficiente," I say quietly. "You should've learned English in school when you had the chance."

"Ehi! Etto!" he calls again, still sweeping his arm back and forth.

The blond girls are staring at me now, too, and Bocca twists around in the chair to have a look. Mimmo is taking his time chatting with sunbathers and children as he makes his way back to me with the money. I shake my head with more violence. Fede, if you think I'm coming over there to translate your stupidaggini, well, think again.

Fede finally gives up and jogs over to me, his hand shading the left side of his face. He's wearing his Terminator sunglasses and those painted-on black trunks with the silver scorpion printed over the crotch. He reaches up to the wooden railing of the boardwalk and gives me the same upside-down handshake the B-boys give each other.

"Why the poser handshake, Fede? And why are you shading your face?"

"Ugh. Medusa's here." Medusa is what he calls the Milanese woman who has rented an umbrella at Bagni Liguria for the last forty summers and who insists on going topless as if this is France or something. I look over his shoulder.

"At your own risk, Etto," he warns. "At your own risk."

"Whatever, Fede. I feel so sorry for you, having to look at women's bocce all day. Maybe you can apply for a disability stipend."

"Listen, I would much rather be staring at raw meat and gristle all day than at that lady's seventy-year-old cold cuts." He laughs, grabs the railing of the boardwalk, and leans back, stretching. "Why don't you come off that boardwalk and talk to these Australian girls I found?"

"No thanks. I think I'll just laugh at you from here. What are they, nannies?"

"One's got a German uncle. They're preparing the vacation homes for him and his friends. You coming over to Camilla's later?"

"Who's going?"

"Who always goes? Everybody."

"I'll think about it."

"Come on. I'll buy you a beer."

"You always say that."

Mimmo reappears and hands me the money for the sandwiches. "Etto, you should go put on your trunks and come out here. We've got extra umbrellas until the end of the week."

"Thanks, but I have to make some deliveries."

"When you're finished."

"Then I have to mow the field."

"Ah . . . sì, sì . . . I heard it looks completely abandoned."

"It's not that bad."

"I've got to go, Etto," Fede says. He points at me as if that will pin me down. "Tonight. Camilla's."

"Maybe."

"Listen, I'm tired of these halfhearted 'maybes.' You're coming. End of the story."

"Maybe."

He gives me one last glare through his sunglasses. "See you there, Etto. No excuses."

I walk up the hill to Pia's, the bag of meat banging against my leg. There are only a few people out walking the terraces during the afternoon break—German hikers mostly, with their ski poles and their vigor and their heavy "Buongiornos" that land on you like a wool blanket. The sun is compact and hard, pounding away at my head like a blacksmith's hammer. I can't tell you how much I hate the sun. My eyes hate the sun. My skin hates the sun. My brain hates the sun. By the time I get to Via Partigiani, my shirt is soaked and my breath is chugging in and out of my lungs.

"Ciao, Etto."

I jump.

"I didn't mean to scare you."

"You didn't scare me, signora." It's Signora Sapia, sitting on the rock under the traffic mirror with her sunglasses and her cane. "How did you know it was me, though?"

"At this time of day, it's either German hikers or you doing your deliveries." She laughs. "Then I heard the wheezing and I knew it was you."

"I wasn't wheezing."

She laughs again. "When you're our age, Etto, you'll be used to this old hill . . . watch out!" She points with the red tip of her cane, and I step aside just in time. The Mangona brothers come by on their racing bikes, with their stealth aerodynamics and the orange flame helmets they special ordered from the Netherlands.

"Come on, Etto, train with us, you lukewarm piece of shit," one of the Mangona brothers shouts at me, the backdraft carrying his words. The other one throws his head back and laughs.

"Hey, vaffanculo!" I call after them. "Your auntie!" I add.

They disappear around the corner, and I turn back to Signora Sapia. "Sorry, signora."

"Oh, Etto" is all she says. A few years ago, she would have given me a lecture about cursing and showing lack of respect for the family, and she would have done it swiftly and unapologetically under the statute that allows the nonne to correct the behavior of anyone they are old enough to remember as a child. But nobody ever says a harsh word to me anymore, as if they think I've already done penance enough for a lifetime. Sometimes I wish they'd tell me off like they used to. Just once I'd like to hear it.

I keep walking, crossing over to the top half of the hill. On the bottom half are the nicer villas, the ones with iron fences dropped in plumb lines straight from the sky and brick paths swept as clean as the floor in the shop. These are the people who spend most afternoons and weekends cleaning their land, spitting on and smoothing nature's cowlicks, and waxing the new growth as aggressively as the Eastern European women who work in all the salons in town. It's not until you get above Via Partigiani that the villas start to get more dilapidated, the people more insane. The walls crumble, the cisterns bubble out of nowhere, and the generators growl. These are the people who train their guard dogs to kill, who loudly refuse the services of the comune, who stockpile gold and root vegetables in their cellars, and talk about the cataclysm as if they can't wait.

Pia used to live with her parents on the bottom half of the hill until she married Nello and moved above Via Partigiani. Through the rickety gate, I can see her sitting on the edge of the garden hammock with her sunglasses on. She's trying to pretend she spends the entire afternoon break on this hammock, but I know she only comes outside so she won't have to answer the door in her sunglasses. Someday I'll tell her she's not fooling anyone, that the purple bruise is pooling past the edge of the frames.

"Ciao, Etto."

"Ciao, signora."

"What's this 'signora'?" she says. "Call me Pia."

Pia has brought her purse out to the garden, too. She counts out the money and gives me a little tip as if I'm ten.

"It isn't necessary, Pia."

"Take it. Please, Etto, for your trouble."

"It's no trouble at all." I hand it back to her. "And you know Papà would kill me if I took a tip."

She flinches. Maybe this is your first instinct if you live with a guy like Nello. Maybe it's because of the word *kill*. People will go around entire verbal mountain ranges to avoid particular words with me now. Kill. Death. Drown. Crash. Even Fede with all his cazzate and vulgarity will never say a curse that has to do with mothers or brothers even though it castrates half his usable vocabulary.

"You know, signora . . . Pia," I say, "if you ever need me to bring you anything from town . . . if you ever need anything else, anything at all . . ."

Her dark eyebrows twitch above her sunglasses, slashing my sentence out of the air like Zorro.

"If I need anything, Nello will get it for me," she says sharply.

"Sorry. I was only offering. . . ."

She stays silent, and as I leave through the gate, I can feel her eyes trying to follow me out. Everyone in San Benedetto knew Pia was doomed even before she herself knew it, but Mamma was one of the only women to befriend her. One time when Luca and I were ten or maybe eleven, she even convinced Pia to leave Nello, and Pia stayed at our house for a few nights while Mamma sorted something else out for her. I remember, as a bribe, Mamma told Luca and me we could stay up and watch television if we gave Pia our room, so we were downstairs watching Supercar in our sleeping bags when the intercom rang.

I think Mamma and Papà were expecting it, but they both went immediately quiet, so all you could hear was KITT's fake voice saying, "One man can make a difference, Michael," or whatever it was he used to say. Mamma and Papà whispered for a minute, until the intercom rang again. But instead of answering it, Papà went out through the other apartment, which belonged to Nonna and Nonno back then. We heard their door bang, and then Nello's and Papà's voices out on the street, arguing so loudly that lights started to go on in the palazzo next to ours. And just when we thought Papà was winning, Pia came floating down the stairs like a ghost, as if the heavy jacket and small suitcase she'd come with were her only mass.

Mamma, of course, started to argue with her, and pretty soon it got to be like an opera—tenors on the street below, sopranos above, Mamma pleading with Pia to stay. Just one more night and she'd see how much easier it was. Luca and I turned up the volume and tried to keep our attention on the TV, but it was no use. Mamma's voice rose over it, her Italian splintering under the stress. In the end, Pia floated right out the door, and Mamma threw herself on the sofa next to me and started to cry. I remember Luca and I looking at each other and using that twin telepathy thing to decide to turn the television down and give her a hug because Mamma didn't cry that often, at least not back then, and it was an episode of Supercar we'd both seen before.

Anyway, ever since then, Nello has been a complete stronzo to all of us. To Papà and me, I mean. But in her single act of defiance, Pia continues to buy our meat.

I must have gone on autopilot down the hill because instead of the paths leading me back to the town and the beach, they've delivered me like a chute to the field and the old liceo. After the liceo shut down, it took me a while to reset my routines and shift the center of my world first to the liceo in Albenga and then the shop, but the muscle memory is still there somewhere. I wade through the grass and sit down next to Luca, the lizards scurrying out of my way.

"Ciao, stronzo."

I lie back in the goal and stare at the blue sky rippling through the net. Nothing in San Benedetto ever changes. Especially in the summer. The sun is always shining, the temperature hovering in the same range. They rarely ever lose a day on the beaches. Maybe every few weeks there's a squall out at sea that will bring in some fog or a light rain at night, and once a decade, we'll get a dusting of snow, leaving a few dwarfed and dirty snowmen that quickly melt into the sand.

My phone lights up. Fede, of course.

WHAT ARE YOU DOING SATURDAY?

MY LONG-LOST FAMILY IS ARRIVING FROM RUSSIA.

YOU HAVE FAMILY IN RUSSIA?

IT WAS A JOKE.

BOCCA AND I ARE GOING TO LE ROCCE WITH THE AUSTRALIANS.

HAVE FUN.

YOU'RE GOING TOO.

I'LL THINK ABOUT IT.

COME ON. DAI.

MAYBE.

NO MAYBES.

LEAVE ME ALONE, FEDE. I'M UP HERE MOWING THE FIELD.

FINE. BUT SATURDAY. LE ROCCE. YOU'RE COMING.

I shut my phone off. I'm not mowing the field today. It's too fottuto hot, and I have no desire to die from gasoline fumes as I creep behind the mower like a Vietnamese farmer yoked to a water buffalo, stopping and starting every time the blades choke on a fist of grass. Nobody comes up here anymore anyway. And it's the afternoon break. I don't know how many times I've heard Nonno complain about people eroding the national identity by not observing the break. I'm just doing my part.

I take off my glasses, and everything turns green and soft, set in gentle motion around me. The sun spins and throws off sparks. I close my eyes, listen to the breeze through the cypresses, and drift off into that pleasant limbo between sleep and wake.

I hear the laughter of a girl, and I bolt upright.

"Who's there?" I pat the grass until I find my glasses. "Who is it?"

"I am sorry for waking you," she says in Italian.

The girl is about my age, dressed in a green T-shirt and shorts that look like they came from a school gym class, and there are two guys flanking her like her fottuto guardian angels. They're both older than she is, one dressed like her, and the other like one of the devil's minions—black shorts, black shirt, black Adidas, and a black tattoo swirling up his arm.

"This is your field?" the girl asks. She's obviously not Italian. Her accent is off, the middles and ends of her words sharp like elbows.

"Mine? No."

"Is this . . . somebody's field?"

I don't want to stare at her legs, but I can't help it. She's got great legs, muscular thighs and calves, tapering down to delicate ankles.

"Well, it used to be the field for the liceo," I say. "But the liceo was shut down, so I think it became the general property of the comune. But then the comune leased it to my father for one euro a year—well, the mayor, actually, who was doing my father a favor, leased it to him . . ." Her forehead is straining under the weight of this information, her eyes squinched shut like flower buds in the sunlight. "And we're supposed to be responsible for the maintenance, but nobody really comes up here anyway . . ."

One of the men asks her something, and she answers him in some other language.

"Do you speak English?" she asks me.

"Yes."

"We are new in town. Can we play calcio here, or not?"

I shrug. "Hey, it's a free country. The field's not in great condition, of course. No one's played here in a while. There's another field in town that's much nicer than this. Right behind the Standa. Astroturf. Painted lines. No horrible walk up the hill."

The two men turn to her, and there's a short conference, after which she turns to me.

"Thank you. You are very sympathetic. We are sorry to disturb your nap. We will come back later."

The three of them turn around and disappear into the tangled weeds and scrub, as quickly and completely as they appeared. I sit spooked for a minute, the afternoon cicadas screeching around me.

"Who the cazzo was that?" I ask Luca, but he only stares back at me and gives me his mysterious smile.

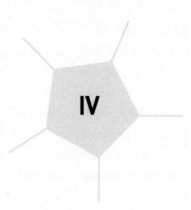

IV

hen I open the door to Martina's, it sounds like the roar of the sea. The flat-screen is turned up to full volume, with prosecutors and publicists looming like mountains and booming like cannons, each man in the bar trying to overlay his own commentary. Most of them have been here since Sunday night going over the forensics of the Genoa-Venezia match in minute detail. Charon used to call them the "small-souled," these men who have been blessed or cursed with early pensions from the railroad or sons to run their businesses. They are permanent fixtures at Martina's, subsisting on a constant drip of coffee and grappa, their days spent doing a dead man's float over their newspapers, their evenings spent shouting at the flat-screen.

"Do not be sucked into the vestibule of their apathy," Charon would bellow at us. "Look and pass." He would pause a moment to allow his voice to travel the length of the aula. "*Look* and *pass.*"

And Casella and I would nearly get sinus infections from holding back our snorting.

"Ciao, tesoro," Martina says. I take my seat at the bar, and she leans over and kisses me on the cheeks. The flat-screen flashes shots of a few players and managers shading their faces and ducking into doorways, then stock clips of courtrooms.

"What's all this?"

"You haven't heard about the scandal?"

"Still?"

"It's only just begun. They've announced that there's going to be an official investigation. Your papà is beside himself."

I pick him out in the crowd of men, his face heavy with anxiety.

"Anyway, I'm sorry, tesoro, but they started coming early this morning, and I haven't managed to cook anything all day. I called Belacqua. He said he would be over with a pizza for you, but that was an hour ago."

I make the silent calculations in my head. Belacqua's uncle's pizzeria is at the other end of the passeggiata. He'll stop and have one joint down on the rocks, maybe two, and by the time he gets here, the pizza will be cold as stone.

The commercials come on, and someone turns down the volume. This is always a sign of calcio arguments ahead, which you who call it soccer instead of calcio might find hard to keep up with. As long as you understand that this is just an infinitesimal fraction of the pain I suffer having to listen to this cazzate every day.

"It is the ultimate injustice," Papà thunders. "The *ultimate* injustice. Yuri Fil didn't leave the field because of match fixing. He left because of his ankle, an old injury from his Kiev Dynamo days. So they are singling him out for having a *disability*? Where is the justice in that?"

"Amazing how those old ankles act up when it's convenient, isn't it?"

"And what if he left the field because he wanted no part in the match fixing?" Papà presses. "If he went off because he didn't want to shoot on a keeper who was going to step aside and let the ball go in no matter what? This is called sportsmanship. This is called integrity. What would be wrong with that?"

"What would be wrong with that? It would show that he knew about the fix. That's called de facto participation." Cazzo, how they love their Latin when they're arguing.

"Well, who's to say that Genoa wouldn't have won anyway? After all, that new Venezia keeper is so young he's still trying to find his *own* balls."

Everyone laughs.

Waiting for Belacqua to show up with my pizza, I find out more about the scandal than I ever wanted to know: the wiretaps at the hotel, the briefcase of money found in the Venezia manager's car, and of course, Yuri Fil's controversial self-substitution only thirteen minutes into the first half. On the surface, it's the same shouting and waving as on every Sunday night during the season, when they make the weekly reordering of the calcio scarves above the bar—victors and heroes on the left, losers and sons of whores on the right. It's the same pinching and thrusting of various combinations of fingers, the same insulting of mothers, aunties, first-grade teachers, and ancestors all the way back to the Romans. Only tonight, the room is creaking under the weight of grand abstractions. Integrity. Sportsmanship. Tradition. Honor.

"I don't *care* about the technicalities!" Papà shouts to the others, wringing his hands as if he's making patties out of them. "I still say Yuri Fil did the honorable thing."

"And *I* still say that Yuri Fil refusing to play is an admission of guilt," Nello says. "That means he knew about the fix and didn't say a word."

"And what about everyone else? Are you telling me no one else on that team knew?"

Gubbio, the mayor, shrugs. "I don't see why it's such a big affair anyway. Genoa needed the win. Venezia didn't. And so Genoa should get the win. For Venezia to lose the game is the honorable thing to do."

"If it's so honorable, why do they need a briefcase full of money?"

"A quarter of a million euros in calcio these days is nothing. A gratuity. A tip."

"Aha, you see? That is exactly the problem," Sordello chimes in from one of the card tables. Sordello's cousin is a second-string midfielder on some Serie C2 team in the south, and he tries to slip in his pedigree wherever he can. "I was talking with my cousin about this a couple of weeks ago, and he agrees with me—calcio has drifted into complete anarchy. A ship without a pilot, a whorehouse where ultras can turn stadiums upside down, players change allegiance every season and will do anything for fame or money. Where is the love of the game, I ask you? The old guys would be *ashamed* if they could see what has become of calcio in this country. And where is the leadership to right the ship? The teams are all run by tyrant businessmen, by a bunch of bossy peasant clowns."

"Ah, but if only it were the individuals." Mimmo takes his turn, and everyone faces him. "It's the *system*. It's this unchecked capitalism eroding everything. Money, the root of all evil."

"Eh, eh, eh . . . I'm surprised you're not handing out leaflets, Mimmo."

"I'm having them printed," he says, and continues, "Look at the financial doping of calcio, the corruption in the government, the breakup of the family, this tabloid-reality-television nonsense—it's all related, and there wasn't any of it back in the old days when a calcio player made the same as his brother in the factory, and they played purely for the love of the game."

There is a general murmuring of agreement around the bar. "Ah . . . sì, sì . . ."

My phone lights up. Fede again.

WE'RE AT CAMILLA'S. COME ON OVER.

I'M AT MARTINA'S.

WELL, EAT AND GET OVER HERE.

"Don't be ridiculous," Farinata's voice booms as he rises slowly from his stool in the corner. He's the oldest fascist in town, and people call him Il Duce, which I think secretly pleases him. "It's not the money. It's not the system. It's not the lack of leadership. It's the *foreigners*. Think about it. We didn't have any scandals until the foreign players started pouring in. 1980. Liam Brady. That's where it all began and ended. And so goes calcio, there goes Italy."

"Euh. Come on!" Papà waves him away. "Are you joking? Liam Brady was squeaky clean. A sportsman and a gentleman. A bella figura if ever there was one!"

"Here, here!"

"And 1980? 1980 you said? Are you out of your mind? Have you for-gotten about Totonero, the scandal of all scandals? Pellegrini, Cacciatori, Albertosi, Paolo Rossi!" Papà counts them off on his fingers. "You hear any foreign names in there?"

"Hey, leave Paolo Rossi out of it. He did his six goals of penance dur-ing the '82 World Cup."

"Ah . . . sì, sì . . ." everyone murmurs again.

The door opens and the scarves flutter above the bar. Signor Cato in the corner reaches for his hair as if for an imaginary hat, his eyes never leav-ing the computer screen. After his wife died, Mamma and Martina tried to keep him busy by making him take those computer classes for old people. Now he spends every day dredging the Internet for the trash of the world.

Belacqua sets the cold pizza down on the counter.

"It's about time," Martina says. She goes to the kitchen and comes back with a plate, a fork, a knife, and a napkin, still fighting the losing battle of trying to civilize us.

"Hey, boss." Belacqua grins and sits down on the stool next to me. "Sorry the pizza's a little cold."

"Have a nice smoke?"

"How do you know I smoked?"

"You're reeking of it."

"A guy's got to rest. What's that Aristotle said, 'the soul that rests be-comes wise'?"

"You must be a *fottuto* genius, then."

He grins. "So, what's all the commotion here?"

"Eh. Calcio, what else?"

"All I'm saying"—Farinata is shouting now—"is that the calcio scan-dals are only the symptom of an *epidemic.* I don't care if you're talking about Liam Brady or fucking Ian Rush and his fucking baked beans and pudding or these damn Moroccans selling their coconuts on the beach!"

"Farinata!" Martina shouts. "Language!"

He waves her away.

"Don't you wave me away, Farinata! I'm warning you!"

"Calma, calma, everyone," Nicola Nicolini says, holding up his manicured hands, his ten-gazillion-euro watch glinting in the light. "It's only calcio. No reason to string anyone upside down in the gas station."

"I'll bet *he'd* like to be strung upside down," Signor Cavalcanti says under his breath. "That finocchio." Laughter ripples down the bar.

But Farinata keeps going. Once he gets onto his fascist shit, he can't be stopped. "You people are in a constant state of denial. *First* they took over the stadiums, *then* they started working in our streets and our piazzas, *now* they're buying up businesses and diluting the gene pool! Don't you see?"

"If we're still producing people like you, Farinata, maybe we should be trying to dilute the gene pool." The bar shakes again with laughter.

"That's it . . . keep on laughing. You'll see. You'll see. It's not their homeland so why should they care what happens to it? And once it stops resembling the Italy we know, the Italy our children and grandchildren know, our young people will stop caring what happens to it, too. And if we, the leadership"—here, half the bar snorts—"aren't the tiniest bit vigilant, one day we're all going to be sitting around here drinking Turkish coffee and bowing to Mecca, and Serie A will be nothing more than a fucking third-world, dirt-and-chicken-fence calcio league."

"Farinata!" Martina shouts, but he ignores her.

"Fari!" a voice from the corner booms. This time, everyone turns in the direction of the computer alcove. Signor Cato's skin is almost transparent, his face glowing as brightly as the monitor. He glares at the offender across the room, one bushy, white eyebrow cocked above his eye. Like all the other old guys who fought in the resistance during the war, Signor Cato is afforded a long list of liberties, including but not limited to drinking wine in the mornings, calling middle-aged men by their diminutives, and being listened to when he wants to say something. Which should not be underrated.

"Fari," he says again, his voice coming from the depth of all his years. "No one wants to hear your fascist cazzate."

Farinata holds his palms out in his best martyr pose. "Look, all I'm saying is that everyone in this room saw Luca play. It was a miracle. A vision. But even at the academy, Luca was third-string behind a Brazilian and an African. And every day, good Italian boys like Luca grow up admiring the Paolo Rossis and the Dino Zoffs, rooting for the Azzurri, dreaming of playing for a Serie A team, and then? Third-string."

The room goes silent once Luca's name is invoked, and everyone turns toward Papà to see his reaction.

"I'll thank you to keep my son's name out of your mouth," Papà says calmly, but then again, he always sounds calm when he's about to explode.

"Carlo's right," Nello calls out from the corner. "That was a bad example, Farinata. Luca was half *American*."

Papà's chair vibrates against the floor as he stands up, and before anyone can do anything, he grabs Nello by the collar. They both go down, grunting and pushing, punching and kicking, Papà delivering a head butt squarely in Nello's gut, Nello baring his teeth and pulling Papà's forearm like a turkey leg toward his gaping mouth. Pretty soon, everyone in the bar is on their feet, and all I can see is a tangled, writhing ball of limbs, the chairs jumping as they slam into them.

"Whoa . . . fight . . ." Belacqua says.

"Stop it! Stop it!" Martina shouts, and I feel her grip on my arm. Which is funny, actually, because the last thing I would do is get involved in this. And Signor Cato is apparently thinking the same thing because he throws up his hands and turns his attention back to the computer.

Finally, Silvio and the others manage to pull Papà and Nello off each other, and they both end up sitting on the floor like little children, legs spread, huffing and panting, faces covered in sweat and dirt.

"Nello, get out," Martina says, her entire body pointing the way to the door.

"What?"

"Get out."

"Why me?"

"You know what you said. Get out. Go. And don't come back until I send for you."

Nello stands up with a grunt and brushes himself off. He looks around for allies, but no one speaks up.

"Oh, is that how it is?" He waves his hand dismissively at the entire bar. "Cowards. Well, vaffanculo, all of you." He puts his hand in the crook of his elbow and thrusts his fist into the air. "Vaf-fan-cu-lo."

It's only as he leaves that I notice the girl from the field this morning standing in the doorway next to Signora Malaspina's ugly niece. Silence blows through the room, like everyone taking a breath at the same time.

"We didn't mean to make such an entrance," Signora Malaspina's ugly niece says, cackling, clutching the girl's arm like they're best friends.

"Come in, girls, come in." I don't know how Martina does it, but she somehow manages to give fifty grown men the evil eye at the same time, and like schoolboys, they start picking up chairs and fetching brooms.

"Carlo, you're a mess," she scolds Papà. "Go to the toilet and clean yourself up."

"Did you hear what he said?" Papà protests. "Did you *hear* what he *said*? You can't let that stronzo in here ever again."

"Let's get one thing clear, Carlo. I saw two stronzos. Grown men fighting like teenagers, tearing up my place, my *parents'* place, peace to their souls. Go on." She pushes him toward the bathroom and turns to the girls. "Sometimes I wonder why I even bother."

The girls look at the whole scene and shrug, like they expect no less from our gender. I can't for the life of me remember the name of the niece, but I know she lives with her aunt, spinster-style, in an apartment in Albenga, taking care of her and helping to rent out the villa.

"We wanted to use your Internet, Martina. The cable guy was supposed to be at the villa today, but he never showed up."

"Go right ahead. Signor Cato was just logging off."

"I was?"

"Yes, you were." Martina shows the girls back to the alcove, and Signor Cato wanders out into the main room and sits next to me at the bar, grumbling about how all he wanted was a little peace in his golden years, and instead, he's being forced to sit and keep company with a bunch of sons of whores.

"What you got there tonight?" he says in dialect, leaning over my plate. I get a good look inside his ears, the hair so prolific it's like small, arctic animals hibernating in there.

"Pizza. You want some?"

"Nah."

"I'll have some." Ciacco appears on the other side, but Martina shoos him away.

"Would you let the boy eat in peace?"

The girl sits down at the computer, and Signora Malaspina's ugly niece leans against the arch of the alcove, facing the rest of the room like a guard dog. I try to glance generally in the direction of the computer, but every time I try, I only manage to catch the eye of the niece. The conversations around me resume at a low, buzzing tone, but no one turns up the volume of the flat-screen. I can tell they're waiting for them to leave so they can start gossiping about who the girl is. After all, you can't expect to show up at Martina's and remain a nobody, a nonentity, when the rest of us are forced to stoop under the weight of everything we and our fathers and our fathers' fathers have ever thought, said, or done in the region.

The girl gets up from the computer and moves toward the bar, and I can feel the eyes in the room silently tracking her. Signor Cato scurries back into the computer alcove, and they fill in his space at the bar, the girl resting her hands on the edge of the wood. She's wearing a light scarf looped around her neck like a nest for her head, and a green warm-up jacket, the sleeves pushed up, the brown freckles on her arms chasing each other into the sleeves. Signora Malaspina's niece stands on the other side, trapping me in between.

"Ciao, Etto," she says. She tries to hand Martina a euro, but Martina brushes it away.

"Don't worry about it. She was on there less than five minutes."

"You sure?"

"Sure. Believe me, it's just nice to see some women in here once in a while."

"Amen," someone at the bar says, and there is some restrained laughter.

"What are you eating, Etto?" Signora Malaspina's niece asks.

"It's this new thing called pizza," I say, and she laughs. She's our age, but I don't really know her. She was in the hospitality program with Fede and Bocca. They say she always aspired to be the puttana of the class, but nobody would sleep with her.

"Is this your uncle's pizza, Belacqua?" Signora Malaspina's ugly niece asks, and Belacqua gives her a lazy smile in return.

"You have to go there," she instructs the girl over my head. "Belacqua here may be nothing more than a stoner, but his uncle makes the best pizza in the region, right, Etto?"

"Right." I can feel my face turning red. I know whatever I say is being recorded by fifty pairs of eyes, the owners of which will play it back to me mercilessly and with commentary every night for the next month.

"We just saw Fede and the rest of them over at Camilla's. He said you were all going to Le Rocce on Saturday night."

"I haven't decided yet."

"You should. It'll be fun. Who knows? Maybe we'll even meet you there."

I can feel the girl looking down at me, but no matter how much I try, I can't look up at her, like her face is some fottuto solar eclipse and I need a cardboard box with a pinhole.

"What's the matter, Etto? You forget how to speak Italian?" Signora Malaspina's ugly niece laughs again. She has one of those hyena laughs, sucking in air.

"With girls, he only speaks Awkward," somebody shouts, and they all laugh.

Signora Malaspina's niece steps back from the bar, and I'm about to sigh with relief when the girl taps me on the shoulder and says in English, "Hey. Don't you remember me?"

Shit.

"The field? This morning?"

I hear the whispers behind me.

"Ah, yes. Sorry, I didn't recognize you."

"Did you have a nice nap?"

"Yes, yes."

"I'm sorry again that we disturbed you."

"Come on, let's go," Signora Malaspina's ugly niece says, and she pulls the girl by the sleeve like she's a child. "Ciao-ciao, Etto. We'll see you Saturday night."

"I never said I was going."

She waves vaguely to the room, weaving through the chairs. "Ciao, everybody!"

"Ciao!" the whole room shouts back.

"He has a stable job!"

"And he likes children!"

"And he's a virgin!" Mino shouts after them, mercifully in dialect, but Signora Malaspina's niece is laughing her hyena laugh, and I know she will translate everything later. Shit. I bury my head in my hands, and the sea air hits me in the back as they leave. The others start in on me immediately.

"What's the matter with you, Etto? Cat got your pisello?"

"Porca miseria! Not one but *two* girls trying to talk to you, and all you could do was play the mute."

"Youth is wasted on the young."

"Isn't it?"

"I thought we were going to have to commit a mercy killing!"

"Who is she? Anyone seen her before?"

"Probably one of Signora Malaspina's renters."

"She looks a little grubby for that, no?"

"Maybe she's a nanny. She looked Irish to me."

"Ha! Etto looks more Irish than her."

"German, then."

"Euh. She can't be German. Germans always travel in packs."

"Or battalions. Or brigades," someone calls out, and everyone laughs.

"Maybe she's American."

"Not fat enough to be American."

"Maybe *you* should move to America, Ciacco."

"This?" Ciacco pats his belly. "All muscle. Feel it. Go on . . . feel it."

"I'm not touching anything. Who knows where that's been?"

Around and around they go. Blah, blah, blah. She can't be English because she was wearing a scarf against the drafts, and the English, especially since Iraq, have it in their heads that they are like the Americans and suddenly above such European principles as drafts and air pressure. She can't be Canadian, Austrian, or Australian because Canadians, Austrians, and

Australians always announce themselves in the first minute so they will not be mistaken for Americans, Germans, or English. Not bitchy enough to be Russian. Not snobby enough to be French. And on and on.

"What's all this?" Papà is back from the bathroom, his face shiny, the damp clinging to the bristles of his hair.

"Some girl came in with Signora Malaspina's niece and started flirting with Etto."

"Just now?"

"Just now."

"Who is she?"

"No one knows."

For a second I think Papà might show some interest, but as soon as he sits down, they're immediately back to the scandal. After every interruption, every argument, every tragedy, it all goes back to calcio. I'll bet even before the smoke cleared in Pompei, the two surviving goat herders dusted off a skull or a string ball or whatever they used in those days and started kicking it around in the ashes.

"Is everything okay, tesoro?" Martina asks, because she is the queen of all women and has a sixth sense about everything.

"Fine, fine."

"Do you want some fruit? I have plums."

"No thanks."

She clears away my plate. "How about a Coca-Cola, tesoro? Or a chinotto?"

"Thanks, Martina, but I think I'll go over to Camilla's."

"Okay, then. See you tomorrow."

"Until tomorrow."

I go over to Camilla's, where the average age of the small-souled drops at least a generation. It's only Camilla's second year running her bar, so she still has a makeshift boardwalk, hammered together out of wooden skids and sunk into the sand, the lights from the passeggiata providing the only illumination. Fede, Bocca, Claudia, and Sima are all sitting in plastic chairs around one of the outside tables.

"Ciao, Etto."

"You made it."

Sima looks up at me with the same expression of confusion Nonna has. "Ciao, Etto," she says, but her voice is like an echo, and before I can answer, she lowers her head.

"Where's Casella?" I say to Claudia.

"Why are you asking me?" Claudia says. "Casella has his own life. I don't control him. It's perfectly feasible that he would be out somewhere on his own."

"He's in the toilet," Bocca says.

"I still can't believe you let him go to the toilet without asking permission, Claudia," Fede says. "Who's going to wear the pants in your family? You can't just have him up and going to the toilet whenever he feels like it."

"Very funny." She crosses her arms and leans back in her chair. "So, Etto, I hear you, Fede, and Bocca have some hot Australian dates at Le Rocce on Saturday night."

"I didn't say I was going."

"Fede did."

"Maybe Fede thinks if he tells enough people, it will come true."

"Come on, Etto, don't be such a downer," Fede says. "One night at a disco won't hurt you."

"You only want me to come and translate for you."

"What makes you think that?"

"Do they speak Italian?"

"No."

"And I already know what your English sounds like."

"English is overrated." Fede grins, the same grin that gets the girls. "We have the language of the scorpion."

"Porca vacca." Claudia rolls her eyes. "Are you still wearing that suit?"

"What's wrong with it?"

Claudia looks out over our heads, down the passeggiata. "Oh, look. Here comes Francesca with her brand-new bocce. I'll bet she's still got the bandages on underneath."

"Those aren't real?" Bocca asks.

"Of course not," Fede says.

"How can you tell?"

Fede shrugs. "I just know."

"I heard she went to Nice and got the two-for-one."

"Really?"

"Don't you remember The Nose?" Claudia hisses, then smiles at the girl as she passes by. "Ciao, Francesca."

"Ciao," Francesca answers, but you can tell she gossips about Claudia behind her back, too.

"I will never understand how she ended up with Gianni. He's so ugly."

"That depends on what you mean by 'with.'"

"What do you know?"

"Ask Paolo."

"She's cheating on him with Paolo? As in, his *brother* Paolo?"

Bocca shrugs. "You didn't hear it from me."

"I can't believe it!" Claudia says, her mouth gaping wide. "I can't believe it. How did *that* happen?"

"Gianni asked Paolo to tutor her in English before their vacation to London."

"Tutoring . . ." Fede says. "Why didn't I ever think of that?"

This is how they will squander the entire night, pretty much like they've squandered every night since puberty, on bickering, gossip, and other stupidaggini—who has and hasn't had work done, who's gotten together or broken up, what happened at the beach or at Claudia's parents' restaurant. Claudia in particular is always pointing out people's plastic surgery, as if no one noticed when she came back from the "Bahamas" that one Christmas and her nose was half the size.

I watch Claudia's sister Camilla through the front windows of the bar, which are flung open to the night air. She's rushing back and forth, pulling out bottles, greeting people, and giving instructions to the bartenders. She bought this bar at nineteen with her own money, and now it's the most popular one for the under-thirty crowd. Sometimes it's hard to believe that she and Claudia come from the same parents. I wonder if Luca and I would have anything in common by now, or if his life would be a string of matches, interviews, girlfriends, and parties. Maybe he would still be with the French girl, or maybe he would have found himself a proper showgirl to hang his arm on. Maybe he would be playing for Milan, or abroad, in England or Spain. I wonder if he would still call home like he used to at the academy, or if he would fade away and come back to San Benedetto only when he had a girl to impress or felt some nostalgia for the holidays.

Fede changes the subject to the topless woman at the beach, and Casella finally comes back from the toilet.

"Ciao, Etto. Glad you could make it. How'd that band saw blade work out?"

"Fine, fine."

I try to remember how it used to be with Casella, when it was just the two of us hanging out, talking about life or the girls we liked. We'd laugh about the comic books we used to make, which became our joint obsession for at least six or seven years. I would do the drawing, and Casella would do the writing and the lettering. We were young and stupid, so most of them were rip-offs of something else. There was one called *SuperBunny*, about a rabbit that was impervious to everything but carrots. Then *Crabman*, the mild-mannered teenager who turned into a crab and swung from the tops of buildings with his crab hands, and of course *Cin-Cin*, the flame-haired reporter who traveled the world with a dog and a drink in his hands, toasting the death of tyrants and stereotyping the natives. Jacopo's mother would let us use the copier at the Hotel Paradiso, and we'd walk the whole length of the beach, right behind the Algerians and their fake purses, selling copies for a thousand lire apiece.

"I mean, they're just so ugly . . ." Fede continues, still going on about Medusa.

"The Spanish say there is no ugly," Claudia says, "only strange beauty."

"Then no one in Spain has ever seen a chest that looks like a pair of wet pantyhose hanging on the line. She should need a license for that, or at least special dispensation from Father Marco. Those things have got to be worth a couple of Hail Marys at least."

"Fede, does Father Marco even know who you are?" Claudia asks.

"Sure. I go to confession every couple of weeks."

"*You do?*" This gets the same stunned look from everyone at the table.

"But, Fede, you don't even go to Mass."

Fede shrugs. "Hey, you can't let that stuff build up."

"Let me get this straight. You—Fede—go to *confession*?" Claudia demands.

"Why is that so surprising?"

Claudia rolls her eyes at him. "Well, I hope you confess your beach attire sins. If that poor old woman is condemned for going topless, I have a long list of men who should wear out their knees begging for forgiveness."

"Who?"

"Number one—Mimmo and Franco and those tiny suits. Number two—you and your scorpion. Oh, look, not as long a list as I thought."

Fede smirks. He crosses his arms, and his muscles pop to the surface. "Did you hear that, Casella? Your girlfriend's looking at my scorpion."

"You know, I've had enough of you for one night, Fede. Come on, Casella, let's go inside and talk to my sister." Claudia stands up, and Casella follows.

"Good plan, Casella," Fede says. "Maybe if you trail behind her long enough, she'll accidentally drop some sex your way."

"Shut up, Fede." Claudia throws a coaster at him, hitting him on the shoulder.

But Fede doesn't stop. "You see? I just got closer than you ever will."

"You're a stronzo, Fede," Claudia says, and she marches off.

Bocca and Fede laugh, and Sima looks up from her phone.

"What was that about?"

"Nothing."

"Oh."

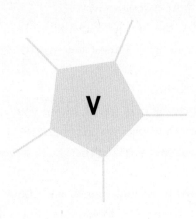

V

ow, I think, is as good a time as any to tell you the tragic history of eligible women in the region.

In the beginning, right after God created the Azzurri, God created the temptation for the Azzurri and all the rest of us. Not apples. Women. And not just functional women like the English and Germans have, but decorative ones, mermaids and Nereids, gifts from the sea, muses for poetry, painting, and a lot of late-night, under-the-covers pulling of the saw. For a while beauty begat beauty, and generations of eligible women flooded through the Roman aqueducts and Etruscan irrigation ditches into even the smallest seaside towns like San Benedetto. But in the normal course of evolution, the women were forced to adopt survival mechanisms to protect them from their predators, id est, the men.

And so by the mid–twentieth century, most of the remaining women had grown cat's-eye glasses to distort their eyes, sprouted dark hairs on their lips, and developed an affinity for granny pants, which pleased their pious mothers and protective fathers but no one else. The herds of young, eligible women thinned, and the entire coast started to swell with nonne.

And as the men in the region sat around the bars, desperately trying to think of a way to seed the clouds, one man appeared, a hero and a savior, though disguised as an enemy foreigner.

That man's name was Martin Malaspina. As in, Martin Malaspina the Italian-American Hollywood director. Maybe you've heard of him. Anyway, he fell in love with one of the few remaining genetic aberrations who had survived the cat's-eye-glasses and granny-pants mutation, and as he fell, he hit his head and mistook the concussion for an idea—the absurd idea that San Benedetto was a worthy setting for a Hollywood movie. And in the brittle newspaper clipping tacked to the wall of nearly every restaurant and bar in the region, Martin Malaspina is standing in front of Signor Cato's fishing boat, a prophet in sunglasses, pronouncing San Benedetto the last spot on earth that is simple and pure, where his ancestors' bones sanctify the ground, the light is brought down from on high by angels, and those Italian fishermen, well, they really know how to, you know, *live*.

So just like that, Martin Malaspina waved his magic wand—and rumor is, it was a big wand—and brought money and fame to San Benedetto. For a few short, blissful years, everyone in the world knew this town, and every woman wanted to come here—Roman society girls, Hollywood starlets, Parisian models swanning down the pedestrian zones in their scarves and sunglasses. Even *Playboy* Bunnies, who came to shoot an entire issue on the beach. *Playboy* Bunnies! Can you imagine?

Of course, this was heaven on earth for the men of San Benedetto, who were suddenly getting attention from unfathomably beautiful and exotic women. No one worried about money anymore. They let the fishing industry sink, chopped the long stretch of public beach into private bagni, crammed the pedestrian zones with crap shops, crapatorie, and Krapkauf-hausen, and began dropping hotels into construction craters.

And then? Bam! After six or seven summers, it was over as quickly as it had begun.

Because just as it had started with one man, it ended with one man. The same man. Martin Malaspina, who had an affair with his guru's daughter, and up and left the newly minted Signora Malaspina in the lonely villa on top of the hill, only surfacing some months later in India to announce his next film. And somewhere there is a stretch of teahouses with clippings of him standing on the banks of the Ganges, enthusiastically declaring that Calcutta is the last place on earth that is simple and pure, where the ground is sanctified by the spirits of his reincarnated ancestors, the light is brought down from on high by devas, and those Indians and their cardboard slums, well, they really know how to, you know, *live.*

With the glamour taken away from San Benedetto, the foreign women evacuated with such speed that it left a powerful vacuum, sucking the middle-aged Milanesi families out of the concrete and pulling busloads of old German Herrs and Fraus from all the way across the Alps. And where did these crowds of eligible women foreigners, these dense crosshatches of XX chromosomes, go? Some followed Swami Malaspina to the banks of the Ganges, but the others wandered up and down the boot like restless ghosts, looking for the myth of Italy. First to Rome because of some other movie, then Florence. The American ones eventually migrated farther down the coast, where locals in Portofino, the Cinque Terre, and Positano, like all good prostitutes, made them feel like they were the first ones ever to plant a flag in their land. And the divorced ones began to hole up in broken-down villas in Chianti-shire, loudly declaring their independence and still quietly hoping for some young, shirtless stallion to appear at the half door with a box of Barilla. There was a flash of hope again when the iron curtain creaked open, but the flood of blond girls rushed right past San Benedetto to Monaco and Monte Carlo, where the men let them throw money around and gave them something to prove. You'd be surprised how many beautiful women are masochists like that, only living to prove themselves to other people. Cazzo, how many people. Really.

And what happened to the domestic ones? While everyone else's attention was diverted, a few strains had quietly survived. Not only survived but become stronger and even more beautiful, like a tree that has been pruned to within an inch of its life or a superbug surviving generation after generation of antibiotics. They'd grown up with Italian men, were wise to our pathetic tactics, and knew we weren't anything special. So they came to be at a premium, settling into a strict rotation through the Serie A clubhouses, of which George Clooney's villa on Lake Como seems to have become an honorary member.

Anyway, I blame the decades-long shortage for this sudden weakness inside me, for this strange feeling that Kryptonite can come in the form of a bright green warm-up jacket, and a head full of dark curls can be like blood in the water, my mind circling the poor girl until I can almost hear the *Jaws* music starting up in the background. Nuh-NUH. Nuh-NUH. Nuh-nuh-nuh-nuh-nuh-nuh-nuh-nuh-nuh-nuh.

The Milanesi arrive on Friday, and all afternoon, there's a slow stream of cars and buses clogging up Via Londra, each one releasing the stink of Autogrill sandwiches and fake-pine air fresheners as they pull to the side, dropping off wives and children who whine to have their first look at the sea while their Vatis or papàs unload the luggage and park the car. By Saturday morning, they're already making themselves at home, the adults staggering under the weight of sand buckets, snacks, and SPF 70 for the delicate skin of their precious Pasquales and Adrianas.

I stand outside on the balcony on Saturday morning, smoking my first cigarette of the day. The sun is shining, and the waves are sparkling. Franco's dog is lying in the shade of the entrance hut at Bagni Liguria, and I can hear Fede, Franco, and the others joking around on the beach as they set up the chaises and umbrellas. The Mangona brothers are already doing a brisk business in their huts, which sit across from each other like the ceremonial gates to the molo. They sell the exact same stock of candy and Coca-Cola for the exact same price, and they put all the profits into a joint bank account that pays for all the custom bicycles they could ever want. But from May through September they keep up a fierce competition and separate tallies, and the loser has to keep his hut open for the seven dead winter months, blowing on his hands in front of a space heater while the winner sits comfortably at home or at the bar. Because of this, after each transaction, they exchange a flurry of vaffanculos of both victory and defeat. I watch them for a while, middle fingers and fists and palms flashing in the morning sunshine, twisting birds, figs, and umbrellas high into the air until they look like they could take flight.

"Ciao, Etto," Franco calls up from the passeggiata. "You on strike today?"

"I wish."

I go downstairs to the shop and flip on the fluorescents. The vitello and the side of beef have already migrated from the back walk-in to the front walk-in, broken down into commas, parentheses, and question marks of flesh. Papà prefers to do all the real butchering alone during the break, finishing the smaller jobs between the trickle of customers from four thirty to six. Every morning when I walk in, it feels like the meat fairy has visited the night before.

I set up the banco and put on an apron. The first hour is slow, so I take the time to string up two young roosters in a face-off, wings fastened back with toothpicks as if they are about to draw imaginary pistols. I cut and tape together white paper boots, white holsters and belts, even cowboy hats where their heads should be. Regina Salveggio's kids press their grubby faces to the glass to get a better look as I wrap up their prosciutto and chicken breasts.

"Could you cut the chicken into strips, Etto? The kids won't eat it if the chicken looks too much like chicken."

Next is Signora Sapia, led around now by the daughter-in-law she used to gossip about.

Then Signora Argenti, who asks me every day what's fresh.

"Everything is fresh, of course."

"That is what your father always says."

"That's because it's true."

Signora Costanza, the smallest and oldest of the nonne, is the last customer of the day. I have to stand on the points of my toes to see her over the banco, and she grins up at me like a little kid.

"What can I get for you, signora?"

"Well, Etto, I was thinking about making a nice roasted chicken today . . ."

"Chicken, coming right up."

". . . but then I thought, well, what am I going to do with an entire chicken? It'll take me a week to eat with my appetite, and besides, all that skin is deadly for my cholesterol." And Signora Costanza launches into some story about her dead husband, her daughter in England, her cholesterol, and how Signor Cato told her about this strange fishing net or spiderweb or something who can answer all of her questions instantly— have I heard of it?

I white-knuckle the top of the banco and look past the poof of her hair. I don't know what it is about her dentures, but she whistles when she talks, the air passing through her as easily as through the bare branches of a tree. Some of the Milanesi fathers wander by the front window, stooping over their BlackBerries and shuffling blindly down the passeggiata, the weight of the banking world placed squarely on their shoulders. They say Milan is just like any small town, fathers and grandfathers bequeathing their professions to their sons, along with the cell numbers of their psychiatrists and chiropractors. Maybe in a hundred years, their lineages will develop their own genetic adaptations, their fingers shrinking to fit the tiny keyboards, their pupils square instead of round to make the computer screens easier to read.

"Etto?" Signora Costanza is looking up at me, wide-eyed. "Is everything okay?"

"Sorry, signora. A chicken breast it is, then. I'll take the skin off for you."

"I said I've decided on the rabbit."

"Half or quarter?"

"Quarter . . . are you sure you're okay, dear?"

"Yes, yes, signora. Just meditating on the meat. Part of the business. Fore or hind?"

"Hind."

"Very well, signora." I pull the rabbit out of the case and take it to the block in back. I turn it on its side and pinch the furry feet together. WHACK goes the tail. I press down on its spine, spreading it on the board like the bad guys when they get arrested in the American cop shows. WHACK, WHACK go the back feet. Lucky for you, were they, bunny? I bung them into the garbage box and press down on the bunny's back until the small bones give way and make a satisfying crack. WHACK. And again the other way. WHACK, WHACK. I can see Signora Costanza flinching through the bead curtain. I rip a sheet of paper off the roll and wrap up one of the tiny quarters. I put the other three on a tray and slide it into the case.

"You know, Etto, you're always welcome to come over for lunch sometime, you and your papà. You only have to let me know so I can prepare enough. I don't make as much as I used to now that it's only me. . . ." I try to imagine the three of us hunched in Signora Costanza's tiny kitchen, Papà's head hovering over his plate as he shovels it in, Signora Costanza and me having the same nonconversation we have every morning.

"That's very kind, signora, but I usually only have a sandwich in the afternoon."

"Well, perhaps in the evening, then."

"I would, signora, but then Martina would be insulted."

"Well, if you ever change your mind . . ."

I give her my best fake smile. Not a chance, signora. Not a chance. I hand the package over the banco, and she has to stand on her toes. She takes forever to count out the money, and I stand behind the register with the drawer open, the impatience nibbling away at me.

"You know, I can open a conto for you anytime, signora. You could pay once a month."

"No, no," she says, "I don't believe in this credit thing. What you buy, you pay for at once. That is what my father taught me. That is what I've always done." She finds the last coins in the bottom of her bag. "There you are. Tell your papà hello, Etto. He's such a good man."

"I will, signora."

"And I may not be in every day next week. You know, Signora Malaspina told me that she would have me over for dinner sometime soon. Bless her, she's done that once in a while ever since my dear Roberto died. Of course, she can't do it all the time since she still has that spinster niece to look after."

"All right, signora." I look at the clock: 12:35. Yes, yes, signora. Parting is such sweet sorrow. Really. Ciao-ciao. Good-bye.

"Well, then. Until Monday. Arrivederci, Etto."

"Arrivederci."

"Ciao."

"Ciao."

"Ciao-ciao."

I lock the door behind her and turn the sign. I empty the banco in record time, and I'm just scrubbing down the block in back when I hear a knock on the window. At first, I ignore it. We are supposedly a literate country now. People have stopped signing their names with Xs and bringing letters to the parish priest. They should be able to read a simple sign on the door, a sign that has been there since my bisnonno hand-lettered it in the last epoch.

Monday–Saturday 8:00–12:30.
Monday–Friday (Summer) 4:30–6:00.

Fede knows to come around to the back door. If someone is looking for Papà, they should know they'd have better luck going over to Martina's, or calling Silvio or Nonno, or better yet, convincing Papà to join the rest of the first world and get a fottuto cell phone.

I dry off the block, and there's a second, more insistent knock, a solid tap that makes the window ring like a heavy bell. I look through the bead curtain. It's her. The girl from the field. Shit. I try to get out of the line of sight, but she already has her face pressed to the window. Behind her is a blond woman wearing aviators and a pink leather jacket even though it's a million degrees outside. She's talking on a cell phone and pushing one of those super, all-terrain celebrity strollers, no doubt the first in a long line of correct parenting decisions that will culminate in a spot at one of the northern universities and a job that doesn't involve standing behind a banco. The seat of the stroller is heaped with bags, and trailing behind the two women is a boy clearly too old for a stroller.

I observe all of this while hiding in the shadows behind the bead curtain, but the girl must see me because she raises her eyebrows and gives a little wave. She taps on the glass again and points to the banco. Shit. I wipe the sheen of fat from my face and take the dirty apron off. When I go up front, she's still waiting patiently, her hands cupped around her eyes and pressed to the window. I take a deep breath and open the door.

"Buongiorno," I say.

"Buongiorno. I'm sorry to make you open," the girl says in English, "but we came all the way from the top of the hill. We thought in summer the shops might be open through the break."

"It's no problem. No problem at all. Come in."

The blond woman is yapping away in a language that sounds like Russian or one of those other languages made for giving orders, and she doesn't even look at me. She and the boy stay on the passeggiata while the girl comes inside. I can't think of the last time I was alone with a girl. My heart starts to hammer away in my chest, and I try to stop it by thinking about the mighty and indestructible Chuck Norris. Chuck Norris can slam a revolving door. People say, "I was scared to death." Death says, "I was scared to Chuck Norris." Chuck Norris's tears can cure cancer.

Too bad he never cries.

I go behind the banco on instinct even though there's nothing in it now but the calf's head. I probably don't have to tell you that in this country we have a long tradition of smooth talkers whose first nature it is to flirt and who will talk up every girl they see just to stay in practice. Romeo, Casanova, Rudolph Valentino, Francesco Totti, Silvio Berlusconi. Cazzo, Berlusconi has proven his ability to chat up 60 million people at the same time. And then there are all the regular guys like Luca and Fede, the mere mortals who can get the American college girls to drop their panties for the slightest nuzzle against the ear, the most watered-down declaration of love, the most uninspired "ciao, bella."

I am not one of them.

Luca and Fede used to try to coach me. It's easy, they'd say. All you have to do is get a girl to share the smallest thing about herself, open up the tiniest crack in her fortress, the most minuscule break in her cell wall, and then you can invade and replicate yourself like a virus until you've collected the whole code to her security system. After that, it's just a matter of pushing buttons. Luca and Fede, they probably would have thought to ask about the English, the accent, the blonde with the cell phone, the little boy dragging behind her like an anchor, and where in Italy she's been that the butcher shops stay open through the break. They would have at least gotten her name. But I ask you, what in this grand tradition of flirting do I manage to say to her?

I say, in exactly the same tone I reserve for the nonne every morning, "And how can I help you?"

She looks down at the empty case and smiles. "It looks like the shops in Ukraine. During Communism."

And again, I should laugh at her joke or ask her about Ukraine or the butchers over there. Anything. Instead, I feel myself crouching down, using the banco like a bunker and flattening myself into a cardboard cutout, a vague outline of every other shopkeeper she's ever met so that if she ever saw me on the street, she would never mistake me for a man.

Her face goes serious, and she clears her throat. "I'd like a filetto, please, and a half kilo of prosciutto."

"Cotto or crudo?"

"Crudo. The longest-aged you have."

"I have twelve months."

"That's fine."

"Thin?"

"Extra thin."

I go back to the walk-in to get the prosciutto, and she watches me intently as I snuggle it against the blade of the slicer. My bisnonno bought the slicer when he started the shop, and it has warped over the years, so when I flip the switch, it sings ever so slightly, metal on metal. I can feel her eyes on me as the slices fall.

"And now for the filetto . . ." I narrate like the deficiente I am. I brush through the bead curtain and into the front walk-in, digging around in the packages. Shit. There it is, vacuum-packed but still white. Papà's head must be so wrapped up in the scandal, he's absentmindedly put it away without taking the silver skin off.

I go to the front empty-handed. She squints like she's bracing herself for bad news, and my insides flinch. The thing about me is that I will say all kinds of cazzate in my head, but I have never been one for telling people what they don't want to hear, even something as small as an unskinned filetto. Mamma used to call it "sensitivity." Fede calls it "being a pussy."

"I'm sorry, but we don't have one. I mean, we do, but it hasn't been trimmed up or had the silver skin cut off yet."

"No problem. I will wait."

"Maybe you can come back later this afternoon?"

"It doesn't take so much time to cut the silver skin off a filetto, does it?"

Shit.

"Okay, so I'm going to tell you the truth." This is also from Luca and Fede's playbook, making even the smallest things sound like grand confessions, like you have given the girl access to the darkest corners of your soul. "You see, my father, he doesn't like for me to touch the veal or the beef. Chicken and rabbit, okay. Mop bucket, no problem. But not the veal. Or the beef."

She keeps staring at me, and my mind records every blink of her eyelashes in slow motion, like the beating wings of a giant, prehistoric bird.

"Not that I'm an idiot or anything," I continue, trying desperately to fill the silence. "But my father, he is a perfectionist, and he takes great pride in his meat. He would rather not sell it at all than sell it in a substandard condition."

"Your father is not here now, is he?" She props her arms on top of the banco and balances her chin on her hands, like she has been given lessons in flirt by Totti himself. "I think you can do it by yourself, no?"

I can count on one hand the times a girl has flirted with me, and I always expect it to be a grander occasion, accompanied by a parade or a flotilla, a horn section, and shouts of "Du-ce! Du-ce! Du-ce!" I am unprepared, that's what I am trying to say. I'm unprepared, and this is what causes me to act like a complete pignolo.

"I don't know if it's such a good idea."

"I won't tell." She raises three fingers in a Scout pledge.

"Maybe you can come back for it later this afternoon? After my father has been here? Or I can deliver it to you?"

"What's your name?" she asks.

"Etto."

"Etto, my brother just arrived an hour ago. He has had a very, *very* hard week, and he needs a good meal. My filetto is his favorite."

I can feel the droplets of sweat collecting on the surface of my skin, as if they've sounded the alarm and decided to jump this sinking ship. I think of what Papà would say, and I look at the clock. What are the chances he will come by in the next five minutes or even realize he packed away the filetto in haste with the silver skin still on it? It wouldn't even cross his mind that he'd made a mistake.

I go back to the walk-in and bring the filetto up to the board. Yes, I admit it, I am going to try to salvage my manhood by showing a girl I can cut the silver skin off a filetto. I take the knife in hand, and I look out at the passeggiata, where the little boy is jumping and kicking at an imaginary ball in the air. The blond woman is holding the phone to her heart, screeching the little boy's name over and over, wearing it down to a nub. The girl is on her toes now, peeking over the banco at what I'm doing. My hands begin to shake, and I make a silent prayer not to slice my fingers off. At least not in front of her.

"Everything is okay?" she says.

"Fine, fine. Tutto a posto."

Just so you know, I am not a complete incompetent, and I've watched Papà and Nonno take the silver skin off a filetto hundreds of times before. I ease the knife under the white and wiggle it a little to get some room, then pull it down the length. Shit. I've made a small gouge in the muscle, so I even it up. And then I even that up. And then I'm not sure what happens, but the board starts to look like Calatafimi after Garibaldi attacked the Bourbons.

"Shit."

"Everything is okay?"

"Yes, yes. Tutto a posto."

I keep going. Rome or death. I don't know why my hands aren't listening to what I'm telling them to do. Even for battlefield surgery, it's unacceptable. I can only hope to hide the filetto as quickly as possible, wrap it up and clean the board before Papà comes back and realizes what I've done. And while I'm at it, I will communicate telepathically to this girl that she must never, ever come here again and make these absurd requests to buy meat.

"It's okay," she says, answering an apology I'm too ashamed to make. "I'll do it." And I swear on my nonno's and bisnonno's portraits that she *comes behind the banco* and takes the knife out of my hand.

Let me be clear. We do not run some kind of casino operation here. People do not just *come behind the banco*. Since the war, there have only been about ten people back here, all of them either health inspectors or with the same last name printed on the awning outside. But she smiles at me and takes the knife from my hand like it's the most natural thing in the world.

"Don't worry. I used to work in a restaurant."

The little boy flings the door open, runs in, and heads straight for the banco, pressing his face and hands against the glass so he can see through to what the girl's doing. She says something to him, and like magic, he steps away, clasping his hands behind his back. I watch the knife flash in her hands, and I can feel the weight of everything in the shop bearing down on me—the loops of sausages, the scale, the slicer, the stool Mamma used to sit on next to the register, the portraits of my bisnonno, Nonno, and Papà wearing expressions of perpetual disapproval.

"So," she says, cocking her head and smiling. "You and your friends will go to the disco tonight?"

I swallow hard and try to channel Luca, Fede, Totti, Chuck Norris, and all the rest of them. "Probably. Are you?"

She looks back at the filetto and shrugs. "I will talk to my brother. Maybe." She holds up the filetto. It looks as good as when Papà does it.

"See?" she says. "Tutto a posto."

The little boy watches me wrap it up, and the girl walks back to the sink and washes her hands as if she works here. Please, God, don't let anyone have seen her through the front window. Please don't let anyone have seen her completely and irreparably emasculate me behind my own counter with a few swift strokes of Papà's knife.

"So, you are a fan of calcio?" she says, pushing through the bead curtain.

"Oh. The shrine back there? That's my papà. He's crazy about calcio."

She stares at me as I ring up the order, and I can feel the heat creeping into my cheeks. The little boy says something in their language and she answers him. Outside, the blond woman snaps the phone shut and lifts her purse from the seat of the stroller. She wanders in like she's never been in a butcher shop before, and she looks at everything curiously, as if she's strolling around a museum. The girl glances back at her, and I can tell they don't get along.

"It's forty-two fifty," I say. The girl hands over a hundred-euro note, and as I'm making change, the two of them go back and forth in some kind of Slavic summit. Finally the girl speaks up. "We would like to make an account. If it is okay? We are here for three weeks."

"And you are staying in Signora Malaspina's villa?"

"Yes."

As I pull the notebook out from under the register, I try to calculate how much rent they must be paying.

"The name on the conto?"

I hold the pencil over the page, waiting. She hesitates. Maybe it's a mafia thing. Maybe this brother is a godfather or whatever they call it in Ukraine. They say the thugs over there make the Italian mafia look like children on a playground.

"Maybe you want to put your own name on the account?" I suggest.

"Yes, yes, I will put my name. Zhuki."

"Again?"

"Like 'zoo,' except 'zhoo' and 'key.'" She makes a twisting motion, like a key in the lock. "Z-H-U-K-I." She traces the letters on top of the register.

"Zhuki . . . ?"

"Yes, Zhuki."

"No, I mean, what's your surname?"

"My surname?"

The blond woman behind her starts to laugh. She takes her sunglasses off with a flourish and stares at me as if I'm supposed to recognize her. "Yuri Fil," she says, tapping the register with one long fingernail. "Money. Pencil. Yuri Fil."

She snatches the hand of the little boy and pulls him out of the shop, leaving the girl, whose face turns bright red.

"Grazie. Arrivederci." She tries to say it as smoothly as she can, but she stumbles on every single syllable.

"Arrivederc'."

My hand hangs in the air, midwave, as I watch them disappear beyond the edge of the window, the blond woman and her stroller leading the way, the girl—Zhuki—hugging the package of tortured meat under her arm like a calcio ball.

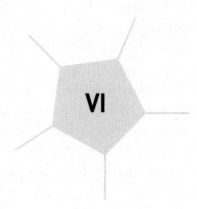

VI

*I*t's probably unnecessary by now to explain who Yuri Fil is. My lack of enthusiasm for the game of calcio aside, he is, I will grant you, one of the greatest strikers out there today, one of those players who can't be quantified by a simple recitation of statistics or loop of clips replayed on *The Monday Trial* and YouTube. It would be beside the point, anyway. Because the point is not how much he means to the Dynamo fans, the Tottenham fans, the Celtic fans, the Genoa fans, or the fans of the next team who will inevitably buy him for a sack of euros. The point is Papà's unwavering devotion to him. I think he would sell me, Nonno, Silvio, the shop, all of us, for an audience with Yuri Fil. After all, this is a man whose photo has earned a coveted place over the grinding counter in back, sharing company only with Dino Zoff, Maradona, and a handful of others. A man whose first three teams have been the only foreign scarves to hang above Martina's bar. A man whose transfer to the Italian leagues inspired another man who has never been east of Trieste to teach himself the fottuto Ukrainian national anthem and keep singing it over and over until his son learned it involuntarily, through osmosis.

Shche ne vmerla Ukrayina, ni slava, ni volya.

When Papà bursts through the door, I'm still sitting on the stool behind the register, my mind digesting the situation. Papà doesn't even say ciao—he simply continues his perpetual list of things I haven't done. Grind the bucket of scraps for the sausage. Clean the gunk out of the cracks in the sink. Reorder the vacuum-pack bags. Make the involtini. He counts them off, levering his fingers back so it looks like they might break off.

"Did you hear me, Etto? Did you hear anything I just said? What's the matter with you? You look like you're barely there. Are you drunk?" But he doesn't even wait for an answer. "I know you can't be tired. You've barely done any work around here. Why are you sitting around like that?"

And maybe this is why I let the moment pass. Because it's a rare chance to withhold from the know-it-all the thing he would most want to know, a way to finally torture the torturer for holding me hostage in this shop, for treating me like a slave instead of a son.

That doesn't mean I do it easily, of course. The guilt of it hangs over me for the rest of the afternoon and into the evening as I sit on the sofa in our apartment listening to Nicola Nicolini getting ready on the other side of the wall, the darkness collecting in the spaces between the shutters, the footsteps of the crazy divorcée who lives above us clacking back and forth across the floor, back and forth, back and forth, enough to make you go crazy yourself.

My phone lights up.

ME AND BOCCA ARE LEAVING IN HALF AN HOUR.

WHERE ARE YOU GOING?

YOU'RE KIDDING, RIGHT? THE AUSTRALIANS. LE ROCCE. I'VE BEEN TELLING YOU ALL WEEK.

I DON'T FEEL LIKE IT.

YOU DON'T HAVE TO FEEL LIKE IT. JUST COME.

YOU JUST WANT ME TO TRANSLATE.

OKAY, WE JUST WANT YOU TO TRANSLATE. COME ON. FORZA. DAI. DON'T BE
A FINOCCHIO.

I never should have taught Fede how to put that fottuto word anticipation on his phone. I should have left him to sweat for every letter like the
ten-year-olds and the old people.

I open the shuttered doors to the balcony and listen to the clinking
of dishes as the tourists finish their Saturday-night dinners up and down
the passeggiata. The waves are weak tonight, slapping halfheartedly against
the pylons all the way down the molo. I stare at the sign on the lamppost
between the bagni and the Mangona brothers' huts. Silvio put it up the
week after they pulled Mamma's body from the water, as if that would have
protected her. As if she would have obeyed a fottuto sign.

VIETATO TUFFARSI—
PERICOLO: TUBAZIONI AFFIORANTI DAL FONDALE.

And in English, for the tourists:

DIVING FORBIDDEN—
DANGER: PIPELINE EMERGING FROM THE SEABED.

The morning Mamma disappeared was one of the coldest and raini-
est of any June I remember. She came into my room before dawn, a dark
shadow perched on Luca's bed, cupping one of his cleats in her hand.
When she stood up, she seemed taller in the darkness, and the thick material of her wet suit pinched her body into an alien shape, her middle
spread, her limbs scrawny since the last time she wore it. I don't remember
what either of us said. I only remember her standing there in the dark,
pulling the piece of fishing net off her wrist, and leaving it on the dresser. I
only remember her hands ruffling my hair and pulling the blanket over me,
the rain pinging against the roof outside my window.

When I woke up the second time, it was already light out, and the rain
had stopped. I took my time getting up. It was a Sunday, and when I went

downstairs, Mamma and Papà were both gone. I remember thinking maybe they had gone for a walk or to Mass or to get a coffee. But I should have known. Her first swim in months and she took it in the rain.

My phone lights up again.

COME ON, ETTO. DAI.

You have to believe me, the last thing I want to do on a Saturday night is go to a disco and watch a thousand kids on Campari and hormones rubbing up against each other to the "Macarena" or "La Vida Loca" or whatever cazzate the posers are listening to these days. And I have zero desire to stand around and watch as Fede and Bocca bludgeon some Australian girls into submission with their stupid lines and their bad English, dragging them to the back door of the Hotel Paradiso by their thong straps. But I think about Papà coming home, and having to sit in the empty apartment all night with him, staring at the television, my omission squatting on me like a goblin or an imp.

"Okay, okay. Cazzo, Fede. I'm coming, I'm coming."

I put on my Chuck Taylors and tie Luca's favorite hoodie around my waist. As soon as I step out the front door, I get sucked into the current of tourists on the passeggiata, the faces of my neighbors surfacing like shining fish.

"Hey, Etto!" Pietro and Bernardo call out to me as they pass. They are carrying their tackle boxes and poles out to the molo for a bit of night fishing. "Fede is looking for you. He says to remind you not to chicken out on him tonight," one of them says, their cackling laughter fading into the darkness.

Silvio is the next to appear, clomping along in his thick police-issue shoes even though he's off duty.

"Ciao, Etto."

"Ciao, Silvio."

"Fede's looking for you."

"I know, I know."

I look up at the hill, the terraces stacked to the sky. My phone lights up again.

"Porca puttana. I'm *coming*."

"Everything okay, Etto?"

"Ciao, Franco."

"Where you headed?"

"Out with Fede."

"God help you."

"I know."

Bocca rents one of the boxes at the other end of the passeggiata, and when I get there, Fede and the girls are gathered around outside, waiting for Bocca to pull his precious truck out.

Fede puts me in a headlock and rubs my head. "I knew you'd come. I knew you wouldn't pussy out on us."

He introduces me to the three girls, who are actually from Austria and not Australia. They're students, and their English is all right except for their sharp little swastika accents. One of them is pretty, but the other two are just so-so and trying to make up for it by dressing slutty.

"Out of the way!" Bocca hangs one arm out the window and backs out of the garage, the brake lights flashing as he taps at the pedal like one of the nonne.

"So you decided to show up after all, eh?" Bocca says.

"What the cazzo did you do to your hair?"

"It's a fauxhawk."

"It's ugly."

Bocca pushes his tongue into his lower lip and grunts, caveman-style. "Euh. It's the style now, idiot." I guess this is Bocca's burden in this world, to change his style whenever any magazine or television show tells him he should. Now it's a fauxhawk and Pumas; last summer, retro Nikes and seventies shag; before that, Adidas slides and a buzz cut; and—for the month he endured the merciless teasing—sandals and a Bob Marley slouch hat. When we look at old photos, we only have to look at Bocca's hair to tell which summer it was.

"Wipe your feet before you get in. And don't smudge the handles. I just had it detailed."

There isn't a word for this kind of love. Disturbing. Maybe that's the only word for it. Bocca loves this truck more than anybody or anything in the world. It's the thing that gets his tent poles up, the thing that completes him. It's an American truck. Imported. White. It's already three or four years old, but the bumpers are still unscuffed, the bed virginal. Bocca lives, dies, and suffers for this truck, washing it, polishing it, and buying it little accessories so it will know it's loved. It nearly killed him when he had to use it every day to drive us all to Albenga our last year of high school. When the starter needed to be replaced a few months ago, Beppe ordered one from America, and he had to enforce visiting hours at the shop because Bocca went to see the truck every day like it was in the hospital.

I climb in back, where there are two small seats facing each other, and the girl who pulled the short straw climbs in after me. Fede and Bocca start arguing about where the other two girls will sit, but Bocca should already know it's pointless. Whenever we meet girls, there's a silent division that takes place. As soon as I walked up, I knew which one Fede would get and which ones were the scraps Bocca and I were expected to fight over. The girl facing me arches her back and sits up straight. She's wearing a silky black top cut almost to her belly button, and if I were a complete stronzo, I could reach in and touch her breast on either side as easily as reaching behind a curtain.

"I am Tisi," she says in English. She reaches her hand over the space between us, stiff like a businesswoman, just to confirm that she's not interested in me in the slightest.

"Etto."

"This is a strange name."

"So is yours."

"I am named after a princess." She giggles. Deficiente.

"It's my truck, stronzo, and I say she sits next to me." Bocca is trying in vain to put the prettier girl next to him.

"Not a chance. That one gets the seat belt. You want that pretty face to go through the windshield, you selfish bastard?"

"So the other one does?"

You can see the lights of Le Rocce as soon as you pull onto Via Aurelia, and Fede points it out to the girls, who coo and sigh. I guess it's pretty from a distance—a wide circle of lights on top of an open cliff. When the Cavalcantis decided to make a disco, it was just a piece of rock, but they blasted seven levels of staircases leading down to the water, and if you walk all the way down, you end up on a private strip of sand with caves carved out like small pouches, the perfect size for two people. Three if you're messed up like that. In the winter, it's mostly locals and a couple of bored French kids who follow the lights, but on summer weekends, everyone is here. People will drive all the way from Milan just to crowd in on the dance floor and make out on the staircases. Fede says he's seen the Botox anchor from Rai Uno here, and the goalkeeper for Sampdoria.

Little Mino is one of the bouncers tonight. They call him Little Mino, but he's as big as a bull. "Ehi! Ciao! Etto! What are you doing here? Haven't seen you in a lifetime. I can't believe they got you to come out." He shakes my hand, squeezing it into powder.

"Yes, yes, ciao, Little Mino."

"I'll let Guido know you guys are here. He'll be glad to see you."

The wind is fierce up here, whipping over the open cliff, and the dance floor is a mass of untucked dress shirts and long hair flapping around in the wind. We shuffle around inside the entrance gate until Guido appears wearing a cream-colored suit and a Patek watch so large it could knock a man out with one blow. He's followed by a couple of salon blondes, their bocce pushed up to their chins.

"Well, well," he says. "Look at what we have here."

Fede introduces the Austrian girls, and they swoon over Fede and Guido as if me and Bocca don't exist. Bocca puffs out his chest and tries to look taller. I look around for Zhuki and Signora Malaspina's niece, but there must be a thousand people here tonight, all of them dressed identically.

"Welcome," Guido says to the Austrian girls, with perfect tact and that sissy British English he brought with him from Milan. "You are in very good hands with these three," he says, "but if you find anything lacking, your every wish is my command."

The girls clinging to him giggle and clap their hands like trained monkeys.

"I have no idea what any of that meant," Fede says, and Guido laughs and switches back to Italian, turning his full attention to us and leaving the girls to dissolve into the night.

"I can't believe they got you out here, Etto-grammo. Nice of you to stoop to hanging out with us posers tonight." He slaps me on the back. And this is what makes it hard for you to hate Guido, even with his preppy, branded clothes, his loaded parents, and his snotty English. Even when he swooped in from Milan with his transfer-student mystique and became the Benjamin of every teacher and the crush of every girl in our class, you couldn't help but like him. He was the kind of guy who made up nicknames for everyone, always shared whatever exam questions he had, and spoke well of us to whichever girl we liked at the moment.

"Over here," he says, leading us toward the dance floor and the VIP cabanas. He takes the Reserved sign off one of the tables and calls a cabana boy over.

"Whatever they want. Gratis."

"Thanks, Guido."

"Anything for friends. Have fun! Drink! Dance! Drink some more! And I'll be back to check on you soon."

He disappears in a wake of blondes, and soon the cabana boy brings over two bottles of champagne. We drink a few clichéd toasts that Fede and Bocca make me translate, and everyone starts stretching and preening and jockeying for position. The music is moaning and wailing out of speakers as big as the walk-ins in the shop, and before I know it, Fede and Bocca have dragged Hansel and Gretel off to the dance floor, leaving me with the same one from the back seat of the truck. She must be freezing, even with the generous padding on her arms, but I don't offer her my hoodie. She arches her back, and I can see she's rubbed glitter or something into the downspout between her bocce.

"I don't dance," I say, cutting off any ideas she might have.

"No?" She grabs her shoulders and shivers, like Jessica Lange in *King Kong*. I know it's not for me. I know she's just biding her time and using me as a prop so another guy will look over and see how much fun she is. Well, he can have it. The giggling, the half-open shirt, all of it. The wind picks up, flapping the edges of the cabana.

"So, then, Etto-who-does-not-dance," the Austrian girl says, trying to create a conversation where there is none, "what *do* you do, then?"

I shrug. "Try to put one foot in front of the other, you know. Try to make it from one day to the next. But that's basically what we're all doing here, aren't we?"

She smiles, a tight-lipped, condescending smile, as if she's sliding it grudgingly over a counter. "I mean, what is your *profession*?"

"Oh, you mean how much money do I make and how interesting am I, and am I worth the time it took to put your makeup on?"

"Do you always invent what other people are thinking?"

"I work for my father. He's a butcher."

"See?" she says. "That wasn't so bad."

She's actually not as ugly as I first thought. She's got loads of makeup on, but I'll bet if you shot a fire hose at her and put her next to an uglier friend, she might make out all right.

"Actually, it's pretty soulless," I say. "Maybe not as bad as being a lawyer or something, but all you're doing is chopping up dead animals and trying to make them look nice."

She smiles widely—again, not for me. I look toward the dance floor, but all I see is clothes and hair, tanned limbs and flashes of jewelry. No sign of Fede or Bocca or anyone else.

"Well, it's probably interesting to talk to everyone who comes into the shop, then," the Austrian girl continues. This must be torture for her, but we both know she has to keep the conversation aloft at whatever cost. I could get up at any moment, leaving her to sit alone like a zero, and everyone knows zeroes don't get hit on.

"Not really," I say. "It's basically the same conversation over and over, forty times a day, six days a week. Buongiorno. You're looking well, signora. How can I help you? Why don't you try the chops? Have a nice day. See you soon. Nobody really means any of it anyway."

She stares at me, her mouth slightly open, deciding what to say. She has those prominent dog fangs a lot of Germans and Austrians have, just to the right and left of center.

"You know," she finally says, "you're not a very nice person."

"I know."

We lapse into silence. I down two glasses of champagne like shots, one after the other, and she lifts her glass delicately and sips her champagne like she's giving me fottuto etiquette lessons. Each time she takes a drink, she lets her eyes roam the room, looking sullenly for her escape, but then, it's as if she realizes this is not the fun! fun! fun! she wants to project, so she forces her pout into a smile. She glances down to check that her shirt is appropriately slutty but not downright whorish, then fixes her eyes on a spot over my left shoulder.

I turn around to see who the poser is.

"Ehi. Ciao, Etto."

"Aristone?" And not only is it Aristone, but Aristone-back-from-university-and-twenty-kilos-lighter-with-new-glasses Aristone. Shit, he actually looks good.

"It's just Aristo now. You know . . . lost some weight."

"Shit, Aristone, you actually look good."

"You mind if I sit with you?"

"I think you would be her savior if you did."

"Aristo," he says, leaning over and taking the girl's hand.

"Tisi," she says.

"German?"

"Austrian."

And then Aristone, he kisses her hand and says, "Es ist eine Scheisse deine Wiener zu schnitzeln," or something that sounds really überpolite and makes her bocce stand up and take notice. And before I know it, they're jabbering away in German or Austrian or whatever, and I remember that Aristone has been in Genoa studying languages for the past three years, though none of us ever thought to ask him which ones. The girl leans forward and hunches her shoulders. I think for a second that her shirt is going to part like the Red Sea, but she must have some secret contraption holding it together. Ah, Tisi, you have gotten the last laugh. I feel the champagne swirling around and coating the inside of my skull.

"I didn't know you studied German, Aristone," I mumble, but I might as well be invisible. Aristone orders a bottle of vodka, that skinny big shot, and when the cabana boy comes, he pretends it's a surprise to him that Guido is comping us, and he gives the cabana boy a big tip like he's an American, flipping his wallet wide open. Good for you, Aristone. Good for you that you are thin now. Good for you that you speak Kartoffel and that you might get something tonight. Tutto bene. Salute. Cin-cin. Vaffan'.

We do six shots. Bam, bam, bam, bam, bam, bam. Actually, they do one, I do six. And it helps. It waters down my vision, making all these obnoxious stronzos on Campari blur into a nice, soft, harmless haze. I can feel the hard edges inside me melting a little, until I'm actually happy for Aristo. I should drink more often. I'm not much of a dancer, but I'm a pretty good drunk. At least I don't get obnoxious like Bocca.

"May I have this dance?" Aristone asks the Austrian girl. This time in English. Show-off. She leans back and crosses her arms. "I don't think I'm in the mood to dance," she says.

Aristone stands up, holds out his hand, and pouts. "Oh, please. Just one. One tiny, little dance." So pathetic. Aristone, please don't beg. Everyone knows it's an amateur move. It's much better to pretend you don't care. Ignore a girl long enough, and she will come to you.

"Well . . . okay," Tisi says, grinning, and she's on her feet.

They walk out under the circles of lights. The song is a fast one, and everybody's hopping up and down and slamming together like idiot prisoners on some chain gang assigned to have fun. I spot Griffolino and Capocchio circling around, looking for customers.

"Hey, Etto, you want to fly tonight?" Capocchio asks me on his fourth or fifth lap.

"I'm high on life, can't you tell?" I answer, and Capocchio laughs, the pockmarks that riddle his cheeks stretching into lines.

I take another shot of vodka and wait for the song to end, but when it does, they stay out there. Two songs. Three. For every song, I take a shot. Couples on their way from the dance floor to the staircases stare at me in pity, and the cabana boy starts to smirk every time he passes. But just as I'm about to feel sorry for myself, I happen to look up at the deejay booth, where Guido is standing behind Nicola Nicolini, who, when he's not turning people's living rooms into fashionable deserts, moonlights as a deejay.

It's hard to tell if Guido is looking at Nicola Nicolini, the soundboard, the crowd of thrashing people, or out onto the endless sea, but I don't think I've ever seen anyone as lonely as Guido in that moment, hovering high above the dance floor, unmoving in the wind.

"I didn't expect to see you here, Etto." Signora Semirami slides onto the divan next to me, her hand already massaging my knee. Shit. I feel my jeans pull tighter, and I slide farther down the divan.

She laughs, flashing her teeth. "What's the matter, Etto? I won't bite," she says. She's about the same age as Mamma would be, not unattractive, but with the look of a bad remodel that shows the previous attempts.

"And what brings you to Le Rocce, Signora Semirami?"

She laughs again, flipping her long, dark hair over her shoulders like a curtain. "I don't know. Maybe I'm here because I heard there is a too-serious but not unattractive young man who needs to be not so serious for a little while." She slides over until she's pressing up against me. She's wearing a short, white denim skirt, the bony valley between her breasts framed by an open white shirt and a black bra, the aging flesh falling off her chest and thighs. "And you can call me Valeria."

"Your bra is showing, Valeria."

Again the laugh. She reaches over me for the bottle of vodka and two shot glasses. "You know, Etto, your friends did not complain when Valeria came to cheer them up. Your brother did not complain."

"As if."

She raises her eyebrows at me. "Believe what you want, then."

They say Signora Semirami keeps the newspaper lists of the middle school graduations, seducing the boys one by one through their years in high school. No one admits to having been with her, but I know from how she pursues me that I am one of the few left on a list she wants to retire. She pours two vodkas and pushes one in front of me.

"Here," she says. "Have a little drink. It will relax you."

"And where is Signor Semirami tonight?" I ask.

"Ah, ah, ah, ah." She wags her finger at me. "Don't you worry about Signor Semirami."

She grabs my knee and draws her nails slowly up my thigh. The hair on my neck tingles, the charge enough to ignite the pool of accelerant in my stomach. I jump up just before her hand reaches my crotch.

"I have to go."

Signora Semirami shrugs and raises her eyebrows. I push my way through the crowd on the dance floor, still pounding out their reel, and I end up a couple of staircases down, facing the sea, on an empty stretch between the shadows of two couples making out. One of them is a girl from Laigueglia who went out with Bocca for a while, but the rule on the staircases is never to acknowledge anyone just in case they are not with the person they are supposed to be with. I light a cigarette and lean forward against the ledge. The cold stone hits my thigh, and I feel my pisello slowly deflating.

The music has been cycling from French crap to Italian crap to Spanish crap to American crap all night, but here, the sea washes over the melodies until they sound like whale songs, distant and haunting. An edge of wind blows a part in my hair, and the waves roil around the rocks in the cove, turning it into a pot of bubbling acid, as if anything dipped into it would come out a skeleton like in the old 1950s alien-ray-gun movies. I stretch my arms out on the stone ledge, and I imagine taking a swan dive and hitting my head on one of the rocks below, which thanks to the vodka have become a moving target. Papà would hear about it immediately from Silvio, and the two of them would rush over here. Guido would close the disco for the night, and a thousand drunken kids would squeeze through the exits, speculating about me with fake concern.

"Etto, what the cazzo are you doing?" It's Fede and the pretty Austrian.

"What?"

"Well, for a second, you looked like you were about to jump."

"No, Fede, you deficiente, I was not about to jump."

The pretty girl giggles, and I wonder how they've managed to communicate all night.

"Come on, let's go back to the cabanas," Fede says.

"Where's Bocca?"

"Still working on the other girl. I think it's going to be a while." The pretty girl is clinging to Fede's side, her hand practically down his pants.

"I'll wait here," I say.

"Why? You scared of Valeria? Don't worry, she just left with Aristone's little brother. Come on, let's go have a drink."

"I'll be there in a minute."

Fede stares at me.

"I said, I'll be there in a minute."

"All right, but don't think too much, and if you're not back in five minutes, I'm coming to get you. You're having fun tonight, Etto, whether you like it or not." The girl giggles.

The last thing I want tonight is to be pitied, to sit around the table and play the violin to their fottuto Noah's ark, everyone paired off two by two, Fede, Bocca, and Aristone laughing because they already know the night will end up with Jacopo sneaking them a room key at the back door of his parents' hotel. And sure, I could probably find some girl out of the hundreds here and take advantage of Jacopo's offer for once, but there's something so pathetic and Neanderthal about it—two people banging up against each other like flint, hoping for a spark to warm themselves. Cazzo, if that's how it is, I'd rather be alone for the rest of my life. A cold shot of air slaps me right across the face, and I can feel the vodka leaking out my eyes.

"Ciao."

I turn, and suddenly I'm looking into those eyes of hers, flashing, even in the darkness.

"Everything okay?" she says.

I wipe my eyes. "Fine. Fine. Tutto a posto. The wind . . . my glasses . . ."

She's wearing jeans and the same green warm-up jacket she was wearing at Martina's the other day, and for some reason, the fact that she didn't put on a miniskirt and a glob of makeup to come here makes me feel less alone. She leans against the ledge and looks down at the rocks in the cove. The alcohol in my stomach and my head sloshes around, one clockwise, the other counterclockwise, and I have to look at the horizon to realign everything.

"It is so beautiful here," she says, her dark curls in motion around her face like a school of small, black fish.

"I guess."

"We have a nice seaside in Ukraine, too."

"You do?"

"I know, nobody knows anything about Ukraine."

"I know some things."

"Really?"

And before I can stop myself, I start mumbling about Stalin and the mass starvations of 1932, Chernobyl, that politician who got his face burned off with poison, and then—thank you, Papà—I start singing the fottuto national anthem. Shche ne vmerla Ukrayina, ni slava, ni volya. The words come out loose and watery, and it feels like I'm gargling on them. She's smiling by the end of it, but I can't tell if it's because she likes me or if she's just amused by this babbling, drunken deficiente in front of her.

"So, do you want to dance?" I ask her.

"I'm not a very good dancer," she says.

"Please?"

"All right."

I push off the stone. It gives way like an unanchored boat, and as I walk up the stairs, each step is in motion, sinking under my feet. Zhuki takes off her warm-up and ties it around her waist. She's wearing a white polo underneath, and under the freckles, her skin is lightly tanned. We reach the top of the cliff, and the full volume of the music hits me. It's actually a not-bad song by the White Stripes, regrettably ground down by Roma and Azzurri fans into a one-word calcio anthem chanted over and over in stadiums around the world.

Po . . . po-po-po-po-po . . . po . . .

Po . . . po-po-po-po-po . . . po . . .

Luca used to tell me that when I danced, I looked like a fish on the line. He and Fede tried to teach me, but I never improved. I flail. I thrash. I flap. I flounder. But Zhuki is smiling at me, and I don't care anymore. I reach out, and my hand fits easily at her waist. I try to pull her close, but she spins away from me.

I'm gonna fight 'em off . . . a seven-nation army couldn't hold me back.

I play it cool for a while and dance my fishing-line dance from a safe distance, waiting for my moment. My eyes drift to her chest. Her bocce are only the size of anthills, but her small shoulders and her rounded hips make her look feminine even with the short hair. I force my eyes up to her face. The whole crowd behind her is jumping up and down and shouting, and I get dizzy watching them. I shut my eyes, but my head starts to spin.

Po . . . po-po-po-po-po . . . po . . .

Po . . . po-po-po-po-po . . . po . . .

She's smiling again. I take my chances and pull her into another collision, and for a split second, I can feel her weight against me.

Po . . . po-po-po-po-po . . . po . . .

Her face is flushed now, and her lips are saying something, but I can't hear over the music and the crashing of the waves between my ears. Kiss her, the voice inside my head tells me. Go for it. I squeeze my eyes shut like I used to do in chickadees when the ball was anywhere in the vicinity of my face. I grab her around the waist, press her against me, and feel her body go rigid in my arms. Open your eyes! Open your eyes! Papà used to shout at me, and I do, just in time to see her face pinch into a look of panic. Her hands push at my chest, levering me backward. Hard. The dance floor is spinning. Sorry, sorry. I hear the words echoing inside me, and then . . . thud.

Po . . . po-po-po-po-po . . . po . . .

Po . . . po-po-po-po-po . . . po . . .

I open my eyes, and she's gone. There's a circle of people bending over me, including Aristone's Austrian girl, whatever her name was, whose cleavage finally takes pity on me and gives me a little glimpse behind her swinging drapes.

"Shit."

"Shit is right." Fede pulls me up off the ground and puts my arm around his shoulders. "Come on, stronzo, you're going home."

They end up putting me in a Jeep with Cangrande and his pock-faced girlfriend from Ceriale. Shit, I don't know what happened to her, but her whole face looks like it's been quilted, stitched down to the bone, and it's all I can do not to ask her why her face is such a mess. I drift back to the dance that's still going on in my head, my hand following the bump of Zhuki's hip.

"So, champion." Cangrande leans back from the front seat. "You going home to your papà like this?"

"No chance. To my nonna's," I say. "Better yet, drop me off on Via Partigiani and I'll walk."

"I don't think you want your nonna to see you like this. Better to go home."

"No. To Nonna's." I start rambling, something about how Nonna always forgives and forgets, and isn't it ironic that she's lost her mind but she's the only one who understands me. Cangrande and his girlfriend are only half listening to me, instead discussing between themselves what to do. You can tell by their voices it's a monumental decision, and in the back of their minds, they're probably thinking about what good parents they'll make someday. We stop on Via Partigiani, right next to the nonne's rock.

"You sure you're going to be okay up the paths, Etto?"

"Sure."

"Be careful, eh?"

"I'm fine. No worries. Thanks. Ciao. Ciao-ciao. Ciao-ciao-ciao."

I slam the door hard, and the whole Jeep shakes.

They sit idling with the brake lights on as I start up the path. I try to make a straight line so they won't come back for me, and finally, I hear the motor rumbling down the road. The homemade lights up the path have already been shut off for the night because no respectable person would be wandering around at this time, and I stumble a couple of times and curse more than a couple of times. I stop to light a cigarette, but the match gets blown out by a breeze that sneaks out of nowhere. And if it can't get any worse, Mino's stupid dog crashes against the iron gate to my left, snarling and barking.

"Shut up, you stupid dog."

But he just keeps barking. Always barking. Always on the attack.

"Serby!" I hear Mino's wife calling through the darkness. "Serby! What's the matter, a bunny scare you? Come here, my little puppy!" The dog's collar rattles as it runs off toward the house.

The dark path closes in on me, and the foliage pulls low and tight like a cordon between me and everybody else in the world. Branches and vines reach out to finger my throat and claw at my face, and I lose track of where I am. All I know is to keep going up. When I get to the field, I lie down on Luca's grave and sink into the grass.

"Shit, Luca, I'm so fottuto drunk."

In the light of my phone, his photo sparkles above me. Luca never drank or smoked. When he was at the academy, he ate, drank, slept, and pissed calcio. His only vice was girls, and never in Milan because he said they took his power, like Samson. But when he came home on weekends or holidays, he more than made up for it. He and Fede would go out on sprees, like serial killers, Luca pulling his "home from the academy" routine, bedding girls all over Liguria and, apparently, even into France.

"I'll bet if it was you trying to kiss her, she probably would have gone for it." The light on my phone goes out, and his photo darkens. "Stronzo. You always got the girls. Even Mamma in the end, eh?"

I let this thought marinate with all the other hundred-proof toxic shit sloshing around in my head. I can feel the self-pity squeezing up my throat and out my eyes, so I pull myself off the ground and grab the ball off his grave. I jog back to the penalty spot and take a couple of shots. Bend it like fottuto Beckham, right? But I'm so drunk, I can't keep the ball under control. Luca and his headstone block the first seven. Shit. He's dead and he can still beat me. Finally on the eighth, I manage to bounce one off the post and into the net.

"Goooooooooooooooooooool!" I whisper to the trees, and I take a couple of victory laps around the field, the damp night air splashing my face.

"Goooooooooooooooooooool!" I say, a little louder this time.

The cypresses bow to me and I flip them off. I flip off Luca's headstone. I flip off death. I do it with as much vigor as the Mangona brothers in their huts. Ha-ha! Vaffan'! Victorious!

"Goooooooooooooooooooool!" This time I shout it for real, not caring who hears. "Goooooooooooooooooooooooooooooooooooooooooool!"

And then I toast them all with my middle finger, rattling off a litany of their wrongs.

Vaffanculo, you Austrian slut with your curtain shirt.

Vaffanculo, Aristone, with your trilingual begging and your university Wiener schnitzel.

Vaffanculo, Fede and Bocca, for guilting me into going to Le Rocce in the first place.

Vaffanculo, Zhuki, for making me feel like a stronzo for just wanting to kiss you.

Vaffanculo, Papà, for not caring where I am right now.

Vaffanculo, Mamma, for leaving me.

Vaffanculo, Luca, for taking her with you.

Vaffanculo to you all.

I take a long bow to the universe.

Bravo.

Grazie tante.

Salute.

Cin-cin.

Good night.

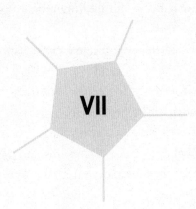

VII

*I*n the morning, I wake up bathed in sweat and shivering against a hard floor, the remains of a nightmare fleeing my head. My whole body is stiff, with something barbed embedding itself into the small of my back. I crack open my eyes, and the sharp point of light through the window starts stabbing away at my eyeballs.

"What the . . ."

I'm lying on the floor of Charon's aula, staring up at the plaster vault, the five globe lights suspended down the arch, still on from the night before. I haven't been in here for four years, ever since the liceo closed down. In the weeks before we started school in Albenga, they indentured Casella, Aristone, and me to clean and pack the teachers' supplies in boxes, which most of them never bothered coming back for anyway. Casella, in a flash of brilliance, copied the master key. I extract my key chain from my back and sit up.

Shit.

The room starts spinning, slowly at first, then picking up speed. The vein on the side of my head is like a pipeline pumping champagne, vodka, and bile, and the contents of my stomach start to creep up. I swallow hard and pull myself over to the wall.

Ahh. Relief. The solid wall does the trick, cool against my back. This is how they used to build, Nonno would say. Not these shoddy affairs nowadays that can be put up in an afternoon and destroyed in a year, but thick stone walls covered in lime wash, with soaring ceilings and arched windows that would have made the Romans proud. Charon's aula is the only room in the school like this. All the other classrooms got redone in the seventies with dropped ceilings and the calming turquoises and aquas of mental institutions. Charon alone insisted that his walls remain the same stark white, the ceiling curving into an infinite nothingness so when he talked, it was like God's voice echoing down, and when you gave an answer, it felt like it hung suspended under the great arched ceiling forever, like a clay pigeon waiting to be shot down.

Oh, he had such high hopes for us. It makes me laugh when I think about how annoyed he used to get when the other teachers would take us to the art museums in Genoa or the aquarium for the day. To make up for it, he would rush through his lectures and pile on the homework, as if he was in a race to impart all the fottuto secrets of the universe. Even now you can see it, the walls crammed with pull-down maps, etchings of the Divine Comedy, and charts of Latin conjugations and English irregular verbs.

"Go, went, gone," I say, and my voice does a lap around the empty velodrome of a room before returning to me. "Amo, amare, amavi, amatus." My voice takes another lap.

I'm actually surprised to see that no one has broken in here. I mean, I recognize that the thirteen-year-old B-boys are fundamentally lazy shits, and for them, this hill is too steep to walk up for any reason, especially with a skateboard under your arm and a joint in your mouth. But I'm a little disappointed in the baby-fascists, who talk like they would stomp any head, climb any hill, and break any window just to prove what stronzos they are. In fact, this is one of the things the men at Martina's talk about on the rare occasions when they are not talking about calcio—the downward spiral of the world, each generation worse than the next. Father Marco wants to build a recreation center to give the kids something to do.

Papà and Nonno want to lock them up in the jail for the whole summer and scare the shit out of them.

I stand up and slide my feet slowly across the dusty floor, the pain in my head flaring with any sudden movement. I sit down in the wooden chair behind Charon's desk and look out at the rows of tables, far more than we could ever fill. And I don't know if it's in the room or in my mind, but suddenly I catch a whiff of something. Must or decay. I'm not sure, but it's enough to bring back the nightmare that has been lurking just out of reach. Slowly, it comes out in pieces from behind the curtain, reassembling itself center stage.

It was horrible. One of the worst dreams of my life. Even worse than the ones I had as a kid that would send me running down the stairs and into my parents' bed. There was a woman walking toward me from the end of the molo, her skin so wet and pale, it looked pickled. She was cross-eyed, with stumps at the ends of her arms, and she was limping and lurching forward like both her ankles were sprained. I turned to run but it was then that she began to talk to me, or at least open her mouth and gesture. I don't remember which. I only remember the feeling as I stood there paralyzed, the smell of rotting fish and seaweed emanating from the sea.

I shudder and breathe in deeply to clear my head, but the smell is still there, and my stomach starts inching up my throat for real this time. I manage to keep it down as I run through the corridor and out the front door, the acid stinging the back of my nose. I fall to my knees in the bright sunlight and let it out, watching the grass and weeds slowly absorb it and feeling the relief take over my body. Maybe not relief, but at least emptiness. I breathe in the clean air and listen to the sounds of the terraces—the chirping of the birds, the scuffing of the cicadas, and the church bells pealing across the face of the hill.

It's Sunday morning.

Shit.

I forgot about Nonna.

I get up off my knees and shuffle toward the path as fast as I can. Nonno and Nonna used to live in the apartment connected to ours, the one Nicola Nicolini now brings his showboys home to. But about five years ago, Nonna's mind really started to crumple up, and we found her a few times wandering the streets and crying, or jumping into the sea with all her clothes on. So Nonno retired early from the shop, and they moved to a small villa up on the hill with a high fence and a gate, where Nonno could tend his vegetables and keep a better eye on her. Somewhere along the way, it became my job to bring Nonna down the hill to church every Sunday.

I drag myself up to their gate and ring the bell.

"Who is it?" Nonno's voice is scratchy over the intercom.

"It's Etto."

"You're late."

"I know. Sorry."

He buzzes me through the gate, and I stand under their giant, gnarled lemon tree to wait. The villa is named after it—Il Limone—but the tree has been completely barren since the day they moved in. Nonno is always trying different fertilizers and pruning methods, but he says the tree is constipated, and I imagine one day splitting it open and finding the inside flush with blooms and lemons at various stages of development, like the chute of eggs inside a hen.

Nonno eventually opens the front door, Nonna standing behind him. She still wears black every Sunday even though she thinks it's for her sister, who died ten years ago.

"Where've you been? I was about to take her myself."

Right. He would have just told her it was Saturday.

"Ciao, Luca," Nonna says, and kisses me.

"It's Etto."

She pulls away.

"Luca's brother," Nonno says. I offer Nonna my arm, but she eyes me suspiciously. Her mind has elbowed out all memory of me. I try to push the hair out of my eyes and straighten my clothes.

"I'm Etto. Your grandson. Luca's brother. Carlo and Maddy's son."

She relaxes when she hears my mother's name. She treated Mamma like a daughter from the day Papà brought her back to San Benedetto.

"And where is she today? Where is Luca?"

I used to tell her the truth, but then she would become confused and start to cry, and I would spend the rest of the day consoling her and feeling bad about it, as if I'd killed them myself.

"Mamma's in California. With Luca."

"Why is she in California?"

"Because she's American. She's from there. And Luca has a tournament there," I add.

"Oh." Nonna takes a minute to process this. She searches my face again before taking my arm. She is the bravest person I know, every day to trust in strangers, to take the arm of someone who could be a serial killer. I could not do it.

"We should probably hurry, Nonna. We're late."

"Whose fault is that?" Nonno calls after me. "Did I ever tell you the story about the girl who was late to her grandfather's deathbed?"

"No, Nonno."

"I'll have to tell you later."

Great. "Come on, Nonna," I say. "Mass starts in fifteen minutes."

But Nonna can't be hurried. Down the path, she has the eyes of an English referee, picking out every dropped coin, loop of wire, matchbook, and lotto card along the way and stashing them carefully in a plastic sack that was probably also at one point scavenged. She hums as she does this, different songs every time, so softly I can't tell the tune. Could be the Miserere. Could be Metallica. But you can tell she's perfectly content. Even if she forgets who she is and who she's with, where she's going and why, she has this internal homing device telling her she will get there eventually. Wherever *there* is.

"Oplà!" Nonna says, reaching out and touching the wall of the path to steady herself. Vaffanculo, it shouts back at her. Raffaella has big tits. Superbang. Fall Out Boy. Fall Out Boy sucks. Ultras suck. Life sucks. Blank-eyed skulls stare out at her. A backward swastika drawn by one of the illiterate baby-fascists. It makes me ashamed of the world that Nonna has to see this. She's an old lady and has already served her time. She should be able to scavenge the ground and hum in peace.

My blood feels thick and slow as I plod past the graffiti and around the broken bottles and used condoms ground between the stones. I think about last night at Le Rocce, replaying each stupidity in my head, and the nightmare

I can't seem to shake. I think about what a terrible son I am for not telling Papà about Yuri Fil and what a terrible grandson I am for making Nonna late. Each thought makes my head a little fuller and my shoulders a little heavier, until it feels like I'm stooped under the weight of the entire hill.

"Aha!" Nonna turns around, a triumphant look on her face as she holds up a one-euro coin. I smile at her, and she goes back to her search. Sometimes I wish I could be like her—wipe my mind clean and keep moving ahead instead of always throwing down these mental anchors into the past and floating back to them. Nonna doesn't suffer over Mamma or Luca. She doesn't constantly replay the outtakes in her head—the one where the paramedics get to the tunnel in time to save Luca, or the one where Mamma is found in the pool of a searchlight, her muscular arms clinging to the rocks of Whale Island, exhausted but alive. Nonna doesn't slosh all her emotions together like a great toxic lake. When she's happy, she smiles. When she's sad, she cries. When she's angry, she yells. Nonna stops her humming for a minute and puts her hand on my back as if she knows exactly what I'm thinking.

The hill flattens. We pass people Nonna doesn't recognize, and I answer for both of us.

"Salve."

"Salve."

"Ciao."

"Ciao."

"Buongiorno."

"Buongiorno."

When we finally get to the church, Nonna looks up at the sweeping archway over the entrance to the courtyard. There are two ancient palms on either side, the giant trunks like elephant feet stomping the earth, the bark peeling and curling away.

"Here we are, Nonna."

Her eyes void just before the moment of recognition. "Ah, yes. Here we are."

The doors of the church are flung open to the air, and I can hear the other nonne warbling along to the dirge of the organ. "Go in the middle door, Nonna, and I'll see you after Mass."

She looks at me, confused.

"Your friends are waiting for you right inside," I say. "They'll see you. Go on in."

"And what about you?"

"I already went to Mass this morning."

"With Maddy?"

"By myself. Maddy and Luca are in California."

She kisses me on the cheek. "You're a good boy."

And this is probably why Nonna is still a believer. Because in her ravaged mind, Mamma and Luca are vacationing in California, the ground is full of treasures, and I am a good boy.

I sit on the bench just inside the courtyard and pull the hoodie over my head against the blinding sun. We used to go to church together sometimes when Mamma and Luca were still alive, mostly for baptisms and Christmas, but Papà and I haven't kept it up. It's not that I'm an atheist. I'm not defending any grand principles or anything like that. There weren't any nuns who humiliated me in school or priests who messed with me. It just all feels silly to me. Wishful thinking. A childhood fantasy meant to make you feel better, like Superman or Santa Claus, too perfect to be believed. I'd rather be a realist about it now than wake up later feeling like a chump.

I close my eyes and try to clear my head, but the chatter inside won't stop, and the nightmare, instead of melting away, only grows, looming over every other thought. I try to keep myself from playing it to the end, but it has a momentum of its own. The corpse keeps staring at me and motioning to me, and I stare back, unable to either move toward her or look away. Finally, I recognize that it's Mamma, or at least the corpse they dragged from the water and never let me see. She smiles as if she can read my mind, and as the minutes pass, she seems to be warmed by my gaze, her skin drying out and turning pink before my eyes. Her feet straighten. Her arms grow hands. And she starts singing this song, one of her favorites by Umberto Tozzi, and dancing around on the molo in her bare feet.

I know. You're probably asking, what's so bad about that? And you early-rising cheerful optimists out there will probably even interpret this dream to mean that Mamma is in heaven or whatever, doing fine, and she only wants to reassure me that she's happy. And I grant you, maybe the fact that I don't see it this way shows you how crooked and bent a person I am. Because to me, the dream is a message from her that it was all my fault. That if I'd really looked at her, really seen what was going on that year, I could have stopped it. That if I'd been a better son, a son worth living for, she would have found the will to live.

The irony is, if I *were* a better son, this thought would make me sad. Instead it only pisses me off, as does every other thought about Mamma. I guess when it happened, I expected to feel like I felt after Luca's accident—the sadness and the loss, the what-ifs spiraling backward through my mind, undoing that morning and bringing him back to life for a few minutes at a time, like a myth or a legend. Saint Luca—killed by the world, killed by his own weaknesses or by that French puttana he was with, who was thrown clear of the wreckage and walked away without a scratch.

Nobody ever tells you that with suicide it's different, that you will be so pissed at the person from so many different angles. First, of course, you get pissed at the part that did the violence, then at the part that acted as a helpless victim and didn't fight back. And then again at the part that stood by watching, a gawker who knew full well what she was going to do and never raised the alarm or gave you the chance to swoop in and save her. You get pissed at the fact that she made the final action of her life eclipse every other happy moment you had. And then you realize you can't even tell other people you're pissed at her. She's checkmated you. Because when other people ask you how you feel, they expect you to act pitiful and sad like on TV, and if you tell them that instead you're pissed off at your own mother, they will think you're a cold, unfeeling traitor, deserving of the lowest circle. More Judas than Judas. More Brutus than Brutus.

My phone lights up in my pocket.

YOU STILL ALIVE?

NO THANKS TO YOU.

WHAT'S THAT SUPPOSED TO MEAN?

I turn my phone off and close my eyes, but now that the tourists have clogged the pedestrian streets, all the locals apparently detour around the church at this hour. Two trans from Albenga I recognize poke their heads cautiously through the archway, like they're afraid of a hidden guillotine dropping on their necks.

"Salve."

"Salve."

Sima wanders past, but she doesn't see me. Then Franco, who I never recognize when he's wearing pants and shoes.

"Etto, is that you?"

"No, Franco."

"Very funny. Tell your nonna I said hello."

"Okay."

Inside, the nonne are chanting. I pull the hoodie farther down over my eyes, but people are somehow determined to pester me today.

"Etto, is that you under there?"

Regina Salveggio actually has the nerve to reach in and pinch back the edge of my hoodie. I open my eyes and she's peering into my face, her kids clinging to her legs like barnacles.

"Boundaries, Regina, boundaries," I say, and I reposition the hoodie. She's already fifteen minutes late for Mass, the lazy cow.

"Oh, don't be such a pedant, Etto. Did you bring your nonna to church today?" The little boy reaches out a tentacle and grips my knee. I give him a dirty look.

"Just like last week, Regina. And the week before."

"Are you okay, Etto? You look kind of pale this morning. Paler than usual, even."

I narrow my eyes at her. Am *I* okay? Doesn't she realize she's the only one in Europe still having kids? Doesn't she realize that at twenty-two she's already doomed herself to a life of stretch marks and IKEA furniture?

"I was just going to ask you the same thing, Regina."

She laughs. "Oh, Etto, you're so funny." And she goes inside the church with her brats.

Father Marco must have made a joke because I hear the nonne

laughing. He starts with his serious tone now, the words themselves inaudible, like he's in there telling secrets. More people pass by.

Ciao, Etto.

Ciao.

Salve.

Ciao, Etto.

Ciao.

Ciao.

How many times can you say "ciao" in one day? You might as well say "vaffanculo." It basically means the same thing: I see you, I acknowledge you, but nothing more than that. Finally, the organ starts up again, and Casella and Claudia lead the stampede out of the church.

"Your nonna's still in there," Claudia says.

"I know."

"Then you also know that it's going to be hotter than hell today and you look like a child molester in that hoodie, right?" Claudia asks, and Casella laughs. I hate it that he laughs at her jokes now and not mine.

"Good. That's the look I was going for. Where are you two lovebirds off to today anyway?"

"Abu Ghraib," Casella says, which is what he's started calling Claudia's parents' house because each week, he's asked in a hundred different and unsubtle ways when he's going to propose to Claudia.

"Don't call it that." Claudia slugs him on the shoulder, and they play slap their way out of the courtyard.

I slouch against the archway, out of the way of the clean-scrubbed people, their spines straight as ships' masts, their laughter as clear as Christmas bells. The crowd today and every Sunday is mostly nonne and youth groupers who swarm around Father Marco like hungry pigeons as he comes down the stairs. Nonna and her friends are usually the last because before they leave, they have to make their rounds of the statues. As I wait for her, I imagine Nonna looking up at some patron saint of this or that, some spooky guy on a pedestal, her scrambled mind mistaking a candle for an ice cream cone or a hairbrush, the fire catching and spreading through the other nonne's dandelion hair like the burning of Troy, setting them all to high-pitched screaming like those plants in *Harry Potter.*

I know. Sometimes I feel like I'm one thought away from the asylum.

Father Marco takes up his position at the bottom of the stairs. He's in his full penguin finery, those blue eyes glittering in the sunlight, that smile that could be on a billboard selling coffee or sunglasses or even swimsuits. Why would a guy that good-looking take a vow of celibacy? He must know he could get as much as Fede if he wanted it. Father What-a-Waste is what the girls at school called him, and when he first came to San Benedetto, there was a solid month when they all packed the pews before eventually realizing he was never going to get over this guy Jesus. He sees me under the archway and corners me.

"Ciao, Etto. Good to see you."

"Great homily today, Padre," I say, but I can tell he's not buying it.

"Are you waiting for your nonna?"

"Yes."

"You know, you're always welcome to sit inside." He looks through me with those piercing blue eyes, which scares me a little, like my sins will show up as bright spots on an X-ray, a coin I've swallowed or a toy magnet I've stupidly stuffed up my own nose.

"I know," I say, squirming out of his gaze. One of the youth groupers comes and pulls him away, and I breathe a sigh of relief. The nonne finally come down the stairs in a line, clutching each other by the arm. Nonna is giggling and whispering in Signora Costanza's ear. I wonder how far back she's gone today. Twelve years old? Fourteen? When most people take on a new age, they leave the others behind, maybe carefully pack one or two of them away, saving them in tissue and mothballs. Cazzo, the thirteen-year-olds these days fling them away and move on to the next ones before they're even completely unwrapped. Nonna, though, keeps all of her ages accessible, hung up in the closet of her mind, every morning pulling out a different one.

I reach up to wave to her, then yank my hand back down to my side. Because behind the line of nonne, squinting in the sun, is Zhuki. I duck behind the giant palm and watch her coming down the stairs. She drops something, and bends down to retrieve it.

"Ah, there you are, Etto," Signora Costanza says. "Why are you hiding behind the tree?"

"I'm not hiding." I put my hand on Nonna's back and hustle her toward the sidewalk. "Come on, Nonna."

But maybe I've moved too abruptly because Nonna looks up at me, alarmed, and starts shouting for help. "Aiuta! Aiuta! He's going to sell me to the gypsies! He's going to sell me to the gypsies!"

Everyone in the courtyard turns to look, including Zhuki.

"Nonna, it's me. Etto. Your grandson."

"You're not my grandson! You're not my grandson!" Nonna shouts. "Aiuta! Aiuta!"

Fortunately, when the nonne aren't gossiping, they are busy meddling in other people's business, so it only takes a few seconds for a group of them to swoop in, explain everything to Nonna, and calm her down.

"Zita, it's your grandson."

"It's okay. He's the one who brought you here."

"You remember Caccia, your husband, and Carlo, your son . . . well, this is Carlo's son."

I glance back into the courtyard. Zhuki and everybody else are still staring at us.

"Nonna?" I say.

Finally the fear melts from her face and she grips my arm.

When we get back to the villa, Papà and Nonno are sitting in their undershirts beneath the wide branches of the lemon tree, their wine glasses carefully balanced on their knees, their voices low and serious, though they talk low and serious about everything—calcio, of course, but also the deficienti in parliament and Nonno's slovenly neighbors who don't know how to trim and clean their own property. Nonno's chair is facing us, and he points a finger in our direction as we approach. Papà gets up to open the gate, and Nonna heads into the house with her treasures so she can spread them out on the kitchen counter and systematically put them away. A bit of wire goes into the drawer with her twist ties. Change gets dropped into a slot in the lid of a large jar in the front hall. Nails and screws that Nonno will use for repairing arbors and loose boards are sorted into smaller jars, the cigarette butts shaken into the garbage, the plastic bag washed and set on the drain board.

"Everything went okay at church today?" Nonno asks. I know someone has already called to tell about Nonna yelling at me.

"Fine. Why?"

"No reason."

Papà sits down and they continue the conversation. About the scandal. What else?

"I don't understand," Nonno says. "It's been a week. If he didn't do anything, why doesn't he come out and declare his innocence?"

"Only the guilty man declares his innocence," Papà says.

"But he doesn't even show his face. Where is he? All he has to do is go out for ice cream with his family and give a little wave to the paparazzi."

"He's Eastern European. They don't wave. They don't eat ice cream."

Nonno takes a long drink of wine. He makes it himself, a few liters at a time, then siphons it into cloudy green bottles. "Well, what are you standing around for, Etto? Pull up a chair."

My nemesis, the sun, is out in full force now, beating down into the yard. I take Luca's hoodie off and wrap it around my waist, pull the third chair under the shade of the lemon tree, and join their inner sanctum.

"Now what was that story I said I was going to tell you, Etto?" As if he has forgotten.

"The one about the girl who was late to her grandfather's deathbed."

"Ah, yes." And Nonno starts grinding into the story he's probably been working on since he saw me this morning, about a girl who was chronically fifteen minutes late to take her grandfather to his chemotherapy appointments, those critical fifteen minutes allowing his cancer to take root.

None of this would happen during the thirty-eight weeks of the calcio season, of course. By this time, Papà and Nonno would've already taken their last piss of the day and arranged themselves on the matching recliners pointed at Nonno's flat-screen, listening to the pregame commentary in reverential silence, the only noise the squawking of the leather every time they shifted their weight. But this is the thirty-ninth week, and they finally have the time to sit outside under the nonlemon tree and instruct me about my failings.

". . . but the granddaughter, she eventually got her due because the old man died without being able to say good-bye, and"—here Nonno leans forward and pauses dramatically—*without* being able to tell her where the safety deposit box was. Because the granddaughter"—he holds his finger in the air like Charon used to hold his pointer stick— ". . . was ten. Minutes. Late."

He stabs these last three words with his finger, pinning them to the air, where they hang between us. I look over at Papà, but he only nods gravely.

I'm used to Nonno's parables. When I was younger, I thought it was a coincidence that he knew so many people who possessed the same defects in character and made the same bad choices as Luca and I did. When Papà told him Luca was thinking about getting a tattoo, all of Nonno's navy friends suddenly got horrible, skin-rotting diseases from their tattoos, often rendering them impotent. When I was sixteen and mentioned that Casella and I were thinking about going to the animation institute in Milan, he spontaneously remembered all the children of his friends who had gone to the city and become prostitutes, drug addicts, or liberals. When I wanted to take a beach vacation down south after graduation, he remembered everyone he knew who had been murdered, dismembered, or sold into slavery by Camorra or Cosa Nostra.

"What was the name of the girl, Nonno?" I ask. "The one who was late."

"Oh, you don't know her."

"You never know."

He takes a drink of his wine. "Why don't you go see if your grandmother needs help?"

I follow Nonna's faint humming into the house, where she's hovering over a tray of zucchini flowers, stuffing them and lining them up. There's still a corner of her brain that knows how to cook. Just like how paralytics can have erections on pure reflex, Nonna's rotted mind instinctively knows what moment to flip a frittata or check on a roast.

"Can I help you with anything, Nonna?"

But she only looks up at me and smiles, as if I am nothing more than a distant but pleasant memory.

We eat dinner at the old wooden table that is probably from my bis-nonno's bisnonno or even before. Nonna has made a feast, the same as every Sunday, and Papà and Nonno silently eat their way through the zucchini flowers, the pasta, and the roast, too much talk being bad for the digestion. I poke at my food as I watch them across the table, their heads bobbing up and down above their plates like birds keeping time, and my mind goes back to Zhuki's frozen face as she stared at me in the courtyard. After last night, she will probably never come to the shop to buy meat again. She will settle for the meat in the freezer case at the Standa, or at Benito's, the other butcher in town, who brandishes his knives like swords and belts out Dante and Puccini to the tourists. It's probably for the best. What would I say if I saw her anyway? I'm sorry. I was drunk. I was a stronzo. See, I have this medical condition . . .

After dinner, I help Nonna with the dishes while Papà and Nonno have their digestivos in the yard. After they decide their postdinner conversation is officially over, I'm obligated to help with whatever projects Nonno has set aside for us. Today, these include cleaning out the second cistern, which for the past two weeks has been belching up an inhuman stench that Nonno swears is an indication of sabotage by one of his jealous neighbors. By the time we've finished and washed up, the sun is setting over the terraces and Nonna has already prepared a second meal. And it's in the middle of the second meal that Papà looks up at me and says, "By the way, I ran into Silvio this morning. He said he went by the field, and it was perfectly clean. He said it looked like a professional mowing job."

At first I think he's being sarcastic, but then Nonno chimes in.

"Gubbio said the same." Nonno clutches his knife in his fist and waves it in my direction. "You see? It just goes to show, a little hard work makes all the difference."

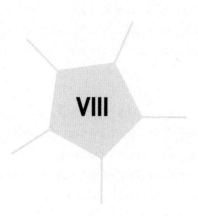

VIII

I don't believe it even when I see it with my own eyes. It starts as a diffused light rising up from behind the cypresses as I walk up the path, like the landing lights of a spaceship or a second sun resting on the field. I find a spot behind the cypresses and crouch down. It's incredible. They've made an entire calcio field out of light, four floodlights as big as babies sitting at the corners, shining in perfect ninety-degree arcs, creating touchlines and end-lines as sharp as chalk against the dark grass, rolling out like a lush green carpet, the bare spots turfed over and all the dead stuff raked out of it.

And in the middle of the field is Zhuki, her cheeks flushed, her silky shorts fluttering against her thighs like the flag of a mythical country where there is no pain or poverty. She's dragging the little blond boy around by the feet, his arms flung high above his head, leaving a swirling wake in the shadowy grass. They are going in circles around the enormous man I saw her with the very first time, and the other guy is near Luca's headstone, kicking a ball back and forth with Yuri Fil himself. They look like dance partners mirroring each other's movements, the white-and-silver ball dart-ing and hovering between them.

I stay frozen, listening to her and the boy's laughter, also rising with the light, and I'm only vaguely aware when my thigh cramps up and I shift my weight. A twig breaks beneath my right foot, and the crack resonates across the terrace.

Shit.

The enormous man swings his head like a wrecking ball and stabs a thick finger in my direction. He charges at me, and I run like a wild animal, breaking through the brush to the path. I can hear his voice booming behind me, and he catches up to me in no time, gripping me by the back of my shirt, my arms and legs flailing, like the masked criminals in *Batman*. He carries me through the cypresses like a shield, the needles and branches scraping the shit out of my face and hands, and he sets me down in front of Yuri Fil like a cat leaving a mouse at the back door. Zhuki's face changes immediately, from soft flesh into stone, and the little boy tips his head to have a look. There's a Ukrainian commotion between the three men, lots of shushing and regurgitation of vowels, as Yuri Fil holds the ball patiently against his hip. The little boy cocks his head at me in curiosity. His eyebrows are round like scythes, Zhuki's flat like plows, her face blank and expressionless, a Closed sign on a darkened door.

Finally, she says something—just a couple of words in Ukrainian—and like magic, the back of my shirt is released.

"So . . . you are the butcher?" Yuri Fil says in English. "Like Materazzi?"

"Who's that?"

"Who is Materazzi? Materazzi the Butcher? He is your Italian defender who is not nice with his elbows." His accent in English makes him sound like a little kid. I'll bet his teammates in Tottenham and Glasgow gave him shit for it in the locker room.

"Actually, I am the *son* of the butcher," I say.

"I will be honest," Yuri Fil says, "we do not care who you are. Only is important for us that you are not paparazzi."

I try to straighten myself out, smoothing my shirt and raking my hand through my hair. I look over at Zhuki and the hard muscles of her jaw, still set against me.

"Well, I'll be off, then," I say.

"Oh, no, no, no, no, no." And this Serie A striker wags his finger at me like one of the nuns in asilo. "You cannot go nowhere. We need a six."

"What?"

"We need a six. We want to play match, and we have only five." I feel Zhuki's eyes drilling through me, and my head feels like it's swelling, like any second it might pop off my neck and roll down the hill, playing pinball down the path and coming to rest in the English garden.

"No thank you, Signor Fil." I back away.

"Yuri," he says, advancing toward me. "Call me Yuri."

"No thank you, Yuri." I turn around and head toward the path.

"But why not?"

Because your sister loathes me, I want to tell him. Utterly and deservedly.

"I don't play calcio," I say instead.

Yuri Fil laughs. "In Italy? *Impossibile.*"

I shrug. "Ask anyone. My brother, he was the calcio player in our family."

"Where is this brother, then?"

I look toward the goal.

"Aha."

I glance at Zhuki's face, and I think I see a slight ripple, a break in the defense. Luca's dead, and he can still soften up the girls.

"Anyway, have fun." Have fun. A former-Serie-B-now-Serie-A striker, who I'm sure could rip out my eyeballs and swap them for my palle, and two guys who would help him, and his sister, who in one sentence could give them the motive to do it. The five of them are probably about to play the best match this field has ever seen, and I say to them, *have fun?*

I hear the grunting and shushing of their language behind me, and then footfalls. Shit. I close my eyes and prepare for the fetal position.

"Hey, relax, relax," Yuri Fil says, putting his hands up. "I am not the man you should worry about. I am your hero. I save you from Ihor. One second more and Ihor was biting your head off . . . biting your head and . . . *ptooh.*" He spits on the ground and laughs.

Ihor stands off to the side chuckling, a rumbling in his chest that sends aftershocks through his limbs.

"I am sorry," Yuri Fil continues, "but you have made me curious. You really do not play calcio?"

"I really do not play calcio."

"You do not like calcio?"

"No."

"You do not watch calcio on television?"

"Not if I can help it."

"No fantasy calcio?"

"What a waste of time."

"And you never even *dreamed* of becoming calcio player? When you was little boy?"

"Never."

He thinks long and hard about this, his finger over his lips as if to show me that I have just spoken the unspeakable.

"Play with us," he says. "One time. One time, and I promise, you will like calcio."

"It's kind of late, isn't it?"

"It is never too late for calcio," he says. "Half a match. Forty-five minutes."

I look back at Zhuki, who hasn't moved either to encourage her brother or to protest. I know I've already blown it with her, but maybe if I indulge her brother, she'll come away thinking that I'm not a complete stronzo. I don't know why I even care. I just do.

"Half a match," I say.

Yuri Fil steps forward and shakes my hand like we're making a deal. He introduces the others. Mykola, his trainer. Ihor, his bodyguard.

"And this is Little Yuri," he says. "Captain of Ukrainian national team 2024." The boy gives a salute, as if he's used to being introduced in this way. "And you already know my sister?"

"Yes," I say, and then for no other reason than that I am a complete pedant, I add, "from the butcher shop." I don't dare look at her.

"Very good." Yuri rubs his hands together. "So, Etto-Son-of-Butcher, we have three rules." He says something to Little Yuri, who clamps his hands over his ears.

"Number one . . ." Yuri counts off on his fingers just like Papà. "Do not be a stronzo on the field . . . number two, do not be a cazzone . . . and number three, do not be son of whore. Everything else okay."

He nods to Little Yuri to release his ears and holds up his wrist to reveal a watch that would put Guido's and Nicola Nicolini's to shame. At least fifty thousand euros of metal links and springs.

"I keep time."

"What position am I playing?"

There's a storm of consonants, this time initiated by Zhuki.

Yuri Fil turns to me. "You will start here," he says, taking me by the shoulders and shifting me into place like I'm still in chickadees. "Mykola and Ihor are on your team."

I smile, looking at the mismatched three who are left, but no one else on the field seems to think it's funny.

"We will give you smaller goal to defend," Yuri says, pointing to Luca's headstone.

He says a word to Little Yuri, and Little Yuri hustles to the far goal like the calcio players on television. You can tell by how he moves, by how he cocks his knees and shifts his weight, that he has inherited whatever miracle gene his papà has, and he will probably spend the next thirty years of his life under the deafening roars of crowds, the desperate sighs of girls, and the admiring love of not only his papà but papàs everywhere.

Yuri sets the ball in the middle of the field and retreats. Zhuki steps up, one foot tensed behind the other, her eyes dark, two blank circles where the arcs of light will not reach.

Behind me, a whistle blows.

Technically, I did play calcio until I was about ten, but during matches I warmed the bench, and when we did drills I was nothing but target practice for Luca. Even if I had played clear through to the junior leagues, I still would have been no match for Zhuki. When her shoulders fake one way, her hips move the other, as if her feet are disconnected from the rest of her body. I trip over myself trying to gauge which direction they're headed, but it's like watching the blades of a fan, and I'm left chasing the breeze. She scores the first goal in two minutes flat.

"You're really good," I tell her, my breath already shallow and quick.

"Like I need you to tell me that." Her breath is coming in little puffs, her face flushed.

"That was supposed to be a compliment."

"Oh, a compliment. Yes, I am good for a girl, right? Is that what you wanted to say?"

"That's not what I meant."

"Who do you think played with Yuri back in the village for all those years? Who do you think blocked his shots?"

"Look, I'm sorry. And I'm sorry about the other night."

"*Last* night," she corrects me. She steps back, her arms crossed, staring me down.

"Look, I was drunk. I was a stronzo." She widens her stance. "See, I have this medical condition . . ."

"Come on, come on," Yuri Fil shouts. "This is not tea party with *Alice in the Wonderworld*. We are playing match. And you, Etto-Son-of-Butcher, lift your head. You are staring at your feet like if you don't they are going to disappear." The whistle blows, and her legs blur.

I don't need to recap the rest of it. It's the longest half ever recorded in the history of calcio. Nine goals. Nine goals she scored on me, the chatter and laughter of Yuri Fil and the others growing louder with each one. Even Ihor grins, though without any movement in the top half of his face. Zhuki doesn't crack a smile.

"Sixty seconds!" Yuri calls out as Zhuki steamrolls me to another goal.

"And injury time?" Mykola shouts back, laughing.

"No injury time!" Yuri Fil taps at his chest with his middle finger. "Only injury is for ego, right, Etto-Son-of-Butcher?"

We're near the floodlight in the corner closest to Charon's aula, and Zhuki dribbles the ball back and forth, alternately blocking the light and letting it hit me right in the face. I think she might be doing it on purpose. She feints and dribbles around me like I'm a stationary object, does the same thing to Ihor, and ricochets the ball off the corner of the headstone and into the net.

The whistle blows.

"It is finished! It is finished!" Yuri shouts like the announcers on TV. I fall to the ground. I wish I could say I do it to make her laugh, but no, I fall to the ground because I feel like I am going to die.

And what does she do? She comes over and stands between me and the corner floodlight, the photons swirling up behind her. I think for a second she's going to pull me up off the ground in a show of sportsmanship, or at least pity, so I reach my hand out to her, but she leaves it hovering, begging in the air.

"*That* was for the disco," she hisses. "Do not fucking touch me again."

And as if to punctuate this, Little Yuri comes charging across the field at me, yelling, "AAAAAAAAAAAAAAAAAAAAAAAAAAAAAAAAAAAA." He takes a running leap and flops across my chest like a cat.

Shit.

"Yurichko!" Yuri Fil shouts, peeling him off me. He says a few stern words to Little Yuri in Ukrainian, then offers me his hand. He pulls me up off the grass like a dead weight. "I am sorry. He watch too much Mexican wrestling. Satellite television. Sorry."

"It's okay." I stagger a few steps until I get my balance.

"Well, I hope you are better butcher than calcio player," Yuri says. "You know what your problem is?"

"I can't play calcio?"

"You must look up. I tell you before. You are always looking at feet. Feet are only tool. Match is up here." He taps his heart.

But I'm only half listening. I'm too busy watching Zhuki stomp toward the terrace wall, only slowing down to hook her jacket from the ground as she passes the sideline. Yuri Fil shouts something after her, and she shouts something back.

He laughs. "You have pissed her off very much. I don't see her play like this since Ukraine. But no problem. In few weeks, she will only score five goals on you and not nine. In few weeks, you will play better, you will see."

"I'm sorry, Signor Fil, but I just retired."

"Yuri. Call me Yuri. And do not be afraid. We say in Ukraine, bottom of mountain is most difficult. I and Mykola, my trainer, we are here for two more weeks, and in two weeks, we can make you a champion calcio player. Promise. Not Serie A, but maybe Serie CI or C2. . . ."

"I'm sorry, Signor Fil, I can find you five hundred men in this town who would cut off their arms to play with you, but I'm afraid it won't be me."

Yuri scoops his son onto his shoulders. He grips Little Yuri's calves, and Little Yuri hugs the top of his head. Ihor and Mykola go to the four corners to collect the floodlights.

"Ah, but I know we will see you again," he says. "Because you are man. And you will not let the woman win." He looks toward the spot where his sister disappeared into the darkness and he raises his eyebrows. "Especially not that one."

The field goes dark, and the bells from the churches on the hill ring eleven o'clock, each one in turn. Ihor shouts something, and Yuri looks at his watch and starts walking toward the back of the terrace.

"Tomorrow night," he calls over his shoulder. "Ten o'clock. And please—do not tell nobody. *Nobody.*"

Once they are gone, I lie down next to Luca, the fresh-cut grass pricking my skin.

"How about that, eh, Luca?"

He grins back at me.

"And the girl?"

Another grin.

"Zhuki." I say it again in my head. Zhuki. Zhuki-Zhuki-Zhuki-Zhuki. If you say it fast over and over, it sounds like a circus, like one of those dances that involves a lot of hopping around before collapsing into your partner's arms. But if you say it slowly and quietly, *sul serio*, it's like the waves foaming up on the beach in the winter.

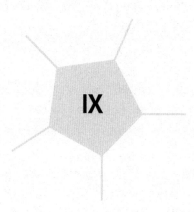

IX

I go down to the shop early on Monday morning, and I can feel Papà, Nonno, and my bisnonno watching me from the wall as I pull in the crates of bread and clean linens from the passeggiata and take the grinder out. Papà is a perfectionist about everything, but especially about his sausage. He won't get one of the electric grinders because he insists the meat tastes better if he uses the same hand crank my nonno and bisnonno used.

I fit the blade and the plate in place and look up at the pantheon of calcio players over the grinding counter, who smile down from their frames and give a benediction to every sausage, soppressata, and kilo of ground beef that comes out of this place. I try to conjure Zhuki out of her brother's face. The features are unmistakable—the narrow nose with the bump at the bridge, the full cheeks and the thick, dark eyelashes, like reeds circling a pond. I can feel the tight muscles at her waist. I can see her rounded hips floating in front of me up the steps at Le Rocce, the pinch of her eyes as they slam shut against me, and the grimace as she gives the ball a kick.

Once I finish clamping the grinder in place, I go out to the back alley, pull up a crate and light a cigarette. I close my eyes and lean back against the cool stones of the building, replaying the events of the past two nights, one a nightmare, the other a dream.

"Et-to." A deep voice echoes in the alley. "Et-to, this is your conscience talking."

I trace it to the pile of empty boxes stacked up behind Chicca's shop. "Fede, if that's you back there, I'm going to beat the shit out of you." I peek around and there he is, his knees drawn up to his chin, a grin on his face, stupid like an owl.

"What do you want, Fede?"

"Why didn't you answer me yesterday? I SMS-ed you fifty times."

"You SMS-ed me three times. What happened, the girl didn't work out and you were calling for a backup?"

"You wish. I just wanted to make sure you were still alive."

"Well, I'm fine."

"I mean, I've seen a lot of drunk people in my life, but you . . . cazzo, there was nothing left of you but the stink."

"Well, you can see I'm fine."

"I mean, you were loaded like a donkey . . ."

"I get it, Fede."

"Sbronzo, disfatto, ubriaco marcio . . ."

"Enough, Fede! I *get* it." I stamp out the cigarette. Fede stands up and follows me back into the shop. I can already tell he's in one of his lost-puppy moods, when he desperately wants to talk about his feelings but instead follows you around, getting underfoot until you ask him what's wrong. Well, forget it. If you can't tell people your feelings, not my problem.

He wanders around the shop, touching everything like a deficiente—the beaded curtain, the top of the case, the register. He leans against the banco and crosses his arms.

"Thanks a lot, Fede. Now I have to clean it again."

He shrugs off the glass. I get the cleaner and the paper towels and start wiping away at the imaginary smudges. Fede crosses the room and reaches a hand up to the portraits on the wall.

"Cazzo, Fede, would you stop *touching* everything."

Fede grins, sweeping his arms like a fottuto showgirl. "Someday, eh, Etto? Someday . . . this will all be yours."

"Hooray."

He sits down on the stool behind the register, hunching his broad back and swinging his legs, his muscles unable to relax, popping out above his knees and at the backs of his arms.

"Okay, Fede. Fine. What is it? What's wrong?"

"What do you mean?"

"I mean, you have your constipated face on, and you've been following me around like a puppy."

He stares at me. I stare back. I can hear a little German kid whining in front of Chicca's shop, his mamma's voice counting, rising with the numbers. Eins . . . zwei . . . drei . . .

"Did you hear Bocca got busted by Jacopo's mamma yesterday morning?" he says.

"I told you it would happen one of these days."

Fede stares at his feet and hooks them over the rung of the stool. I remember when Mamma worked the cash register, and how she never sat down. She was always greeting people at the door, bending down to talk to the kids, and sending them on their way with a "Bye-bye! See you tomorrow!" It was so different from how she'd thought her life would turn out, nothing to do with art history or California or the people she'd spent the first twenty years with.

"Apparently, Jacopo's mamma brought the maintenance guy in at six in the morning to take a look at the air-conditioning, and Bocca and that girl—how was she called?—were just snoozing away, naked like their mothers made them."

"I told you it would happen."

I go into the front walk-in and carry the two buckets of scrap back to the grinding counter. Papà premixes the right proportion of veal to beef to fat for each of the sausages he makes, and he labels the buckets with masking tape and a thick black marker so I don't mess it up. Fede follows me. Sometimes I wonder why he's so dead set on hanging around me all the time. Sure, when Luca was around, we would all go out together, but it wasn't until after Luca died that he started to seek me out on his own. Maybe he misses Luca and I'm some kind of surrogate. Maybe he feels guilty about loaning him the motorcycle, and telling himself he's looking after me helps him get to sleep at night.

Fede leans against the band saw table.

"Not the smartest idea to lean against a band saw, Fede."

He shrugs but doesn't move. I wipe down the grinding counter and scrub my hands before feeding the scrap into the maw of the machine. I turn the crank, and the pink squiggles fall into a loose pile on the counter.

"Cazzo, what *is* it, Fede?"

He looks up at me with those pathetic eyes and runs his hand through his hair. When he's eighty, he will still have that hair.

"What *is* it?"

"I don't know . . . it's just so . . . I don't know . . . depressing sometimes."

"What's depressing?"

"The whole thing."

"What do you mean, the whole thing?"

"I don't know, maybe *depressing's* not the right word. Maybe *boring* is more like it. I mean, it's not even a challenge anymore."

"Wait, by *the whole thing*, you mean *sleeping with girls*, Fede? You're telling me that's *depressing?*"

"I know it sounds crazy." He stuffs his hands into his pockets.

"Listen, Fede, I've got work to do, so if you just came by to brag . . ."

"That's not it at all."

"Then what is it?"

"I don't know . . . I mean . . . every time, it's the same thing. The same stupid lines, the same stupid moves. I feel like I've got to live up to some imagined something in her head, and she feels like she's got to pull out these ninja moves that she's seen in some movie or learned from some other guy . . ."

"*That's* what's bothering you? Fede, there are whole continents of men who are doing it with girls who learned on you first."

"That's not what I'm saying."

"Cazzo, what *are* you saying, then?"

"Forget it. You don't understand."

"I don't understand. . . . Look. I'm crying for you, Fede. Really. I'm crying into my fottuto pillow every night for you and how much sex you get, and how it's not even a challenge anymore. Yes, that's the saddest story I've ever heard, having to sleep with all these too-willing girls who will leave town in ten days. Tragic. Utterly tragic."

Fede shakes his head and starts for the door, his hands stuffed into his pockets, his shoulders hunched like I'm the one who's wronged him.

"Forget it," he says. "I'm sorry I said anything. Next time I'll just keep it to myself."

"Don't try to make me feel guilty, Fede. You're the one who ditched me the other night."

"You know what, Etto? Vaffanculo," he says, and his sturdy chin gives me a poke from across the room.

"Vaffanculo yourself."

He lets the door slam behind him, and I watch him cross the passeggiata to Bagni Liguria. Like I'm supposed to feel bad when *he's* the one who packed me into a car just so he could get rid of me and stay with some girl that now he's complaining about. I go over it in my head as I grind the sausage, getting more annoyed with Fede with each turn of the crank.

Papà comes in just as I'm finishing. He's out of breath, as if he's run all the way from Martina's.

"Have you heard?" he gasps.

"About what?"

"They think Yuri Fil is in San Benedetto! Yuri Fil! In San Benedetto!"

"Who's Yuri Fil?"

"What do you mean, who is Yuri Fil?" He points to the photo on the wall. "*This* is Yuri Fil."

"Oh."

"Oh. Yes. Etto, listen to me carefully. If you hear anything, you must call *immediately.*"

"Sure."

"Not just 'sure.' I mean it. Immediately. It is imperative. Anything at all, call me. Imperative."

"You don't have a phone."

Papà throws up his hands. "Just call me on Silvio's. Or Martina's. Or anyone else's. Everyone is over at Martina's already."

"Fine."

"*Imperative*," he says, stabbing a finger in the air—just like Nonno—before he hurries out the door.

"*Imperative*," I mock. "*Imperative!*" But my insides twist as I say it, and I get a whiff of the meat in my hands. The smell of death. It starts as a subtle sweetness hidden behind the earthy, metallic scent, encouraging you to breathe more deeply. Only when you do, that's when the acidity uncoils and strikes. You can work for months at a time without smelling it, until you convince yourself that your job is the same as selling books or cell phones or neckties. Papà will even tell himself he's doing something noble. Nourishing families around their dinner tables. Feeding the world. Only once in a while does it really strike you that you are, in fact, peddling flesh. Flesh chopped off an animal's bones and ripped from their sinews, flesh that every second is going more rancid.

All day long, I try to breathe through my mouth. The flow of customers starts as soon as I open the front door, and all anyone wants to talk about is Yuri Fil. But as I think about Zhuki surrounded by the gossips and vultures and vampires, my stomach churns, and this strange protectiveness surfaces inside me, an inexplicable desire to hide her away or punch someone out for her.

"Hey, Etto, have you heard the news?"

"What news?"

"There's a rumor Yuri Fil is staying in Signora Malaspina's villa."

"Who?"

"Yuri Fil."

"The calcio player?" I raise my eyebrows convincingly.

"Yes, from Genoa. The Ukrainian."

"He's in San Benedetto, you say?"

"That's what I've heard. He's brought his entire family. You haven't seen him, have you? He hasn't come by for any meat or anything, has he?"

"No, I haven't heard anything."

At this point, they lean over the banco conspiratorially. "You would tell me if you had, wouldn't you?"

"Of course," I tell them all, holding up three fingers in a Scout pledge. But what I'm really swearing is an oath to Zhuki, that as long as she's in this town, I will never let her or her family's name dissolve on my tongue. I will never sacrifice her to the circle of chairs at Martina's or let her be dissected by the dull blades of the gossips.

I should have been an actor. I fool even Chicca.

"You hear anything about this Ukrainian guy everyone keeps talking about?" Chicca asks me as we puff away at our cigarettes.

"Nope. You?"

"What would I hear? I'm stuck in this shop all day." She shakes her head. "Let's just hope he'll be good for business."

X

*O*ne of the things you'll find out when you lose somebody close to you is how complex a network of wires and cables you've built from your life to theirs. When Luca went off to the academy in Milan, our lines fell into disrepair and disuse one by one, but when Mamma died, the whole network came crashing down in one terrible storm. It took months for my brain to learn that there was no connection on the other side, and it kept spontaneously sending out impulses every time I thought of the smallest anecdote to tell her or the most minuscule piece of gossip to spread. By the time I remembered that there was no one on the other end, it would be too late, and I would have to watch all those impulses go down the line, fizzling and crackling into a void.

Strangely, it's not as much of a problem when your life is going badly, because there are any number of people in the world who are happy to step in and listen to you gripe and complain. But you learn the hard way that there are precious few you can share the good things with. The hopeful feelings. The lucky turns. The invitation to play calcio from the brother of a girl you never thought you'd see again. And since you have no way to transmit these bits of good news outward, the only option left is to swallow them like a chicken would—a pebble here, a stone there, grinding against each other in your stomach until even the good things become a reminder of all that's gone wrong.

I don't feel like going to Martina's on Monday night, but if I skip dinner, it will look suspicious. They will start talking, and the thing will never end.

"You're late," Martina says. On the flat-screen, there's a cycling race on mute that no one but the Mangona brothers is paying any attention to. "I was about to send someone after you."

"Sorry."

She smiles and ruffles my hair. "I've got fish for you today." She sweeps past Signor Cato and disappears into the small kitchen.

Nello's sneering at me from down the bar, like he's bored with drinking and he's going to try to pick on me the first chance he gets. Unfortunately, Martina doesn't believe in banning people, even Nello, so he's been allowed back in after only a week's exile, though carefully assigned a seat far away from Papà.

"You look like shit, Etto," he starts.

"Thank you."

"Why don't you get some sun once in a while?"

"Don't you know? We half-Americans are allergic to it."

"Ah, ah. Very funny."

I glance over at Papà and the other men and eavesdrop on their conversation. They're still talking about Yuri Fil, but this time, it makes me squirm in my seat.

"But if he is in fact here, why would he choose San Benedetto of all places?"

"Why not San Benedetto? Let's not forget—San Benedetto is the last place on earth that is simple and pure, and those Italian fishermen, they really know how to, you know, *live*."

Everyone laughs.

"I grant you, it's not a bad place to live, but it's not pedigreed like in the old days. It's not as if we have models and actresses mincing down the passeggiata anymore."

"Or *Playboy* Bunnies. Don't forget the *Playboy* Bunnies." There's some chuckling.

"Exactly. Why would he come here? To ordinary little San Benedetto."

"Doesn't anyone remember?" Signor Cato calls from the alcove, and everyone turns in his direction. His eyes are still scanning a screen full of tabloid headlines. "Don't you remember?" Signor Cato repeats. "Right after Martin Malaspina left Signora Malaspina, she had that long romance with the Dutch calcio player."

"That Van-der-Basten-velt-huisen-elftal guy?"

Everyone laughs.

"The other one. Ajax versus Liverpool. The fog game. Walked off the field because he thought the game was over."

"De Born."

"Ah, yes, De Born. Now there was a playboy."

"What is it with women and Dutchmen?"

"It must be their windmills." Another chuckle.

"Aha. So, that De Born who warms the bench now for Genoa is related?"

"His son."

"Ah . . . sì, sì . . . he must have passed on his father's fine memories from San Benedetto."

Mystery solved.

Martina comes back with plate after plate, and I bolt down the food as fast as she can put it in front of me. A dish of olives. Trofie with pesto. Fish in some kind of orange-colored sauce. Nello watches me eat for a few minutes, then tries again.

"Be careful you don't ruin your girlish figure there, Etto."

"That's enough out of you, Nello," Martina chides.

"What did I say? I didn't say anything. I'm merely looking out for his health."

"Don't think I won't ban you."

Martina leans across the bar and puts an apple fritter in front of me. "Etto, you're quiet tonight. Are you sure you're okay?"

"Fine. Maybe a little tired."

"Well, make sure you get some sleep tonight." She reaches over and ruffles my hair.

I wish I could tell her all about Zhuki. I really do. But I know she would tell Papà or at least Silvio. Instead I sit on the turf in front of Luca's headstone, my fingers plucking out a few blades of grass that are already tall enough to threaten the neat edges of the stone.

"So, what do you think my chances are?"

Luca's photo smiles back at me, his mouth pinching into a dimple at the corner.

"I borrowed your shorts and cleats today. I hope you don't mind."

I dig a cigarette out of my pocket and sit still for a minute, listening to the sounds of the hill.

"I know. I shouldn't lie to Papà. *You* would never lie to him like this."

And I swear I see his little shoulders shrugging under his jersey like he used to do whenever he scored a goal. Each time he did it, it caught me off guard. It was the simplest and humblest gesture possible, as if to say, "And so it is." I stare at his face, forever the fresh face of a twenty-year-old. I think this is one of the things that bothers me the most—that I'm already two years older than he'll ever be, and life will keep piling up on me until I'm an old, bitter man looking at an exuberant kid who bears no resemblance to me at all. Maybe that's exactly what Mamma was scared of—life moving on. The year she was depressed, I would come home from the liceo in Albenga, sit on the end of the bed, and recount every detail of my day. I would turn off the TV and open the shutters, tell her stupid jokes, and put on her favorite songs. In my mind, I guess I figured if I kept chucking life rings at her, she would eventually have to grab one. But maybe it was too much—too much clanging of the everyday world being let in, too many mundane thoughts and ordinary churnings returning to her own body. She put it off for almost a year by staying in bed and submerging herself in the endless television programs, but she had to know it couldn't last forever. Maybe when she looked out onto the flat sea, she saw the permanent solution—a field more fallow than the comforter of her bed or the flat screen of the television, where Luca's memory would never be plowed under and replanted with everyday life.

Shit. I wish I could stop myself. Stop trying to get inside her head. Sometimes I really hate myself for going over and over it. It's pointless anyway. I mean, if I never knew something as basic as the fact that she was capable of ending a life, what did I really know about her at all?

I hear them rustling through the vegetation on the next terrace. I stub out the cigarette and jump to my feet.

"Look at who is here to play calcio!" Yuri shouts.

Zhuki, Yuri, and Little Yuri are all wearing the yellow-and-blue jerseys of the Ukrainian national team with the name "Fil" perched over the number on the back. Ihor and Mykola are in the green-and-white horizontal stripes of Celtic, Yuri's last team. Zhuki walks right past me without a word.

"I see you have proper shoes today," Yuri announces. "Good! We bring you jersey, too. To make it official."

A handful of green-and-white material is thrown in my direction. Zhuki says something in Ukrainian and everyone laughs.

"She say, it is green and white," Yuri translates. "For hope and faith. When you do not have ability."

I steal a glance at her. She has only the smallest glint in her eye, but my mind has already begun to magnify it.

"Joke," Yuri says, slapping me on the back. "It is only joke."

I turn around and change into the jersey so she will not see my chicken-carcass chest.

"And these are for you also." Yuri holds up what looks like two pieces of coal in the moonlight, but when I get closer, I see they are those clip-on sun lenses the old Germans wear, the kind that flip up and down on your glasses.

"What are those for?"

"For you."

"To block out the glare from the moonlight?"

He holds out his hand.

"What?"

"Your glasses."

I reluctantly hand them over. Luca and Fede used to tell me I looked like a turtle without my glasses, one of those old ones that live on the Galapagos. I always feel incredibly vulnerable when they're not on my face, like at any moment, anyone could jump out of the bushes, crush them, rob me, and leave me for dead. Yuri Fil and his trainer hunch over the glasses muttering, and when I get them back, the dark lenses are clipped to the bottom instead of the top, flipped out at ninety-degree angles.

"What are these? Ukrainian sunglasses?" I laugh.

"So you will look up," Yuri explains. "So you will not want to keep eyes low to ground."

They set up the floodlights and the match starts. Everyone scatters, leaving the goals open. Yuri, Little Yuri, Ihor, and Mykola are all whooping and shoving each other as they play. Zhuki and I are the only serious ones, Zhuki because she wants to prove she can kick my culo again, and me because I'm trying to prove that I don't always get my culo kicked by girls. The clip-on lenses do help. I don't look down at all. Partly because it's dark down there, but also because I want to stay ultra-attentive to who's running at me and avoid any collisions that would jam the lenses into my sockets, scoop out my eyeballs, and serve them up like hors d'oeuvres. It takes all my concentration to worry about this, to think about my feet and the ball, to stay in the light of the field, and to not get distracted by all the people around me, real and imaginary—Zhuki ahead of me, Luca in the ground, Mamma in the sea below, and Papà sitting in my head, yelling everything he used to yell at me from the sidelines.

Give it to Luca!

Don't jog. Explode!

Ah, come *on*, Etto!

For God's sake, open your eyes!

I run so hard, my glasses fog up, and my hair feels like a poof of reddish-brown smoke above my head. My stomach, lungs, spleen, whatever's in there, tighten, every organ squeezed to half its size, and the tracks of sweat are running in torrents down my back. The other men strip off their shirts, but I keep mine on. Now that Ihor and Mykola are not letting Zhuki run over me, Team Fil has only scored five against us, and Mykola has scored one for our side. Zhuki kicks the ball out of bounds. It gets caught in the brush on the next terrace, and Ihor runs after it. I put my hands on my knees, trying to cough up the phlegm weighing me down. Yuri jogs over to me.

"You must quit smoking."

"How do you know I smoke?"

He hunches over and pretends to cough up a lung, then stands up laughing.

"Very funny," I say.

"Aha! And this is another thing we must teach you. Have fun! Like you say before. Today you look like animal who run away from hunter. Like you be eaten if you lose." He reaches over and rubs my head. "Have fun!" he repeats. "Calcio is not so serious."

The whole time he's talking, all I can think is, non me ne frega, Yuri Fil. I don't care if I get better at calcio or not. The only reason I'm showing up here is to prove to your sister that I am not a vampire and a stronzo, and possibly, just possibly, to get back at my father, *neither* of which requires me to be good at calcio.

"Etto!" Ihor shouts from the sideline, and the ball comes sailing into the light. Yuri jumps up in front of me and snags it with his chest, letting it roll down his body before flicking it away. I go after it, but he traps it and dribbles circles around me, keeping it away from the desperate stabs of my toes. And I don't know exactly what happens next, but somehow the ball ends up behind him, and I wind up on the ground. Little Yuri dribbles it to our unguarded goal and puts it in.

"Goooooooooooooooooooooooooooooooooooooooooooooooooooooool!"

Yuri sweeps Little Yuri up on his shoulders and circles the field, shouting, Little Yuri riding his papà like a bull, whipping an imaginary lasso in circles around his head. I lie down in the grass, flat on my back, trying to recover the collapsed sections of my lungs.

"You must get rid of this laziness, Etto." Yuri stands over me, smiling, Little Yuri's face rising up over his papà's like a great, two-headed calcio monster. "You will never make Serie A if you are always laying on ground taking naps."

The rest of them gather around, and it feels like I'm looking up from a deathbed at their faces, Mykola's thin and gaunt, Ihor's like one of those great Soviet ironworker statues. And then there is Zhuki, her face rising like the moon, her cheeks made slightly pouchy by gravity, her eyes resisting and opening like blooms. I see the smallest twitch at the side of her mouth, and it crumbles the darkness of her face, like weeds breaking through the concrete. I hear the shush of Ukrainian, and I know the night is over.

"We must go. Tatiana wait for us," Yuri says, pulling me up off the ground. "Maybe paparazzi are sleep now."

"There are paparazzi?"

"Only one tonight. He came from Rome in the afternoon. A little guy, skinny, with six senses. No matter what, he always know where we are. It is strange, very strange."

"How did you leave the villa?"

"Oh, we know how to systemize the paparazzi. Easy. I tell Tatiana, wear the bikini and go on balcony. Then we go out back door. It is my hope, this little paparazzo, he will not be here for long time. Many people say Ilary will be have Totti's baby." He scoops a pregnant belly out of the air in front of his own flat stomach. "If is true, all paparazzi will be in Rome from this weekend. If we are lucky, they will be marry and there will be wedding. Then paparazzi will be in Rome whole summer, and everybody will forget about stupid Ukrainian striker."

Zhuki says something to Little Yuri, takes his hand, and heads toward the path. "Ciao," she throws over her shoulder in my direction, and I lap it up.

"Ciao!"

Yuri heads toward one of the floodlights. "We will see you again tomorrow. Same time."

"We'll see." I try not to sound too eager. "I'm not sure if I can."

"Ah, but I am sure," Yuri says, laughing. "I am sure we see you tomorrow."

The floodlights go off. I hear the rustling as they climb up to the next terrace, and suddenly, I'm alone again. I sit down next to Luca and light a cigarette.

"Did you hear that? She said 'ciao.' Clearly to me. She wouldn't have been saying it to anyone else. And that smirk." I twist around, and the photo stares back at me, cold and unblinking.

I rest my back against the stone as I listen to the midnight bells and watch the lights blink out across the hill. I catch a flicker of light coming through the row of cypresses. Shit. I must have left one of the lights on in the aula the other night. I heave myself up from the grass and push through the second line of cypresses that divides the field from the liceo. I fumble with the keys and pop each of the three locks in turn.

"Anybody there?" I call into the corridor, and my own nervous laugh echoes back to me.

When I was little, I was always the last to get ready for bed, and when we watched movies together on a Friday or Saturday night, sometimes I was too scared to go upstairs on the commercials to brush my teeth or put on my pajamas. So Mamma started a system, calling to me at regular intervals from her seat on the sofa, like the pinging of a submarine.

"Are you there?"

"I'm here!"

"Are you there?"

"Here!"

"Are you there?"

"Here!"

She would keep it up for as long as I was away, until I was safely tucked next to her on the sofa again.

I walk down the corridor, past the rows of class portraits, white with dust, shrinking with each graduation year. Nonno had forty or fifty classmates filling the frame, dressed smartly in jackets and skinny ties. Papà's is down to twenty-five, squeezed into tight sweaters and flared pants. In my class, there were only eight of us fourth-years in the classical program, only six in the class below. I guess we should have known it was coming, but the closing of the liceo caught everyone off guard. They posted the letter from the regional education office in August, right before our fifth and final year was supposed to start. The letter said it would be temporary, one year, maybe two, until they could figure out the funding to open it back up. For the rest of the week, everyone was red-faced and waving their arms around, planning strikes and tax boycotts, but in the end, they just shrugged their shoulders and forgot about it. That's how everything happens in this fottuto country—depth charges of outrage and then apathy stretching as far as the eye can see.

In the end, we were taken in by the schools in Albenga, the classical and scientific students to the liceo, the hospitality students to the institute. The teachers, who once seemed to us an indivisible unit, were unceremoniously disbanded. Charon had qualified for retirement eons ago, so he moved back in with his mamma in Rome, and Professoressa Gazzolo went to Milan, where to the torment of every boy at school, she had a muscly boyfriend with a Ferrari. Et tu, Professoressa Gazzolo? The rest of our teachers went directly from their vacations to jobs teaching other delinquents in other backwaters of the empire, with no interruption in pay.

I walk past the bathrooms and more classrooms, down to Charon's aula at the end of the corridor. I stop at the doorway and reach up to touch the frame, where someone in some previous class had scratched a message with a sharp knife or a pen nib.

"Abandon all hope, you who enter here . . ."

And for the first time I notice that the quote has been finished, only the second part isn't carved in the jagged gouges of some high school kid. It's written in sharp pencil, in the restrained loops that once crowded out the margins of my essays. Charon always wrote in pencil, he told us, in order to emphasize the permanence and infallibility of words themselves.

". . . for you have lost the gift of understanding."

I read the words again and I can't help laughing, imagining old Charon up on a chair, vandalizing his own doorway for a joke only he would get. It was hard to see Charon doing anything for a joke. He had wispy white hair that looked like it was leaping away from his skull in sheer terror, and he was so old, he talked about ancient Rome with the same affection the other teachers had for their childhoods in the sixties and seventies. I think the other teachers were even a little scared of him. None of them were allowed to use his chalk, his chair, his books, or his aula. Pete the Comb Man could go in there to clean and do maintenance, but no one else.

I open the door and it's dark. My brain, my logic, whatever, tells me it must have been the reflection of the moon I saw, bouncing off the windows, but something else inside nags at me. I sit down in my old seat. For four years, we begged Charon to change us out of alphabetical order. For four years, we stared at Sima's bra straps and Claudia's smashed culo that miraculously re-formed when she stood up, and we made the same joke of kneeling on our seats, pretending Aristone's head was too big for us to see past to the chalkboard. For four years, every time we had a test, we would take turns whistling softly from the second row until Charon looked up from his book with those burning embers of his eyes and said, plainly and calmly, "Stop it."

I let the silence sink into me.

"Mamma, are you there?"

My own voice echoes down from the vaulted ceiling.

"Did you see me tonight, running around out there? I'll bet you couldn't believe it."

No answer.

"You would like her," I continue. "She's not like Luca's floozies. Remember that one who stalked him all the way from Milan? She was a masterpiece, eh?"

If I could have only one thing back, it would be her voice. The way she put the accent on the wrong syllable in Italian or amputated all her *g*'s in English, and the mix of both that only the four of us could ever completely comprehend. She and Luca are probably up there right now, floating around, laughing and talking in La Lingua Bastarda. Sometimes if I think about it too hard, I feel like a chump. I thought we were a team, I really did. Me and Mamma. Papà and Luca. That's how it was supposed to be. When we followed Luca to his matches on the weekends, Papà would go to the stadium at the first light of dawn. He could spend the whole morning there, talking to coaches and scouts and scrutinizing Luca as he trained. Mamma and I would spend those mornings at one of the art museums. That was our thing. Mamma used to be as passionate about art as Papà is about calcio. It was the reason she came to Europe in the first place, because she said she was tired of learning art history from slides, and tired of being in California, where there was nothing older than she was.

She could make any museum interesting, even when I was a kid. She would take me around to each sculpture or painting as if she was introducing me to old friends. She taught me how to tell the difference between a Greek statue and a Roman one and how to crack the code of the Dutch still lifes. She told me endless stories about the sculptors who had a competition to the death over some commission, or the painter who was stone blind but chose colors by tasting them. When I got tired, she would hide behind some old caesar's bust and make him talk to me as I passed, or she would attach us to a tour and pretend I didn't speak Italian or English, translating everything to me in some babbling, made-up ape language while I nodded my head and tried to keep from laughing.

The Sistine Chapel was by far her favorite, and every time Luca had a match in Rome, we suffered the Metro, the long lines, and the souvenir vendors to see it. When I was little, all I remembered was the scaffolding and what looked like worms—a writhing mass of pink, naked bodies pinned to the ceiling like larvae, muscles straining, faces contorted, trapped for all eternity. By the time I was eleven or twelve, I looked up at the same ceiling and saw only breasts. Large breasts, small breasts, full breasts, sagging breasts, lopsided breasts, breasts with nipples like fingers, breasts pointing in opposite directions like signs at a crossroads. London, Paris, New York, Milan, Breasts. Breasts and, briefly, piselli, which I only let myself glance at for half seconds at a time and only for comparison's sake because God knows I didn't want to end up a finocchio like Nicola Nicolini.

But I remember the time when it finally made sense to me, and when I figured out why she liked it so much. It was right after Luca moved up to the U16s, and it was the hottest summer ever recorded in Rome. I woke up in my bed in the pensione already sweaty and annoyed, and I only braved the Metro across town to humor Mamma and because the museums were air-conditioned. That day it seemed like we stood in the chapel forever, our necks wrenched back, tour after tour squeezing in on us from all sides, every language in the world piling up around us like the great rubble of Babel.

Mamma had probably explained it to me a hundred times before, and I already knew every story there was about Michelangelo. How the pope forced him into it. How everyone thinks he painted it lying on his back, but really, he was standing up the whole time. How he painted one of his critics into *The Last Judgment* as a demon with a snake biting off his pisello. Thanks to Mamma, I had long ago learned the strict organization of it all—the ancestors of Jesus above the windows and the hulking prophets anchoring the spaces between them. I already knew the nine central scenes from Genesis by heart and in order. First, there was the creation of everything good—light, sun, water, Adam, Eve—and then the descent: God kicking Adam and Eve out of the garden, God flooding the world, Noah ending up in a pathetic, drunken heap at the end.

But this time Mamma said something new, or at least something I hadn't listened to before. She said the ceiling was the most human work of art ever created. Human. That was exactly the word she used. Not *divine* or *beautiful* or *meraviglioso* or any of the synonyms we made up in La Lingua Bastarda. No. She called it *human*. And finally, that day, I saw what she saw, that this great work of art was just people doing human things—crying, blushing, sewing, primping, suckling, reading, playing, lifting, struggling, smiling, grimacing, thinking, and doing those things with wool and weaving that no one knows the words to anymore. All of them intertwined.

Before we went to Luca's match that afternoon, we had enough time to have lunch in some beat-up caffè in Trastevere, and I remember looking around at the other customers, the waiters joking at the bar, and the pedestrians walking by. And because this was the old Trastevere, before the hipsters and the developers got their hands on it, they were ordinary people doing ordinary things—walking their dogs, carrying their groceries, pushing baby strollers, or humping around on canes. And for that one, perfect hour, the world reordered itself the same way the ceiling had, the vulgar herd separating into individual and noble lives. Husbands and wives, mothers and daughters, customers and clients, friends. For that one hour, everything was as it should be, and it all made sense.

I went home after that weekend and started drawing. Not comics or copies of magazine pages like I was used to doing, but real people from real life. I would sit out on the molo or the balcony during the afternoon break and draw the men fishing or the tourists lying on the beach, the waiters in the restaurants along the passeggiata, or the Mangona brothers leaning out the windows of their huts. I filled notebook after notebook, showing no one, not even Casella. Not even Mamma. Sometimes I wonder what she would have said.

I look up at Charon's blank ceiling, and the chatter in my head stops. I get a strange feeling, like someone else is doing the thinking for me, and I no longer control my own head. Suddenly I'm on my feet, dragging the heavy tables across the floor with a deafening vibration.

Porca miseria. I see it in a flash and all so clearly.

The scaffolding that takes shape over the next couple of hours is a marvel of engineering and a testament to Professoressa Gazzolo's physics class. I pull extra tables from the other classrooms, levering and heaving them, two by two, layer by layer, with some invisible strength. In the end I build what looks like two fortresses, three layers high, one taking up the front half of the aula and the other, the back. I tear apart the boxes in the art room that were left in limbo, and I collect every pencil, every brush, every can of paint and roll of paper. I find three posters of the Sistine Chapel, rubber-banded and forgotten, and I take the best one and climb the scaffold of tables, crouching and contorting until I'm at the top. I look down at the floor. My knees rubberize, and I start to feel a little sick. My fingertips cling to the plaster, digging in, looking for a handhold.

"Easy there," I say. I steady my legs and have a good laugh at myself. I stretch my arms out like in *Titanic* when they are at the front of the ship, Kate and Leonardo DiCraprio, as we used to call him just to annoy the girls in our class. I look down the length of the aula, the globe lights dangling a meter from the ceiling.

"I'm the king of the world!" I shout. "The king of the world!"

I laugh. The echo fades and a sober silence sets in. I dig the pencil out of my back pocket and wrap my fingers around it. It feels gigantic, like when the nuns first taught us how to write our names back in asilo. I roll it around between my fingers and stare up at the vast, blank space. I look back and forth from the poster to the smooth ceiling, and I plot out the first of the nine central panels in my head. I've decided to start with the last one, suspended over Charon's desk at the front of the aula. *The Drunkenness of Noah.*

I haven't drawn anything in two years. My hand shakes as it follows the curve of Noah's back and thigh as he lies slumped on the ground. I draw and redraw the pockets in the cloth as it falls and bunches beneath him. I try to copy his sons' young muscles as they stand around pointing, deciding what to do. It takes me all night just to get the basic outline down, and trust me, it's no masterpiece. The sons end up looking like a bunch of bickering women with curlers piled on their heads, and the lines of the drapery are a mess—smudged and wobbly, some of them feathering out into false ends like a frayed wire after several attempts to get the curve right. Michelangelo himself would have thrown me out onto the stones of the piazza with all his other assistants. But I have a strange feeling of satisfaction, and as I look down the clean, white arch, I can see the other panels emerging from the plaster on their own.

I will give her a resting place as beautiful as the tombs of the Roman emperors or the popes in the Renaissance. Not some flat, anonymous stone in a nondescript cemetery next to dead relatives in a country she never loved. But here, surrounded by her favorite painting and overlooking the sea. And, Mamma, wherever you are out there, you will finally see how much I loved you, and how much you threw away.

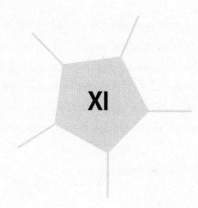

XI

I know, I know. You are probably shaking your head, thinking, what kind of deficiente thinks he will be able to paint a copy of the Sistine Chapel on the ceiling of a classroom? What kind of arrogant stronzo? What kind of naive child? Believe me, it's nothing I don't ask myself as I walk down the hill in the early morning light. Papà is already leaving for Martina's.

"Where have you been all night?"

"Out with Fede."

"I thought you and Fede had an argument."

"Who told you that?"

"Nobody has to tell me anything. I am your father. I know what you are thinking before you even think it." He looks at his watch. "When you and Jimmy are finished unloading the truck, send him over to Martina's. I need to talk to him about the July orders. And of course, if you hear anything about Yuri Fil, anything at all . . ."

"I know, Papà."

"Try to get it out of that niece of Signora Malaspina if you see her."

"Yes, Papà."

I go upstairs and change my clothes, make myself a coffee, and bring it down to the shop. I drink it staring at the portraits on the wall—my bis-nonno, Nonno, and Papà, lined up like a firing squad. I grip an imaginary cigarette between my lips and shut my eyes beneath an imaginary blindfold. Pow. I slump against the banco, and the imaginary cigarette falls to the floor.

My phone lights up. Fede, from the beach, ten meters away.

HEY, STRONZO. YOU LOOK LIKE HELL.

This is Fede's way of apologizing.

YOUR AUNTIE.

And that is mine.

The wall phone rings just before eight. It's Papà, calling from Martina's.

"Did you forget what I said about Jimmy?"

"Jimmy didn't come."

"Didn't come?"

"He must be running late."

"Running late? When is the last time that happened?"

"I'm sure he'll be here."

"Make sure you send him over." Click.

My mind stays up on the hill and in the aula all morning. The only time I come to is when someone asks if I've heard anything about Yuri, and when Papà calls every hour on the hour to see if Jimmy has shown up yet.

"Not yet. Maybe you should call his papà?"

"Yes, maybe."

The wall phone rings again at noon. "He hasn't come yet, Papà."

"Hello?"

"Hello?"

"Hello, is this the macelleria?" She says it in Italian, but her accent is unmistakable.

"Yes."

"Etto?"

"Yes."

"There is a problem at the villa today," she says in English. "Paparazzi. We cannot come down to the shops. Can you bring the meat to us? To the villa?"

"Of course. At your service." At your service. I sound like a fottuto eunuch.

She wants a whole rabbit, a whole chicken, six steaks, a kilo of ground beef, and six hundred grams of prosciutto, unsliced. I go upstairs and get my rucksack, pack up the order, and start taking apart the banco early. As soon as the last customer is gone, I flip the sign and lock the door, step out onto the passeggiata, and pull the floodgate down. The sun is blinding today, bouncing off the waves, and with no breeze, the hot air stays trapped against the land. I weave through the crammed streets and try to stay in the shade of the awnings and the mandarin trees. As I walk, I feel conspicuous, as if everyone is watching me from their windows and they know exactly where I'm headed.

On Via Partigiani, the Mangona brothers go by in a blur.

"Ride with us, Etto!" one of them shouts as they pass.

"Tomorrow!" I shout back.

"It's always tomorrow," and they both laugh.

Sometimes I wonder if Luca and I would have been as close as the Mangona brothers if I'd stuck with calcio. Maybe I should have tried. Maybe at least I would have had more stories about him instead of this awful blank slate of the last five years of his life.

I trudge on under the weight of the rucksack, past Nonno and Nonna's path, past Mino's house and the field, the sun now pounding away at me like a spike being driven into the ground. My back is soaked and my legs are tired, but I fight the hill every step, and I push myself as fast as I can go so the Ukrainians will not have lukewarm rabbit and sticky prosciutto. As Papà always says, we are judged on the condition of the meat when it comes out of the package and not only when it goes in.

At the villa, there are four black cars with tinted windows parked on the access road alongside the iron fence. There's no movement as I walk past the cars, but when I near the gate, I can hear the muffled slamming of doors. The villa rises in front of me with its columns, balconies, and arbors, and as the creeping shadows in my peripheral vision make their way toward me, I try to focus on the front door.

Shit. Stay calm. Keep your hands visible. They are only paparazzi. Then again, maybe it was a lie to protect me. Maybe they are really mafia coming to collect a debt, and I am the collateral damage. Maybe in a few minutes, I will be nothing more than pieces scattered along the road, a few bits of hair and trace that the crime channel will reassemble into a suspenseful, hour-long forensic elegy in my memory. Blessed are the contents of his stomach and the DNA results, blessed the identifiable tool marks from the custom-made nunchucks they used on his face.

The front door of the villa sweeps open, slowly and dramatically. Behind me, I can feel the shadows closing in, the rapid-fire of the camera shutters like lizards flicking their tongues.

"Out of the way," and they press their lenses through the bars of the gate.

It's not Zhuki drifting toward me but the woman on the cell phone who came into the shop. She's wearing a gold bikini and a long, white robe as thin as a spider's web. Tatiana the Showgirl. Yuri Fil's wife. I don't know where she came from, if she's originally Russian or Ukrainian or what. All I know—all anyone knows—is that she started out as a humble showgirl, a simple vehicle to deliver breasts to the masses, and has graduated to become a calcio player's wife, one of the sequined blondes floating through the tabloid pages, haunting VIP access areas at the stadiums and dimly lit parties at night. Once in a while I'll see her in a WAG roundup or an interview, but whatever clichéd musings she might have are immediately eclipsed by her giant and mesmerizing breasts.

She smiles and reaches her hand through the bars as I take the packages out of the rucksack. But like the Austrian girl, she isn't smiling *at* me, only over my head, her gold breasts like hovering Ufos, hypnotizing me. She holds out a hundred-euro note, dangling it in front of my face, and I freeze.

"Take," I hear her say, in English, through her clenched smile.

"Oh, no, no, signora. You have a conto at the shop."

"Take. You. Euro."

"But we do not accept tips, signora."

"Euro! Take!" she hisses, and her gold breasts suddenly look menacing.

I take the bill and slip it into my pocket with as little fanfare as possible, my face burning, the shutters still firing around me.

"Oh! Oh! Paparazzi! Paparazzi!" she exclaims, even though they have been less than a meter from her the entire time. A look of alarm crosses her face, and she covers her collarbone with her hand, knocking her knees in a fake Marilyn Monroe. My eyes finally break from the spell of the gold breasts and are drawn upward to the veranda, and there is Zhuki, laughing at the whole scene, or maybe just at me. I let my hand flap free from the pocket of my jeans in an almost imperceptible wave, and she lifts her hand slightly from the railing before turning and disappearing behind the roofline. It's only then I realize that Tatiana the Showgirl has gone back into the house as well. The door of the villa closes with the quiet precision of a German car door, and the paparazzi stop taking pictures and leave my side, drifting back to their black sedans. The heat closes in around me, and I come to.

Shit. If Papà sees this, he's going to kill me, bury me, and then resurrect me, just so he can kill me a second time. For not telling him in the first place. For not calling over to Martina's and letting him make the delivery. For taking a tip from Tatiana the Showgirl. And for other reasons he'll make up with the shovel in his hands. Shit.

"Ehi!" I shout to the last of the photographers as he's about to get into one of the cars. "I'm not going to be in the tabloids or anything, am I?"

And the guy gives me a look like I'm the biggest deficiente he's ever met, rolls his eyes, ducks into the car, and slams the door.

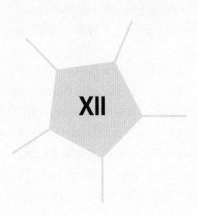

XII

*T*he next morning, I'm still lying in bed when I hear the truck pull into the alley and shut off abruptly. Usually, Jimmy lets it idle while he smokes a cigarette and waits for me. When I get down to the shop, Papà is there—not with Jimmy but with Jimmy's papà, who I haven't seen in at least a couple of years.

"Sorry about the mix-up yesterday, Etto. It's been a stressful week."

"Where's Jimmy?"

"He didn't say anything to you?"

Papà looks at me intently.

"Nothing. Why? What happened?"

Jimmy's papà shakes his head and sighs. "He's left us."

"What do you mean, left?"

"I mean, he came down to breakfast on Friday morning and told his mother and me it was going to be his last day of work. He said he and his friend have gotten themselves jobs."

"Doing what?"

"Who knows. He's calling himself a consultant. Some company based in America. He said they have conventions to sell video games all over the world, and he and this friend will be going to them and doing demonstrations."

"That's going to be their job?" Papà says. "To play video games?"

"That's what he said . . . I know. What kind of job is that?"

"And where is he going to live?" Papà asks.

"I asked him that, too. I said, if these jobs are all over the world, where are you going to live, and you know what he said?"

"What?"

"Hotels. One night here, one night there. Who would want that? Can you imagine waking up in a different bed every morning only to spend all day in a hall with no windows, staring at a screen? Why would he want to do that when he could be out in the sunshine and the fresh air, working on the land?"

"It sounds fishy to me," Papà says. "Do you want me to have Silvio investigate it?"

"I don't know. He showed us the contract, and it looked legitimate enough. Signed. Notarized. Heat stamped. I didn't even know he had any friends besides me and his mother. In fact, I asked him, and you know what he said?"

"What?"

"He said he met this friend online. What does that even *mean*? How do you become friends with someone you've never been in the same room with, much less make plans to go around the world with them?"

"How long is he going to be away?"

"This contract is for six months, but who knows?" He looks at his shoes and shakes his head again, like he's trying to puzzle it out. "Boh. I guess he never liked the slaughtering part." He says this matter-of-fact, but when he looks up, I can see the terror in his eyes, the fear that he's going to lose Jimmy for good.

Papà and Jimmy's papà move the carcasses into the back walk-in and hook them—the full vitello, the nose swinging ten centimeters from the floor, and the side of beef.

"Pass me a pan, Etto, will you?" Papà says.

I bring him the pan and he puts it under the nose of the vitello. There's nothing more to do, but Jimmy's papà is still standing around looking lost.

"Don't worry," Papà tells him. "He will soon realize that he never had it so good as when he was at home, surrounded by his family, working in the security of the family business. He will be back. Mark my words, he will be back." I know this speech is more for me than for Jimmy's papà, and I'm sure when Nonno finds out about this, I will get one of his special stories about the girl who worked for her parents' restaurant, left them in the lurch, and lived unhappily ever after.

"I hope you're right, Carlo." Jimmy's papà reaches over and puts a hand on my shoulder. "Anyway, you are lucky to have such a good and loyal son."

For the rest of the week, I do what I need to do in order not to be missed. I open and close the shop on time. I eat at Martina's and try not to seem rushed. I answer Fede's SMS-es and meet him and the rest of them at Camilla's a couple of times. But I wake up every morning knowing that I am only waiting for the sun to set and darkness to fall, for my eyes to take in the sight of her running back and forth across that floodlit field.

I think I'm making progress. Each day I record the angle of her mouth curling up at the corner and the number of words she speaks to me.

"You sure were a hit with the paparazzi." Eight words.

"Don't feel bad a six-year-old blocked it. Little Yuri isn't a normal six-year-old." Thirteen words.

"I was wondering if you would mind bringing us a girello and a few steaks tomorrow?" Sixteen words. Yes, I know a meat order shouldn't count, but I'll take what I can get.

Every morning, I hide their order under the piles of vacuum-packed cuts in the front walk-in, and every night, I sneak into the shop, pack it into a cooler, and tote it up the hill.

"How much do we owe you?" Zhuki asks me.

I shrug, as if my father and I are gentlemen butchers and money is of no consequence. "You have a conto. We can settle up before you leave." And I can't look at her, so I look at my shoes and pretend I'm working a stone out of the ground. "When *are* you leaving anyway?"

"I don't know. Now Yuri is talking about staying longer."

"Really?" I find another imaginary stone to work at. "Don't you want to get back to Genoa?"

She shrugs. "It's not like I have anyone waiting for me. Yuri, Mykola, and Ihor, they are my friends. Wherever they are, that's where I'm happy."

Yuri comes across the field toward us, clapping his hands. "Enough chat, enough chat. Back to work. Back to work."

From my first day on the field, Yuri and Mykola have approached me like a mental patient, their calcio experiments like deprogramming, as if this is my last chance at rejoining the normal, productive, calcio-loving society. They teach me all the things I should have learned on this field ten years ago. How to kick with the laces for power, the inside of the foot for accuracy, and the outside for spin. They teach me how to read the keeper and bait the defenders. And they make me practice. Practice, practice, and more practice. Attacking, defending, passing, shooting, running, and more running. I feel like the fottuto Karate Kid.

"I thought you said calcio was going to be fun," I say, clutching my knees and trying to spit the weakness out of my body.

"Ah, for you, maybe is not fun yet. Your body have much to learn. But when your body know what to do, your head will stop thinking he know everything, and when head stop thinking he know everything, you will see that calcio, it is simplest and most beautiful game in whole world."

On Saturday night, there's a full moon, and each blade of grass stands out in high relief against the others like an army on the march. I don't know how the field stays so meticulously mowed, if they've hired somebody or what, and to be honest, I don't care as long as I don't have to do it. I try different positions for when they come through the hole in the terrace and she catches the first glimpse of me. I sit cross-legged in the middle of the field, then on top of Luca's headstone, then against it with arms crossed, then apart. Luca is probably laughing his head off.

"Hey, shut up, brother. Some of us actually have to work at it."

I hear the rustling of the brush and the sputtering of their incomprehensible language, and I recross my arms. When we were twelve, Fede and Luca taught me how to put my fists behind my biceps so they seemed bigger. I look down to check the effect, but the bulges look like air bubbles traveling up a straw. I uncross them and put my hands on the edge of the headstone as if I am a coiled spring, virile and ready for action. I realize the talking has stopped. I hear a click, and one of the floodlights blinds me.

"Shit!" I throw my hands in front of my face to a gale of Ukrainian laughter. Ihor in particular can't get enough. He does six or seven instant replays, each one with as much fling as he can make his solid arms do, each one with the "Shit!" as high as his voice will go. All to the delight of Yuri, Little Yuri, Mykola, and Zhuki. But you know something, Ihor, and anyone else who's listening out there? I don't care if she's laughing at me. Because at least she's not scowling anymore.

Yuri bowls the ball at my feet. I try to stop it, but it rolls right past me. "Shit."

"Hey. No more of this 'shit.'" Yuri says. "I am tired of it. From now on, you say, 'I work on it, Yuri, I work on it.' Here, I show you how to control ball." He gets down on the ground, turning and shaping my feet into a position they are somehow incapable of finding on their own. No one would believe it if they saw it, this Serie A calcio player tending to my feet.

"Like this," he says.

It's then I notice a little girl hiding behind Zhuki's legs. She's wearing a baseball cap with blond curls frothing around her face, and she peeks around to see what Yuri's doing.

"Well, hello, hello, Principessa," Yuri says.

"What's her name?"

"Principessa. My wife, she wanted Italian name, not Ukrainian or Russian. She think if she have Italian name, she will have easier life."

"Well, it's not exactly an Italian name. . . ." I say. Shit. Maybe the fottuto French are right, naming their entire population off an approved list of ten names. Who the cazzo names their kid Princess?

"I told him that when she was born," Zhuki says, and she nudges her brother with her foot. "But he does not listen."

"Not important," Yuri says, standing up. "Only thing is important is that you never saw Principessa here. We have much trouble sneaking away from villa with her."

"Because of the paparazzi?"

"No, no. The paparazzi went to Rome last night," Yuri says. He stands up and opens his arms to the sky. "Thank you, Er Pupone and Ilary. Just as I imagined. She will have baby, and he is Catholic mamma's boy, so there will be wedding. Story about handsome Roman striker much more interesting than story about old Ukrainian striker. I must telephone to the Little Golden Boy and say, 'Thank you that you are so handsome and Ilary is a blonde. You save my family from paparazzi.'" Yuri laughs.

"Why did you have to sneak out, then?"

"Aha, because we take Principessa with us tonight. Tatiana, she worry that if girl play calcio, she turn into boy. Or lesbian. Like my sister."

Zhuki shoves him hard, and he loses his balance.

"I am only joking. Only joking."

Mykola shouts something in Ukrainian from the other side of the field, and the last of the floodlights goes on. Zhuki and Yuri laugh.

"What did he say?"

"He say, 'And God make the light!'" Yuri rubs his hands together. "So! You are ready?"

"What torture do you have planned for me tonight?"

"Torture? Being with us is torture?" Zhuki smiles. God, I love those teeth. Small and rounded, like milk teeth, but they might as well be fangs for all the destructive power they carry.

"Etto, I tell you, tonight is big night," Yuri says. "For you, and for the world. Tonight, we teach you—an Italian man—to throw away the catenaccio."

"What are you talking about?"

"The catenaccio. This silly game of defense you Italians play that makes the boring scores and pisses off rest of world. You know why they play the catenaccio, the Italian teams?"

"Why?"

He nods to Little Yuri, who dutifully clamps his hands over his ears.

"Because they are pants shitters! Because they scared. They think there is limited number of goals in season, and they scared other team take them all. So they try to lock the door. But tonight we say, no afraid, no afraid! Enough of the catenaccio! Attack! Attack! Attack!"

"And how exactly are we going to do that?"

Zhuki says something to Little Yuri, and he sprints over to their pile of things on the sideline and comes back with a bag. Zhuki smiles as she hands it to me.

"What's this?"

"It's for hockey," she says. "Here." It's a goalie's helmet, and she helps me slip it over my head. I can feel her fingers brushing against the back of my neck. I think she could have asked me to put on a pink ballet thing that was two sizes too small and I would've let her do it.

"Ready?" Yuri says.

"For what?"

And cazzo if he doesn't kick the ball straight into my stomach, so hard that it doubles me over and bounces out of bounds.

"Shit! What did you do that for?"

"No 'shit,' remember? And do not worry. We are professionals. When we are finish, you will no be scared of nothing. There will be no catenaccio inside of you. All will be left is attack."

He lines the ball up again, and I fold my arms across my stomach. "Wait! Wait! Let's at least talk about this."

"No talk. No wait. Trust me. Zhuki, say him."

"It's fine. He did the same to me when I was ten."

"And look how good she play now." I look over at Zhuki. There's no way out of this without having to cash in the chips of my manhood. "Come on," Yuri says again. "No afraid."

I stand up to my full height. Wham.

"Now open your eyes this time. You have mask. Come on. No afraid."

Wham! Wham! Wham! Wham! He hits every one right in the stomach. After about the tenth one, I stop flinching. After five more, the sting is gone, and after another five, I wonder if I should undergo psychoanalysis or something because it actually starts to feel good. Wham! Wham! Wham! Wham!

"Now," Yuri says. "*Now* you are ready. Now you got nothing to lose, nothing to fear. Say it: Enough of the catenaccio! Attack! Attack! Attack!"

I look around at the others, but no one else seems to think this is crazy. "Enough of the catenaccio. Attack, attack, attack."

"Louder!"

"Enough of the catenaccio! Attack! Attack! Attack!"

"Louder!"

He makes me repeat it twice more. I look across the hill, but no lights go on in the houses around us. Up here, you are not your brother's keeper. Whatever your brother does is none of your fottuto business.

We fan out across the field. Zhuki kicks off from the center spot, and as I'm chasing after her, I feel stronger than before, actual muscles working beneath the surface, the swamp monster that was trying to share the air in my lungs last week now shrunk to a manageable size. I don't score any goals, but I can tell I'm making Team Fil work a little harder, their breath and their steps quickening around me. We play almost until midnight, when Principessa is asleep behind Luca's headstone and Little Yuri is so tired, he starts laughing hysterically and falling down every time he touches the ball.

"You are coming tomorrow, yes?" Yuri asks.

Every night I check Zhuki's face to be sure. "Yes. Tomorrow."

"Good." Yuri slaps me on the back. "Good work tonight. You are improving. Stronger."

"Yes," Zhuki says, "not bad for a butcher's son. Not bad at all."

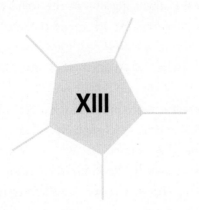

XIII

I know now what it means to lead a double life. To chase after a shouldn't, with a should dragging like an anchor from your neck. Prince Charles, President Clinton, Prime Minister Berlusconi, I never liked any of you. Really. But I understand you now. Sometimes you just can't stay away.

So I save an entire column in the ledger of my conscience before I even commit the individual infractions. Not that a prayer exists that can give me absolution anyway. Me secretly playing calcio with Yuri Fil is worse than if Mamma and Silvio had had an affair, worse than if Luca had gone to play for Juventus. It's so far beyond the actuarial tables of penance and forgiveness, I know that if I don't want it to squat in my head for the rest of my life, if I don't want to drag it around behind me or live in the shadow of its bulk, I must somehow incorporate it. Pretend the lie is simply a part of me. So I pull at it, twist it with logic, thin it with rationalizations, shrink it by comparing it to all the other messed-up things people do these days, and keep working at it until it seems minuscule, a nanofabric that can be knit right into my skin, the lumpiness and itchiness unnoticeable to everyone but me.

After Martina's every night, I go up to the aula. I don't have the nerve yet to fill in the first panel with paint, so I start on the second. This time, I use a giant sheet of paper from the roll and measure out a meticulous grid of squares to match the smaller grid I've drawn on the poster. After that, it's a simple matter of multiplication and diligent copying. When I'm finished with the drawing, I tack the paper onto the ceiling and poke along the lines with a pushpin, then rub charcoal into the holes until it creates a perfect dotted outline.

I look up at the results. It's probably the hardest panel of the nine. The most complicated. *The Deluge.* Forty days and forty nights cooped up with your family in an ark. No wonder Noah got trashed on vat wine when it was all over. These days they would make a reality show out of it, each person driven slowly insane by their loved ones and jumping overboard. I darken the lines on the island and the bank before starting in on the people. There are maybe a hundred figures in the picture, some of the true deficienti cowering under a sheet, trying not to get wet, the rest realizing the threat and panicking to save themselves, scrambling up rocks and trees and the side of the ark, holding bundles of belongings above their heads, a few even trying to tread water or pile into a rowboat. Every man for himself. Every man doomed.

At ten o'clock I go outside and wait for the Ukrainians. I sit on the fifth-year bench, looking down onto the town. The bench used to sit at the entrance of the liceo, but my first year, the fifth-year boys clustered around it and dragged the whole thing ten meters, concrete base and all, right to where the terrace drops off. I remember they were so fottuto pleased with themselves. On breaks, seven or eight of them would squeeze onto the bench and look down on San Benedetto like Romulus looking down on the city of Rome, victors over their brothers, masters of all, the world laid out submissively at their feet. What a joke. Now when I see those same fifth-years on the street, they're just like the rest of us, living at home and working for our papàs or our papàs' friends.

I watch the lights and the people in the town, small as crumbs, filling in the meticulous rows of restaurant tables along the passeggiata, a few crawling along the empty beach. I imagine a giant tsunami coiling up on the horizon and roiling over all of it, like the one in Indonesia last Christmas, wiping out the entire population and scrubbing the town clean. The water would build and climb steadily up the hill, terrace by terrace, and Charon's aula would be released from its foundation, floating up on the waters to the level of Signora Malaspina's villa. I would be trapped in the aula for days, forced to eat splinters of wood and plaster chips to survive. Eventually, the water would recede, and somehow Zhuki and I would be the only survivors, stumbling out of our respective arks into the embrace of a rainbow, vowing immediately to start the civilization over from scratch. None of the cazzate of modern society. Just the two of us. Purely for the good of the world.

Over the past week, I've found out that the Ukrainians are not a punctual people, but tonight they're so late, I worry they won't come at all. They told me they have a friend from Genoa staying for a few days. Maybe he does not play calcio. Finally at ten-thirty, I see the bright, white beacon of a cell phone sweeping through the brush. This time the voices are in Italian. Ah yes, the friend from Genoa.

And can you even guess who the "friend from Genoa" is?

Vanni Fucci.

Vanni Fottuto Fucci. The other star striker who plays for Genoa, who represented the Azzurri in the last World Cup, and no doubt will again for the next one in Germany. Vanni Fottuto Fucci, Armani underwear model, *Playgirl* centerfold, and the man who has the panties of all the women on the continent hooked to his eyelid, so when he blinks a half second too long, four hundred million thongs, bikinis, and even granny pants simultaneously drop to the floor. Vanni Fottuto Fucci, the bastard who for an hour and a half of emotional injury time makes me look like a stumbling idiot in front of Zhuki and, with his crossovers and his foot stalls and his fancy drag-backs, even manages to tangle the feet of the great Yuri Fil.

Oh, he has all the moves—the flaunted familiarity with her family, the shameless use of Little Yuri as a prop of his tenderness, and the pathological urge to take his shirt off. When he pulls it up over his head and reveals a set of tortoiseshell abs, it feels like a bandage being ripped off my skin. They say he has a painting of himself as a centaur hanging above his bed for all his conquests to see. Could it be any worse? Vanni Fucci staying in Signora Malaspina's villa, steps away from Zhuki's bedroom door.

I search her eyes for any sign of attraction. But she doesn't dwell on Vanni Fucci any longer than necessary in order to read his next move, and her eyes stay straight ahead in such perfect concentration that it would make both Marcello Lippi and the Dalai Lama proud. You can tell, she's in this one to win. Still, three minutes into the first half, Vanni Fucci manages to get behind her and score.

"Gooooooooooooooooool!" he shouts, making double figs with his fingers and running around the field, laughing in her direction as if it's one of their inside jokes. "Goooooooooooooooooooooooooooooooooooooool!"

Like I've said, I'm no expert on women, but it seems like a poor way to win her over.

And sure enough, I hear her mutter something in Ukrainian, which I convince myself means "stronzo among stronzos," and it gives me a small pinhole of hope. If she can see the stronzos, maybe she can see the good guys, too.

At halftime, Vanni Fucci replays his best moves for us, and Little Yuri starts doing his limp-limbed dance in the middle of the field that he does every night at this time because he's six and should be in bed by now.

"How long are you staying in San Benedetto?" I ask Vanni Fucci.

"I'm going back to Genoa with them on Tuesday."

Suddenly the world stops spinning, and the stars swirl and fall from the sky in a burning rain around me. "Tuesday?"

"Yuri must go for the process," Zhuki says. "With the sporting judges."

Yuri hangs his head in shame.

"Only for a few days," Zhuki adds. "And then we'll be back."

"Don't worry, Yuri," Vanni Fucci says, laughing and hitting him on the arm, "if it doesn't work out, you can always retire to the glue factory in America."

Yuri looks up and shrugs. "I think America is not so bad place for calcio player. Not so much competition, and nobody on the street know who you are. Do you know Ronaldinho went to America last year, walked around for two weeks, and nobody recognizes this is famous man? Whole world know his face, his hair. Europe. South America. Asia. Africa. Australia. But not America. Can you imagine? Ronaldinho! Walking on streets in Los Angeles. No bodyguard, nothing."

"Sounds like hell to me," Vanni Fucci says.

"To me? Like heaven. I would go to America tomorrow. No problem. I have aunt in Chicago. She love Chicago. But Tatiana, she say she can no leave Europe. She think they are animals in America, eating with their hands and wearing cheap cloth-es."

Yuri backpedals into the center of the field, blowing the whistle for the second half to begin. Thank you, Tatiana. I take back every bad thought I've ever had about you.

For the entire second half, I chug up and down the field like a referee. We are winning, mostly because Vanni Fucci won't pass anyone else the ball. And then, in the last few minutes, he decides to chip the ball to me. I'm not expecting it, and I trip. I go down hard, nothing graceful about it, just tangled feet and whump! I look up at the sky full of stars, my whole body aching as Vanni Fucci swoops in and scores the goal.

"All okay?" Yuri reaches a hand down to me and pulls me vertical.

"I'm alive."

We watch Vanni Fucci take his victory lap, thrusting figs into the air.

"You know," Yuri says. "I know my sister very well. And Zhuki, she does not interest with Vanni. I tell you, since we are children, she never like strongest, most handsome man in room. When she was little girl in village, she always take care of three-leg puppy, two-head chicken, cow that give no milk . . ."

"Thanks. I get the idea."

"Good."

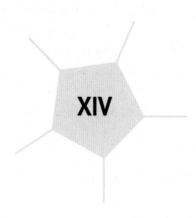

XIV

*F*ede has let me know with an infinite number of SMS-es that he thinks I've been blowing him off, so after the match on Sunday night, I track them down at the Truck Show. The Truck Show is a small, cheap amusement park at the back of town with a giant picture of a truck at the entrance. It's also Bocca's part-time job. I try not to come here often because the clientele is mostly thirteen-year-old boys ramming into each other in bumper cars for hours on end or head butting the punching bag to see if they can get the lights to go halfway up. I guess it's a good place to go if you want to see why the Roman Empire fell.

"Well, if it isn't Etto."

Bocca throws the basketball straight at my chest, and I catch it without flinching.

"When did you get reflexes?"

I throw it back at Bocca and sit down on the bench under Michael Jordan's luminous foot, part of a giant light box. If you're sitting at the exact right spot on the passeggiata, you can see it from pretty far away, his scissoring legs suspended in midair, the illuminated orange ball an extension of his arm. Bocca is supposed to be taking tickets for the basketball game. Instead, he and Fede are in the middle of a never-ending shoot-out.

"So why aren't you down at Camilla's tonight, Fede?"

"Eh. I need a break from watching Claudia and Casella make fish eyes at each other."

Bocca sinks a free throw. "Look at that! Look at that!" he shouts. "Seven!!"

"That's *six*," Fede says.

"What are you talking about? I've got seven, you've got six."

"Bullshit."

"Where'd you learn how to count?"

"From your auntie."

"Deficiente."

"Cretino."

"Finocchio."

"Vaffan'."

Bocca finishes up his round. His last shot bounces off the backboard and into his hands. He tosses the ball to Fede.

"Thirteen—twelve. What're we going up to?"

"First one to a hundred. Winner plays Etto." They both laugh.

A crowd of thirteen-year-old boys has been forming a safe distance away, their arms crossed with their fists pressed behind their biceps. Some of them have cigarettes dangling at their sides, and they pinch them and inhale thinly to make it look like they're smoking gangia and not tobacco. But you can tell they're getting impatient, creeping closer and shifting their weight.

Fede's turn. He shoots another ten, and half of them go in.

"Come on, you're hogging the game," one boy finally says, and it emboldens the others.

"Yeah, Bocca, you're supposed to be working here, not playing."

Fede throws the ball back to Bocca, and Bocca shrugs. "I'm testing the equipment. Safety check. And after that is my lunch break." His first shot bounces off the rim.

"It's not lunchtime. It's after midnight."

"You should be home in bed, then."

"Come on, let us shoot. If you don't, we're going to tell your boss on you."

"Well, we're going to tell your mammas you're smoking," Fede says.

"Then I'm going to say your mamma left the cigarettes on the nightstand after we . . ." The other boys laugh.

"Come here," Bocca says to the leader. He hesitates, so Bocca uses the magic open sesame of thirteen-year-old boys everywhere. "What's the matter, you scared?"

The boy can't back down. He takes a few cautious steps in Bocca's direction, glancing back at his friends. Bocca waits until he's only an arm's length away. He pulls the rims of his eyes down with his fingers until you can see only red, and he forces his voice up from the back of his throat.

"I'm gonna eat your soul," he says.

The kid jumps back. "Freak."

Bocca and Fede double over laughing.

"Loser," the kid continues once he's a safe distance away. "Grown men hanging out at the Truck Show. Probably don't have any girlfriends."

"Yeah," his friends chime in. "Losers."

"Come on, let's go clobber the punching bag."

"Yeah."

Fede and Bocca are still laughing hysterically. They try to slap fives, but miss because they're laughing too hard.

"I'm gonna eat your soul . . . good one, Bocca, eh, Etto?"

"Eh."

Fede stops laughing. He tosses the ball to Bocca and sits down on the bench next to me.

"Okay, Etto, why the serious face?"

"I'm not allowed to have a serious face?"

"Not unless you tell us why."

"I'm just thinking, that's all."

"About what?"

"Nothing." I can hear the Sicilian Bull Ride bellowing from the other side of the park. Ride it for ten seconds as it bucks and shoots fire from its nostrils, and you can win a stuffed bear. Fede stands up, walks over to the line, and eyeballs his next shot. It rolls around the rim and goes in. Bocca retrieves the ball and throws it back to Fede.

"Have either of you ever thought about living somewhere else?"

They both turn to look at me. Fede shrugs. "Where?"

"I don't know. Somewhere else."

"And do what?"

"I don't know. Nothing in particular. I've just been thinking lately that it might be nice to have the abstract possibility to leave."

"You can leave whenever you want."

"I mean, without the guilt trips or the gossip or becoming my nonno's next cautionary tale. . . ."

"I don't know what the cazzo that word means, Etto. *Abstract.*" Fede sinks another shot and laughs. "Yes, of course, an abstract life would be easier. Abstract people. Abstract choices. But what's so bad about your real life, Etto? What's so bad?" Fede takes the rest of his shots, and all but one go in.

"Lucky," Bocca snaps, and he snatches the ball away.

The shoot-out comes down to the last shot. Bocca makes a clean swish, his hands suspended in the air.

"Eat it!" he says.

"Double or nothing," Fede says.

"You're on."

I sit through the next round, watching them, and I feel a little like Nonna must feel, like I've got my face pressed to the glass looking in on everybody else.

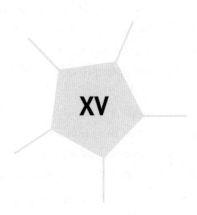

XV

*O*n Monday morning I wake up to the sound of a door slamming. "Papà?" I call downstairs.

Nothing. I look over at Luca's bed and listen to the silence. Papà still has our cleaning lady, Rahab, change the sheets, so they're always perfectly smooth, pulled tight like a drum. When Luca first went off to the academy, sometimes I would sleep in his bed just so it wouldn't look so abandoned.

I go downstairs. There's a nice breeze circulating through the apartment. Papà is a big believer in fresh air, so he always leaves the windows and shutters flung open. I make a coffee and stand out on the balcony. The beaches are empty this early in the morning, the sea so flat, I could fold it up into an envelope. I remember when I was a kid and I used to look at the spread of the sea and pretend I was Marco Polo or Christopher Columbus, imagining all the possibilities. Now all I see is a vast, unending boundary.

"Ciao, Famoso!"

I look down, and there's Mimmo waving at me from the beach.

"I said, ciao, Famoso!"

"Are you talking to me?"

"Who else?" He grins. "Your papà is looking for you!"

The front door of the shop is open. The banco is already set up, and Papà is standing in front of it, waiting for me, his arms crossed like a barricade. I go to the back, grab a clean apron from the crate, and put it on.

"You're here early," I say.

"I'm here early? It's my shop."

"I'm just surprised to see you this early."

"Surprised? *You* are surprised? I'll show you surprised." He pulls out a magazine, gripping it in front of him like a hooligan he's collared on the street. He thrusts it in my face, and it takes me a second to refocus. It's a tabloid, *Gente* or one of those, folded open to a spread of photos, and my eyes scan the page: one of Cristiano Ronaldo's girlfriends walking and drinking coffee from a paper cup. Francesco Totti and Ilary Blasi leaving some mall near Rome, the imperceptible bump circled in red ink. And then I see it. The bottom right corner of the page. Tatiana the Showgirl, her golden breasts eclipsing most of the frame. But down in the corner, my hair is unmistakable, the sliver of my profile, my pale hand reaching up to take the hundred-euro note, which is circled and magnified to five times its size with the caption "One hundred euros! What kind of meat is he delivering?"

"Well? What is this? What?"

I look at Papà. There's no point in trying to talk to him now. He has the entire arsenal out. The Contrapposto of Impatience. The Small Pupils of Accusation. The Eyebrows of Disdain.

"It's a delivery," I say, as quietly as I can.

"Do you know who this is?"

"No."

"No? How can you not know who this is? It is the wife of Yuri Fil!"

"Oh."

"And you are taking money from her? Please tell me that is not you taking money from the wife of Yuri Fil."

"It was a tip," I mumble. "I tried not to take it, but she made me."

"She made you? She made you?" he says. "She is a woman! How can she make you do anything?"

"I'm sorry, Papà. It happened so fast. I didn't know who she was. Some woman called for a delivery and I said, of course."

"You didn't know who she was? The wife of Yuri Fil and you didn't know who she was?" I consider changing my plea to temporary insanity on account of the breasts.

"Well," Papà continues, "even if, as you say—and I doubt it—that you did not know who this is, it does not matter who she is. We do not do our jobs for bribes."

"It wasn't a bribe. It was a tip."

"Bribe . . . tip . . . respectable people don't take either. If you want tips, go and work for Benito." He hangs his head. "I am so ashamed. So ashamed."

"I'm sorry, Papà."

And then he says something he has never said before, not even in his worst bout of anger, not even when I came home the night of my sixteenth birthday, completely drunk with the front of my pants wet.

"Go."

"What?"

"Go." He steps behind the banco and gestures to the portraits. "I can't even look at you. I certainly cannot force your nonno and bisnonno to look at you all day long."

"I said I'm sorry, Papà."

He points to the door. And there it is—the Head Turn of Disownment. "Go."

I stand rooted for a few seconds and give him a chance to take it back, but I can feel the lump rising in my throat, and I almost strangle myself trying to pull the apron over my head. I fling it toward the back, and it hits the beaded curtain, which shivers as if to say, "Aya. You're *really* in trouble now." But I don't care. After everything—all the hours I've stood behind that stupid banco just so he could sit at Martina's and talk about calcio and other stupidaggini, all the deliveries and walking up that fottuto hill. Maybe if *he* were here to answer the phone once in a while, maybe if *he* made the deliveries once in a while, well, maybe it would be *him* in *Gente*, maybe it would be *him* making the acquaintance of the breasts of the wife of Yuri Fil.

As I step out onto the passeggiata, the sun strikes me across the nose.

"You okay, Etto?"

I hurry past Chicca and everyone at Bagni Liguria, who must have heard the whole thing. I put my head down. I just want to disappear.

"Hey, Etto, you okay?" Fede calls out.

I don't stop. Even if I did, they would all tell me the same thing. Don't worry about it. That's just how he is. He'll cool off by tomorrow. As if he is the only one allowed to get pissed off, the only one allowed to lose his straps and say whatever he feels like saying, whenever he feels like saying it.

I can feel my legs pumping through Via Londra, my breath emulsifying in my lungs, weighing them down. Yes, Papà, I took a tip from Tatiana the Showgirl. And you know what else? I play calcio with the man himself every night. And one of these days, I might even have the palle to try with his sister again. Suddenly, I feel strong, like a steam locomotive charging through the gauntlet of tourists and busybodies, sweeping them out of the way with my cowcatcher.

"Ciao, Etto, what's the hurry?"

"Nice picture in *Gente!*"

"Ciao, Famoso."

"Ciao, VIP."

"Etto! I just saw it."

"What kind of meat *were* you delivering?"

I light a cigarette and puff away at it up the hill. The sun feels like a firebrand in the sky, pressing itself into my forehead.

"Etto, is everything all right?"

"Sì, Signora Sapia."

"You sound like you're stumbling."

"It's only the heat."

"I know. Awful. And no rain. Heard about your picture in *Gente.* Everyone is talking about it."

"Sì, signora."

"I hear they caught you looking awkward."

"Who said that?"

"But you always were an awkward-looking boy. Since you were little."

When I get to the aula, I lie down on the floor, but the cool wood does nothing to calm my anger. I look to the ceiling, but the drawings seem weak and impotent, the bodies limp, the expressions pinched and cauterized.

"Vaffanculo, Papà," I say through my teeth. You'll see how hard it is to do it by yourself, to work the entire day alone, to be chained to that banco like a dog to a tree and have to ask Chicca to watch the shop when you have to run upstairs just to go to the toilet. He has never done it alone. First there was Nonno. Then Mamma. Then me. I don't think he's worked a full day in three years, ever since I finished liceo.

The anger courses through my veins, and then I hear the words of Yuri Fil in my head. No afraid, no afraid. Enough of the catenaccio. Attack! Attack! Attack!

I move swiftly up the ziggurat of tables, a few sharpened pencils gripped between my teeth. I imagine tripping on a loose nail in one of the tabletops and taking a fall, hanging in the air for a couple of seconds before dropping like an anvil and crashing through the floor of Charon's aula, leaving a perfect outline of my body. As the camera hovers over the hole, I would climb out, stars and birds swirling around my head, the pencils having knocked out a few teeth, splitting my mouth into a smile like the Joker's.

I boost myself up on the top table and stand up, holding my hand against the ceiling until the coolness fills my pores. I know exactly what I will draw today. Right on the ceiling—no paper or pinholes to buffer the anger or slow me down.

The sixth panel. *The Tree of Life.*

I'm not cautious with the lines, and they hold nothing back from me, either. As I draw, I can feel the rough bark of the tree rising to the surface, my fingers chasing the fleeing shadows of the pencil, smudging in leaves and branches. I run my hand over the skin of the snake and feel its coil and the ripple of its scales as it twists around the trunk, choking it. I feel the taut muscle giving way to the soft bosom of Tatiana the Showgirl, her chest swelling almost to her elbow, her hand dangling the hundred-euro note between the branches. My feet slide across the table, my neck cocked back at the angle of a man whose throat has been slit. I draw my own hand reaching out to take the tip, bribe, whatever. I fill in my arm, my chest, and my stomach, then stop, leaving my entire torso dangling in the air, holding on to that hundred-euro note for dear life.

The first two panels, I'd drawn everyone as Michelangelo did—mostly naked. And you know, it really is a nice metaphor. Nakedness, purity, vulnerability, whatever. Until you find yourself contemplating the shape and color of your own junk. So I move to the other end of the table and start on the second half of the drawing. The After to the Before. The snake blooms a second head, Papà's scowling face instead of the angel's, his boning knife showing me the way to the desert. I draw another version of myself slinking out of the garden, hunched and wrinkled, shadows stamped around my eyes and across my forehead. But again, I can't get past the waist.

My foot scuffs one of the pencils, and there's a delay before I hear it hit the floor. I lie down on the table and stare sideways at the tree, from this angle now fallen. Tiiiiiiiiiiimber. Did it really fall if I'm the only one who seems to notice it? I stare at both figures, at the smooth, white plaster below my waist. Half man, half nothingness, hovering in the air. And you know what? I'm tired of being the eunuch, of hearing myself say, "How can I help you?" and "What can I do for you?" and "Yes, Papà," and "Sorry, Papà." I'm tired of listening to Fede's woes of getting too much sex. I'm tired of being the only guy in the region to turn down Signora Semirami, instead trailing behind a girl who barely talks to me, like a chivalrous knight on an imaginary quest, pledging my loyalty and waiting hopefully on the sideline. I am tired of being a slave instead of a son.

So in the blank, white space between my legs, I draw the biggest penis anyone has ever seen. Bigger than Luca's. Bigger than Fede's, even. Bull-sized.

I will not go back. I will not go back until he asks me. Begs me.

I work the rest of the afternoon in a frenzy, filling in the figures. I try to remember Tatiana the Showgirl's face—her hollow cheeks and her swollen lips. I spend a lot of time getting the junction right where the scales of the snake melt into Papà's skin. I fill in the landscape in the background: the cobbled driveway of the villa, the iron gate, and the massive columns.

By the time I climb down, it's already dark. My eyes burn. When I turn my head, I hear the crack of the vertebrae, and when I pat my stomach, it thumps like a drum. I haven't eaten all day, and I've cycled past the grumbling stomach and the hunger pangs. My body is already starting to hollow out the cells, filling them with adrenaline and lactic acid, speeding up the process of consuming itself.

Eat up, brother. Buon appetito.

My phone lights up. Fede.

MARTINA'S LOOKING FOR YOU.

I don't answer.

SHE'S BEEN HOLDING YOUR DINNER.

Martina has made dinner for Papà and me almost every night since Luca died, and the thought of her waiting for me and wondering is the only thing that makes me answer.

TELL HER I'M SORRY, BUT I'M NOT COMING.

WHERE ARE YOU?

I'M FINE.

I shut off my phone, go outside, and sit on the fifth-year bench. I take out a cigarette and stare at it in my hands, then put it back in the pack. The stars over the sea are infinite tonight. They say that since the big bang, the universe has been in constant motion, expanding at an accelerating rate, the spaces filled with dark energy and dark matter. And what we can see either by looking through telescopes or formulating equations only makes up five percent of what's actually out there.

Five percent.

And the rest? No one knows. I was listening to this astrophysicist on TV a few years ago, and they asked him about it—what exactly this dark matter and dark energy was. Now, this guy won a Nobel Prize or something, and he's supposed to be on TV as an expert, and you know what he said? He said it's a complete mystery to him, too. And then he shrugged. This Nobel laureate. And it really didn't seem to bother him. He went on to say that there have always been and will always be things the scientists don't know, and it's only the simpletons and amateurs who try to wrap everything into a neat little package, who try to explain away the mystery.

I hear a rustle in the bushes from somewhere near the path.

"Etto, you up here?"

I can see the glint of his glasses and the heavy beard that makes him look like a monk instead of the chief of police.

"Ciao, Silvio."

"I've been looking all over for you."

"I guess you win the prize."

"What are you doing up here?"

"Making bombs."

"That's nothing to joke about, Etto." He sits down on the bench. "Are you okay?"

"Fantastic."

"I heard you and your papà had an argument."

"There's no argument. He told me to leave the shop, so I did. Finished."

"Come on, Etto. You know he didn't mean it."

"He sure sounded like he meant it."

Silvio swats at the air and leans back against the bench. "Etto, he doesn't know what he's doing. It's the middle of the tourist season. He can't possibly run the shop every day by himself. He'll have to work fourteen hours a day."

"He should have thought about that before he said it."

"He would not be human if he always thought about things before he said them."

"Then it shouldn't be a problem for him to ask me to come back."

"If you go to the shop tomorrow morning, I am sure he will apologize, Etto."

"I'm not."

Silvio sighs. "You're a good boy, Etto. And your father is a good man. But sometimes you two need to be a little easier on each other." He looks out at the sea, waiting for me to agree with him, but I let the silence sit instead.

"Are you going to stay up here for a while?" he says.

"Probably."

"Not too long, eh? Marinating in it isn't going to make it go away."

"Maybe I don't want it to go away. Maybe I want him to admit that he's wrong for once."

Silvio sighs again. He puts his hand on my knee and stands up. "You know, your papà and you have more in common than he and Luca ever did. Both of you, paralyzed by your own pride. Stubborn as mules."

Hee-haw, hee-haw, I say in my head as Silvio makes his way down the path. Papà couldn't even come to do his own dirty work. He had to send Silvio. That's what he did when they found Mamma, too. He couldn't even do that.

"What is wrong with you tonight?" Yuri asks, ten minutes into the game. "You play like you have the ropes around your legs. Are you sleep? Are you drunk?"

"Bad day."

"Bad day?" Yuri blows the whistle. "Stop the clock! Stop the clock!" he shouts, even though he's the one keeping time. He jogs over to me. "What is this 'bad day'?"

"I don't want to talk about it."

He stares at me for a minute, then holds up a finger. "Wait. Wait here." He goes to the sideline and fishes around in the pile of jackets and shoes.

"Here," he says, and he holds out an iPod, the earbuds wrapped carefully around it. It's one of the new ones, small as a pack of gum. He presses the button in the center, unwraps the earbuds, and hands them to me. "Give your head rest. These problems you think about, they will be not so serious after game of calcio." He taps his finger against the furrows in my forehead. "No worry."

The iPod is turned up to full volume, and it's almost all in Ukrainian or maybe Russian—Soviet anthems, folk songs, classical music, arena rock, chanting monks, and bad hip-hop. But it works. With Yuri's sound track booming in my ears, I don't hear Papà's voice criticizing me. I don't hear the wheezing of my lungs begging me to stop, or the clock ticking away Zhuki's days in San Benedetto. She and the others appear and disappear in front of me, their movements unfolding slowly and gracefully, and the field seems like another world, floating out in space, the floodlights at the corners penetrating into my heart and taking away its weight.

I score a goal. It's the first goal I've ever made. Ever. Granted, it's not a pretty one, bouncing off my knee and barely dribbling across the line. And granted, there's a six-year-old defending the goal. But a goal is a goal is a goal is a goal.

"Goooooooooooooool! Goooooooooooooooool!" I shout over the music as I run around the field, and I can feel the blood coursing to my head. I do it Vanni Fucci–style, leaning in around the corners, hands in the air. "Goooooooooooooooooooooooooooooooooooooooooool!"

The others stand by, at first smiling, then staring at me in disbelief. Ihor moves his shadow over Little Yuri to protect him. On my third lap, I slow down and realize they're not staring at me at all but at the line of cypresses.

Shit. I yank the earbuds out of my ears, and the music stops abruptly.

"Papà . . . what are you doing here?"

Yuri and the bodyguard conference in Ukrainian while Papà quietly surveys the scene. I wait for his face to change into anger, or at least that look we used to get as kids, the look that said, I know we are in public now, but just wait until we get home. But the look never comes. Instead, he sets a small paper bag on the ground and starts back toward the path, his shoulders slumped, not even raising his hands to protect his face from the scratch of the cypresses. I feel the muscles in my legs loosen, and I sink to the grass.

"Shit."

Yuri covers Principessa's ears, and Little Yuri clamps his hands over his own.

"Shit, shit, shit, shit, shit." I sit down on the ground and start rocking like the kid who ate the paste back in asilo. The Ukrainians hover over me.

"Are you okay?" Zhuki asks, cautiously, in English.

"Yes. Sorry. Shit. Sorry. Shit."

"What is it?" Yuri asks. "What is this 'shit'?"

"Nothing. It's nothing."

"I do not believe you," he says. "No hands on head, *this* is nothing. One hand on head, this is problem. Two hands on head, this is Chernobyl."

"It's Chernobyl, then."

"I don't understand."

"That was my papà."

"And this is so bad? He is your papà. You will ask him to keep secret, and he will not tell no one we are here. Anyway, paparazzi are already in Rome, chasing Totti and Ilary. No worry."

"It's not that."

"Then what is the problem?"

"It's a long story."

"We are Slavs. We like long stories."

I look up at Zhuki's face, pale as the moon in the dim light, and I start babbling like a deficiente, telling them everything. Well, the edited version of everything. I tell them that Luca and Mamma died in an accident, and calcio is really the only thing Papà has left that makes him happy. "And now he's going to think I've been seeing you every day behind his back."

"You do see us every day," Yuri says.

"Yes, but he's going to think we're best friends or something."

"We are not best friends?" Yuri puts on a pout and laughs, then stops himself when he realizes I'm not laughing.

"You don't understand. Papà is obsessed with you."

"Obsessed?"

"He is a big fan of yours. Your biggest. He remembers every goal you ever scored and every interview you ever gave. He's had your picture up in his shop since your days at Dynamo, and he fights with the knife between his teeth for your honor every time someone says you are guilty. When he found out you were here in San Benedetto, it was one of the greatest moments of his life."

"You exaggerate."

"No."

"And you play calcio with us every day and you do not tell him this?"

"Yes."

"Oh, you are a bad son," Yuri says.

"Yes."

Ihor has retrieved the paper bag and is eating Martina's chocolate cake with his fingers. He walked all the way up the hill to bring me a fottuto piece of chocolate cake.

"Well, it is finished now," Yuri says. "But no worry. Tomorrow we fix."

"Trust me. There's no way you can fix this."

"Ah, ah, ah." He wags his finger at me. "Trust *me*. Calcio fix everything. You do not know the power of calcio. Calcio put back order in universe. Calcio make everything better."

The church bells scattered over the hills take turns ringing midnight. When I stand up, the Ukrainians seem relieved that the vigil is over and they can finally go home and go to bed.

"Will you be okay?" Zhuki asks.

I hesitate. How fast things change. This morning I was a rebel. Tonight I am a refugee. Yuri can see it in my eyes. Zhuki says something to her brother, and he nods.

"Come with us," he says. "You come with us to villa and we relax a little before you go home. Everything will be fine. You see. No worry."

They collect the floodlights and start toward the scribbles of brush and brambles that conceal the breach in the wall at the back of the terrace, that rabbit hole they disappear through every night. Ihor goes first, his voice reappearing somewhere above, and Yuri hands Little Yuri and Principessa up into the darkness. Zhuki scrambles up behind them and holds out her hand to me. It's a steep slope strewn with rocks and a few crumbling steps, and I'm surprised by her strength as she pulls me up onto the next terrace.

I don't know what I'm expecting when Yuri opens the front door of the villa. A flash of light? A flock of white doves? An earthquake? Instead the door opens into an ordinary front hall. Ordinary for a Hollywood movie director or a calcio star, at least. The walls glow a soft yellow, with white moldings piped around the edges of the room like icing. Baroque or Venetian or rococo, or whatever that style was back in the 1600s. Or maybe it was the 1700s I'm thinking of. I can never keep that stuff straight. The floors are cool white marble, a crystal chandelier hangs from the ceiling, and on the right is a giant portrait of Signora Malaspina sitting coquettishly to the side in one of those low-hipped, one-piece bathing suits from the fifties or sixties. She really was a good-looking woman, even in that suit.

Mykola and Ihor line up the floodlights along the wall, ready for the next day.

"Have you ever been in here before?" Zhuki asks.

"Never," I whisper.

"You don't have to whisper," she says, almost purposely loud, and her voice echoes down the long hallway in front of us.

"Isn't Tatiana already asleep?"

"Don't worry about Tatiana. She takes enough pills to keep a bear asleep all winter."

"And Vanni?"

"He's in the guest wing. He can't hear a thing."

"Why didn't he play tonight?"

"He say air is too dry here," Yuri says, shifting Principessa to his other shoulder.

"By the sea?"

"He say something about salt. Salt is bad for his skin, and bad for his French cosmetics contract."

"He is not allowed to get wrinkles," Zhuki says, smirking. "It says so in the contract."

I want this on record. Vanni Fucci, dream of every woman in Europe, has been cowering in the villa all day long, rubbing two-hundred-euro lotion into his skin.

They all change into slippers. Zhuki gives me a pair of beat-up slip-on Adidas from a pile, and I follow the others down the long hallway. It opens into a massive living room and kitchen, with sleek divans like the ones at Le Rocce and a flat-screen bigger than Martina's.

"Sit down, Etto," Yuri says. Principessa is still fast asleep on his shoulder, and Little Yuri is walking like a zombie, his eyes half closed. Yuri says something to him and holds out his hand, and in slow motion, Little Yuri reaches up and tucks his fist into his papà's palm, which closes over it like a ball-and-socket joint. I remember when Papà used to take Luca and me up to bed, each of us sitting on a foot, wrapping our arms around his thick calves, laughing the whole way as he went stomping up the stairs.

"Say ciao, tutti. Buona notte."

"Ciao, tutti," Little Yuri says, his eyes closed. "Buona notte."

Ihor flops down in one of the chairs flanking the divan, puts his socked feet up on the coffee table, and makes a noise like an animal lying down in the hay for the night. I hope for a second Zhuki will come and sit next to me on the sofa, but she chooses the other chair, sliding off her slippers and tucking her feet beneath her.

"This is a nice place," I say.

Mykola looks around the room and shrugs. "It is okay." Everyone laughs.

"It's definitely not Strilky," Zhuki says, and they all laugh harder.

"What's Strilky?"

"It is the village Yuri and I are from."

"I thought you were from Kiev."

"That is only what Yuri says to the interviewers. Tatiana makes him because she does not want him to be from the village."

"What's there?"

"In Strilky?"

Strilky. I try to practice it in my head.

"Five streets," she says, "four hundred people, two hundred cows, a hundred orphans . . ."

"You and Yuri grew up in an orphanage?"

"No, but there was a big orphanage at the end of the village. With a field. It was a terrible field, like when we saw this field the first day. But this is where Yuri learned how to play calcio with the older boys. Every day after dinner, we would play calcio at the orphanage."

"Tell him about the radio," Yuri says from the doorway. He is back from the hinterlands of the villa.

"Ah, yes, the radio. When he was about twelve . . ." Here she stops to consult with Yuri. "Yes, twelve, my father somehow was able to buy us a transistor radio, which was just incredible for a child at this time. We had fights about who could hold it. We would walk through the main street of the village, and . . . oh, we thought we were so cool." She laughs. "On Sundays, we put the radio next to the field, so everyone could listen to the real matches while we played. We used so many batteries. This was all we asked for on our birthdays and for New Year. Batteries and football stickers." She laughs. Yuri translates this back to Mykola and Ihor, who have no doubt heard the story a hundred times before. They both smile.

"By the time Yuri was a teenager, the whole village would come, mostly to see him play."

Yuri laughs. "No, no. They come to see my sister play. They never see a girl play so good in all their lives."

Zhuki says something to him in Ukrainian and turns back to me. I get the feeling that she's telling these stories in order to cheer me up, and maybe it's working. Not the stories themselves, but the fact that she even cares.

"Anyway, it was quite beautiful. The whole village came to the field to make picnics, and for four or five hours every Sunday, the people from the village and the children from the orphanage were together, like the orphans had parents and aunties and uncles again. When it was dark, the children had to go back to the orphanage, and everyone else went home. Only Yuri and I stayed. This is why he likes to play in the dark."

"The ball," Yuri says, in the shorthand of siblings Luca and I used to have before he left for the academy.

"Yes, I was going to tell about this. We had a special ball with stars on it, you know, these stickers for putting on the ceiling, to learn the names of all the patterns . . . how do you call them?"

"Constellations?"

"Constellations. We put them around the ball so we could see it, because there were no lights on the field. And then we would pretend Yuri was Oleh Blokhin and I was Lev Yashin."

"Who's that?"

She laughs. "Who's that? Two of the greatest Soviet players of all time. You do not know Oleh Blokhin and Lev Yashin?" There's a small conference in Ukrainian, and they all stare at me in disbelief.

"Anyway," Zhuki continues, "the ball. It was like kicking the ball through the whole galaxy. Like we were not in Strilky anymore."

Yuri says something to his sister, and she gets up and goes into the other room. Mykola starts telling a story in equal parts Ukrainian, broken Italian, English, and mime, which seems to be the play-by-play of a pickup game from when they were in England or Scotland. From what I can understand, the grass was wet and Ihor made a spectacular fall, which is endlessly replayed by Mykola and Yuri, the gales of laughter and snorting growing louder each time they do it.

"Shhh . . ." Ihor holds a finger to his lips and points to the ceiling. "Tatiana sleep." And everyone bursts out laughing again.

Zhuki comes back from the kitchen with a stack of bowls, a handful of spoons, and a carton of ice cream. She serves the ice cream, Mykola batting away Yuri's hand when he reaches for it, both of them bantering back and forth each time he takes a bite.

"They are making an agreement, how many minutes Yuri must stay on the treadmill tomorrow," Zhuki explains, smiling.

The ice cream carton scoots back and forth across the table, leaving streaks of condensation as they retell their stories and private jokes. The empty bowls get plunked on the table, and Zhuki picks up the carton and scrapes the corners with her spoon. I would give anything for this night to stretch on, but I can feel the time bearing down on us. The conversation is sinking, and I try to bat it aloft.

"So, when was the last time you were in Ukraine?"

Zhuki licks the spoon and flinches like it's medicine going down. She glances at Yuri.

"Long story," she says, shaking her head. "My mother's boyfriend . . . long story."

"We Italians like long stories."

They laugh.

"You see?" Yuri says. "You make a joke. You are feeling better." He stands up and stretches, and Ihor and Mykola do the same. Yuri's not much taller than Luca, only Luca had that classic striker shape—the small upper body and huge thighs, every muscle on him distinct enough to do a pencil rubbing. Instead, Yuri has the build of a goalkeeper or the statue of David—all heavy marble, his hands and feet disproportionately large.

Yuri sighs. "I am sorry, but we must sleep. Tomorrow morning we go to Genoa. I must go to sporting judges and answer questions." There's a heaviness in the room. Yuri looks at me, and then at his sister. "But we will return to San Benedetto. Soon. And we will finish your calcio diploma."

He says something in Ukrainian, and Zhuki stands up.

"My sister, she will show you door. And do not worry about your father. We will fix."

I pull the iPod out of my pocket. "Here."

"No, no," he says. "You keep. Your brain, I think, need vacation. Every time, not only on calcio field."

"Thanks."

"No problem. No worry."

Ihor says something, and everyone laughs.

"What did he say?"

"He say you be careful. My sister, she have very fast left hook for Italian men."

I can feel my face flush as Zhuki and I walk down the long hallway in silence. I don't want to leave. Not only because of Zhuki, but all of them. The whole night has softened me, dulled my anger. I take my time changing from the Adidas slides to Luca's cleats.

"Are you thinking about your father?" Zhuki asks.

"What? No." I stand up and look back down the long hallway. "I was actually thinking about how if there's another ice age and the Libyans cut off our oil supply, you could probably survive for a year in here by burning the picture frames and the chairs."

She laughs. "You're a strange one, Etto."

"I know."

"Will you be all right going down the hill? Maybe you would like a flashlight?"

"I'm fine. Thanks."

"I hope everything will be all right with your father."

"I hope so, too."

She smiles. "Give me your number. I will SMS you when we return from Genoa." I watch her punch the numbers into her phone. As simple as that.

"Buona notte."

"Buona notte." And she shuts the heavy door behind me.

I don't go home. I think about Papà and the look on his face as he stood between the cypresses, and I imagine what he'll say about me if I'm not in the shop tomorrow. I know I'll never hear the end of it. Martina, Silvio, Franco, Mimmo, everybody will come by and try to intervene. They'll tell me how much he's already suffered, and that he didn't mean it anyway. How we only have each other left, and we should not waste a day because you never know. Ah . . . sì, sì . . . you never know.

I sit down on the fifth-year bench and look out over the terraces of warped olive trees, twisted grapevines, and knotted pines. The waves are foaming around the molo and bubbling up in my head. I think about how I'll feel if I don't go down to the shop tomorrow, how the lump of pride I will have to swallow will grow a little every day until I'll vomit just thinking of it.

I lie down and close my eyes. I take out a cigarette and roll it between my fingers, then put it back in the pack and lob the whole thing over the edge of the terrace.

Pow!

It explodes like a grenade in my mind, lighting up the whole landscape.

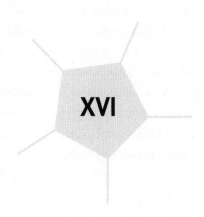

XVI

I sleep in the aula, and it's still early when I get to the shop. Not even Franco and Mimmo are out yet, only Pete the Comb Man standing next to the beach cleaner, doing his tai chi. When he's finished, he'll start up the engine and ride up and down the beaches like a Riviera farmer, plowing wide, clean furrows in the sand, perfect for sowing the next generation of German and Milanesi pedants, irrigated by their own sweat. I know he sees me, but I try not to meet his eye. They say he prays for everyone who meets his eye.

I start setting up the case with the lights off, and I'm about halfway done when I hear the clank of the back door lock and see his stocky silhouette against the light of the alley, his hair sticking out like a porcupine, its defenses always up. He props the door open to let the air in.

"Ciao, Papà," I say. As if nothing ever happened.

He flips the fluorescents on and comes up front. "Etto?" He looks surprised. He doesn't kill the fatted calf for me, but he doesn't tell me to get out, either.

"Ciao," he says, and that simple word stamps and seals the truce.

He puts on his jacket and washes his hands like any other day. He sharpens his scimitar, pulls the hacksaw off the wall, and goes into the walk-in to start a rough carve of the vitello. He's done it so many times, he can do it while it's still hanging. I finish setting up the case and start scrubbing down everything in the shop, polishing the glass until it's invisible, and oiling the stainless steel until it's shiny enough to deflect a laser. We work in silence, the only sounds from the spray of the disinfectant and the muffled rasping of Papà's scimitar against cold flesh. This is my apology, my reassurance to him that maybe we are not going to win any father-son awards, but at least I won't come down one morning and announce that I'm going to play video games on the other side of the world.

It's already quarter to eight when I look up and see Little Yuri and Yuri in matching sunglasses and baseball caps, waiting patiently outside the door. I turn the lock and open it a crack.

"What are you doing here?" I whisper.

"I told you, I come fix everything with your papà."

"I don't know if it's such a good idea anymore. Things seem okay now."

He tips his sunglasses, and his pupils pierce right through me. "Trust me. You will see."

It sounds like such a simple thing, doesn't it? Trust me. Fidati di me. Three words as wide as the ocean, and the title of a not-bad song by Laura Pausini. And what Yuri Fil's eyes are urging me to do right now. Trust me.

"Papà? Could you come here a minute?"

He says something, but the walls of the walk-in muffle his voice.

"Papà?"

He taps at the door with his foot, and it eases open a crack. "Can it wait? I'm in the middle of something here."

I look at Yuri, and he raises his eyebrows at me, amused.

"I really think you need to come out here, Papà."

He comes out of the walk-in, wiping his hands on his smock. The bristle of his hair is glistening with sweat. I think he's the only man alive who can sweat in a refrigerator. He takes his handkerchief from his pocket and mops his forehead.

"Can I help you?" he says.

"Excuse. I don't want to bother you," Yuri says. He takes off the base-ball cap and the sunglasses, and Papà's eyes widen, like the eyes of a little boy looking into the sky.

"Signor Fil?"

"Yuri." He stretches a hand out, and Papà looks down at his own hands, which are speckled with blood and grist. He shakes his head vio-lently, as if he's directed this moment before in the film of his mind and this is not it.

"One moment." He holds up his finger. "Moment, moment." He pushes through the bead curtain to the sink in the back room, and I hear the water run.

Yuri looks at me and I shrug. We wait for Papà to come back, wiping his hands on a towel.

"Sorry, sorry. It is an honor to meet you, Signor Fil. Truly an honor." He grasps Yuri's hand in both of his and kisses it like the ring of the pope. I can feel my face getting hot, but Yuri and Little Yuri don't even flinch, as if this happens to them every day.

"I come to explain you," Yuri begins. "Yesterday. Your son, he come and find me. For you. He tell me you are number one fan of Yuri Fil in the world. He ask me to meet you."

Papà looks at me, then back at Yuri.

"It is true, it is true," Yuri says. I can tell right away he's not a skilled liar. "Your son, he was up on the field. He cut the grass."

"I thought you said that he found you."

"Yes, exactly, he found us." I can see Yuri's face flush. "And he tell me right away you are my number one fan, and he ask me to meet you. He say he want me to do this as present to you. And I tell him, if you want that I meet your father, you must do something for me. You must show me ten minutes of your best calcio. And he say, no, no, I do not play calcio good."

"That's true," Papà says.

"And I say, well, that is payment I want. If you do not play with us, I do not meet your father. So he do it. For you. He is good son," Yuri says, and he claps his hand on my shoulder.

My father is speechless.

"Yes, good son," Yuri continues. "And big honor that your son follow you, that he choose your profession. For the father, it is greatest honor in the world. Come here, Little Yuri." Little Yuri hustles from the front of the case, where he's been staring at the calf's head. "This is Little Yuri. Captain of 2024 Ukrainian national team."

Little Yuri salutes, and there's an awkward silence between these two men, these men who have absolutely nothing in common besides one's obsession with the other.

"I want to show you something," Papà finally says.

He leads him through the beaded curtain to the grinding counter and nods with his chin at the row of photos. Yuri's eyes dart back and forth in silence. He stretches out one cautious finger and touches the frames, first his own photo and then the others.

"But . . . I do not . . . I am not so good like the others."

"But of course you are!" Papà laughs.

"Hagi should be here. Ronaldinho. Baggio. Kaká." He shakes his head and looks at the floor. "I thank you. I thank you. But I do not deserve this."

"Don't worry," Papà says, putting a hand on his shoulder in the same way Yuri put his hand on mine. "Your name will be cleared from this scandal. They will ask their questions and realize you had nothing to do with it. Don't worry."

Yuri raises his head, and maybe if I hadn't looked at that face every night for the past two weeks, I wouldn't have noticed the doubt worming through the surface of it.

"Ach," Yuri says, clapping his hands together, his face brightening. "I forgot. I bring present for you."

Yuri reaches into Little Yuri's backpack, pulls out a dark bundle, and shakes it out in front of Papà. It's a Genoa home jersey, split down the middle into dark red and blue, the griffin seal over the heart, the block letters spelling out "Fil" on the back.

"Oh, it is too much, too much," Papà says. "You will sign it for me?"

"Of course." We both stare at Yuri while he signs the shirt with one of the pens we use to mark the orders.

"I have a present for you, too," Papà says, beaming, and motions Yuri over to the counter. He sweeps his arms in front of the case. "Anything, anything at all. Gratis. Free."

"No, no. Grazie, grazie. No, no."

"But you must. I insist." And Papà begins choosing things on his own, scooping them out of the case and wrapping them up. "Here, this is a nice roast."

"No, no. It is not necessary." But as Yuri keeps up his protest, Papà weighs him down with more packages—all the shish kebab we have made for the day, the roast, a rope of sausage long enough to save someone from drowning.

"Real kielbasa," Papà says proudly. "A Polish butcher taught me. It will remind you of the old country."

"Thank you," Yuri says quietly. "Very generous. Thank you. Thank you, but we must go now. We go to Genoa today."

"Before you leave," Papà says, holding one finger up. He takes a deep breath. I know what's coming. "Shche ne vmerla Ukrayina, ni slava, ni volya . . ."

At first, I want to crawl under the grinding counter and liquefy in embarrassment, but then I see Yuri's eyes welling up. I wonder how much the tabloids would pay for the photo of a Serie A calcio player brought to tears in a butcher shop from a caterwauled version of his national anthem.

"It is great honor you do for me," Yuri says when Papà is finished. He puts his baseball cap on and takes the hand of Little Yuri. "We go to Genoa for few days now, but when I come back, we play calcio together. You, me, your son, and my son."

"It would be my honor," Papà says.

"No, it is my honor, my honor," Yuri says, and they both start to sound like the fottuto mafia.

"My honor."

"*My* honor," Yuri repeats.

I wish you could see Papà's expression as he stands in the afterglow of Yuri Fil, watching him disappear down the passeggiata with his armful of meat. As long as I live, I will never forget it. After all, how many times do you get to witness the best moment of a man's life? Surely not as many times as you witness the worst.

For the rest of the day, Papà shuttles between Martina's and the shop, bringing everyone by who wants to see the jersey, which now hangs at the end of the line of portraits, the shoulders squared on a hanger.

"To Carlo and Etto," Yuri signed the jersey. "My favorite father-son team."

Of course, when Papà tells the story, he forgets to mention anything about me, or even that I was in the room. You'd think there were no witnesses with the way he embellishes.

"And then he said to me, 'No, you are wrong, it is my honor, my honor to be in such a noble shop as this, with such a noble man . . .'"

I sit down at the bar, and Martina leans over and kisses me on the cheeks.

"How's it going, Martina?"

"Ay, ay, ay! Yuri Fil, that's all they've talked about all day long. Leave the poor man in peace, I say." She rolls her eyes. "It is nice to see your papà so happy, though."

It's true. He hasn't been this happy in a while. His face is flushed and his hands are fluttering lightly in the air.

"And then," Papà brags, "he said as soon as he gets back from Genoa, we are going to play a match together."

I'm ashamed to say it, but I'm secretly pleased when they burst Papà's bubble.

"He's only saying that because he doesn't have anyone to play with up there."

"I guess it gets really lonely at the top, eh?"

"After all these weeks of ignoring the entire town. Who does he think he is anyway?"

"He's a cheater, that's who he is. And who wants to play with a cheater?"

But Papà sits there and takes it, his mouth sewn up into a tight seam, a distant look in his eyes as he stares up at the calcio scarves.

Martina disappears into the kitchen and comes back with a steaming plate of sausage and beans. Gubbio sits in the empty seat to my left, and Ciacco appears at my right, fanning the steam toward his nose.

"Is that rosemary?" Ciacco asks.

"Maybe a little garlic?" Gubbio adds.

I curl one arm around my plate in defense, and Martina waves them away like stray cats. "Shoo! Shoo! Via! Let the boy eat in peace."

"Oh, come on, Martina. There are no scrapings left in the pot?"

"You both have wives at home to cook for you."

"Tell that to my wife."

"Come on, Martina. Why don't you put us out of our misery and start serving food again? Your parents made a good bit of money in the old days."

"Are you joking? I can't get rid of you as it is. If I started serving dinner to all of you, I might as well set up a hotel."

"I'll go get my pajamas."

"Ay, ay, ay! Imagine!"

"Why are you so quiet tonight, Etto?" Nello calls from the end of the bar.

"Leave him alone."

"I'm just trying to make conversation with the star. It's not every day you get to meet someone whose photo turns up in *Gente.*"

"Ignore him, Etto."

"So, what kind of meat *were* you delivering?" Nello asks, leaning toward me, collapsing into laughter.

"Ask Pia," I answer. "She just ordered from us the other day."

The next morning, I wake up to the sound of the front door slamming and Papà's footsteps headed up the vico. There's no light sifting through the shutters yet and no noise outside except for the waves. I check my phone. Five thirty.

He leaves at the same time the following morning.

On the third day, I'm ready. I go to bed fully dressed, jumping to my feet as soon as I hear the door slam.

Outside, the sky is the color of ink, a thin puddle of watery blue leaking from the horizon. I follow the silhouette of his hair and the tap of his cleats against the cobblestones as he heads toward the back of town, across the railroad bridge, and up the hill. He's fast for fifty or whatever he is now, and the distance between us expands until his silhouette disappears and I only have his footsteps to follow. I pass Via Partigiani and Mino's gate. Mino's dog is fast asleep, and as I come up the last stretch, I can hear the familiar thump of the ball. I look through the gaps in the cypresses, and sure enough, there's Papà in his undershirt, running back and forth across the field.

He stops and holds the ball steady under his foot, as if he can sense me there, and I hold my breath as he looks around, only releasing it when he starts up again. He sticks to what looks like a prescribed routine some coach gave him decades ago. First, he takes penalty shots, then switches to running drills—hopping over imaginary lines, skittering sideways, and twisting around imaginary cones. When he messes up, he makes himself do it over.

After an hour he looks exhausted. Finished. Ready to quit. But he plays on. The rising sun fills in his features and his clothes, and he takes his shirt off and starts an imaginary match against himself, faking out imaginary defenders and passing to imaginary strikers. He runs in great, galloping arcs toward the goal, changing direction in an instant, all while keeping the ball firmly under control. I can't believe how quick he is, how strong, how relentless, how . . . good. I wonder if in his head he is playing against Yuri. Or Luca. I wonder if this is where Luca got his talent from.

And then it occurs to me that this is the first time I've actually seen Papà *play* calcio. I've seen him watch calcio and argue about calcio of course. I've seen him read the twenty-five pages of calcio coverage in *Gazzetta dello Sport* every day. I've seen him coach us in chickadees, back when we were kicking with our entire shin, and yell through Luca's matches. But I've never actually seen him play.

After about an hour and a half of this, Papà abruptly jogs to a stop, locks his hands on top of his head, and walks a few erratic circles. He picks up his shirt from the sidelines and throws it over one shoulder. He puts the ball on Luca's grave, stands back, and crosses his arms. I'll never know what he says. I wish I could understand the words, or that I knew him well enough to imagine what he's saying, but I can only hear the faint whispers and stops. I can only watch the morning light falling to the ground around him, seeping into the field.

When I see him in the shop, I don't say anything. But during the break, I work on a new panel on the ceiling of the aula, floating in the middle of the white space, out of order with the others. The fourth panel. The one you see cropped and framed on the walls of dentists' offices, banks, and summer rental apartments. The one with God's finger stretched out to Adam. E.T. phone home.

I start with the porcupine hair, the ham hands and the sausage fingers, Papà's chin thrust forward fearlessly despite everything that's happened to him. I pencil in his gray pants and his white smock, the top button open at the collar. The immaculate jacket, Silvio calls it. I draw directly on the ceiling, my knees sturdy, my hand steady, the lines sucked from the tip of the pencil like smoke from a wick.

When I'm finished, Papà is flying high in his great swirling half shell, a dozen San Benedettons propping him up. Down and to the left, I'm lounging on a grassy field in the same contorted pose as Adam. I stare at the panel in the shifting light, at Papà's arm outstretched toward mine and at our fingertips, only millimeters from their target. One minute, the muscles of his arm seem completely rigid, his stiff finger pointing at me accusingly, and the next, it's like he's reaching out to get my attention. The only thing that doesn't change is our expressions. The cynicism on my face and the intensity in Papà's, just like when he's breaking down a side of beef or charging toward the goal.

I stretch my hand up to the ceiling and touch the space between our hands. That synapse. That fottuto synapse.

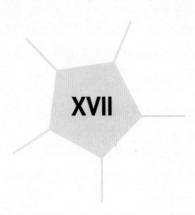

XVII

*Y*uri said a few days. I thought that meant two or three, but it's already five. I worry that he's managed to clear his name with the prosecutors, and now they will stay in Genoa, send for their things, and never return.

On Sunday afternoon, I dry the dishes while Nonna washes, the secret song vibrating on her lips. We never talk, but when I'm with her, I telepathically communicate to her all my deepest thoughts and feelings, and she always smiles back at me like she understands.

"Etto! Come out here!"

"Etto!"

I put the bowl I'm drying into the cabinet. "I'll be right back, Nonna." She nods.

Outside, Nonno and Papà are sitting under the barren lemon tree in only their undershirts, their glasses of lemonade—made from store-bought lemons—propped in the grass at their feet. Papà has been on a high all week, relaxed and tan. He's a different man since Yuri came into the shop, as if the warmth of Yuri's calcio supernova has incubated all of his best characteristics. I'm not even sure how to deal with this Papà.

"Come sit with us, Etto," he says, and he gets up to pull the third chair under the tree.

I sit down, wary. I have one of Luca's old jerseys on. Not the last one, which is framed above his bed, but one from a tournament a few years back. There have been shouting matches about me wearing Luca's clothes, but either Papà doesn't notice or he lets it go.

"What is it?"

They look at each other and then at me.

"Nonno and I have been talking."

This can't be good.

"We think you're ready to learn the real butchering," Nonno says. "Not only taking care of the banco, but nose to tail, animal to plate."

They both beam at me.

"When?"

"We can start this week," Nonno says, rubbing his hands together. "Tuesday morning, as soon as the carcasses arrive."

We all stare at each other for a minute.

"Well?"

"I have a choice?"

"Of course you have a choice!" Nonno says.

But to have a choice, of course, you need two things to choose between. They continue to stare at me.

"Okay."

"Okay!" Papà repeats.

"I'll get someone to look after Nonna," Nonno says.

"You're coming down to the shop, too?"

"Am I coming? Am I coming? It will be one of the biggest moments of your life. I wouldn't miss it."

I have two people to thank for this, I know. Yuri and Jimmy. Yuri for opening Papà's eyes to our continental drift, and Jimmy for showing just how far that drift could take a son. I remember now that last week, I walked in on Papà and Jimmy's papà in the middle of a very serious and hushed conversation that broke off as soon as I came in. Papà never wanted me to do any of the butchering before. This is just his way of anchoring me in place, of holding my feet to the terraces until they burrow and grow roots.

On Tuesday morning, I wake up before the sun and lie in my bed until I hear the truck rumbling down the alley.

"Etto!" Papà calls from downstairs. "Etto, you awake?"

"Yes, Papa."

"The cow has arrived!"

"Okay, Papà." The diesel engine gives one last sputter before it shuts off. I look over at Luca's bed.

"Here goes nothing." And I heave my feet to the floor.

By the time I get down to the shop, Papà and Jimmy's papà are already jammed inside the back walk-in with the vitello, the nose of the animal pressed to the floor as they try to maneuver it onto one of the hooks. Papà is wearing an apron over a T-shirt, both stark white next to the deep brown of his skin. In the summers, it takes only a gentle lashing of the sun before his melanin stands at attention. Luca and Mamma were the same. Then there's my skin, compliments of some raping, pillaging Viking ancestor. By Ferragosto, my face will look like I've been burned by a hot iron, red welts all over my cheeks and nose.

"Ready? Heave!"

"Porca miseria."

"Let me," I say. I squat and hug the calf around the shoulders, Papà gets around the belly, and we manage to hook it.

"Bravo. Bravo," Jimmy's Papà says. "Etto, when did you get so strong?"

"Boh."

"So, I heard today is the big day," he continues.

"Big day for who?" I say.

"For the calf." He laughs. "For *you*, Etto. For *you*."

"Ah, yes. Big day."

Papà and I unload the side of beef and barely manage to get it hooked when Nonno bursts through the front door like a television host through a flock of showgirls.

"Ciao, tutti!" He's wearing his old smock, which has his name stitched over the heart, like there's anyone in this region who couldn't recognize him. At his side is a large leather bag, which he sets on the marble next to the vacuum-pack machine. He looks like a doctor making a house call.

"Are those the famous knives?" Jimmy's papà asks.

"The very ones." Nonno claps me on the shoulder. "So, are you ready?"

"Ready as I'll ever be."

"Ah, if only my Jimmy were so keen."

Nonno unpacks his old leather and chain-mail aprons, and Papà and Jimmy's papà bring in the rabbits, the chickens, the young roosters, and the boxes of "goodies," as Papà calls them—the slippery insides that stay in vacuum packs in the back walk-in until the Algerians or the Sicilians request them.

"Here," Nonno says. "Put these on." He holds the chain mail in front of me, and I brace myself for the Dungeons and Dragons jokes if Fede or anyone else happens to walk by.

"Is this really necessary, Nonno?"

"That depends. Do you want to cut your nuts off?"

Jimmy's papà laughs. So this is how the baton is passed. I let Nonno layer the leather and chain mail on me while Papà washes up in the back. The weight drapes over me, from shoulder to knee, like lugging an extra body around. Thanks a lot, Jimmy, wherever you are. Until you left, Papà was perfectly happy to let me stand behind the banco and grind the scraps. And now, thanks to you and your stupid video games, they feel they have to weigh me down with metal aprons and legacy knives.

"Who's taking care of Nonna?"

"She's at Martina's."

"All day?"

"She'll be fine. It's good for her to get out someplace besides church once in a while."

I put a cotton apron over the leather and the chain mail, and my body takes on the square proportions of Nonno and Papà. The two of them don't wear anything but the cotton one anymore. The safety catches are already built into their joints and muscles, telling them when to stop the knife. Papà pulls the hacksaw off the wall and sharpens his scimitar, the rasp of steel against steel cutting through the air.

"First we show you the primal cuts."

"Wait, Carlito, not yet," Nonno says.

He takes me by the shoulders and looks into my eyes. The whites of his eyes are cream-colored and cloudy, his eyelids caving in. "Etto. This is a very important day for you. I want you to remember this day for the rest of your life. This is the day you truly join the line, both of our family"— he gestures dramatically to the portraits behind him—"and of the noble butchers stretching back to the Middle Ages."

"Can we hurry this up, please?" Papà says. "The customers will be here soon, and you still need to set up the banco."

"Thank you, son, I know quite well what needs to be done. This was once my shop, you know."

Papà rolls his eyes.

Nonno clears his throat and continues. "And so . . . to designate the magnitude of this day, I would like to present you with a gift." He reaches into the leather bag and takes out a roll of cloth, thick as a salami. He unrolls it slowly on the marble, extracting knives as he goes.

"First, your boning knife. This one will become your best friend, and when your wrist starts to hurt, your worst enemy." He hands it to me, the tip squeezed under his thumb. The hilt is smooth and warm, and it fits the shape of my hand perfectly.

"Your scimitar . . ." I can feel the pull of the shifting chain mail on my shoulders as I take the scimitar, the edge of the blade like a mirror.

Nonno pauses then, unrolling the rest of the knives, then rolling them back up just as quickly. He gives it a squeeze and tucks it back into the leather bag. "Eh, you'll find you don't really need the rest of them, but they're all yours anyway. From your bisnonno to your nonno to you. Congratulations." He gives me a bone-crushing hug.

"Can we start now?" Papà says. "Or do you have some sort of benediction prepared? A eulogy for the calf perhaps?"

Jimmy's papà smiles. This whole time, he's been leaning against the grinding counter, watching the spectacle, a wistful look on his face.

Papà carries the hacksaw into the back walk-in. "Okay, let's go, Etto."

"I'm leaving," Jimmy's papà says. "Good luck, Etto!"

"One more thing." And Nonno hands me a hairnet.

"Seriously, Nonno?"

"Seriously. And go put on a glove. A metal one."

I dig around in the cabinet under the grinding counter for a mesh glove. I put it on and squeeze my hand into a fist, the metal recording every millimeter of movement. I catch a glimpse of myself in the glass of the photographs.

"I look like a complete pedant," I say out loud, and I wonder how hard it will be to avoid the sight lines from the window all day.

"Nonsense," Nonno says, patting me on the shoulder. "You look good."

They must have coordinated all of this on Sunday afternoon, sitting under the shade of the lemon tree. They must have played paper-scissors-rock for the one who got to tell me I had to wear a hairnet. I go into the walk-in, a man accepting his fate, and Papà pulls the door behind us so it's just him and me, the vitello, the side of beef, and a couple of Parma hams.

"The first thing now is to count off the ribs." His voice echoes against the smooth white walls as his thick fingers run down the inside of the carcass. Nonno pokes his head in to see what's going on.

"You want to make your first cut between the eleventh and twelfth rib," Papà instructs. "Right here."

"Between the twelfth and thirteenth for the cow," Nonno adds, and Papà nods.

Papà takes the hacksaw and starts sawing across the hanging carcass.

"Except you want to put your energy into the *push* and not the pull," Nonno adds. "The pull rips. The push slides."

"Do you want to do it?" Papà sets the saw on the upturned crate next to him.

"No, no. You're doing fine. You're doing fine."

Papà pulls at the hook and it swings on its length of chain. The hook makes me shudder. Every time.

"Then, you want to hook it right here." He takes my hand in his and finds a spot under the eleventh rib, just next to the backbone. "You feel that?" Papà hooks it, and yanks on the chain to make sure it's securely looped around the pipe that runs overhead. My stomach churns, and I swallow hard.

"Here." He hands me the hacksaw, and I continue the cut. The backbone stops me, and Papà takes his boning knife out of its scabbard and pops apart the joint. I start sawing from the other side, Papà and Nonno scrutinizing my movements.

"Now, counter the action of the saw with pressure from your other hand."

The saw slips and comes loose from the carcass. "Shit."

"You see?" Nonno says. "That's what these stupid aprons are for."

The door opens and I hear the noise from the passeggiata. Nonno disappears, and I can tell by the tone of his voice that the customer is a tourist, not someone we know. I keep sawing away, and finally, the foresaddle swings free. Papà yanks on the chain, hoisting it and fastening it to the pipe. Then we lift the hindsaddle from the pipe and carry it to the long table across from the grinding counter.

"Slowly, slowly. Gentle, gentle," Papà says as we ease it onto the table. "A bruised vitello is not a happy vitello, and an unhappy vitello is not a tasty vitello."

"I thought that was only when it's alive."

Papà raises a finger. "Ah, but you must always respect the meat. Rule number one, two, three, and four. Allora . . . first we will find the filetto."

He guides my hand inside the carcass until I can feel the soft flesh. It's strange standing close enough to him to hear his breathing and the small grunts as he stretches and maneuvers. Like he's pulling me closer with each little sound.

"There. We just detach"—he reaches in with his boning knife—"a little scrape of the tendon and . . . ecco fatto! There we are." He sets the smooth pocket of meat on the other end of the table.

I hear the last bits of conversation between Nonno and the customer. They're talking about the weather and the lack of rain. The door opens and shuts, and Nonno wanders back again.

"Next we take off the loin." Papà raises his knife in his right hand as he fingers the back of the carcass, looking for the precise spot to cut.

"I thought the idea was for Luca to do it," Nonno says. "For *Etto* to do it," he corrects himself. Papà steps back without a word and hands me the knife, and Nonno and Papà lock eyes as if to conclude a conversation they had when I was not around.

It takes me six hours to break down the hindsaddle under Papà's close supervision, Nonno's super-supervision, and my bisnonno's beady eyes from the wall in the other room. Cazzo, I think even Dino Zoff gave his opinion when it came to the disastrous extracting of the fesa, which will have to be cut up now and sold as stew meat. By the end of it, Papà and I are both exhausted. Nonno tells us he will do the rest of the vacuum-packing and the cleanup, and he sends Papà to Martina's and me to Bagni Liguria with an order of sandwiches.

"That wasn't so bad, was it?" Nonno asks as I wash my hands at the sink in back and wipe the sheen of fat off my face with a wet paper towel. I take the leather and chain mail off, and I feel like I might float away.

"It took a lot longer than I thought it would."

"Ah, don't worry. Ten years from now, you'll be as fast as we are."

Ten years. It rings in my head like a death sentence.

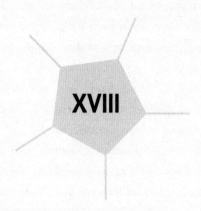

XVIII

*O*n Wednesday, the sporting judges hand down the sentences at noon. Five-year bans for the president of Genoa and the managing director of Venezia. Both teams kicked down to Serie CI with three-point deductions. Six months for the Venezia keeper. Three months for Yuri.

"Madonna!"

"Maradona!"

"Porca vacca!"

"Mamma mia!"

"Dio Cristo!"

On Martina's flat-screen, high-definition smoke billows over downtown Genoa. Via Balbi is up in flames, cars are flipped on their backs like houseflies, and the police are stomping out in riot gear. All because of the demotion. The screen flashes to footage of the Venezia keeper ducking behind the curtains in his villa, then to Yuri and Ihor throwing luggage into the back of an SUV, Tatiana in the front seat hiding behind a pair of giant sunglasses.

At Martina's, everyone stares at the screen in a stupor. They look like a defeated army, the ripples from the bad news etched into their foreheads. I'm the only one celebrating, gilding the next three months as I count them off in my head. August. September. October.

Shit. Please, God. Please let them come back here. Please. Just give me a chance. Please.

For the next few days, Papà and I both hold our breath. Papà keeps his vigil by running back and forth on the field every morning, and I hold mine at night, up on the scaffolding in the aula.

The year before the liceo closed, the art teacher, Professore Latini, had big plans for a mural that all the scientific and classical students were going to paint together along the corridors of the school. Casella's papà donated fifty cans of paint, and Professore Latini did the design. It was one of those peace-and-love hippie murals, and by making us do it, I'm sure he thought he was going to cure cancer and eliminate war. But one day Charon heard us talking about it, and he started to ask us questions about how much class time would be missed and what the mural looked like, and before we knew it, he had marched down the hall to the director's office and quashed the whole thing. I don't think he and Professore Latini ever spoke again.

Anyway, working on the aula is the only thing that speeds up the time. I pop the lids of paint with a screwdriver I find in the janitor's closet and mix the colors on panes of replacement glass. I concentrate on the tip of the brush, and before I know it, the first swipe of gray-blue has spread into a sea, and four hours have passed. It's like dropping through a wormhole in the universe or stepping out of my human skin and letting it fall like a robe to the floor. I don't get hungry or thirsty or have to go to the toilet. I don't have to deal with other people or fight my own thoughts. It's like being trapped inside the belly of a whale or the pocket of snow under an avalanche, and when I finally hear the voices of the Ukrainians coming down the hill ten days after they left, it feels like a rescue team sent to save me.

I climb down the tables, my heart banging away at my chest like a silent bell. I wonder if Luca ever got nervous for a girl, or before his matches. I never asked him. Lots of things, so obvious, and I never asked him.

"Ciao," she says.

"You're back."

"Of course we're back."

"I thought maybe you would stay in Genoa."

"Ach. What is there for me to do in Genoa now?" Yuri says.

"I heard. I'm sorry."

"Eh. As the Americans say, shit happens. You are ready to play? We have new torture for you." He rubs his hands together and forces a smile, but his face looks almost sinister, and I can see something dark pooling just beneath the surface.

Still, I roll my eyes and play along. "So what is it today?"

"Today, we are going fishing," Zhuki says, and Mykola holds up several meters of bright blue polyester string. The kind they use for fishing nets. The kind Mamma picked up on the beach in Vigo and wore around her wrist for twenty years until she left it on my dresser. Mykola ties a loop around my wrist as deftly as if he were winding a bandage.

"What's this for?" I ask, and Mykola ties the other end to one of Zhuki's wrists.

"This is so you stop running around field like cat with no home," Yuri says. "You must learn to work in team. You must pass. You must run plays. It is no good for man to be alone, to be lonely wolf on field. You must listen to voices around you. You must teach body to know where are your teammates. All time you must know."

"If I promise to think about it more, can we forget about the string?"

"Think about? If is only in the head, so what? Body must learn."

"Don't you think it's kind of dangerous? If I trip, or . . ."

Yuri shrugs. "Do not trip."

Zhuki shakes out the line between us, ten meters or so. Little Yuri hustles to the center of the field, the only place where the light runs out and the darkness forms a blurry diamond. Yuri blows the whistle, and the match is under way.

When Yuri plays calcio, it's much easier to read his emotions than when he's standing still, and it's as I watch him running back and forth that I realize just how pissed off he is. He's going all out at Serie A pace, running and dribbling as if we're professionals playing the last seconds of injury time in an elimination match. I feel the tug of the fishing line cutting into my wrist as I try to keep up with Zhuki. Yuri steals the ball from her and dribbles toward me. He feints to my left and I follow as he cuts back and dribbles easily around my right side.

"Stop," he says, and everyone on the field jogs to a halt. "Stop, stop, stop!" I feel the line around my wrist go slack. "Etto! What are you doing?" Yuri spits out his words like nails. "You followed me *left*. I can't *go* left." He plucks at the line between Zhuki and me, his eyes firing blue sparks. "If I go left, my head get cut off! You must learn not to buy everything your opponent sell!"

Zhuki says something to her brother in Ukrainian and Yuri hangs his head.

"Forgive him," Zhuki says. "He's upset over the ban."

"I'm sorry," I say, and Yuri looks up.

"You are sorry? Why are *you* sorry?" He laughs. "Are you sorry that calcio is crooked in Italia and the game is destroyed for money? Or are you sorry I am a stupid cazzone?"

"Yuri . . ." Zhuki says, and she puts her hand on her brother's arm.

Yuri looks down at his son and covers his face with his hands. He turns around a couple of times, like a dog looking for a place to lie down, then trots up to the ball and kicks it as hard as he can. Through the darkness, I listen to it crash into some vegetation several terraces up. We all stare at him in silence.

Yuri swings around and looks straight at me. "Tell me, Etto-Son-of-Butcher. The people in the town. What do they say about me?"

I hesitate.

"Tell me," he says.

"Well, they are big fans, and they think this ban is completely unfair."

His eyes stay fixed on me and he shakes his head. "You know, Etto," he says quietly, "when you are calcio star, there are many, many people who say you what they think you want to hear. But there are very, very few people who tell you the truth. I want that you tell me the truth. What do they say?"

"You really want to know?"

"Yes, I really want to know." He hunches his shoulders as if he's preparing for the blow.

"Well, they say that you keep to yourself."

"They do not say it so polite, I know. Tell me what they really say."

I look at Zhuki, and she shrugs.

"Well . . . they say you are a snob. That Tatiana is a . . . well, a not-nice woman."

"What else?"

"That you both think you're better than everybody and don't want to dirty your hands on our town. That you're scared to leave the villa because you think the common people are going to jump you and rob you in the street like gypsies. That you do not respect them, and your silence is because you are guilty. . . ."

"Okay," he says. "That is enough."

"Except my papà," I add.

"Yes?"

"Yes. Papà will defend you to the death."

"He thinks I am innocent?"

"One hundred percent."

Yuri looks down at the ground and shakes his head. "I am sorry, Etto. I cannot play today. We play tomorrow. Tell your father to come also. I will have better spirit tomorrow."

Mykola and Ihor go around and collect the floodlights, and Yuri heads up the hill, Little Yuri running after him. Zhuki and I are left standing in the darkness.

"I'm sorry," Zhuki says. "He is not himself today."

"It's okay."

"It's not. But he didn't mean to yell at you. He likes you."

"Don't worry about it. Really, it's okay."

She stares at me, her lips pursed in another apology. "We will see you tomorrow, I hope?"

"Tomorrow."

She turns toward the back of the terrace, but she only takes a few steps before our arms jerk up in an involuntary wave. She looks at her wrist and laughs.

"I forgot," she says. "This stupid fishing line."

We work at the knots, which are more complicated than they looked when Mykola was tying them.

"I will kill that Mykola," she mutters. "He did it on purpose."

We end up having to sit down on the ground, hunched in the dim moonlight, her hands working to free me, and mine, her.

"Finally!" She rubs at her wrist. But instead of jumping up and running after the rest of her tribe, she flops back on the grass, wriggling a little to fit her back into the ridges of the earth. I lie down next to her, my heart thumping in my chest.

"I just wish I could do something for him," she says. "Something that would make him happy. These past few days have been terrible for him."

She turns her head to look at me, but I don't dare look her in the eye. I can feel us crashing toward the moment when something has to happen, and I'm scared I already know what it is. I have, since puberty, always been the Friend. Maybe it was because I was always standing next to Luca and it was a simple process of elimination. Who knows? In its best case, the Friend is the guy the girls go to when they need to cleanse their palates between Stronzo #1 and Stronzo #2, but at its worst, being the Friend is a perpetual purgatory—the guy who always gets the brotherly grip around the shoulder in all the photos and the kiss on the cheeks instead of the lips. I know multiple variations of the Friend speech, enough to know that I feel it here, stalking around the terrace in the dark.

"Look, there's the Big Bear," she says instead. "And Venus."

"Where?"

"Right there." She scoots closer to me, and I smell the mix of soap and sweat on her skin. It would be so easy to reach over and put my hand on the bump of her hip, lean over and kiss her, but I can't get the night at Le Rocce out of my head. Or what she said to me the next day. My muscles lock, my arms pinned to the ground.

"How can you tell?" I ask.

"Venus is easy. It's the brightest one. The earth only reflects half the light Venus does."

"I didn't know you could see any planets without a telescope."

"You can see five of them. Mercury, Venus, Mars, Jupiter, and Saturn.

Not tonight, because the moon is bright. And not all at the same time. But if you look for them, they appear."

"How do you know where to find them?"

"The same way you find everything else. You look where you last left it. Most of the time, they have the same orbit. Sometimes they go back and . . ." She draws a loop with her finger. "But if you keep looking, it gets easier every time."

I stay quiet as she tells me about the Perseid showers in the middle of August, and how most people think shooting stars are actually stars, but really they're only flaming bits of rock and dust. Her hand hovers in the air, hypnotizing me as it floats above us in space, drawing arcs across the sky.

"I'm sorry," she says suddenly. "I'm boring you."

"Not at all."

"Yes, I am."

"You're not. It's interesting. How do you know so much about stars anyway?"

"We all knew a little growing up. You are in the country, and you see them every night. But I had a friend in Scotland who taught me properly. When Yuri was playing for Celtic. He went and got his PhD in America," she adds, and I can tell by the way she says it that he was an old boyfriend. "I like it because wherever you are in the world, you can see the same stars. Glasgow. London. Kiev. Genoa. Strilky."

"San Benedetto," I add.

"San Benedetto."

She tilts her head to the side, and her eyes flash a distant freedom, like they have seen and encountered it all and still manage to find wonder in the world.

"Do you like moving around?" I ask.

"It is good for some things. I think it has made us closer, me and Yuri."

"And why don't you ever go back to Ukraine?"

"Ah, my mother is with a man now who is . . . let us simply say that he is not a good man."

"Your stepfather?"

"Nooo. He is only her boyfriend. But he acts like she is his property. He drinks a lot. And he tries to make money from Yuri."

"How can he do that?"

"Oh, he finds ways. One year we came home for Christmas and he made Yuri sign a hundred calcio balls for him. The next time, there were things missing from our room. Things of Yuri's. School notebooks. His old cleats. His favorite toys. We found out this guy had sold them on the Internet. He says it is because Yuri does not give our mother any money, but that is only because Yuri knows she will give it to this man and she will never see any of it." She shakes her head. "Now he makes my mother borrow money from the neighbors and say the next time Yuri comes home, he will pay them back. These are our neighbors, the people we know since we are children. And now when we do not come back to Strilky anymore, they think Yuri is the good-for-nothing one, who is cruel to his mother and is not paying back the money he owes."

Whenever they've mentioned Ukraine, I always think of it as a big gray lump with lots of poor people standing in bread lines. I try to revise the image now to include the Internet.

"So, why is your mother with him?"

She shakes her head. "I don't understand her. Sometimes I think she must be the stupidest person in the world."

"I don't know. I think there's probably some stiff competition for that."

She laughs. "I'm sorry, Etto. It must be difficult for you to listen to people complain about their mothers."

"No, no. It's fine."

She looks at me for a minute, and it seems like she wants to say something else. Instead, she sits up. "I must go."

"I'll walk you back."

She hesitates.

"It's dangerous for you to go walking around up here on your own," I say. "There are dogs and . . . other things up here. Your brother would kill me if anything happened to you."

A smile teases at the corner of her mouth. "I don't know. Maybe it is more dangerous to go walking with you."

Her boldness catches me off guard, so I act on the instinct of twenty-two mostly girlfriendless years, holding up my palms as if to show that I am unarmed of the usual attractiveness, charm, whatever, that she has found elsewhere in our species.

"Trust me," I say. "You've got nothing to worry about here."

Shit. I'm such a pignolo.

She smiles. Amused. Like she wants to put me in a jar of chloroform and stick a pin through my thorax. Ah, yes, the elusive Italian pedant. Here he is. And what a fine specimen she's found.

I follow her up the path to the next terrace. As we walk, the bell towers bang out midnight, and the lights below are snuffed by an invisible hand. I imagine everyone in the town turning in for the night. Papà walking home from Martina's to an empty house and turning on the television just for the noise. Mamma-Fede rubbing Fede's hair and telling him what a good boy he is. The Germans and Milanesi drinking their fourth or fifth digestivo along the passeggiata, the waiters clenching their jaws to stifle their yawns.

I try to make the walk last as long as I can by zigzagging across the terraces. We go Indian file in the narrow parts, taking turns leading each other through the ramshackle yards of the lazy good-for-nothings and the neat garden rows of the families of good breeding, as Nonno would say. We lead each other under grape arbors and around cisterns, listening to the swish of our legs through the high grass and the crunch of our shoes on the stones. The walk is easy tonight. There's no weight pressing down on my back and no steepness rising out of the hill to strike when I least expect it. No, tonight it feels like rising is the most natural thing in the world, like hot-air balloons or the moon or angels on their way back to heaven. It's as if someone has called a temporary suspension of all the natural laws of the universe. Gravity. Time. The inevitable Friending.

It starts stalking behind us again as we round the path to Signora Malaspina's villa. As we near the gate, the air pressure plummets. Zhuki punches some buttons on the keypad, the gate swings open, and I feel a sudden pressure in my chest. I hear the collective gasp of the imaginary crowd in anticipation of the final moment when the iron bars rain down like enemy spears, slamming into the ground and separating us on either side.

"Etto. I've been thinking."

Shit, here it is.

"I want to organize a match for Yuri. On Sunday. Not a serious match, but like we used to play in Strilky. It will be a surprise. Maybe it will help him not be so depressed." She holds one of the buttons on the keypad down, and the gate stays open.

"You think he's really depressed?"

"You would not be depressed if you were accused of something you did not do? If someone forbid you to do the one thing you love for three months?"

"If you put it that way."

"The worst part is that his suspension is also for his position on the Ukrainian national team, so he will miss playing in the World Cup qualifier in September."

"Ukraine is still in the running?"

She gives me a soft elbow to the stomach. "So. What do you think? Can you find ten or fifteen people in the town who would like to play with us on Sunday afternoon?"

"I think I could find five hundred."

She laughs. "Better start with fifteen."

"Done."

"Thank you, Etto. I really appreciate it." She flashes one more blinding smile my way, turns, and hustles to the front door as if she's running onto the field for a substitution.

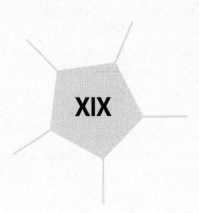

XIX

hen I wake up in the morning, my stomach starts to hurt thinking about what I've promised. I feel something being ripped away from me in slow motion, and there's nothing I can do to stop it. The truth is, I don't want to share any of it. Not with Papà or anyone else. I don't want to share the camaraderie or the boundaries of light, the inside jokes or the stupid calcio experiments. I don't want Yuri to dole out his advice to anyone but me. I don't want anybody to see the determination in Zhuki's eyes or the sweat catching in the dark hairs at her temples, flat and inky like a drawing. But most of all, I don't want to share the part of myself that runs across the field after a fottuto calcio ball, my arms and legs flailing, completely free.

Papà is already setting up the banco when I go down. I put on an apron and go into the front walk-in for the cold cuts.

"So why don't you set up any of those crazy things in the case anymore?" Papà asks, his head still ducked into the banco, arranging, always arranging.

"I thought you didn't like them."

"I don't. But the kids seem to. Especially those German kids. Who knows? Maybe it brings the mothers and nannies in like you said."

So I take one of the rabbits and string it up, stretched out and leaping over the ribs like a superhero. And as I'm fussing with the paper cape, I say it as offhandedly as I can.

"I saw Zhuki yesterday. Yuri's sister. They're back from Genoa."

"Oh?"

"She wants to plan a surprise calcio match for Yuri. Sunday afternoon. I thought I'd ask Fede and Bocca. Maybe you could ask Silvio and a couple of others. Not too many. We don't want to turn it into a circus."

Papà tries to keep his cool. "No, of course not. We can't let him think we are a town full of maniac celebrity-chasers. It must be dignified. A few men playing a match." He says this with as much old-world-butcher gravitas as he can manage, but I can see a flash of the old Papà's excitement in his eyes—the one who used to play with us in the surf and take us in the walk-in and tell us scary stories. The one who used to make plans for the future. For half an hour, he paces from the banco to the grinding counter to the vacuum-pack machine to the walk-ins, moving and removing things, but not getting any work done.

"I just remembered—I need to get a part for the slicer," he says finally, pulling his smock off and throwing it on the hook. "Casella's holding it for me." He practically runs out of the shop, and I don't see him for the rest of the morning.

At twelve thirty, I close up and cross to Bagni Liguria with a delivery Mimmo called in. They have the wooden gate shut today for some reason, and when I knock, Franco peeks out of a book-sized door cut into the gate, his gray hair mussed like the wizard in Oz.

"What's the password?" he asks.

"Tiny swimsuit."

"Ha-ha. Very funny." He opens the gate and closes it right behind me.

"So you've got security now, eh?"

"We've always had security. This is a very exclusive beach."

"I thought you were a Communist, Franco. I thought Communists didn't have exclusive anything."

He laughs. I hand over the bag of sandwiches.

"It's for the Ukrainians," he says.

"The Ukrainians?"

"Yuri Fil. Not him, but his sister and the kids. They've been here a few hours already. Really nice girl. She invited me to play calcio with them on Sunday. Maybe you want to come?"

My heart sinks, and as I watch Franco take the bag and make his way through the rows of striped chaises and open umbrellas, I realize that the Ukrainians no longer belong to me. Our midnight matches, our inside jokes, our secrets are no more. They belong to my neighbors now. They belong to the rest of the world. Franco's dog shifts and sighs.

"Etto! Ehi!" I shade my eyes and squint. "Etto! Over here!"

It's Fede, shouting from the red rescue catamaran. He's perched on the seat, the oars dragging in the water. Little Yuri and Principessa are sitting in two life rings at his feet, and Zhuki is in the front between the two floats, dangling her feet in the water. She's in a bikini, but one of those athletic ones like Mamma would wear, her stomach flat, her arms tanned and muscular as she grips the edge of the boat.

"Etto! Ehi!" Fede hooks one of the oars and whistles with his fingers. Zhuki is smiling and shading her eyes, bobbing with the sea.

"Stronzo," I mutter. Fede takes kids out on the rescue catamaran only if he's interested in their nannies, and I feel the jealousy surfacing inside me like a great sea monster, unhinging its jaws and clamping down on the boat, tossing Fede into the water.

"Here you go." Franco hands me the money.

"Thanks."

"Vieni!" Fede calls. Come here. And Zhuki and Little Yuri start up, too. "Vieni, Etto! Vieni!"

"I think they want you to come out there," Franco says.

"Well, they'll be waiting a long time."

A few of the Germans and Milanesi raise their heads from the chaises to see what the commotion is about, then let them sink back down. Bocca twists around in the lifeguard chair and gives me a slight, cool hand raise. Ihor is watching from the shore, but he doesn't break a smile. He's on the job today.

"Vieni!" they shout again.

If I were Chuck Norris or Francesco Totti, I would strip down to my underwear and strut into the surf, *Baywatch*-style, do a perfectly taut crawl out to the rescue boat, and boost myself up on one of the floats. But I haven't touched the water since Mamma. Not even wading in.

"Forget it," I say, and I shake my head in their direction.

Fede's shoulders ripple into motion as he starts rowing back to shore. They hit the sand, and Fede jumps into the water and pulls the wobbling catamaran ashore. Zhuki helps the kids clamber down the floats. If you didn't know any better, you could mistake them for a young family, and I search for any signs that Fede's been flirting with Zhuki or that she's been swallowing his bait.

Zhuki jogs over to me. Her whole body is solid, the tan lines stopping where her calcio shorts and the sleeves of her T-shirt fall. She stands at the bottom of the stairs, pulling at her suit.

"Ciao."

"Ciao."

Fede is skulking around near the guard chair. I can almost hear the eyeballs of the mothers and nannies rolling to the edges of their sunglasses to have a look. I wonder if he'll have the palle to come over here and try to play innocent.

"Where's Yuri?" I ask her.

"Ah, he's still upset. Vanni came from Genoa today, and they are sitting up on the veranda drinking."

"And you? Aren't you worried about the paparazzi here?"

She laughs. "They don't want a picture of me. Anyway, the paparazzi will stay in Rome for the next six months, examining Ilary's bump and trying to see if the baby will play offense or defense."

I look over her shoulder. Fede is chatting with Bocca now. He grabs one of the slats of the guard chair and leans back, flexing his muscles and putting on a show.

"So . . . you know Fede?" I try to ask it like I don't care.

"We just met. He remembered me from . . . from the night at the disco."

"Ah, yes, the disco."

She smiles.

"I'm glad you think it's funny now," I say.

"You should have seen your face when I pushed you."

"You should have seen yours."

And as if he's purposely trying to interrupt the moment, Fede wanders over. He's wearing a pair of loose surfer trunks today.

"Where's the scorpion?" I say, hoping Zhuki will ask about it, and I will be able to tease him about it, just enough for her to see that he is not for her.

"The scorpion has been retired."

I snort. "I'll believe that when I see it."

"I told Fede about the calcio match tomorrow," Zhuki says.

"I don't know, I think there are too many people already. You can come and watch, I guess."

Fede cocks his head and gives me a strange look.

"Of course he can play," Zhuki says. "The more we are, the better."

"I thought you said ten or fifteen."

Fede furrows his eyebrows at me. "We were just about to take Little Yuri for a jump off the molo," he says, and it sounds like a challenge. "Do you want to come?"

"I'm not really dressed for it today."

"We'll wait while you go upstairs and change."

"Don't do me any favors."

"I'm just trying to help."

"Fede, you know I'm not jumping from the fottuto molo, and you know exactly why I'm not jumping from the fottuto molo." I try to say it in as much dialect as I can manage, or at least garble it so Zhuki doesn't understand.

"Hey, relax."

"You relax."

"What's your problem today?"

"What's yours?"

"Is everything okay?" Zhuki says.

"I have to go," I say. "I've got some stuff to do."

"At least stay and watch us jump," she says.

"Sorry, I have to go."

I watch the whole thing through the shutters of our living room. Zhuki, Fede, and Little Yuri file out onto the molo and duck through the railing. They hold a quick strategic conference, Zhuki and Fede laughing the whole time.

The summer when I was ten, Mamma and Luca finally convinced me to jump off the molo. I was so scared that Mamma made Franco and Mimmo wade into the water, and she promised to jump in herself and rescue me if I didn't surface by the count of ten. Mamma had been a lifeguard in California all through high school and part of college, and she was always ready to jump in and save someone. She did the Heimlich on Bocca once when we were little and he choked on a piece of coconut, and one day she hauled in one of Luca's little summer girlfriends when she swam out too far. Some of the old men used to call her Pamela Anderson and do the slow-motion running thing even though she looked nothing like her. That's why I didn't believe Silvio when he said it was an accident.

Anyway, I remember hanging on to that railing like a baby koala, and Mamma having to count to three about five or six times, all the people at the bagni watching us. Finally, I got so nervous, I just wanted it to be over. So I jumped. I wasn't even listening to Mamma's count. I think I jumped on two. And it was the scariest fottuto minute of my ten-year-old life. The water closed up around me, and I kept going down and down. I was convinced I was going to sink to the bottom and stay there, and when I finally surfaced, I was gasping for air and trying to clear my eyes with both hands. I remember frantically dog-paddling to the applause from the beach until my toes touched the sand. I remember Mamma scooping me up, wrapping me in a warm towel, and telling me how proud she was.

I spread the slats of the shutters and lean in. Fede, Little Yuri, and Zhuki space themselves out along the edge of the concrete, their arms looped around the railing, their toes hanging off the edge like birds on a wire. I listen to the lapping of the water, the caw of the gulls, and the distant voices shouting along the shore.

Pronti . . .

Attenti . . .

Via!

Splash.

Zhuki and Fede bob to the surface, their hair slicked back, laughing, as Little Yuri steams toward the shore in a determined crawl. Principessa runs squealing toward the stairs to meet them as they come out of the water, and Ihor lumbers behind. I have to squeeze my eyes tight against the jealousy rising inside me, so tight it feels like my eyes are sutured shut, never to open again.

I spend the rest of the afternoon alone in the aula. I paint over the first panel, the last panel, whatever. The one of drunken Noah, the penciled faces of Noah and his sons transforming into the faces I know. I take Noah's place as the drunk sprawled out, spreading like a puddle on the floor, and Zhuki, Fede, and Bocca are the faces standing over me, their eyes bugging out and fingers pointing in horror. The field in the background transforms into the sea, a distant red catamaran bobbing on the waves. I feel like a fool for ever believing she could like me, and I wish I could dive straight into the plaster, leaving nothing but a slick of color in my wake.

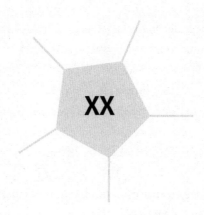

XX

hen Papà, Nonno, and I arrive at the field on Sunday afternoon, there are already a hundred men milling around. Most of them are Papà's age, men whose legs have been atrophying under one of Martina's tables for the past twenty-five years, and who I hardly recognize without a drink or a newspaper in front of them. Silvio, Gubbio, Mino, Ciacco, even Nello.

"Where's Fede?" I ask Bocca.

"Dunno. He was acting really weird at the beach. Said he had something to do."

I look around at the crowd of men warming up, thunking around dirty and deflated calcio balls and wearing the too-tight shorts and cracked cleats from their glory days, the smell of wet leather and mothballs filling the air. I make my way around the edge of the crowd and wait by the terrace wall until I hear the rustling from above. The faces of the Ukrainians appear one by one, wearing the same blinking, startled expression.

"I don't believe it," Zhuki says. "How many people!"

"What is this?" Yuri says. Zhuki starts talking in Ukrainian, and Yuri's smile spreads across his face.

"What the cazzo is going on here?" Vanni Fucci is the last one down, and he lands less gracefully than the others. "Zhuki, I thought you said we were going to play a match today."

"We are."

"This isn't a match. It's a bunch of old men."

"Mister Fucci," Yuri says, smirking. "These are not old men. These are our fans."

"Speak for yourself, Yuri. My fans are better looking. And female."

"Ah, come on, Mister Fucci," Yuri says again. "We are not in Serie A anymore. We play calcio today like we play in our village in Ukraine. Like you play in your piazza in Pistoia."

"Forget it. I'm not blowing out a knee for this. One of them could fall on me, or trip me. What if one of *them* goes down and they sue me for all I've got?"

Yuri pats him on the cheek and laughs. "No worries, Mister Fucci. Even when your calcio career is kaput, you will still have skin like baby to make your money."

"Right. I need to find some shade."

Yuri looks out over the crowd and rubs his hands together. "Now . . . what we will do with so many men?"

Mykola says something, and Ihor laughs.

"What did he say?"

"He says maybe we can do some running and then the few men not dead from a heart attack can play the match," Zhuki says.

"Where is your father, Etto?"

"I don't know," I lie.

"Ah, I see him. Over there." He reaches a hand up to wave, and the crowd immediately goes silent, turning in our direction like plants to the sun.

Yuri is embarrassed, but he steps up to speak.

"Thank you," he says in Italian. "Thank you for coming. I am very happy so much people come to play the beautiful game. But is very many people. We must divide team. So, who wants to play first, you stay on field. Other men, go to side."

There is silence across the terrace. No one moves. Yuri suddenly looks nervous, and Mykola and Ihor say something behind me. I feel a poke in my back.

"Etto," Zhuki whispers. "Help him." She pushes me forward.

"Okay. Um . . . if everyone could listen to me for a minute?" I say. "Please."

The crowd stays quiet, all except Nello, who steps forward, his arms crossed. "Listen to you? And just who put you in charge?"

"What do you mean?"

"Who put you in charge? What gives you the right?"

"I'll tell you what gives him the right." Papà steps up next to me. "Because his father leases this field. His brother is buried in this field. And he does all the mowing and cleaning up here. Who invited you anyway? I know I didn't." Nello grumbles, shuffling off to the side, and Papà continues. "Okay, we're going to do nine on nine. Mangona brothers, you're with me. Guido and Bocca, you go with Etto." Papà picks four old guys and gives me four, and the Ukrainians split up, Zhuki and Mykola on my team, Yuri and Ihor on Papà's. "Everybody else, start forming your teams. We play fifteen minutes at a time, each team rotating out to let the next team in. Score accumulates."

There's chaos for several minutes as everyone scrambles to get on the best team, and then more chaos when someone realizes there are no lines drawn on the field, and the discarded sweatshirts and warm-up pants have to be stretched along the sidelines.

"Okay," Papà says. "We are ready. Signor Fil, would you do us the honor?"

Everyone looks to Yuri, who's hovering over one of the beat-up calcio balls and batting at it with his toes. He balances his foot lightly on top of the ball, then does some quick maneuver so it magically ends up in his hands. He rotates it slowly, smiling to himself as if in a trance, as if he is back in Strilky, holding the old ball and picking out the constellations.

"Ready, Yuri?" I say.

He looks up at me and grins. He puts the ball in the center of the field, pats his chest to find the whistle, and looks around at the men one last time.

Bwwweeeeeeet!

The field quickly disintegrates until it looks like the passeggiata during Ferragosto, or the universe after the big bang. But cazzo if I have ever seen a group of men play so passionately. Men with grown children and bad backs attempting Maradona's evasions, Ronaldinho's elastico, Totti's spoon shot, and Cristiano Ronaldo's Oscar-worthy grimacing and playacting. Pretty soon, between the fake injuries and the real ones, the field starts to look like Monte Cassino, fallen bodies everywhere, the Mangona brothers chugging around lost without their bicycles.

"Over here, Etto," Zhuki shouts, but my foot has already read the field and sent the ball in her direction. I feel myself charging ahead, passing on instinct and leaping over bodies to receive the pass. After a solid month of training with the Ukrainians, the cords in my body have strengthened, and my veins are wide open, delivering rushes of oxygen. Today, I don't need upside-down sunglasses to keep me from looking at my feet. I don't need an iPod to clear my head or a string to tell me where my teammates are. My body somehow knows.

"Pass it here! Pass it here!" Papà calls out. He's the last old guy standing. One of the Mangona brothers flicks it to him, and he weaves down the field, the ball moving ahead of his feet as if by magnetic force.

"Run, Carlo! Forza! Dai!" Nonno shouts from the sidelines, and then, "Tackle him, Etto, tackle him!"

I give him some trouble, but Papà manages to deliver it directly in front of Yuri, who shoots, faking Bocca out.

"Gooooooooooooooooooool! Gooooooooooooooooooooooooooooool!"

The sidelines go wild with cheering and shouting, people sticking out their tongues, rocking imaginary babies, and pointing to the stars. Papà charges toward Yuri, the intense concentration of his face breaking into a grin, and Yuri hooks him with his arm and wraps him into a hug.

The whistle blows and we run off the field, Papà sucked toward one side, a thousand hands patting me in the other direction.

"Good job, Etto," Bocca says.

"Yeah, nice passes out there."

Vanni Fucci decides to join the next round after all, and Yuri's off the field, so there's no one to keep up with him. All the men can do is throw themselves into his path, like revolutionaries in front of an advancing tank. He racks up the score, and the next eighteen men exchange. And the next. And the next. No one wants to go home. Because this is nothing like watching calcio matches or pregame shows or postgame analysis. This is not the calcio market or the calcio variety spectaculars, or the reality shows with the wives and girlfriends of calcio.

This is pure calcio.

Our team is on again. Yuri and Papà have spent the time off the field planning a defense, and for the first ten minutes, we do nothing but go back and forth. I don't know if it's the adrenaline or all the training, but I'm not tired at all. Zhuki passes to me and I slip around Ihor somehow. One of the Mangona brothers comes at me from the side, and I slide, kicking the ball hard at the goal, the net absorbing it like an amoeba.

"Goooooooooooooooooooooool! Gol! Gol! Gol! Gol! Gol! Gol! Gol!"

The crowd cheers. I can feel the grass burn along the side of my leg, and I roll over onto my back. Zhuki comes by and pulls me up off the ground, and it gives me the momentum I need for the last few minutes. I pass to Zhuki, and she scores another goal. Yuri calls time, and I jog to the sidelines for the next exchange.

"Amazing, Etto!"

"Where'd you learn to play like that?"

"Didn't you used to be asthmatic?"

"You're really delivering the meat this afternoon, eh, Etto?"

"Eh."

Zhuki has been sucked into the crowd farther down the sideline and quickly surrounded by a group of nonne, who are no doubt telling her the dangers to one's womanhood that can occur with all that exertion. They've got her trapped pretty well, but if she wants to get away, she shows no sign. We cycle in three more times. The sun goes down behind the terraces, and the air turns grainy and gray. Over five hours we've played, twenty mini-halves in all. I have no idea what the score is when Yuri finally calls the match, but you can feel the disappointment in the air, everyone shuffling around, reluctant to go home. They stand around talking and smoking restorative cigarettes, the red ash like traffic lights in the twilight. I find Zhuki in the milling crowd, talking with Bocca and Silvio.

"I was just telling Zhuki that a bunch of us are going down to Camilla's," Bocca says.

"You should come," I say, hoping Fede won't be there.

"I can't. I have to prepare Little Yuri and Principessa for bed."

"Can't Yuri do that?"

"I promised Little Yuri I would read to him tonight. But we'll be at the beach tomorrow. Will you meet us?"

"After I close the shop."

"Until tomorrow, then." And all of a sudden, she stretches up and kisses me on the cheeks. It's not a romantic kiss. It's the same kiss Martina gives me over the bar, the same kiss I obediently give to the nonne whenever they manage to trap me within arm's length. All the same, it's a kiss.

"Tomorrow," I mumble like some kind of deficiente, and I watch her walk off toward the back of the terrace.

"That looked friendly," Bocca says, and I shrug like it's no big deal.

I survey the field to see if anyone else saw her do it, and I spot Papà, standing alone on the sideline, staring at me. He holds my gaze for only a second before jerking his head and looking away. I wish I could tell how long he's been watching and what he's thinking. Mamma always joked that he only ever showed three emotions—happy, angry, and hungry—and the burden fell to her to interpret everything in between. She would tell us exactly why he was angry, and precisely how long we had to be quiet until he cooled down. She would tell us when he was too preoccupied with a problem to hear our school stories. And she would let us know when he was proud of us.

The knots of men unravel. Bocca and I head toward the path, joining the slow procession down the hill, the faces and voices of my neighbors appearing and disappearing as we pass.

At Camilla's, Fede and the rest of them are sitting around a table outside.

"If it isn't the Azzurri," Claudia says. We pull over two more plastic chairs and everyone makes room. "How was the match?"

"Etto scored a goal."

"I don't believe it."

And Bocca starts recapping the match, alternating between Vanni's and Yuri's best moves and the stumbling old guys trying to vindicate their childhood calcio dreams. When he gets to my goal, he describes it in excruciating detail, and he makes me show the burn on my leg. The entire time, Fede is staring into his beer, and I try to puzzle out his face to see if he's pissed at me, or if he's worried that I am pissed at him.

"Why didn't you play today, Fede?" Claudia asks.

Fede shrugs and takes a long drink.

Camilla comes outside with another tray of beers. "I heard about the match, Etto. How was it?"

"Good. How's the empire building?"

"Good. Busy."

"Claudia says you're taking Internet classes to get a hotel license now."

"Trying to. How's the shop?"

"Euh."

She smiles. I've always liked Camilla. She knows exactly what she wants to do in life and doesn't let anyone tell her differently. I think her parents wanted her to turn out a little more like Claudia—find a husband, take over the family restaurant, that sort of thing.

"Why don't you stop working for a minute and sit with us?" Claudia says. "Casella, tell her."

"Camilla, your sister wants me to tell you to stop working for a minute and sit with us."

"Why don't you get up on her shoulder, Casella?" Fede says. "Polly want a cracker? Polly want a cracker?"

"Shut up, Fede," Claudia says. "He was kidding."

"Polly want a cracker?" Bocca laughs.

"At least Casella knows how to keep a woman happy," Claudia says.

"Ah, yes, the grand theory of love. Always do what Claudia wants."

"Oh, and what's your theory, Fede? Quantity over quality?"

"Not anymore. I'm taking a break."

"I'll believe it when I see it."

"Believe it," Fede says. "Who knows? Maybe one of these days, I'll even start looking for Mrs. Fede."

Claudia laughs so loudly that Sima looks up from her phone.

"Why is that so funny?" Fede demands.

"Are you kidding? That's the funniest thing I've ever heard. You actually think any girl is going to take you seriously, Fede? *You?* Husband material? Really?"

Fede looks at her blankly, goes to say something, then changes his mind. He pushes his chair back, counts out a few coins, and leaves them rattling on the table.

"Oh, come on, Fede, you're not going to leave over that, are you?"

"Lighten up. She was just kidding."

But I look over at Claudia, her arms locked across her chest, and I know we are a long way from kidding.

"Hey, if you can dish it out, you should be able to take it," Claudia says.

I watch Fede walking away down the passeggiata, and suddenly I feel sorry for him. There's something heavy in his shoulders and the flatness of his gait, his perfect muscles like ballast, weighing him down.

I stand up.

"Let him be, Etto."

"Yeah, just let him be. He'll be back."

"Spoiled baby. He's only doing it for attention anyway."

I catch up with Fede on the molo. He's slumped on a bench like Pete the Comb Man when he's on one of his drinking binges, and I sit down next to him, the points on my cheeks where Zhuki kissed me still sparking in the darkness.

"You okay?"

He shrugs.

"What was that about?"

He shrugs again.

"You didn't have to skip the match today, you know."

"I know."

"And I'm sorry for being such a stronzo."

"I know."

The clouds are blocking the moon tonight, and the sky and sea melt together. I spot the swag of a cruise ship parked on the horizon, and it looks like it's hovering in empty space.

"There's something between you and Claudia, isn't there?"

"Why do you say that?"

"There is, isn't there?"

"Not anymore."

"There *was*?"

"We hooked up."

"What? When?"

"Ages ago."

"Shit. How?"

"I don't know. How does anything like that happen? It was the night of Luca's funeral. She found me on the rocks with a bottle of whiskey, and I didn't feel like going to bed. So she stayed up with me. Just talking at first."

"Shit. Does Casella know?"

"Nobody knows. Her. Now you."

"Shit. And then what happened?"

"You know you say 'shit' a lot." He gives me a look of concern, then shrugs. "I don't know. I just couldn't follow through."

"With the sex?"

He smiles at this, his eyebrow cocked in amusement. "No, Etto, not with the sex. With the other stuff. She came to me the next day, talking about what did it mean to me and what did I want, and relationship this and relationship that."

"And?"

"Cazzo, my mind was already so messed up thinking about Luca. I don't know exactly what I said. I guess not what she wanted to hear. And then a couple of weeks later, she started going out with Casella."

"And now? Do you still . . . ?"

"What do you think?"

"But she treats you like garbage. Come to think of it, you treat *her* like garbage."

Fede looks me full in the face, and in the darkness, his skin looks as black as the sea.

"Etto," he says, "if you start to look for logic in these things, you're really fucked."

By the time I get home, the apartment is dark, and I sneak in as quietly as I can. The alarm chirps, and I toe off my shoes.

"Etto, is that you?"

"You're still awake, Papà?"

I come to the top of the stairs and find him sitting on the sofa in the dark with a drink in his hand. He's staring off into space, his cheeks striped by the faint moonlight through the shutters.

"Etto, come here for a minute."

I sit down in one of the chairs.

"You're pretty good friends with that sister of Yuri's, aren't you?"

"Zhuki."

"Zhuki," he repeats. "She seems like a very nice girl. Everyone who's talked to her says they like her."

I have no idea where this is going. "She is."

Papà takes a drink. "You know, Etto, I told your mamma if she wanted to live in California, I would move there for her."

"You? In California?" I try to imagine it. I only went there once when Luca and I were about twelve, and all I remember was that everyone was blond and they smiled all the time as if no one ever had problems or got sick or died. I wonder if things would have turned out differently for us there.

"It seems ridiculous, doesn't it?" Papà continues. "But the point is, I would have made it work somehow. *We* would have made it work somehow."

I still have no idea what he's getting at. "I guess it's lucky she wanted to live here."

"Yes. She seemed to like it here anyway." He runs his hand over the bristles of his hair and exhales. "I don't know, Etto. I don't know. I guess what I'm trying to say is, whatever happens, we're okay, right? I mean, I know it's been a little rough lately, but you and me, we're okay?"

"Of course, Papà."

"I only want what's best for you, Etto."

"I know, Papà."

He clears his throat and takes another drink.

"You played good tonight."

"Thanks."

"*Very* good."

"Thanks, Papà. You did, too."

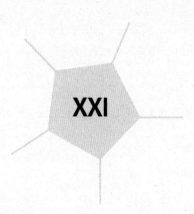

XXI

hen I come down to the shop in the morning, Papà is already back at the grinding counter, stuffing sausages from the last of the ground scrap, a job that is a lot easier to do with four hands than two.

"Do you want me to help you, Papà?"

"It's okay. I'm almost finished."

He won't look at me, as if he's embarrassed about saying those things last night. Or maybe nervous, like I've finally seen through the cracks in his defense, and now he has to wait to see how I'm going to use it. I don't know. I guess I feel the same way.

He leaves as soon as he's finished, and the rest of the morning is slow. Jimmy's papà won't be here until tomorrow, and there's nothing left to break down, chop apart, or grind up. Outside it's almost too hot to breathe, much less cook, so the customers are down to a slow trickle. I spend the morning reorganizing the shelves behind the banco, rooting out the crumpled bags, markers, boxes of spices, and old receipts. As I work, I listen to the sounds of the beach and try in vain to pick out her voice.

At twelve thirty, I close up and go upstairs. I dig around in the back of the wardrobe for my trunks and put them on, but they look like something a little kid would wear, with orange crabs floating in blue life rings. I pull on a pair of Luca's shorts and some of his flip-flops.

"You're dressed for the party today," Mimmo says as I stand at the entrance hut, scanning the beach. "Unfortunately, the party's already migrating." He points to the scrum of men surrounding Yuri, slowly moving toward us. Papà is there at Yuri's side, and Zhuki is hurrying behind, hastily packing up Little Yuri and Principessa, putting on T-shirts and making them rinse their feet under the spigot.

"Ciao," she says. "You're just in time. We've decided to hold practice today." She's wobbling a little, loaded down with a giant beach bag and a kid on each hand.

"Do you want me to take the bag for you?"

"I can get it."

I reach for it, and I instantly regret it. It's got to be twenty kilos.

"What do you have in here—a third kid?"

"I can get it if it's too heavy."

"I'm joking. It's fine."

But only looking at the hill makes my lungs wheeze and my back hurt. If I have to talk the whole way up, I'm done for.

"So, tell me another story about Ukraine," I say.

"What about?"

"I don't know." I spot Mykola and Ihor walking up ahead. "How does Yuri know Mykola and Ihor?" And I silently hope it's a long and convoluted story.

"He met Mykola at the academy," she says. "Strilky was too far, and our family was poor, so sometimes Yuri would spend the holidays with Mykola's family. Mykola's surname is Shevchenko. You know it?"

"No."

"Oh, it is very famous in Ukraine. He has a cousin in the Premier League, and his father was one of the great gymnasts, traveling the world and training with foreigners. At the academy, they were still using the old ways, so Mykola and his father were always telling Yuri what the foreign calcio players did—eat this way, tie your shoes this way, train this way, run on this part of your foot, don't let the other boys make psychological games with you. . . ."

"Why didn't Mykola end up playing for a team?"

"Ach. It is a sad story. Both of them were going to be signed by Kiev Dynamo. But then Mykola, he injured his knee. He tried to rehabilitate it, but his career was finished. When Yuri signed the contract with Dynamo alone, he wrote Mykola in as his trainer. Almost for a joke. But Yuri was so good, they accepted this condition. Each time he was transferred, Mykola was always in the contract. Now he is like family."

"And Ihor?"

"Ihor is the biggest boy we knew from school. So when Tatiana said, everyone I know has a bodyguard, we need a bodyguard, Yuri looked this boy up, and he was only working in a factory, so he agreed. And now Ihor is part of the family, too."

"Strange family."

"All families are strange."

I drop the bag as soon as we reach the field, and Principessa and Little Yuri run off. Yuri has gone up to the villa for the SUV, and he dumps a pile of cones and balls in the middle of the field. The men who stopped at their houses along the way are pulling on their socks and cleats.

"Attention!" Yuri shouts, waving his arms in the center of the field. "Attention!" For the next hour, they practice, first in shaky rows, kicking balls back and forth, then in snaking lines and crisscrossing patterns in front of the goal. Yuri has Zhuki demonstrate from the penalty spot, and she hits the same piece of net over and over, the arc of her shot perfect every time. I watch from the sidelines. It's in-cazz-ibile to me that these men who argue back and forth at Martina's, too stubborn to listen to anything but their own opinions, are suddenly obeying the staccato of a whistle and following meekly in the steps of a woman half their age.

"Etto, get out here, you lazy bum!"

"Yeah. Get off the sideline before it fuses to your culo!"

"Too late," I shout back.

Papà takes his turn and misses, and Yuri claps a hand on his shoulder and talks to him for a while, twisting and contorting his body, making

Papà repeat a series of kicks at an imaginary ball before allowing him back into the line. Zhuki sits down on the sideline next to me and takes off her cleats.

"Yuri seems to be doing better," I say.

"Yes. This is exactly what he needed. A very good distraction."

They stop the drills and organize into a scrimmage, Yuri and Mykola squatting on the other sideline.

"Look up! Look up!"

"Don't think! Shoot!"

"Read the fake! Read the fake!"

"Attack, attack, attack!"

I'm feeling bold. "So how about coming to Camilla's with me tonight?"

"Oh, I can't tonight. Yuri wants to go to the bar, so I must stay at home with Little Yuri and Principessa."

"What about Tatiana?"

"She went to Milan for the week."

"For what?"

"She's going paparazzi hunting."

"Really?"

"She does this every few weeks. Even when we are in Genoa, she must go to Milan or Rome for shopping and to see her showgirl friends. Genoa is not sophisticated enough for her, she says." Zhuki laughs. "This from a girl who grew up in Cherkassy."

"Where?"

"Exactly."

"So why did you come to San Benedetto, then?" I ask. "You could have gone somewhere exclusive, to one of the Portos—Porto Cervo, Portoferraio, Portofino . . ."

"Yuri does not want to go to the celebrity resorts. Prisons, he calls them. He still does not want to believe he is a celebrity. Even the villa as big as a shopping center, that was a compromise with Tatiana. He does not like us living alone, high up on the hill, always looking down. If it were only his decision, he would stay in a small flat next to the sea."

"And you?"

She pulls her knees up to her chest and looks at me intently. "I am a lot like my brother."

When I walk into Martina's at six, the flat-screen is on Miss Italia nel Mondo, mercifully with the sound off so we don't have to hear the interview portion and the serious tones these girls have been practicing for a month in the mirror. The noise in the bar is deafening, the same as it always is during the high-summer season, everyone coming to escape the tourists and the heat. Only tonight, it sounds like a hospital ward.

"I think I did something to my ankle."

"My back feels like someone has been trampolining on it."

"My back is fine, but my thighs. Porca miseria, my thighs!"

"My calves."

"My feet."

"My neck."

"My culo."

"I think even my scalp hurts."

You'd think none of them knew they had a body until today. And after they've made a thorough inventory of every muscle and ligament, they go into the endless recaps and heckling. Some of these men could heckle for the Olympics.

"Silvio, I haven't seen you run that fast since you were trying to chase that rapist down the beach last summer."

"Ciacco, I haven't seen you run, period."

"Only from his wife," someone says, and everyone laughs.

"You should get your wife out there on Sunday."

"They were talking about it."

"What do you mean?"

"All the wives. They were talking about making a picnic of it next week."

"A picnic? This is a serious match, not a picnic."

"What's the matter? You don't want any witnesses to your weak dribbling?"

"Perhaps you didn't notice, but I scored a goal on Sunday."

"I'd be surprised if you didn't. You never pass . . ."

"We'll see who scores the goals next week."

"We'll see."

They start to plan, ignoring even the swimsuit competition flashing behind them, and before long, there's a league of twelve teams, complete with a double-elimination tournament on the weekend of Ferragosto, even uniforms that Signor Cavalcanti is going to try to get for cheap from his brother-in-law in La Spezia.

Martina comes out of the kitchen and plunks two bowls of trofie with pesto on the bar in front of me.

"If you want it, Carlo, it's over here," she calls to Papà. "I'm not going to be your waitress today."

Papà stands up slowly and makes his way over to the bar. He sits down next to me and gives me a look of mock alarm. Martina makes another trip to the kitchen and brings back a rack of clean glasses, which she bangs on the bar and starts putting away with violence.

"Martina?" Papà asks. "Martina, is everything okay?"

But she doesn't look up, so I try.

"Martina? Is something wrong?"

She only thins her lips and shakes her head. The door opens, letting in the passing noise from the passeggiata, and I feel the sea air skittering up my back like the first time Zhuki stepped into the bar. I turn to look, just as everyone else does.

"Buona sera." Yuri's standing in the doorway, flanked by Ihor and Mykola. The entire bar falls silent. I think you could've heard a baby crying on the other side of the world.

"Buona sera," Papà finally says.

"Buona sera!" the entire bar echoes in unison, like some fottuto elementary school class.

"We come to see if anybody need medical attention."

The whole bar laughs, but it feels forced, everyone on their best behavior.

"Do you mind if we have a drink with you?" Yuri asks.

"Not at all, not at all." And there's a deafening scraping and banging of chairs as fifty men try to make room for them at their tables.

Mykola and Ihor choose a table, but Yuri walks over to the bar.

"Ciao, Etto. Ciao, Carlo."

"Ciao."

He nods to the flat-screen. "Miss Italia?"

"Miss Italia nel Mondo."

"What's the difference?"

A few words. That's all it takes to open the room again and resume the chatter.

"It means some Italian guy had a fling on vacation and these are the babies," Farinata starts. "They're not even Italian."

"Who cares, Farinata? They're in bikinis."

"What I want to know is how that stumpy Maradona is going to reach any of their heads to put on the crown."

"They'll give him a stepladder."

"Maybe the Hand of God will come down for him again."

"I will say that Rome diet is working for him."

"Cocaine?"

"I thought that was the Milan diet."

"That's heroin."

"Who put him on television anyway? Let him rest in peace."

"It was the only way to make Paolo Bonolis look taller."

"That's not Paolo Bonolis. It's Carlo Conti."

"Same thing. What happened to that guy anyway? It's like he got locked inside the tanning bed."

"Black makes him look taller." They laugh. The same old jokes, but tonight a strange, new feeling overcomes me. The feeling that I might someday want to be a part of this.

The girls on the screen stay on mute, their mouths gasping like fish when the winner is announced. They do their best fake hugging and I'm-so-happy-for-you faces, and Maradona does in fact have to get on the points of his feet to crown the Filipino one.

"Yuri, would you like a drink?" Papà asks.

"Get them some of that homemade grappa," someone shouts.

"Good idea. Grappa, Martina."

"*Please*," Martina answers.

"Please," Yuri says.

"Ah, don't mind her," Nello says from down the bar, lowering his voice to a stage whisper. "Menopause."

Martina looks up and down the bar. She wipes her hands on her apron, unties it behind her and throws it on the counter. "Arrange yourselves. Make sure you lock up when you leave." She heads for the door.

"Uh-oh. Now you've done it."

"She's just making a point. She'll be back."

"Talk about hot tempered."

"Her mother was just like that."

Papà looks at me, then Yuri, then the door. He eases himself off the stool.

"I'll go, Papà."

I head for the molo. I don't know if it's the molo or the sea that draws people to it, that invites them to stand along the railings and fling their unhappiness into the waves. If they drew samples and counted the emotional distress like they counted the bacteria in the harbors or the cocaine residue in the Po, the beaches would be closed all summer. I pick out Martina's sloppy bun among the short, hairdresser perms of the Germans and the salon styles of the Milanesi.

"Martina, wait up." But she either doesn't hear me or doesn't want to.

I finally catch up to her at the gates of Bagni Liguria. The bagni are empty at night, the chaises and umbrellas neatly stacked to the side. "Wait up, Martina. You're faster than half the men."

She stops, and we let the people on the passeggiata stream around us.

"Go back and finish your dinner, Etto. I left the rest of it in the kitchen."

"Martina, you don't have to cook dinner for us anymore. Really. We can fend for ourselves."

She laughs. "You think I'm this upset about cooking a couple of extra plates every night? God, I need to be around women more."

"What is it, then?"

"It's that bastard-of-a-cafone-of-a-husband of mine again."

229

I flinch. I can't remember the last time I heard Martina curse. "What did he do?"

"Took out another loan in my name. Fifty thousand euros this time."

"Why didn't you tell us?"

"Nobody ever asks."

"What does he need fifty thousand euros for anyway?"

Martina sighs. "His sister told me a few months ago he was buying a house in the Caribbean with that puttana from Calabria. I remember thinking at the time, 'Where's he going to get the money for that?' I'm so stupid."

"But he can't do that. He's not even your husband anymore."

"Technically, he still is." And I realize that I know next to nothing about Martina, that she's never burdened me with any of this.

"What are you going to do?" I ask.

"Take it. What else can I do? Hope he pays it back someday."

"What do you mean, 'take it'? You shouldn't have to take it. We'll get Silvio to investigate. We'll have Dura and the other guys from Naples call their friends and chase him down. We're here for you, Martina. Anything you need."

She laughs, shakes her head, and turns to the sea. The waves are calm near the shore, but there are depth charges of spray exploding about twenty meters out.

"You know what I need, Etto? A life. I really need a life."

I'm not in the business of getting lives for people or I would get myself one. But what I can give her is a small piece of a ceiling in a defunct liceo in Berlusconi's Italy. What I can give her is my full attention and concentration as I paint her into the third panel. *The Sacrifice of Martina*. I draw her first, a background figure, standing in the kitchen and putting another pot on the stove. I put a nimbus around her head and make the kitchen glow. Over the next few nights, I start adding figures—Papà with his finger in the air and Signor Cato staring into the screen of the computer. I paint a flat-screen in the corner and swap in the bar for the altar, the calcio scarves waving above it, almost horizontal, as if in a fierce storm. I work on it every night after dinner, holding the faces of my neighbors in my head as I climb the hill.

"Why are you staring at me?" Nello growls one night at the bar.

"I'm not staring at you." But I've been staring at everyone lately, at their worry lines and their laugh lines, their hollowed eyes and swollen jowls, their expressions and gestures and the hundred ways they slump in their chairs, occasionally lobbing remarks over their shoulders and listening for the detonations.

"Yes, you were," Nello insists. "You know I'm straight, right? Hey, everybody! Get this! Etto's trying to flirt with me."

His cackle seals his fate. I vow to save him for *The Last Judgment*. I'll paint him cowering in the boat on the River Styx, being whacked by Charon's oar, just as he whacks poor Pia in this life.

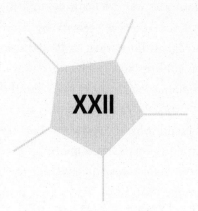

XXII

It doesn't take long before the Ukrainians are absorbed into San Benedetto like long-lost cousins, and I start to dream about crowds, about living in communes and spectating at calcio matches in two-tiered stadiums, about being wedged between the Germans and Milanesi on the passeggiata or trapped in airplanes, cruise ships, and shopping malls. In each dream, I find myself pawing through people, searching for someone or something that remains just out of my sight.

When I go down to the shop on Tuesday morning, Papà, Nonno, and Jimmy's papà are already standing around and talking about Jimmy, who's apparently playing his video games in Japan now.

"He says he is practically a celebrity there," Jimmy's papà is saying. "People ask to have their picture taken with him, and when he walks down the street, everyone turns to look. He says everything there is half the size. Women the size of dolls. Hotel rooms as small as a coffin. And so clean. He says it is so clean you could eat off the streets."

I can tell by how Jimmy's papà talks that he's secretly proud to have a son so worldly, but whenever Jimmy's name comes up, Papà and Nonno get nervous looks, as if they expect me to evaporate on the spot.

"In a month or so, you will be able to break down an entire vitello by yourself," Papà says as encouragement. "It will be a day to celebrate."

"Yes," Nonno adds. "A butcher never forgets his first vitello."

While we work, I sneak glances at the front window, trying to catch the very moment Zhuki emerges from the crush of people on the passeggiata and crosses to the beach. I know Papà is doing the same, parting the bead curtain every ten minutes or so, pretending to ask Nonno some question he already knows the answer to.

By one o'clock, all that's left of the hindsaddle is spread over the back table, and the vacuum-pack machine is running at full blast, the rifle shot and hiss at the end of each cycle setting the rhythm.

My phone lights up. Zhuki this time.

WE'RE AT THE BEACH.

I HAVE TO FINISH UP IN THE SHOP.

COME OVER WHEN YOU'RE FINISHED.

Papà seems to read my mind. "It's all right, Etto. You've done enough for today. You can go."

"Are you sure?"

"Sure. Go."

Mimmo is sitting inside the entrance hut, reading. The beach is mobbed, the umbrellas cluttered with wet swimsuits flung across their backs. Yuri is sitting on a chaise in the front row, surrounded by a group of men, most of them in street clothes.

"I don't see any deliveries in your hand today, Etto," Mimmo says.

"Not today."

He wags his eyebrows at me. "She's over there."

"Thanks."

The sand shifts as I step down from the boardwalk. I feel like I'm walking in slow motion and everyone is staring at me, like my skin is transparent and they can see the folds in my brain and the blood pumping through my arteries.

I find Zhuki knee deep in the water, holding Principessa's hand while Little Yuri and a couple of other boys jump into the crests of the waves as they roll in. I stop at the edge of the dry sand, just out of reach of the bubbling surf.

"Ciao."

She turns around, squinting. "Ciao."

The sun is heavy on my forehead. I wish I'd brought a pair of sunglasses, a hat, something to block it. A monster wave comes in, washing over my feet, eroding the sand beneath them and knocking me off balance. Zhuki laughs. I look up, and there are her eyes pulling me forward.

She picks Principessa up and goes out to where the boys are. The water splashes around my ankles, and I look down at my feet, pale and glowing, distorted by the water. I imagine the flecks of Mamma's skin cells swirling around with the bits of seaweed and sand. One drunken winter night, I finally pressed Fede into telling me where they'd found her body. He said it was concealed in the sand and murkiness between the piers, and the divers had to unhook her from the pipes that lie flush on the sea floor. I don't even know what those pipes are for. Fede said she'd taken one of the hooks from the shop and attached it to her weight belt. I look up at the chair. Fede is watching me, and he smiles and gives me a thumbs-up. My stomach churns.

"Are you okay?" Zhuki calls back to me.

"Fine. Why?" I try to force myself to relax. What is it they tell you when you're seasick? Look out at the horizon, as far you can until you forget the sickness and get your balance back. So I look out at Whale Island rising like a rocky wart from the smooth skin of the sea and let my eyes float to the horizon. It doesn't help. I still have the awful feeling in the pit of my stomach that if I make any sudden moves, the equilibrium of the sea will be upset and Mamma's bloated body will come floating up from the bottom.

Zhuki wades farther out, Principessa clinging to her shoulder. She jumps with every wave, shouting with the boys. I shuffle my feet until the water is up to my calves and the waves splash at the edges of Luca's shorts.

I stop. I can't do it.

Zhuki turns around and motions again for me to follow, but I shake my head. They jump into a few more waves before the whole group turns around and comes back toward me in slow motion, Zhuki's legs fighting the water. I can hear her explaining the tides in both Ukrainian and Italian, how the sun and the moon pull the water up and down. Like getting in and out of a bathtub, she says. She sets Principessa down on the sand and turns her attention to Little Yuri, who's pulling at her arm.

"I told Little Yuri we would jump off the molo. Do you want to come?"

"No, no," I say, trying to play it cool. "No jumping for me."

"I'll save you if you drown." She makes a little diving motion with her hand, and I force a laugh.

"I don't feel like the beach today. How about a hike?"

She looks at Principessa and Little Yuri. "I don't know. I think Little Yuri and Principessa want to stay on the beach for now."

"I didn't mean Little Yuri and Principessa. I meant you."

"But who will watch them?"

"Their parents?"

She pulls at the bottom of her suit and runs her fingers through her hair. She studies my face, and I try to erase the fear and anxiety.

"Wait here," she says.

She goes over to Yuri, parting the crowd, Little Yuri and the other boys following behind. She sets Principessa down on the chaise, and they talk in Ukrainian while the men wait patiently. Finally, she emerges from the crowd.

"Okay," she says. "Let's go."

"Let's go."

I stick my legs under the spigot as Zhuki rinses off under the shower. She slips on her shorts and her T-shirt, waves to Mimmo and Franco and a few others, and in a minute we're alone on the passeggiata.

"So," she says, "a hike. Where to?"

"Up?"

"Where else?"

✳︎   ✳︎   ✳︎

We end up on a bench in the English gardens overlooking the harbor. They were planted a century ago by women who carried parasols and jumped into the sea fully clothed. You can see half the hill and the town from here, as well as the harbor on the back side, the boats lined up and tucked away.

"You are so lucky to live here," she says.

"I guess."

"What do you mean, 'I guess'? Look at this."

"Well, it's not bad if you come here for a few months and you don't know all the stuff that goes on, but after a while it gets tiring, you know, everyone knowing your business all the time. Sometimes it's like you can't sneeze in the morning and not hear about it later in the afternoon."

She laughs. "Calcio is the same."

"Really?"

"Sure. The same players and players' wives moving from Serie A to Premier League to Bundesliga to La Liga. And the paparazzi. They are like the grandmothers in my village, following everyone around, reporting every little thing anyone does."

"At least they have more interesting things to report on."

"Ha!"

"You're telling me you don't meet any interesting people in calcio?"

"I meet a lot of women like Tatiana. And a lot of men who want to be with someone like Tatiana. And then there are the people who only want to get to know me in order to get access to Yuri."

"Why do you think I'm here?"

She laughs and gives what I think is supposed to be a playful shove, but it nearly knocks me off the bench. "You didn't even know who Yuri was."

"Sure I did." And I rattle off the statistics I'd heard Papà cite a hundred times before.

"But you didn't *care* who he was."

"Not really."

She smiles. "So . . . do you think you know the business of everyone who lives on this hill?"

"Almost everyone."

"I will quiz you. Who lives in the house right up there?"

"Which one?"

"The one on the next terrace. The one that looks like Disneyland."

"That's the Cavalcantis' house. You remember Guido, the one who runs Le Rocce?"

"White suit? Lots of girls?"

"That's him."

"He makes so much money from the club?"

"No. It's his father. He went to Milan when he was young, made a lot of money in the stock market, retired at forty, and moved back here."

"It is such a big house. It looks like it might fall into the sea."

"People were angry for a while because they tore down an old, classic villa and put that up. But the Cavalcantis, they are very nice people. Not snobs."

"And this one?"

"Signora Sapia's. She lives there with her son and his wife."

"Ah, I know her from church. She's a very nice lady."

"Now. She used to be a complete . . . witch."

"Really?"

"Especially to her daughter-in-law. She didn't think she was good enough for her son. And then one year she went blind. Suddenly. And now her daughter-in-law is the one to lead her around and do everything for her."

"What about that one?"

"Signor and Signora Semirami."

"Anything interesting about them?"

"Where do I start?"

We keep walking up the hill, through the crooked paths and mule tracks that knit together every villa and rustic hut. I listen to her footsteps behind me as they tread over rocks and grass, the percussion changing, but always maintaining the same steady grace. We end up on the field, which even in this drought is green and lush. Zhuki takes the ball from Luca's grave, slips off her flip-flops, and flings them in the direction of the side-lines.

"Are you in?" she says, and I kick mine off, too.

There are no rules today. No whistles, no experiments, no penalties, no scores, no defense. We run through the soft grass in our bare feet, dodging and weaving, laughing our heads off, scoring goal after goal. Is this what it was like for you, Luca? Did your muscles become liquid, responding to even the slightest bump in the grass? Did you feel like you could run from here to Rome, with leaps and bounds over the tops of the trees?

I score a goal, and I imitate Vanni Fucci, thrusting figs in the air, then falling down on the field in an exaggerated face-plant. Zhuki runs to fetch the ball and dribbles it back.

"Half-time," she says, and she sits down next to me, leaning back on her arms. I flip over, and I can practically hear Luca hissing at me across the terrace. Kiss her, you idiot, kiss her.

"Etto?"

"Yes?"

"Is the reason you won't jump from the molo because of your mother?"

"Who told you that?"

"The nonne."

"Well, the nonne should probably mind their own affairs."

"Like that will happen." She laughs. She picks up the ball and twirls it around in her hands. "It is true that she killed herself in the sea? After your brother?"

"What else did the nonne tell you?"

"That she was American."

"Yeah, she was from California."

"Did you ever go there?"

"Once. When we were about twelve. She didn't really get along with her parents so she only went back every few years. They thought she was stupid for staying here. They kept calling it a phase."

"Even by the time you were twelve?"

"Even by the time we were twelve."

"And where is her grave?"

"Over there. In California."

"Why?"

"I don't know exactly. My papà called her parents up when she . . . when it happened and they . . . well, they said some pretty awful things. They're both lawyers," I say, as if this matters. "Anyway, they demanded that he send her back."

"And your papà did it."

"I don't know why. I think he didn't want to argue."

"Maybe he felt guilty? Like it was his fault?"

"Maybe."

She picks up the ball and tosses it to me. I bat it back to her like a volleyball, and we try to keep it up until it drops and we have to start all over again.

"So what was she like?"

I hesitate.

"If you don't want to talk about her, it's okay. I'll stop interrogating you."

"Actually, it's kind of nice to talk about her. I've just never had to explain her to anyone, that's all. Everyone I've ever known knew her, too."

Zhuki tosses the ball to me, and I catch it. I lean back into the grass and prop it under my head like a pillow. The sun is white-hot today, the shreds of cloud igniting like tinder as they pass over it.

"Well, she loved life. It sounds like a cliché, I know . . . well, it sounds like a lie now, too. But it's true. Every morning, she would get up and go for a swim in the sea. It never got old for her, living here. Spring, summer, winter, it didn't matter. She was always outside, and she talked to everyone on the street. Complete strangers. Tourists. Even people like Farinata and Nello. Sometimes it would take her an hour just to make it down the passeggiata."

"She sounds like an amazing person."

"Yeah. When you were with her, you really understood why people gravitated toward her. There was just something about the way she would look at you that made you feel . . . I don't know, loved. So loved, it was impossible not to love back."

We lie there in silence for a minute, listening to faraway voices somewhere down below.

"It must be really difficult to live without her."

"It is. But it's more than just her."

"What do you mean?"

"Have you ever read the 'Inferno'?"

"No."

"We all read it in school. Our teacher used to tell us these different theories of hell, and one of them is that it's a permanent separation. And you know what? That's exactly what it feels like. Not just from her, but from everybody else."

"God, too?"

"Maybe."

"Is that why you sit outside the church instead of going in?"

I turn my head away from her and spot a lizard hiding out. I pluck a long blade of grass and try to touch the lizard with it, but he scampers away.

"I don't know," I say. "I used to pray. That whole year after my brother died, when my mamma was like that . . . I was like a monk, I prayed so hard."

"But it didn't work."

I look her in the eye. "No. It didn't work. And after that, I just thought, you know, what's the point of it if you can't save one person? If you can't save this one good person. What's the point?"

Silence settles over us and sinks into the field.

"Now can I ask you something?" I say.

"Sure."

"Why do you hang out with me?"

She laughs.

"No, I mean, all I ever talk about is depressing stuff, and when I'm not doing that, I'm kind of a pedant anyway. I should be taking you to Nice, or at least to the bars or the disco or the Truck Show . . . telling you jokes, making you laugh."

She smiles at me. "Etto, all I meet are boys who want to go to bars and talk about stupid things. This is my least favorite part of being the sister of a calcio player. If I want to talk about something important, about the world, about life, they tell me, 'Don't be so serious,' or 'You should smile more.' Ugh. I hate that one the most."

"You *should* smile more."

"Very funny." She tosses the ball at me, and it bounces off my leg in the direction of the cypresses. "See, Etto-Son-of-Butcher? You do make me laugh."

I reach my hand into the space between us, and I can feel her hand sliding into mine, resting comfortably under my palm. We lie there for a long time, just holding hands, and as the minutes pass, it's like someone is kneading a soft spot into my side, parting my ribs and making a path.

XXIII

*F*riday is the start of the Apocalypse. That's what we call the first two weeks in August—the buildup to Ferragosto, when the tourists outnumber us ten to one and there is no bagni, no street, no vico, and no mule track where you can go to escape their voices or their children or their giant beach blow-up animals. It can take you half an hour to shuffle down the pedestrian streets, tourists pressing in on you from all sides.

"What I want to know is where the water's going to come from to flush all these toilets and run all these showers," Chicca says. Papà, Chicca, and I are standing out in front of the shops.

"Franco said the bagni are calling a meeting about rationing."

"Rationing?"

"You were too little to remember how it was back in the eighties. Lines all the way down the passeggiata waiting for the water trucks. Even the hotels had to ration. It was a nightmare."

Officially, there hasn't been any rain in San Benedetto since June. Down here in town, it's easier to ignore, but up on the terraces, Nonno's garden is shriveling away to nothing and his cistern is so dry, even the stench has abandoned it. For the past couple of weeks, the fire helicopters have been chopping up and down the shore, mesmerizing the kids on the beach as they scoop up seawater in their giant buckets and drop it on the smoking brush. There were two fires last week, one just past Laigueglia, and one not far from the campground in Albenga.

I spend the morning at the band saw and the vacuum-pack machine, cutting and packing ribs while Papà works the counter up front. He steps out onto the passeggiata in between customers, chatting with everyone who passes. Every time the door opens, the banco kicks on, chugging like a locomotive to keep itself cold.

Sawing ribs is one of the simplest tasks you can do in a butcher shop. And one of the most dangerous. If you let your guard down, it's easy to catch the bone on the blade, which can set off a few nightmare scenarios, including but not limited to flinging the bone into your face, lodging a chip in your eye, or ripping your hand into the path of the blade. If you're really unlucky, the blade can snap and send two meters of toothed steel whistling and vibrating through the air. But Papà seems to think I can handle the band saw and almost everything else in the shop these days. He doesn't hover anymore. He doesn't microsupervise or talk about hairnets or greet me with lists of tasks, and I've started to see it not only as his shop but maybe mine one day.

I'm moving the last of the ribs to the walk-in when my phone lights up.

"Papà?"

"Yes?"

"The Ukrainians are on the beach."

"Are they?"

"You should go over there, Papà."

"But who will work the counter?"

"It's not so busy today. And I just finished the ribs. I'll be fine alone."

"Well," he says, "only if you're sure." But in the time it takes to say the words, he has already whipped off his jacket and washed up at the back sink, one foot out the door.

The rest of the morning is slow. I close up at twelve thirty, wrap up three sandwiches, and bring them over to the beach. Fede's on duty in the entrance hut, playing with his phone.

"Look who's suddenly coming to the beach every day."

"I'm working on my tan."

"Nice try. I think everybody knows exactly what you're working on."

"What about you? You got your eye on any nannies these days?"

"I told you. I'm taking a break. Why does nobody believe me?"

I look over at the Ukrainians. Yuri's holding court again, Papà sitting in the place of honor next to him, his pants rolled up, his toes digging into the sand. Zhuki is off to the side making a sand tower with Little Yuri and some of the other boys. I put one of the sandwiches on the counter and hold it down with my hand.

"I need a favor, Fede."

He looks at the sandwich, then eyes me suspiciously. "What kind of favor?"

"I need to borrow your moped."

Fede hesitates. After Luca's accident, he sold the wrecked motorcycle and his other one to a guy in Albenga. They were both Japanese models—hypersports—zero to one hundred in three seconds, and to replace them, he bought a used moped that barely makes it over fifty. When he rides it, he looks like one of those clowns on a toy bike, his legs nearly doubled up.

"No."

"Come on, Fede. Dai."

"No."

"Please? I want to take her up to the meadows, and I've got no other way."

He sighs and shakes his head. "I don't know, Etto . . ." He looks over at Zhuki. She sees us and waves, hands her shovel off to one of the boys, and comes over to the boardwalk.

"Ciao." She gives me a one-armed hug around my waist. I let go of the sandwich and plead my case with my eyes.

"Do you swear you won't go over thirty?"

"Thirty? I won't make it up the hill."

"Forty, then. No faster. And both of you better be wearing helmets."

"Thanks, Fede."

"I mean it."

I somehow manage to start it and rock it off the kickstand. We wobble through the alley and onto Via Londra, Zhuki gripping the rack behind her, the front tire rasping against the pavement as I overcorrect. I haven't driven anything since Luca's accident, and it bucks every time I touch the brake or the accelerator.

"Are you sure you can't tell me where we're going?" she says in my ear as we idle at the stoplight, our helmets clacking together.

"You'll see."

The light turns green, and I twist the throttle. She switches her grip to my waist, and I can feel her knees pressing into the backs of mine. I creep around the curves as we drive through town and onto Via Aurelia, the sea on our left, the terraces on our right. No afraid, no afraid, I hear Yuri say in my head. I twist the throttle a little and feel the motor level out beneath me, the rattle of the chain falling into a rhythm. I can feel the breath entering and leaving her body, her weight leaning with mine around the curves.

Shit, God, please don't let us fly over the cliff. Please? If not for us, for Papà and Yuri.

We pass the disco and Laigueglia, and go around the cape toward the valley of the Dianos. I make a quick apology to Fede as we pass fifty, and I open the throttle all the way. The wind whips at my face and hands, the sun reflecting up at me from the metal tank and the tar in the road. The cars are flying by, the sea unmoving to our left, the sun steady overhead. I think about Luca and the French girl, and my eyes start to water in the wind. Because you know what? I think God, he, she, it, whatever, wants this for us—to ride a moped down the coast in the embrace of a girl. Maybe this is exactly what God kicked us out of the garden for.

We turn inland, and the road becomes narrow and ragged at the edges. They didn't make this road until Papà was a boy, and everyone had to give up a small piece of their land to do it. It's nothing but steep rises and hairpin turns snaking through olive groves and along garden walls, dodging around the backs of chicken coops and tiny chapels to the Virgin Mary.

245

We used to come up to the meadows all the time when we were kids. Especially before Papà and Nonno had our side-by-side apartments renovated and installed the air-conditioning. August was the worst. The mugginess would rise up to our room, soaking into our skin until even the salt of the sea couldn't wash it away. Sometimes Mamma would leave the shop early and collect us from the beach. She'd pile us into the back of the shop Ape, and we'd stay up in the meadows all afternoon, leaving just enough light to steer back down the hill. I don't remember the first time or the last, only the habit of it—Luca and I bouncing in the bed of the Ape, the buzz of the motor, and the flush of green that met our eyes as we crested the hill.

Zhuki and I round the final switchback. The hill rears up, then ripples into meadows, the rolling foothills of the Alps in the distance. Zhuki sighs. I cut the motor and let my feet skip along the ground as we coast, the road finally crumbling into dirt. There's a nice breeze up here, like someone has thrown a bucket of water on the broiling sun.

"I can't believe it," she says. She gets off, turning around in wonder and relief. "Who would ever think this is up here? I always thought our villa was the top of the hill."

"That's the thing about the terraces," I say. "They always trick you into thinking you're finally at the top."

I dig the remaining two sandwiches out of the seat compartment, along with a blanket and some matches Fede must keep in there for when he's trying to make nice with some girl. Good old Fede. We spend the rest of the afternoon up in the meadow with no plan, and it's like being a kid again. We shut off our phones and take off our shoes. Zhuki shows me how to hunt for mushrooms, and I bring her to the stream I remember. We skip stones and build leaf boats, and she shows me what she promises are the most popular Ukrainian children's games. There's one that involves chasing and hitting each other with a belt, and one that is like hide-and-seek, only the penalty for being found is to get your arm rubbed until it burns.

"They really toughen the kids up in Ukraine, eh?"

"Most of them have a hard life ahead of them anyway."

"Do you think you'll ever go back there?"

"I doubt it."

"Not even when Yuri's career is over?"

"I don't know. Yuri and I have talked about opening a restaurant. But probably not there."

"What kind of restaurant?"

"Ukrainian food, of course. Vareniki, borscht, blintzes . . . but I would make my restaurant modern. Not so heavy. Euro-Ukrainian. I used to cook at such a place in Kiev." She picks at the grass, extracting small wildflowers and collecting them in a bunch.

"Why do you have to wait for Yuri? Why can't you open a restaurant on your own? I'm sure he would loan you the money."

"But where?"

I swallow hard. "Why not here? In Italy, I mean."

"Oh, it would be difficult to open a restaurant in Italy. People don't know Ukrainian food at all, and there are so many good restaurants. Even in the small towns. And then if Yuri moves to a different team?" She pulls a long blade of grass and wraps it around the stems of the flowers.

"You can always visit them."

"Oh, I cannot imagine this."

"No?"

"Yuri is my entire family. Little Yuri. Principessa. Ihor. Mykola."

"Not Tatiana?"

She makes a face. "Not Tatiana. Tatiana and I, we are very different women."

"Thank God."

She grins. "Yes. And what about you, Etto-Son-of-Butcher? Do you always want to be a butcher?"

"I don't even know if I'm a real butcher yet."

"That's not what your papà says. He was talking to Yuri the other day and saying how proud he is of you. He says you are a natural."

"He did?" I try to imagine Papà saying anything remotely like this.

"You know, Etto, I think you're lucky."

"Why?"

"You have no questions about your life. You already know the answers.

Where will you live . . . what profession will you have. You mustn't keep asking and wondering what is around the corner. Your whole life is under control."

"It sounds really sad and pathetic when you put it like that."

"I don't mean to say it this way."

I've never talked to anyone like this. With Mamma, I just assumed she knew, when maybe she didn't, really. And with everybody else, especially in the last couple of years, it was like a punishment I could dole out, that if they couldn't manage to ask me the right question when I was in the right mood, they didn't deserve to know anything about me. But as Zhuki and I watch the sun go down over the foothills, I feel an urgency to tell her the things I left unsaid with Mamma and Luca, the things Papà and I can only skirt around.

I stand up and brush the dirt and grass off my culo. "I want to show you something."

"That's what all the boys say."

"You're funny."

"What is it?"

"It's a surprise."

"A good surprise or a bad surprise?"

"Trust me."

It's much harder to steer the moped on the way down, and I have to brake almost constantly to fight the pull of gravity. By the time we reach Via Partigiani, the shadow of the hill swallows us up, the headlight slowly opening the infinite road. I drive up the service road, kill the engine, and coast. The kickstand won't hold in the grass, so I balance the moped against Luca's headstone.

"What, you have some new moves or something?"

"I wish."

I lead her to the liceo door and pull out the keys.

She laughs. "We used to break into our liceo in Ukraine all the time, too," she says. "We had codes on our doors, and the director always said they were changing them, but they never did."

I push the door open and flip on the lights in the corridor. They buzz and flicker as Zhuki looks around. She wanders along the class photos and reaches up to touch each one. "Are you in one of these?"

"We never got to take our picture. It closed the year before we graduated."

"Your father, then?"

I show her Papà's and Nonno's pictures, but she lingers on the others, too. The moonlight pools on the wooden floor and casts our shadows on the wall. I lead her down the corridor, but she takes her time, standing on her toes to look into the window of the director's office and opening the door of each classroom along the way.

"This is cool, Etto. Thanks for bringing me here."

I wait at the end of the corridor, in front of Charon's door. My heart pounds as she reaches for the handle.

"What's in here?"

I let her open the door herself, and she stands frozen in the doorway, her eyes darting around the room, taking it in. At first there's almost a look of fear on her face, like I've been in here flaying my victims and sewing their skin into suits. She mutters a few words in Ukrainian and walks slowly around the edges of the table towers, her head flipped toward the ceiling in the same contortion I've held for the past two months.

"You know," I say, like some fottuto tour guide, "by the time he was finished, Michelangelo's eyes were so warped, he couldn't read a book unless he held it above his head and looked up."

"*You* did all this, Etto?" she says, and she starts to climb.

"It's stupid, I know. And I'm probably never going to finish it. I don't even know why I started in the first place . . ."

"Everyone is here. Look. There's Fede. And Franco . . . Martina . . . Tatiana . . . your papà . . ."

I climb up after her. "You recognize them?"

"They're really good, Etto. They look like they do in real life." She stares at the panel of Papà kicking me out of the shop. She screws up her face and breaks into a laugh. "Is that *you*?"

Her eyes are so bright, but I don't look away. I feel her reaching for the front of my shirt, only this time instead of a push, I feel a pull. I put my hands on her waist, and it feels like we're floating on the sea, the wooden table like the deck of a ship buoying us up, sent to right my listing life.

I know, I know. You are used to my generation's compulsion to report everything we do the instant we do it, and I can hear you over there saying, *enough* with the fottuto metaphors—what *happened*? And especially if you are American and obsessed with keeping tallies and statistics on every aspect of your life, you will probably even want to know what base I got to and if I "scored."

And I will answer you as I would answer Fede or Bocca or any of them: It's none of your fottuto business.

But if it were . . . if it were, I would tell you that there is nothing to compare to the touch of another human being. The bridging of a synapse. A spark of life.

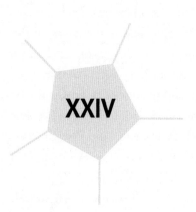

XXIV

hen I wake up on Sunday morning, there's a low buzzing inside my veins, like the home-strung power lines that zigzag between the houses toward the top of the hill. I hear the distant sound of The Band coming closer, and I get up, open the shutters, and poke my head into the morning air. The Band is a bunch of guys mostly Papà's age who go out in the streets and play whenever they feel like it. Sometimes it's for the religious holidays or to serenade someone for a birthday or a new baby, but most of the time, there's no reason at all. Once a summer at the height of the season, when the tourists are packed into every closet and storage room, they do an early morning march-by at full blast. Just to remind everyone who owns the town.

I watch the tops of their heads as they pass by below. Claudia's papà is one of the main organizers, so Casella's been drafted into The Band, and sure enough, I spot his trumpet and his ponytail in the back of the line.

"Looking good," I shout.

"Hey, Etto!" Claudia's papà answers. "Say hello to my new son-in-law."

Casella lifts his head and gives a sleepy grin. He puts the trumpet to his mouth and blows a note that lasts until the end of the vico.

I walk up the hill to pick up Nonna for church, and I don't feel the incline at all. It's like I'm still floating next to the ceiling of the aula, and as I sit in the courtyard of the church, my body fires off celebratory sparks. The doors are flung open to the warm sunshine, and as they cycle through the Holy, Holy, Holy, the Our Father, and the rest of it, I make up my own prayers.

"Shit. Thank you, God. I don't deserve her, but . . . shit. Thank you. Thank you. That's all. Thank you. And sorry for the cursing."

The last song plays, and everyone exits, squinting as the sun hits their eyes.

"Congratulations," I tell Casella, and he smiles sheepishly. Claudia thrusts her hand in my face, the diamond sticking up like a lollipop.

"Can you believe it, Etto? Can you believe he finally did it? He even got down on his knee, just like in the movies. . . ."

But I'm only half listening to Claudia, because behind her, Zhuki is coming down the stairs with the nonne. She smiles at me, and my face must register it like a mirror because Claudia interrupts herself and turns around to look.

"Ah, I've heard the rumor that Etto has a girlfriend, but I didn't quite believe it," she says.

"She's not really my girlfriend."

"Whatever, Etto."

Zhuki comes over to us. She's wearing a blue skirt, and I try to think back and remember if she was wearing a skirt the other times I saw her at church.

"Ciao."

"Ciao."

"How is it going?" she asks.

"Claudia and Casella just got engaged."

Claudia thrusts the ring in Zhuki's face.

"Beautiful," Zhuki says. "Congratulations."

I watch her as she asks all the polite questions about when the wedding will be and how Casella asked her. Claudia talks on and on, Casella clinging to her side, the nonne stopping to congratulate them. But Zhuki is the only one in focus for me, everyone else blurring around her.

"Are you going to the match this afternoon?" Casella asks me.

"Of course. Are you?"

"Sure."

"You're going?" Claudia says.

"Why not?"

And Claudia starts talking again, something about her mother and the wedding, but it must be at a different frequency that only brides can hear, because all I sense is the same low buzzing in my veins as when I woke up.

After dinner, Nonno, Nonna, Papà, and I drive to the field in the 2CV. We pull up through the service road, and Nonno and I meet gales of laughter as we unload two large jugs from the back, sloshing with icy lemonade.

"Ah, but you had to buy those lemons didn't you, Caccia?"

Cruel.

If I live eight hundred years, I will never believe how many people have come up to the field on a Sunday afternoon. Not only the regulars from Martina's but even people like Signor Cavalcanti, who has enough money to buy himself a nice Serie B team, and Benito, the other butcher, exiled for decades by his own arrogance. Even the students home from university for the summer, who usually want nothing to do with these backward old men. They are all out there on the field, chasing a fottuto calcio ball.

While the first match runs, the women unpack blankets and picnic lunches. Tatiana is among them, standing expressionless in her dark glasses and capris, only clapping with her fingertips when Yuri or Vanni scores a goal, as if she's too good to cheer for amateurs.

But I have to say, for amateurs, they're starting to look pretty good out there. The first day, each man tried to be his own superstar, his own Ronaldo, his own Eusébio. But with a full week of practice, they are passing foot to foot, and their bodies have begun to remember the formations of their youth. Today they have enough breath not only to run up and down the field without falling down but to scream out directives and encouragements to their teammates.

"Go, Franco!"

"Take the shot, Gubbio!"

"Faster! Faster!" the Mangona brothers shout. Tired of running, they've declared themselves both the official coaches and referees, and they ride up and down the sidelines on their mountain bikes, shouting at men twice their age.

"Come on, Padre! Get him!"

Vanni Fucci runs down the field, hotly pursued by Father Marco, who has the passion for the game if not the talent. Vanni pulls out his fanciest footwork, and Father Marco ends up in a heap in Vanni's wake as Vanni cruises easily to the goal. And even though it's Vanni, I can hardly believe my eyes when he circles back toward Father Marco, waving his figs in the air.

"Peck at this!" he shouts at Father Marco, who tries to laugh it off as the other men help him off the ground.

The crowd along the sidelines is hushed, except for Tatiana, who's laughing her fottuto head off. The Mangona brothers stop their bicycles and consult, one whispering, the other shaking his head. Finally, they both look up at Vanni.

"Foul!"

"What?" Vanni stops in his tracks.

"Foul!"

"For what?"

"For being an arrogant stronzo." One of them pulls a yellow card from his pocket and thrusts it in Vanni's direction.

"That's not a foul!" Vanni shouts. "You show me the rule book. That is not a foul! Yuri, are you going to stand there and let this happen? This is ridiculous."

But Yuri only laughs. He's on the sidelines with Papà, enjoying the show.

"Your papà seems like he's having a good time," Fede says. He sits down next to me and unwraps one of his mamma's sandwiches.

"I know. I think for Papà, it's a little like having Luca back."

"That doesn't bother you?" he mumbles through a big bite of sandwich.

I look over at Papà and Yuri, heads together, talking strategy. "He's happy."

"You want a sandwich?" Fede asks. "My mamma made them."

"Later maybe."

"Did you hear about Claudia and Casella?" he asks, and he takes another bite.

"Yeah. You okay?"

He shrugs. I watch him finish the sandwich in silence. He wipes his fingers on the paper and crumples it into a ball.

The whistle blows.

"We're on," he says, and he gives the crumpled paper to his mamma, along with a kiss on the cheek, before he sprints onto the field.

Fede's team is playing Papà's, and I watch as the old guys and the young guys blur into the same, universal age of boys playing calcio. Each time they manage to string four or five passes together all the men throw up their hands and shout, "Ole!" I look at the nonne, still gossiping, oblivious to the match, the babies being passed around, the mothers restraining the toddlers from running straight to their papás on the field. And for some reason, all I can think about is Martin Malaspina. And Mr. Malaspina, I don't even know if you're still in the movie business, if you're in India or Hollywood or Timbuktu, but if only you could see this, you would wonder why you left, and you would reproclaim this town as the last place on earth that is simple and pure, where a patchwork of heaving picnic blankets sanctifies the ground, calcio stars are brought down from on high, and those San Benedettons, well, they really know how to, you know, live.

"We're on next, Etto." Zhuki pulls up her socks and double knots her cleats, and the Mangona brothers call out a two-minute warning.

On the field, Yuri passes to Papà, who fakes out Fede and scores a goal. I watch Papà jump up and down, shouting and slapping fives with everyone on his team. When he comes to Yuri, he pulls him into a hug, his bear paws pounding against Yuri's back.

"Good shot, Papà! Good shot!" I shout. And maybe I'm a bad son for even thinking this, much less saying it, but I think it's the first time in two years, or maybe in my life, that I don't resent him. The first time I've felt completely free.

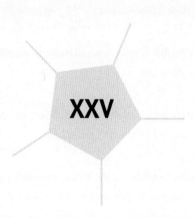

XXV

$\mathcal{T}$he rest of the days until Ferragosto go by in a blur. When I'm with Zhuki, it feels like I'm tumbling through space, nothing under my control. In the afternoons, we wander around the hill paths with the restless Germans, from the public olive oil mill all the way to the harbor, and as far up as the village Nonna was originally from, where from twelve thirty to four thirty, the streets are abandoned and there's not a single shutter open. Places I haven't been in years.

Now that Tatiana is back from Milan, Zhuki leaves the kids at home and comes to the bar with Yuri, Mykola, and Ihor, and she quickly becomes part of the Ferragosto festa planning committee. She and Martina pore over their lists at the bar, organizing the food, while Yuri and Papà work out the calcio tournament and Silvio takes care of everything else. Once a night, the entire bar stops for an update on the progress and to deal with the daily crises. Only in the past few days, Signor Buonconte has said they can't use his land. The festa has been held there ever since I can remember, and it's the perfect setting—a wide field between two torrents. But with no rain, he's afraid of the grass catching fire.

"We'll have it on the calcio field, then," Silvio says.

"What about the risk of fire? All those shrubs and trees?"

"We'll start soaking the ground today. Etto, can you manage that?"

"Isn't there a watering ban?"

"We'll have Gubbio declare an exception . . . Gubbio!" Silvio shouts over to the card tables.

"Yes?"

"We need an exception to the water ban. For the festa."

"Fine with me." And Gubbio raises his hand, giving the benediction of the comune.

"You're going to have the semifinals for the calcio tournament on Friday afternoon, then?" Martina asks.

"And Saturday morning."

"Until when?"

"Three o'clock."

"Three o'clock? How are we supposed to set up in time?"

"We'll have plenty of lifeguards to help."

"Can't we end earlier? Yuri? Carlo?"

"I don't think so. We have fifteen teams now." Papà pulls out a piece of paper and consults with Yuri. "Make that sixteen. The only way we can end earlier is if we start at six in the morning."

This idea is immediately and vociferously vetoed throughout the room, and Martina sighs.

"Don't worry," Silvio reassures her. "It'll all come together. It always does."

He's right. Every year, they start with nothing, and somehow the festa materializes. The bar and restaurant owners along the passeggiata loan chairs and tables, and the bagni owners donate sections of boardwalk and lifeguards to help with the setting up and taking down. Guido sends the backup sound system from Le Rocce, and the Turks who run the Truck Show pack up the bouncing castle for the kids and bring by a couple of generators. Sandro's furniture shop loans out their truck. Father Marco saves up the candle stubs that have burned too low for the holders and hands over the church kitchen to the nonne for two weeks so they can roll enough trofie to stuff the freezer. The villas on the hill loan their grills and what's left of their gardens after the drought. No one trusts the Standa to provide anything but the paper products and plastic cups, which they do with a loud proclamation in their front window testifying to their sponsorship. For the rest of the food, they circulate a list around the smaller shops. There's always competition among the bakers—whose rolls, focaccia, and pastries will be featured. Papà gets the list first and signs up to contribute the sausages, leaving the chicken to Benito. Hollywood chicken, Papà calls it, because who knows what's in those puffy breasts?

"This is our second Ferragosto in Italy, and I still don't understand what it is," Zhuki says. We're sharing one of the chaises at the beach, watching the action. It's so hot out today, even Tatiana is here, lying on the chaise next to us in her bikini and heels, yapping on the phone.

"What do you mean, what is it?"

"I mean, what's it for?" Her head turns to follow the crowd of young boys being led out to the molo by Yuri and Ihor. There are probably twenty of them, and they climb up the stairs and spread themselves out along the concrete ledge, far enough apart not to conk their heads together as they jump. Yuri gives the signal, and they spring off one by one down the line, each bobbing up in a wreath of white foam. The tourists applaud, and the waiters step out onto the passeggiata in their long aprons.

"What's it for? Boh. For August fifteenth. For the holiday. For summer vacation."

"That's it?"

"Maybe before it was religious. Or Communist. Come to think of it, it used to be one of the 'festivals of unity,' but the Communists must've run out of money to throw it."

"You have a lot of Communists here?" She looks alarmed.

"All over Italy."

"*Really?*"

"But they're not real Communists. They're not out there murdering or collectivizing or anything. They don't even get elected that often."

"Then what do they do?"

"They hold festas."

"Will there be any Communists at this festa?"

"Franco and Mimmo."

"Franco and Mimmo are Communists?"

Franco is patrolling the edge of the water, his fingertips absentmindedly rubbing up and down the corrugation of his ribs, feeling the scar that runs up his side like a seam. Zhuki eyes him uneasily. On the other chaise, Tatiana's conversation is becoming more shrill.

"I'm surprised Tatiana is here today," I say.

"There must be a paparazzo around. I think she calls them herself sometimes."

"Who's she talking to on the phone anyway?"

"Her mother."

"What do they talk about so . . . violently?"

Zhuki shrugs. "Clothes. Gossip. Should she get plastic surgery? Why is Ilary Blasi getting more publicity than she did when she was pregnant?"

"Has she always been like that?"

"Not so bad as she is now. But I told my brother in the beginning she was not a good match for him. It was a terrible argument we had. The worst ever. I think he saw problems, too, but he did not want to say."

"Why did he marry her, then?"

She sighs and rolls her eyes. "This is a question for a man, not a woman."

"Zhuki!" Yuri is back on the sand, dripping, tapping the face of his watch. His gestures are so graceful, everything he wears or touches somehow looks like he's advertising it—watches, baseball caps, even the biodegradable shampoo he squirts on his palm as he sticks Little Yuri and Principessa under the showers.

"I should go," she says. "Yuri wants to eat and take a nap before the elimination rounds this afternoon."

"He's really taking this seriously."

"He always takes calcio seriously."

"What about 'Have fun' and 'It is only a game'?"

She laughs. "That was only for you."

✳   ✳   ✳

Three or four hours later we're up on the field for the semifinals. Only three or four hours. But I can tell immediately that something has changed in the time between. Zhuki's face is clouded and dark, and she won't look at me. When we start to play, she runs cautiously around the field, quickly passing the ball away whenever it comes to her.

"Shoot it, Zhuki, shoot it!" I shout, but she only passes it off.

By the half, they are winning, 2–0, and I have no choice but to take over.

"Come on, Luca," I say. "Can you help a guy out down here?" And I know you will never believe this, but I swear, he does. Through the second half, it feels like my feet are acting on their own, reciting moves I've never practiced, my breath washing through me as easily as the wind. I evade. I dribble. I dodge. I bewilder. I score two goals, and we end up winning 3–2, locking us safely into Saturday's brackets.

Zhuki is upset, though. I can tell. I follow her off the field, but she's walking too fast.

"Hey." Fede intercepts me and slaps me on the back. "I never knew you could play calcio like that."

"That makes two of us."

I notice that Zhuki is limping and wincing, headed toward the liceo.

"What's the matter with Zhuki?" Fede asks.

"I don't know . . . hey, Zhuki! Wait up!"

I follow her through the cypresses to the fifth-year bench.

"Hey."

She glances over her shoulder. "Hey," she says. "Nice goals."

"Thanks."

She has one cleat off already, her sock pulled down around her heel. She moves her hand, and there's a wide, red burn through the concave of her ankle, pinpricked with blood.

"Somebody cleated me."

"They're really excited today."

"I guess."

We sit in silence for a minute. There's something about the way she slumps against the bench and clutches her foot that makes me scared to ask, but finally, I do.

"Is everything okay?"

"Not really."

"What is it?"

"It's that suka."

"What?"

"Tatiana. She's talking about going back to Genoa already."

"I thought you were planning on staying here through the fall. Through October."

"That's what Yuri wanted. And what everyone else wants."

"So . . . ?"

"You don't understand. Tatiana is trying very strongly to convince Yuri."

"So talk to Yuri . . ."

"It's not that easy. Yuri's deaf and blind when it comes to Tatiana."

"Well, if worse comes to worst, you can always stay here on your own."

"And then what?" She sighs and looks me straight in the eye. "Look, Etto, I like it here." She sweeps her arm across the view of the sea. "What's not to like? It's great for a summer, for a few months. But this is not real life."

"It's my real life. It's a lot of people's real lives."

"I'm sorry, I don't mean to offend you." She looks down at her foot. There's some clapping and cheering from the field, shouts of "Over here! Over here!" Then finally, "Goooooooooooooooooooooooooooooooool!" We listen to the shouting peak and ebb. Zhuki tucks a corkscrew of hair behind her ear.

"Genoa is not so far," I say. "I could visit you."

"I don't know, Etto. And what if Yuri doesn't stay in Genoa?"

But I don't get a chance to answer because a bloodcurdling scream fills the air. Zhuki's face is immediately scribbled away by panic.

"It's Principessa," she says, pulling her sock back over her ankle. She runs to the field, cleat in hand, and I follow behind.

"Paparazzi! Paparazzi!" Everyone is shouting in general alarm, every man on the field gathered into a tight cluster around Yuri as Silvio and Papà march toward the cypresses.

"This is the police," Silvio announces. "Put your hands up. We know you're back there."

"Porca puttana, Silvio, this is no time for the *law*," Gubbio shouts, following them. "Yes, we know you're back there, you sneaky little mamma's boy! Grow some palle and come out and face some real men." But before the three of them reach the edge of the field, the cypresses begin to shake and scream in Italian.

"Stop it, you crazy testa di cazzo! Hey, hey! Ow! Give that back! Give that back, you dumb gorilla! Ow! I will prosecute you, you figlio di puttana! You hear me? Prosecute you! I have witnesses! Do you see? I have witnesses! Ow! What are you doing? Cazzo! What are you *doing?*"

A skinny emo type in skintight jeans and a thin T-shirt lands sprawling on the sideline, as if the cypresses have spit him out. Ihor appears from behind the trees, chewing something. He advances toward the paparazzo, who scrambles away, and it's only when he's at a safe distance that he turns around and shouts.

"Fine, you stupid Serie CI Ukrainian and your damn mafia here. That's how you want it? Well, you'll have to read about it in the tabloids, I guess. You'll find out soon enough though. You'll find out soon enough."

"Hey, you twerp," Nonno answers. "You're a disgrace to your papà and your papà's papà and your ancestors all the way back to the slime your family came from."

Papà raises his eyebrows at me.

"Good one, Nonno."

Meanwhile, Ihor walks toward the pack of men, and it parts for him like a splitting amoeba, revealing Yuri with Principessa wrapped around his legs. Vanni Fucci is on one side, cowering, and Little Yuri is on the other, crossing his arms defiantly.

"What did he say?" Yuri asks. "What did he say?"

Ihor spits something into his fist. He holds it up and places it in Yuri's upturned palm. It's a tiny, blue plastic memory card, mauled almost beyond recognition.

"But what did he say?" Yuri says again. "What did he say?"

XXVI

*B*ack when Luca was playing in the regional youth leagues, Luca and Fede used to do this thing where Luca would make a complete idiot of himself. He would dribble the ball down the field, doing every fancy move he could think of, and the defenders would be in a panic, triple-teaming him, trying to guess the next of his antics. And then, in the middle of the chaos, Luca would give one imperceptible flick of his foot and kick it to Fede, who'd be shuffling around like a homeless guy somewhere in the periphery, no one watching him. And of course Fede would shoot it straight into the goal. They called the play Keep Your Fottuto Eye on the Ball. And that's exactly what happens in the next week. I keep my fottuto eye on the ball, and I'm left gaping into an empty space where it used to be.

There are four matches on Saturday, and we win ours handily against Mimmo and Franco's team, thanks to a goal I squeeze out in the last few minutes of the match. Vanni and Yuri's match is next, and they go at it like schoolboys, chasing each other around the field, locked in combat. Maybe this refusal to lose is the characteristic above everything else that has allowed them to become the giants of this world, their faces on billboards as big as buildings, the vibrations of their footsteps felt around the globe. Except in America, of course.

Papà wants some time to practice and strategize for the semifinals and the finals on Sunday, but as soon as the last whistle blows, Martina is on the field giving directives.

You wouldn't believe it unless you saw it—a whole festa created out of nothing in a few short hours. The furniture truck is too big to pull up on the service road, so they have to park it on Via Partigiani and chug everything up the hill on human steam. Martina and Silvio stand in the middle of the field splitting the deliveries into two piles—edibles and nonedibles. Chairs: Silvio. Chicken: Martina. Generator: Silvio. Box of eggplant: Martina. We crawl up and down the mule track like ants, then back and forth across the terrace, moving the tent, the folding tables, the grills, and a generator into formation for Martina, then fitting the pieces of boardwalk together to make the dance floor. Guido, Bocca, and Aristone are busy building the stage and setting up the speakers and the soundboard, and the Turks from the Truck Show struggle to inflate the bouncing castle in the far corner. Nicola Nicolini has been appointed the subchair of "atmosphere," and he stands in the middle of the field, his hands on his hips like a traffic cop, supervising us in how to aesthetically scatter the tables and chairs, string the lights in the trees, and set the candles on the tables.

"Allora . . ." Martina says, standing over the mountain of food as Mimmo and Franco light the grills. There are five of us officially conscripted to the cooking tent—Zhuki, me, Fede, Fede's Mamma, and Martina, but twice as many nonne appear and insist on helping. We attack at once, following Martina's orders. We season the chicken, cut up the bread, grate the cheese, chop up tomatoes and artichokes for salads, and make fresh pesto out of a pile of basil the size of a small tree. Mamma used to be part of the cooking team, too. She wasn't nearly as good a cook as Martina, but I have an image of the two of them standing side by side under this very tent, laughing until they were both sore.

"Etto, maybe you can help Yuri get started with the shashlik."

Yuri convinced Martina that this summer, there should be something Ukrainian served at the festa, and he's volunteered to make a special kind of Ukrainian shish kebab. I find him in front of the liceo, squatting over a homemade barbecue fashioned from bricks and a shiny oven shelf that must have come from some ten-thousand-euro oven inside Signora Malaspina's villa.

"Ciao, Etto," he says.

"Martina told me to help you with the shashlik."

At his side are a heap of sharpened sticks and an industrial bucket that looks like it could be plaster or paint. He pulls the top off, and inside is a pile of beef, neatly cubed and nestled in chunks of onion. The aroma puffs up in a cloud under my nose, and it rivals anything I've ever smelled in Martina's or Nonna's kitchens.

"Normally we use pig, but your father does not sell pig."

I start building the shashlik with meat and pieces of onion, leaning them against the sides of the bucket, anchored in more meat. Yuri meticulously stacks branches under the oven rack until it starts to look like art. He finally lights it, the smoke curling up in thin ribbons.

"This is ultimate secret for shashlik," he says. "Green wood, good fire, not so hot. My sister teach me this. She is very good cook, you know. She worked in fancy restaurant in Kiev."

"She told me."

"She is very good woman, my sister. My children are lucky to have her for aunt."

"They're lucky to have you as a papà," I say.

"Eh."

He squats across the barbecue from me, his eyes fixed on the glowing wood, and we work in silence, the aroma from the meat making my stomach growl. He's dressed in ordinary shorts and a T-shirt with a plain blue baseball cap and some beat-up brown sandals, completely stripped of his endorsements and his Serie A. He bows his head, tending to the shashlik in silence for a few minutes before he looks up at me.

"Etto, I tell you something," he says. The smoke and the waves of heat distort his face. "Etto, I am not innocent man. I knew about the fix. The sporting judges, they give me punish I deserve."

"But, Yuri, you got off the field."

"But I knew. And I did not say nothing."

"I'm sure you couldn't have been the only one on Genoa who knew."

"Of course. Everybody knows. The managers, they tell me everybody do this. This is business as usual in Italy, they say. And if prosecutors find out, they will fix. They will fix so nobody will get the ban." He shakes his head. "But these are excuses. I knew and I did not say nothing to nobody. And I will have to tell Little Yuri someday. This is most terrible."

"Why wasn't everybody else banned, then?"

Yuri's face gives a shrug his shoulders don't follow through on. "Because the investigators, they take me into little room. They ask me questions, and I say the truth. The others, they go into little room and they say lies."

"That's so unfair."

"Not fair? How? I did wrong. I was punish. All is fair. For me at least." Yuri stands up in the column of smoke and breathes in deeply. "Anyway, do not feel sorry for me. Feel sorry for the little boy I was twenty years ago, the little boy who runs around field in Strilky and dreams of becoming calcio player. Do not feel sorry for me now."

I wait for him to say something else, but he only bows his head and tends to the shashlik. Martina calls me back to the food tent. The pace is quicker now, with only half an hour until the ticket sales start. I find myself elbow to elbow with Zhuki, coiling and skewering sausages and stacking them into an enormous foil tray. We haven't talked much since yesterday. The words we said are still teetering precariously on top of one another, and I think neither of us wants to be the one to pile on the wrong word and upset the balance.

"So where are the kids?" I finally ask.

"Over by the bouncing castle with Tatiana and Vanni."

"I'm surprised she came down for this."

"Me too. Too many peasants down here."

I laugh.

"It's true. She uses that word. Peasants."

"Ouch."

"Testing, testing." Guido is at the microphone. "Testing, one, two, three."

He starts to croon a Frank Sinatra song, and the lifeguards putting together the boardwalk load him with whistles until he gets off the stage. Zhuki laughs. I look out over the terraces and onto the sea. It's been cloudy all day, the sea below a dense, glossy green, like hard candy poured into a mold.

The ticket sales start at six, and the people come streaming up from the town and from all over the hill. The first wave is the nonne whose husbands have passed away, and who come straight to the food tent to help or at least hover. They reach over the folding table and pat our cheeks.

"So cute you two are."

"The babies would be beautiful."

My face turns red. I glance sideways at Zhuki, and she's embarrassed, too.

After the nonne with no husbands come the nonne with husbands, who sit across from each other at the small tables, holding hands like teenagers. Then the middle-aged couples, who split into camps of men and women, gossiping and complaining about each other just as they did in school. We start dishing up the antipasti: tomato, roasted pepper, and olive salads; vegetable fritters; tiny artichokes sprinkled with parmesan, oil, and salt. Then the trofie, gnocchi, and farinata for the adults, focaccia for the children. Camilla is set up selling tickets at a table to the side, and soon, there are so many people in line, Fede has to go over and help. When the Communists were running the festa, all the money went to the cause; now it goes to fireworks.

Around seven o'clock, the people our age start showing up, skipping the food tent for the drinks table. Guido takes the canned music off, and the first band warms up. It's Belacqua and his band, a bunch of kids two classes below us in liceo who have piercings and flannel shirts and only play American music. In the end, everyone but the tourists will be here. And the thirteen-year-olds. Well, the thirteen-year-olds will pretend they're too cool to come, though toward the end of the night, they will start appearing, beers hidden under their shirts, hovering at the edges of the dance floor.

"Bone down nana dead man town, fur hid a took when ah hidda gra-a-a." Belacqua tries to make his voice gravelly like Bruce, and I imagine

Charon cuffing him upside the head and telling him to go back and study his English.

"Tesoro," Martina calls from the other side of the tent, where she's already frying the frittelle for dessert. "Why don't you two start taking the chickens off if they're ready?"

There are four grills put together, two of them tented with half barrels for the chicken, and two with the nautilus-shaped sausages. Yuri is still tending the shashlik, and every once in a while appears with a handful of smoking skewers. I make myself some towel mitts and lift the half barrels off the grills, and Zhuki and I start an assembly line, me popping the chicken off the skewer and breaking it down, her spraying the pieces with a mist of white wine and wrapping them in tinfoil. When the chicken is finished, we cut the sausage spirals into links and stuff them into a dwindling pile of rolls, start a new shift of sausages, and put the anchovies on. In the meantime, Martina and Fede's mamma are working furiously on the desserts, dipping the fritters in and out of an oil bath balanced between two or three burners, cutting apart squares of grape focaccia, and slathering crepes with Nutella. The crowds surge, exchanging tickets for plates as fast as the nonne can pass them over the counter, and the second band starts—Casella, Mimmo, Claudia's papà, and some of the others, playing all the old favorites. The young people clustered around the stage dissipate, and the dance floor fills with couples and smooth dancing.

"Ciao." Claudia comes around to the side of the cooking tent. The grills have been packing the tent with heat all evening, but finally, the breeze off the sea is starting to pick up.

"I heard the good news." Martina wipes her hands on her apron and leans over one of the folding tables to give Claudia a kiss. "Congratulations. You two make a wonderful couple."

"Thanks, Martina." But I see Claudia throw a nearly imperceptible glance in Fede's direction. I'm the only one who seems to notice, and at first I think I'm delirious from too much time spent under this fottuto tent, but no, it's definitely there. I watch the back of Fede's head at the ticket table. There's a steady line, and Fede and Camilla are working faster than we are, tearing the tickets off the roll and collecting the money in a lockbox Camilla balances on her lap.

"Are you having anything to eat?" Martina asks Claudia.

"Maybe a little later. Got to fit into the dress, right? Everything looks great, though, Martina. You've really surpassed yourself this year."

"Thank you, dear."

Claudia goes off to find Casella, and Martina leaves her station at the back of the tent and hovers behind us.

"Etto, Zhuki, why don't you two take a break?"

"It's okay, Martina, we can stay."

But Martina takes the knife out of my hand. "Go on. Get out of here for a little while. Eat. Dance. I've got plenty of help now. Go."

She loads us down with paper plates and bowls of food and sends us off to the drinks table, where Franco and Bocca are lining up cups of wine and lemonade.

"Where are your tickets?" Bocca demands.

"Your auntie has them."

Franco laughs. I take two plastic cups of wine and hand one to Zhuki. All of Nicola Nicolini's careful planning has gone to hell. The café tables are bunched together against the wall of the next terrace, where the men are clustered around Yuri and Vanni Fucci. Zhuki and I sit on the grass at the edge of the dance floor and stare at the San Benedettons drifting and twirling by. Mimmo's leading the band, his shirt unbuttoned to the waist, and when the bridge of the song comes, he starts calling out to people by name.

"Zeno, let's put some more energy into that step! Napoleone, you'd better slow down before Ale needs to take you to the hospital!"

"Did your parents like to dance?" Zhuki asks.

"My papà, no. But my mamma did. She would always dance with the widowers at the festas and sagras."

"I'm sure they loved it."

"Some too much. But she would only move their hands away from the target and keep dancing."

"She sounds like a very kind person."

"Kind doesn't even cover it."

We watch Nonno and Nonna twirl by, Nonna free of her mind for a while, spinning and laughing, each turn making her more beautiful. I can see them as they were when they met on the beach as teenagers, and for the first time it occurs to me that Nonno doesn't sit around at Martina's like the other old guys and pass Nonna off to the care of a Polish woman every day. Even now when he's in the shop on Tuesdays, he makes sure she's with her friends.

"Etto and Zhuki," Mimmo calls to us over the microphone, and everyone turns in our direction. "Don't think we don't see you over there on the side. Why aren't you dancing? Are you going to be shown up by your grandparents?"

I shrug for both of us, and everyone laughs.

"Dai, Etto. Hurry, before she gets away," Gubbio says, laughing, as he and Signora Costanza twirl past. "Forza. Su, su!"

I think there might be nothing worse in this world than old people heckling you.

"Come on," she says, and we get to our feet.

It's a fast dance, a polka or something. One-two-three, one-two-three, Zhuki counts off as I try to lead her around the dance floor. The entire terrace blurs, and all I can hear is her voice in my ear. The polka melts into a slow song, and Casella comes off the stage and takes Claudia's hand.

"Ladies and gentlemen," Mimmo announces, "I want to call your attention to the soon-to-be Signor and Signora . . . Casella."

Casella takes a mock bow. The couples step apart and applaud for them, then rejoin. The music starts again. Camilla and Fede are out on the dance floor now, too, though Camilla is holding Fede at arm's length, as any smart girl does with a notorious vampire. We glide past the rest of our neighbors, who, clothed in motion and music and the glow of thousands of Christmas lights, seem like different people. Even I start to feel the grace in my body, my feet skimming the boardwalk, Zhuki's legs turning at the slightest pressure from my hand.

She tucks her head into my chest and sighs. "Genoa is not so far," she says.

"Genoa is not so far," I repeat.

The song winds down, and everyone relaxes. A breeze is picking up, riffling through the highest leaves of the trees on the next terrace up, and I feel a slight change in the air pressure. The pause in the music seems to last longer than usual.

"Look," Zhuki says. She points to Yuri climbing up on the stage. At first I think he might be drunk, but Mimmo hands him the microphone, and he walks steadily to the center of the stage.

"Ladies and gentlemen," he says in Italian. The microphone squawks, and Mimmo makes some adjustments.

"Neighbors," Yuri starts again. "I want to thank you for your hospitality these past two months. I also want to thank FIGC and the sporting judges, who give me such pleasant vacation."

Laughter runs through the audience, and a gust of wind blows the skirts of the nonne against their legs.

Yuri clears his throat. "We have enjoyed your music very much, and we very much would like to play for you traditional Ukrainian song." There's applause from the dance floor, and whistling and hooting from the cluster of chairs as Ihor mounts the steps to the stage. Yes, that's right. Slab-faced Ihor, plodding up the steps like he's performing a duty for the motherland. Mimmo hands him his guitar, and for some reason, we all laugh. I look over at Papà, who is red-faced and beaming. I can't tell if he's drunk or just happy.

Ihor sits down on a stool, holding the neck of the guitar delicately between his fingers. A trickle of notes falls from the strings, slow and soft, Ihor's eyes half-lidded, following their descent to the floor. Everyone stops laughing. The couples on the dance floor and the children playing at the edge of the terrace drop their arms and listen. Ihor takes a deep breath, and no one can believe the voice that follows the notes, the voice that seems to pick up the entire terrace and carry us to some secret forest in Ukraine. Yuri is on the stairs, kneeling on one knee, staring at Ihor with absolute stillness.

"It is about the Karpatsky," Zhuki says softly. "The Carpathian Mountains. It is about the rivers coming down the mountains to wash the blood from Soviet oppression." She leans against me, and I try to keep my heart from knocking through my chest and leaving bruises on the back of her head. Genoa is not so far. The wind starts to blow harder, and I look up to

271

the sky. The clouds are piling up, one on top of the other, like extra terraces, but no one else seems to notice. They are too transfixed by this man-child on the stage, who makes them feel like this music belongs to them, the childhood it comes from, and the distant land, too.

"Etto, I need to talk to you."

I feel Zhuki's weight pulling away as we both turn to look at Signor Cavalcanti, his face strained. He's just as stylish as Guido, his shirt perfectly ironed, his titanium watch fitted snugly around his wrist.

"Etto, I need to talk to you," he says again. He's so close I can smell his cologne.

"Right now?"

"Yes."

"What is it?"

"I need to know."

"Need to know what?"

"Is my son gay?"

"What?"

"Is Guido gay? I need you to tell me the truth."

I can smell the leaves unfurling, opening to the sky, the roots beneath the ground creaking as they reach farther down into the water table. It's going to rain. A few people in the crowd look up. The children on the edges grow restless and start to play a game of dodging between the cypresses.

"I need to know, Etto. You've never seen him leaving Nicola Nicolini's apartment?"

"That doesn't make him gay."

"In the morning?"

I look over at the sound table, where Nicola Nicolini and Guido have been sitting happily together all night. Ihor finishes the song and hands the guitar back to Mimmo with a sheepish grin.

"I don't know where he thinks *he's* going," Mimmo says into the microphone, and the crowd laughs.

When I turn back to Signor Cavalcanti, he's still waiting for an answer.

"Signor Cavalcanti," I say, "Guido is your *son*."

Mimmo starts another song, but there's a commotion among the children that's spreading to the adults, and when I turn back around, Signor Cavalcanti has disappeared back into the darkness at the edges of the dance floor.

"What is it?"

"Do you see it?"

"I've never seen one before."

"How many are there?"

The sky is sagging low, and there, toward Laigueglia, are three water trumpets, ambling across the flat plane of sea.

"Shit."

"What is it?" Zhuki asks.

"A water trumpet." I spin my finger in the air. "Three of them."

"Tornadoes?"

"If they decide to come onto the beach."

"Can they do that?"

"They can do whatever they want."

"Will they come up here?"

"I think we're too high." But, cazzo, what do I know about water trumpets? In twenty-two years, I've never seen one.

I hear the rain crumpling the dry leaves overhead and feel the first swollen drops bursting against my back. In a matter of seconds, the entire field is engulfed in noise—plastic sheets flapping in the wind, the clattering of tables and chairs and shouts of instructions. In the middle of the chaos, the Ukrainians crowd around Zhuki and click into their own tongue. I get to work with the others, folding and stacking the chairs around the dance floor as dark circles as big as euro coins start to blot out the light wood of the boardwalk.

"Yasno," I hear Zhuki shout through the wind.

"Dobre," Yuri answers, and he heads up the hill with Little Yuri and Principessa in tow.

"He will take Little Yuri and Principessa to the villa and bring the SUV down to help," Zhuki says to me, wiping the rain out of her eyes. "Have you seen Vanni?"

"I saw him go up the hill with Tatiana."

"When was that?"

"I don't know. A couple of songs before Ihor got up onstage?"

Zhuki, Ihor, Mykola, and I join the army disassembling the festa. The man whose fingers made the rings of heaven vibrate on a few strings is now stomping down the path to the truck, hoisting tables over his head. The rain is heavy now, the sky white like snow, and we troop up and down the mule track, slipping in the mud and reaching out to steady ourselves. I can feel the people catching me and pushing me up the hill from behind as the mud coats my feet, weighing them down. I recognize a few voices and Belacqua's laugh through the rain, but by now everyone is soaked through, and I have to look closely to see who is who.

Finally, the truck is loaded and the brake lights go on. Sandro starts the engine and it gurgles to life. The right tires spin, but ten of us attach ourselves to the bumper and the doors and push it out. I recognize the kids from Belacqua's band, who sit inside with their equipment and pull the door down with a bang. Thunder echoes over the sea and lightning saws the sky in half. People disperse in all directions, but I make my way back up the mule track. The bouncing castle has disappeared, and the entire field is empty except for the dance floor.

"Etto! Over here!" Nonno has pulled the 2CV onto the weedy service road at the back of the terrace. He and Nonna and Martina are squeezed into the front seat, with all the leftover food piled in the back and on Martina's lap. Martina has the window flipped up.

"Where's Papà?" I shout over the rain.

"He's already gone down to the shop. We're storing the food in the walk-ins."

"Have you seen the Ukrainians?"

He points. "Last I saw they were under the tent."

I sweep my hair away from my face with both hands and set out to find the Ukrainians. I find them huddled under the food tent, including Little Yuri and Principessa, who are now wearing bright yellow rain slickers and boots, like phosphorescent ghosts.

"Where's the SUV?"

"Up at the villa," Zhuki answers.

Yuri has an expression I've never seen before, as if his entire face has been deboned, leaving only skin, eyes, and tufts of hair.

"Did you find Vanni?"

Everyone glances at Yuri, and I know even before Zhuki says it.

"They were together."

"Shit."

"Etto, I need to ask a favor," she says.

"Anything."

"Can you find us a hotel for the night?"

Except that.

"It's Ferragosto," I explain. "All the hotels are booked six months, a year ahead of time. They put people in closets and storage rooms. I'm sure there's not a room left in town."

There's another conference in Ukrainian, and this time I pick out the word *hotel*. Zhuki looks distressed.

"But you can stay at our apartment," I say quickly.

Zhuki, Mykola, and Ihor look at each other. It's clear they're the ones making the decisions.

"Are you sure?" Zhuki says.

"There won't be enough beds for everybody, but we'll figure something out."

"Thank you, Etto," she says, and hugs me.

I lead the way. Ihor and Mykola carry the kids, and Zhuki grips the arm of her brother. My phone lights up my pocket almost constantly as we creep down the muddy mule track, holding on to the walls of the path. On Via Partigiani, wide rivulets of water are flowing over the pavement like a glaze of ice.

"I think the torrents have overflowed," I say.

"Is that bad?"

"Very."

By the time we emerge onto the railroad bridge, the sky has gone dark, closing over us like an iron plate. The vicos perpendicular to the beach are all already flooded and deepening every minute, the water having found the fastest route down to the sea. The shop is closed and dark, and as I unlock the door of the apartment, there's another conference in Ukrainian, and Mykola and Ihor trudge back up the hill.

"They think it's better if they stay at the villa tonight," Zhuki explains. "To make sure she doesn't steal anything of Yuri's."

Yuri is still unresponsive, a ghost of himself. The alarm chirps, and we tumble into the front hall, peeling off layers and kicking off shoes.

"Papà?" I call.

No answer. I check my phone. It's filled with messages.

COME DOWN TO MARTINA'S.

ETTO, GET DOWN HERE. MARTINA'S.

ETTO, WE'RE ALL AT MARTINA'S.

Shit.

"Papà?" I call again, but again there's no answer.

"Are you sure your papà will not mind?"

"Not at all." I lead them upstairs to the living room, our damp socks leaving footprints on the wood. I turn around, and Yuri is still standing at the bottom, deciding whether he can make the climb.

"Yuri!" Zhuki calls out something in Ukrainian, and he finally sets his legs in motion.

"Yuri can sleep in Papà's room," I say. "You and the kids can have mine. There are two beds."

"What about you?"

"I think something's happened at Martina's. I might not be back for a while." Even inside the apartment I can hear the palms creaking under the weight of the wind, and the wooden piers of the molo groaning against the force of the waves. "SMS me if you need anything."

"Okay." And we kiss—automatically—as if we've been saying good-bye like that our entire lives.

I go outside, and it's like the crazy divorcée upstairs is dumping a bucket of water on me, like she did to Fede and Luca the time they got drunk and serenaded her. The sheets of water down the vico are thicker, running up to my ankles and shellacking my shoes with a wobbly finish. I run down the passeggiata, my hair slicked back, my shoes squishing with every step. I can see the crowd of people gathering, their figures smeared like charcoal drawings in the driving rain. I run as fast as I can, following the floodlights, and when I get there, it's worse than I imagined. Half the roof is gone, and a third of the walls. It's like looking down the maw of a beast, the tables and chairs mangled and flung around the room, bottles lying smashed on the ground, the liquor mixing into a nauseous cocktail, the calcio scarves blown into the mess. A couple of men are standing around lamenting the deaths of the lotto machine and the flat-screen, which is lying on its back, the whiteness crackling through it like ice.

The rest of the men are already at work, twenty or thirty of them packing everything that can be salvaged into the kitchen and the computer alcove, which still have a roof. A few men with brooms try to push the water back to the sea where it belongs, and Fede is supervising a group of lifeguards on the beach below as they shovel sand into trash bags and shuttle them up the stairs on chaises, like patients on ambulance stretchers. Around the perimeter where Martina's wall used to be, there's a pathetic little pile of black trash bags belching out sand.

"Etto!" Papà catches me by the arm and shouts through the rain. "You're here! Go back to the shop and get some vacuum-pack bags."

"What?"

"Vacuum-pack bags! The trash bags are breaking!"

It's only as I turn to leave that I notice Martina, sitting in a chair in the corner, the same expression as Yuri's on her face, her world eliminated in one stroke.

I run back to the shop. The water in the vico is now up to my shin, and I fight through it. I go around to the back alley, and when I open the door, there's only a small puddle inside. My shoes squeak against the linoleum, and I circle around as the three portraits and the jersey watch calmly from the wall. I pull the pillowcase off the television and stuff it full of the biggest vacuum-pack bags we have. In an instant, I'm back outside, wading with the current down the vico.

The wind has calmed down, and the rain is falling in straight lines now, like beads strung from the clouds. The sea is a blackish-green, heavy as oil, the rain pocking its surface. Casella's Uno is creeping along the passeggiata ahead, the brake lights blinking as he navigates the streams of water. Finally, they hold steady, and I run to catch up.

"Thanks." I get in and slam the door, arranging my legs among the rolls of plastic and tape.

"You've seen Martina's?"

"I can't believe it."

We drive down the passeggiata, steering around the debris, the wiper blades thumping softly. The day Mamma disappeared, Silvio and Papà stayed out on the molo with the coast guard guys. The sea was full of every sailboat, fishing boat, rowboat, and catamaran from Imperia to Savona, but Silvio wouldn't let me help or even go out onto the molo. He did let Casella park the Uno on the passeggiata, and we sat inside, the seats cranked back, people tapping on the windows to offer us food. We spent all day and all night like this, napping and waking in a terrible twilight, time suspended, circling overhead. At around five in the morning, Silvio tapped on the window of the Uno and told us the search was over.

Casella pulls the parking brake, and half a dozen people reach for the door handles. They've sent out for more floodlights, and there are five ladders set up on the tiled floor, reaching into the empty sky. The rain turns to mist, and Papà somehow convinces Martina to go home and get some sleep. I join Fede's crew, filling vacuum bags with sand and piling them against the flooded vico. Five of the young guys are up on the ladders, supervised by three times as many old guys shouting from the ground. It's three in the morning by the time they manage to staple the plastic sheets over the opening and duct tape them together from the inside. The water in the vico has subsided, and the clouds have moved off as if they were never there, opening into a clear, starry night. I'm too revved up to go to sleep, and I remember I don't have a bed anyway, so I end up lying on the deserted molo with Fede, Bocca, and Aristone, our damp socks and shoes peeled off and scattered.

"Cazzo, Fede, you really took charge back there."

"Boh."

"It's so strange to think about," Aristone says, "but someday we're going to be the ones running this town."

"So you're coming back here after university?"

"I don't know. What's a language specialist going to do here?"

"You see? Better drop out now before you educate yourself right out of the region."

"If the liceo opens back up, you could take Charon's job."

We all laugh.

"I really don't know what I'm going to do," Aristone says. "When I'm in Genoa, I want to be here. When I'm here, I want to be there."

We're all silent for a while, thinking this over.

"Hey, what was Signor Cavalcanti's problem tonight?" Fede asks.

"You saw that?"

"It was hard not to."

"He wanted to know if Guido's gay."

"What?"

"You know, with Nicola Nicolini."

"Nicola Nicolini? I thought they hung out because of the deejay thing."

"Maybe at first."

"So you knew all along?"

"We share a wall with Nicola Nicolini," I say.

"Guido, huh? What a shame."

"That he's gay?"

"That he's in love with Nicola Nicolini. If only he'd told us, we could've found someone cooler for him."

We all laugh.

Bocca boosts himself up off the ground. "Well, girls, I'm going to bed. I'm dead tired."

"Me too," Fede says. "You going home, Etto?"

"I don't know. There's no place to sleep."

"Why?"

"The Ukrainians are there."

"All of them?"

"Turns out Tatiana was sleeping with Vanni."

"I don't believe it."

"Believe it. Yuri told her she has until noon tomorrow to move out of the villa. In the meantime, they're staying with us."

"Do you want to come home to Mamma-Fede's?" he asks. "Sleep on the sofa?"

"I'll be fine."

"Sure?"

"Yeah."

I watch as the three of them separate and disappear into the darkness. I lie out on the molo for a while longer, looking up at the terraces. I imagine the small villages just beyond the ridge, the meadows and foothills, the Alps and the rest of Europe. Beyond, beyond, beyond. I think about what Aristone said, about always wanting to be somewhere else, and I wonder if I could do it, if I could ever manage to leave this place for good.

The alarm chirps as I walk in the door, and I hear Papà's voice come to an abrupt stop.

"Etto? Is that you?"

"Yes."

They're sitting in our living room, Yuri slumped in the chair, Papà on the sofa, a couple of glasses between them. They don't look like a calcio star and a fan anymore—just two men, sitting and talking in the dark.

"Why don't you go in my room and lie down?" Papà says.

I never go in Papà's room anymore. It looks like a hotel, the bedspread stretched tight, nothing but the absolute essentials set out. Two lamps. An alarm clock. The dish where he sets his watch every night. As soon as I close the door, the conversation in the living room resumes. I sit down on the edge of the bed and take off my jeans. I stretch across to set my phone on the nightstand, and it's then I see a framed photo of the four of us. I thought Papà had gotten rid of everything that had anything to do with Mamma, but there it is.

I pick it up and slip under the covers. Most of our family photos were after Luca's matches, Luca flushed and smiling, me on the other side, sulking about being dragged to this stadium or that. But this one is of all of us on the beach. It must be right after the season because there are no chaises or umbrellas, but the sun is still strong. Late September, maybe? I have on the Dodgers shirt Mamma brought back from America the year we turned fifteen, so it must have been one of the last photos before Luca went off to the academy. In the picture, we are all squinting into the sun, arms thrown over each other's shoulders. Just like a real family.

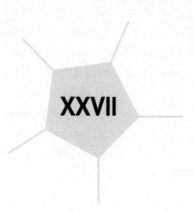

XXVII

I wake up in the morning clutching the photo to my chest like a defibrillator. I hear voices in the living room. One voice, actually. Yuri's.

"I don't care where I transfer," he's shouting into the phone in English. "Yes, I *know* transfer window is closing. Someone somewhere must want Ukrainian striker! You convince them . . . I don't care! Let it be Pescara! Let it be Bari! Let it be Catania! I tell you, I don't *care*! Only no Genoa!"

Shit. Bari? Catania? And each time he opens his mouth, it's the name of a place even farther away.

"Everton, then! Greek leagues! Portugal! I don't care!"

I put on my jeans and go out into the living room. There's no sign of Papà or Zhuki. Little Yuri and Principessa are wide awake and watching a soundless Bloomberg Business while Yuri's pacing between the coffee table and the television. He stops and runs his hand through his hair as he listens to the guy on the other end of the phone. He looks in my direction, and I raise my hand in a half wave, but there's no flicker of recognition. His eyes are like burned-out bulbs. I don't think he's slept all night.

"I tell you. I. Don't. Care. Where," Yuri shouts into his phone. He sinks into the chair and leans his head back. He folds one arm over his eyes and sighs. "Sorry, sorry. Yes, Alfie. Yes. Yes, of course. You always take care of me. You think you can talk to him? All right, I will call this afternoon. I know. Okay. We talk then. You are good man, Alfie. You are good man. Good-bye." He snaps the phone shut and mutters something in Ukrainian, then folds himself forward, his hands cradling his forehead. Little Yuri and Principessa are watching sullenly as two men in suits argue about the stock market in Tokyo, the graphs full of slashes.

"Are you okay?" I ask.

Yuri doesn't say anything. Or move. I sit down on the arm of the sofa. "Yuri?"

He mumbles something unintelligible, maybe even in Ukrainian, I don't know.

"What did you say?"

He picks his head up. "I say, maybe I should have never left village." And he lets his head sink down again.

I pick up the remote, put the sound on low, and switch it to the Disney Channel. The alarm downstairs chirps, and Papà appears at the top of the stairs. I expect him to look as tired as Yuri. Instead, he seems invigorated, his face ruddy, his eyes bright from the sea air.

"Have you been down to the shop?" he asks.

"Not yet."

"We're lucky. Only a little bit of water, and the power never went out. We only have to figure out what to do with all that food from the festa."

"Maybe bring some up to Nonna's today?"

"Ach. Nonno would never allow that. Especially if there are guests."

"Guests?"

"Where else would they go?"

"What about the semifinals and finals?"

"Postponed. The field is soaked anyway. . . . Come on, Yuri. Hup, hup. I told Silvio you and I would go around and check on the old people and make sure they're okay. No power outages or anything. Hopefully you won't give them a heart attack when you show up at their door."

"What about Nonna?" I ask.

"Nonno is taking her to church this morning. . . . Come on, Yuri." He claps his hands together with the inexhaustible energy that used to annoy us when we were kids. "Let's go. Better to be busy when these things happen. Trust me."

Yuri rouses himself from the chair. "I will wake Zhuki."

"Let Zhuki sleep. Etto can watch the kids."

"I can?"

"You can."

Papà and Yuri leave, and I make myself a coffee and stand out on the balcony, listening to *The Lion King* songs cycling through in the background. Outside, the streets look like biblical times, sand covering the passeggiata, dead fish and palm fronds lying everywhere. The tourists are stepping around the destruction in a daze, snapping pictures. I can see the crowd gathering around Martina's even from here.

I go back in and sit down on the sofa, and Little Yuri and Principessa arrange themselves next to me. *The Lion King* is about halfway through, and Principessa starts to shift around, pressing her hands into my thigh as she rearranges herself.

"When are we going home?" Little Yuri asks.

"Probably this afternoon."

"Is that your bedroom we were sleeping in?"

"Yes."

"Why do you have two beds?"

"I had a brother."

"Where is he?"

"He's not here anymore."

"Where did he go?"

"He died."

"And then where did he go?"

"Where everybody goes. Heaven." But I can already tell, I'm not selling this kid on it.

"You don't know, do you?"

"Of course I know. He's in heaven."

"How do you know?"

"Okay, I don't know, all right? But it makes me feel better, and it's a lot easier to explain to you than the alternatives."

"So he could be anywhere, then. He could be under this sofa. He could be out in space. He could be in Ukraine."

"When did you get so chatty?"

"What's 'chatty'?"

"Let's just watch television, okay?"

Zhuki eventually comes down, and as we get the kids ready to go up to Nonna and Nonno's, I pretend that we are a young family off to visit the grandparents. When we arrive, Yuri and Papà are already there, and Ihor and Mykola soon return from the villa to report that Tatiana and Vanni left an hour ago in Vanni's Maserati. Nonna has made a tableful of food, and as we pass it around, Papà plays koo-koo with Principessa behind his napkin as if we get together with the Ukrainians every Sunday.

When I was a kid, I remember thinking that the universe was composed of families like ours, perfect bubbles floating around in space, and inside your family's bubble, you developed your private jokes and your family stories. You were lucky if it lasted, but once your bubble popped, it was gone. Never once did it cross my mind that you could become a part of someone else's bubble, or that two half bubbles could match up to make a whole. A complete whole. Since I woke up this morning, I've felt the presence of Mamma and Luca, not in the empty chairs or the absences, but in our togetherness. As we listen to Nonno recap the history of water trumpets in the region, or as we talk about the World Cup next year, or watch Little Yuri and Principessa run around the yard, Mamma and Luca are here as sure as we all are.

How do I know, you ask?

I don't.

The afternoon stretches, and we drink our digestivos in the yard under the lemon tree. The air is hot and humid, but the branches shade us from the sun, and the leaves help generate a light breeze.

"What kind of tree is this anyway?" Zhuki asks.

"Lemon."

"Why are there no lemons?"

"Ach," Nonno says. "It is the fault of the man who owned this villa before us. He never cleaned or trimmed his land, only left it dirty year after year."

Yuri has been near-catatonic for the entire afternoon, the conversation ricocheting around him. But now he leans back in his chair, squinting and frowning at the branches as if this is the very first tree in the world, the one that led to his demise.

"I've tried everything," Nonno continues, "but once a tree is barren for so long, there is nothing you can do. It simply forgets how to grow." And Nonno starts listing all the measures he has taken to try to bring life back to the tree.

I've heard it a million times before, but I listen politely, and it's only out of the corner of my eye that I see Yuri reach his arm up in slow motion, like a Sky Sport replay, up, up into the mess of branches, unfurling his fingers into the shiny leaves.

"What are those?" Yuri says.

"Where?" Nonno stands up and examines the tree, and sure enough, there's a small cluster of pale-purple buds. And do you know how when you see something once, you get the pattern in your eye and you start to see it all over? That's exactly what happens, and soon, all of us are out of our chairs, examining every branch of the tree.

"Right there."

"And there."

"Over here."

"Here's one."

Nonno is as excited as I've seen him for any match. "Maradona! Maradona! Lemons! Lemons!"

Zhuki beams, lifting our Principessa up to see, our Little Yuri holding on to her pocket as he gazes up and waits his turn.

Pescara is not so far.

Bari is not so far.

Everton, even, is not so far.

XXVIII

*F*or the next few days, the Ukrainians are trapped in the villa as the paparazzi swarm outside. I SMS Zhuki and tell her I can deliver anything they need, but she says they are fine. As the days stretch with no gossip about their evacuation, I start to think that maybe there's a chance they will stay, at least until October. But that dream is shattered on Wednesday morning, when I find myself staring into the cold screen of my phone, the bottom dropping out of my stomach like a trap door.

CAN YOU MEET ME AT THE FIELD TONIGHT?

She's waiting for me on the fifth-year bench. The moon is waning, the horns pointed to the right, casting an eerie glow onto the sea. Even in the dim light, I can tell she's been crying.

"What is it?" I say.

She wipes her eyes with the heel of her hand and looks away. I remember one time Professoressa Gazzolo started crying in front of us in class, the day after she found out her boyfriend in Sanremo had left her for an eighteen-year-old girl. We'd already heard the story, and of course, Fede had been with the girl six months before, so we kept telling her not to cry, that the girl was a cow anyway, but she couldn't stop. And worse, she kept saying, "Sorry, sorry," because she didn't want to cry over this guy, either, and because she was embarrassed to be crying in front of her students in the first place even though, I have to say, it's not often you see that kind of humanity in a school.

Anyway, I get the same feeling watching Zhuki—that it would be less embarrassing for her to stand naked in front of all of San Benedetto than cry in front of me.

"What is it?" I say again. I sit down on the end of the bench. I'm scared to touch her, to release whatever she's going to say next.

"We're moving to Chicago."

"*What?*"

I can feel the universe rushing outward and stretching the space between us, the gulf widening between our bodies. I can feel the atoms pulling apart, the gaps filling with dark energy and dark matter.

"He's being transferred at the end of the month. They're in the middle of their season, and there's a good chance he won't even be able to play right away because of the ban. But he will be able to practice, and to keep his place on the Ukrainian national team." She wipes her nose on her sleeve and keeps talking. "We have an aunt in Chicago. I've met her. She's nice. Principessa will be able to learn English. She was too young when we were in Glasgow. . . ."

"They have calcio in Chicago?"

"They have soccer."

"Is it the same thing?"

"I guess so."

"When are you leaving?"

"I'm not sure."

The words fly up and perch on the horns of the moon like a hawk eyeing us, and she presses her hands into the bench as if she wants to vault herself off it and run away.

"Don't go," I say. She turns to look at me, her face half lit, split down the middle. "Don't go. Stay here. In San Benedetto. We could find you a job, an apartment . . . everything."

She stares at me for a long time, and I hold my breath.

"I'm sorry, Etto. I have to go."

"You don't have to go."

"You don't understand the stress my brother is under. He needs me. Little Yuri and Principessa need me."

No one will ever believe me if I tell them this story. No one will ever believe I have such palle forged of steel. "*I* need you," I say.

The crease appears between her eyes. I haven't seen it since the days after the disco. "You're not making this easy, Etto."

"I don't want to make it easy. Cazzo . . . Chicago? Couldn't he find anything closer?"

"The transfer window was closing. America was all that was left."

Great. My fate is in the hands of a fottuto calcio schedule.

"Look, Etto. I like you. A lot. But let's be rational. How long have we known each other? A couple of months? This is my *brother*. The brother who saved me from this awful situation with my mother's boyfriend. The brother who got me out of Strilky. He's the only one I have left. I thought you of all people would understand that. And now you are asking me to choose between him and you?"

"I'm not asking you to choose between him and me. I'm asking you to choose between him and you. You love those kids, I know, but they're not your kids. Your brother's calcio career is not yours. Your brother's life is not your life."

The furrow between her eyebrows deepens. I look down and realize that this whole time, I've been rubbing her fingers like a talisman. She pulls her hand away.

"Etto, this *is* my life. Maybe it seems stupid and small to you, like I am only following after my brother like a puppy. But it is my life, and those people you are talking about are my family. And they would do anything for me just as I would do anything for them."

I know. I know. You can never win a breakup you don't want in the first place. But I keep going. Rome or death.

"Are you sure about that?"

Her face darkens, and I can almost see the gate rolling down over it. "I'm going, Etto. I didn't want to end like this, but I'm going." She stands up and gives me two perfunctory pecks on the cheek, a chaste punishment for my passion that feels like the final two screws in my coffin.

"I thought you understood me," she says.

Ouch.

She disappears up the hill, and just like that it's over, flaring and burning out like a comet you wait a lifetime for, leaving only darkness, the sea, and silence.

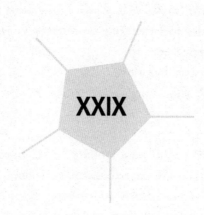

XXIX

By Thursday morning, the streets are clean and the beaches are open again, but no one is allowed in the water because of the bacteria counts. Some of the tourists have cut their vacations short and gone home, but most of them have been wandering around the town like we have, restless and unsettled. Fede comes across the passeggiata midmorning as I'm taking a smoke break. Yes, I'm smoking again. Judge away.

"I just heard," he says. "I'm sorry."

I shrug.

"Do you think you'll still have contact with her?"

I shake my head. "It didn't end so well."

"Maybe you can call her."

I shrug again. "What's the point?"

Fede stares at me, but I can see his concentration drifting. He squints over my shoulder in the direction of Martina's bar.

"Is that . . . Signor Cato?"

I turn to look, and sure enough, Signor Cato is running toward us down the passeggiata, his skinny legs pumping, his white hair flickering in the air like fire. I don't think I've ever seen him move a muscle other than his mouth or his index finger clicking on the mouse, and now, here he is, running down the passeggiata.

"Where's your papà?" he gasps.

"He's upstairs. What's wrong?"

"Martina's gone."

"What?"

"She's gone. A few of us went looking for her to see if she'd serve us a coffee in the open air. We buzzed and buzzed. She's not answering her door. Her neighbor said he hasn't seen her since yesterday morning."

I get Chicca to watch the shop, and Papà, Signor Cato, Fede, and I walk over to Martina's apartment, where she's lived alone since her bastard-of-a-cafone-of-a-husband left her five or six years ago. Papà knocks but there's no answer.

"Martina?" He uses his key. I hold my breath and expect the worst.

"Martina? Are you there?" The echo follows us as we check the other rooms.

"Where do you think she went?"

"I don't know."

"I can't believe she wouldn't tell us."

"What do you think we should do?"

"I'll go talk to Silvio," Papà says.

"I'll ask around the bagni," Fede says.

They both hurry off. I head back toward the shop, and I'm about twenty meters down the passeggiata when I remember Signor Cato, who is still standing in front of Martina's apartment building, staring up at the windows. He has no place to go. No wife, no Wi-Fi. He probably doesn't even have a coffeemaker at home.

"What are you going to do today, Signor Cato?" I ask.

"I don't know."

"You can sit up in our apartment if you want."

"Do you have a computer?"

"No. But we have coffee. And I can buy you a newspaper."

He thinks about it. "You know what? I think I will sit out on the molo today."

I watch him through the front windows of the shop for the rest of the morning. Once upon a time, he spent all his days out there. He was the last official fisherman in San Benedetto, docking his boat along the molo decades longer than anyone else had been allowed to, until the year Gubbio forced him to either join the marina or pay a docking tax, which Signor Cato loudly decried as the equivalent of choosing between Scylla and Charybdis, though he didn't quite use those words. And rather than give in to Gubbio, he decided to sink his boat himself, loudly and dramatically. Mamma, Luca, and me were among a small crowd watching as he stood on the boat and gave his speech, violently chopping a hole in the bottom with an ax, only diving off the prow once bubbles the size of a man's head began gurgling up around him. I remember the bite of Mamma's bangles as we stood there, the scratchiness of the piece of fishing net against my wrist, her hand tightening around mine while we waited for him to surface.

For a while afterward, Signor Cato would go out on the molo to fish, and he and Mamma would often meet in the early mornings, Mamma in her wet suit, Signor Cato with his tackle box and pole. Now he looks stiff and out of place, his back rigid against one of the benches. People greet him like they haven't seen him in a decade, and the ones who haven't been to Martina's maybe haven't. A few of the other regulars from Martina's join him, and the waiters along the passeggiata bring out trays of coffee. Each time I look out the window, the crowd seems to have grown.

At noon, The Band wanders by, playing the Ferragosto dirge that was postponed due to the storm, but they, too, drop their instruments to their sides and join the growing pack of men. Even the Mangona brothers take turns abandoning their kiosks to see what's going on. And to any untrained eye, the same thing is going on that has always been going on whenever two or more are gathered in San Benedetto—moving mouths and flying hands pulling air into air, crafting grand plans from nothing and into nothing.

Papà comes back to the shop with Silvio. "What's going on out there?" he says.

"Who knows?"

They join the crowd, which has grown to about thirty now, their hands synchronized, turning like eagles in the air. All at once, they get up and start moving in the direction of Martina's, gliding like a pool of mercury, absorbing more people as they advance. Mimmo, Franco, Dura from Naples, Father Marco, Pete the Comb Man. Only Papà breaks off and hurries back to the shop.

"We're rebuilding Martina's."

"You're what?"

"We're rebuilding Martina's. All of us. Casella and his papà are going to order everything wholesale, Father Marco is going to set up a collection box at the church, Signor Cavalcanti will donate a new flat-screen, and all the retired men will work on it. Dura used to be a bricklayer, you know."

"Shouldn't you ask Martina about this?"

"Mino said he saw her get on the train with a giant suitcase yesterday morning. He asked her where she was going and do you know what she said?"

"What?"

"Away."

He goes behind the banco, tears off some paper, and grabs a couple of markers. "I need you to pack up the food from the festa for lunch. Anything that's still good. Make some sandwiches if you have to. I'll send Casella to drive it over. Figure about forty men."

"Forty?"

"Forty."

Papà starts leaving me in the shop alone almost every morning again, and the only evidence he's been here at all is the tabloids he leaves open on top of the banco. They start in on Tatiana and Yuri's breakup immediately, hammering away at the one hard clod of truth until it pulverizes into a dust cloud of lies—reports that Tatiana left Yuri for another showgirl, pictures of Zhuki identified as Yuri's new girlfriend, and ridiculous quotes from their mother's boyfriend back in Ukraine. *Gente* calls it the "Ukrainian Circus," and makes it a regular feature, giving it a split screen with photos of Tatiana on one side and Yuri on the other. Tatiana and Vanni behind the darkened windows of Vanni's Maserati vs. Yuri and Zhuki and the kids at a mall in the suburbs of Genoa. Vanni carrying Tatiana's purse as she cuts the line at a nightclub in Milan vs. Yuri and Zhuki and the kids at the aquarium.

In every picture, Zhuki is flinching from the camera flash, pulling Little Yuri and Principessa toward her like baby birds under her wing. But there's nothing about Chicago. Nothing about America. Who knows? Maybe it was just a lie she made up for me.

Now that Martina is gone, Papà and I have to cook for ourselves, mostly sandwiches or boxed pasta with jarred sauce. Once in a while we answer the knock on the shared door and have dinner with Guido and Nicola Nicolini. Guido's parents have cut off all contact with him, and there's a somberness in his eyes now that dulls the flash of metal around his neck and wrists. A bunch of sad bachelors we are. Me the saddest of them all. At least Guido and Nicola Nicolini have each other, and Papà has Silvio and the other regulars from Martina's, who have started spending their evenings sitting under the makeshift tarps, drinking from their own bottles. I try to escape to the aula, but the last time I was there, it was the night with Zhuki, and now, the long room echoes like a crypt.

That's another thing they forget to tell you about grief, that every loss you feel after the first is not added but multiplied, like what they tell you in school about drinking and taking drugs at the same time. And after squaring so many fractions and fractions of fractions, you find out you've used up your lifetime allotment of both pain and joy, and all that's left is an emotional flatline and the deep conviction that you will never, ever try anything with the potential to intoxicate you again.

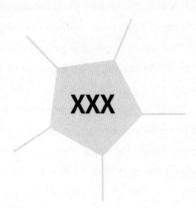

XXX

*T*he new calcio season starts the last week in August, Genoa faced with the uphill climb from the bottom of the league tables. The men listen to the matches on the radio as they work on Martina's, just like they used to back in the old days, when their weekends were spent taking turns on each other's home improvement projects. They lay the brick and nail the boards to the rise and fall of the crowd, only stopping when the announcer's voice accelerates, still as statues, trowels or hammers in hand.

The retired guys make steady progress all week, but it's on the weekends that you can see the real leaps and bounds. The brick walls start to edge out the plastic sheeting, and the windows are installed. The new wooden floor is pounded into place, and paving stones are laid for an outdoor patio. Dura, who everyone used to dismiss as just another immigrant from Naples, becomes both the supervisor and—most people believe—the supplier, mysterious stacks of brick and bags of mortar appearing on the passeggiata in the middle of the night.

In the meantime, the world keeps churning out tragedy. A thousand pilgrims die in a stampede, and a hurricane in America wipes out an entire city. The old men all mutter, ah . . . sì, sì, it could be worse, it could be much worse, and the box of donations Father Marco set up for Martina's gets a new sign on it.

Sending money to America. Has the whole world turned over on its axis?

The first week of September, two letters arrive at the shop. One is a postcard from Martina.

I am okay. Not sure when I will be back. Kisses.

The postcard is from somewhere in Sweden, with a swooping shoreline the same shape as ours, only covered in pine trees and wooden huts. Papà nails it to the wall of the bar.

"Sweden? Why would she go to Sweden?"

"Why not?"

"Why would she leave at all? She had it good here."

"Good? We treated her like an indentured servant."

"We treated her like family."

The second letter is from Yuri, and Papà places it carefully in the bottom of the lacquered box that Nicola Nicolini insisted on for the top of the credenza.

Dear Carlo and Etto,

Thank you for everything you do for me and my family. Someday we will return to San Benedetto and play calcio match together.

Yuri

There is nothing from Zhuki.

Anyway, I'm so busy, I hardly think of her.

Only a couple of times.

A minute.

I miss her, and I wish Mamma and Luca were here to tell me how to get her back. I lie awake in bed at night, trying to make Mamma answer me.

Are you there? Are you there? Are you there? I dig in the bottom drawer of the wardrobe, feeling around in the piles of socks until I find the loop of fishing line. It's twisted and faded, the knot frayed at the ends. I make a double loop and slide it over my hand.

Are you there?

But there's still no answer, so left to my own devices, I do what any other sad loser would do. I paint her on a ceiling. *The Creation of Zhuki.* I dress her in her silky calcio shorts and cleats, and paint myself on the ground like Adam, conked out and swooning, my hand resting on the side where the rib has gone missing. Not a pain or a scar, exactly, but a soft spot. Unprotected. Vulnerable. Zhuki is in the middle of the panel, turned toward an impassive Yuri, clasping her hands and begging her brother to return to San Benedetto immediately. It's pure fantasy, I know. No better than the Dungeons and Dragons nerds behind their locked bedroom doors, painting steel bras onto tiny medieval maidens, trying to conjure up the real thing.

"You've heard nothing from her?" Fede and I are sitting at the bar at Camilla's.

"Radio silence."

It's only me and Fede now. Bocca is working at the Truck Show almost every night, Claudia and Casella spend all their time planning the wedding, and Sima and Aristone have gone back to university. Since Ferragosto, Fede wants to spend every night at Camilla's. At first I thought he was drinking away his sorrows over Claudia getting engaged, but then I started to notice his eyes tracking Camilla around the bar. And she makes him wait for it, but eventually she'll come over and talk with us. At the beginning of the night, she spreads her attention evenly, but as it progresses, she starts to laugh more loudly at Fede's jokes and hardly takes her eyes off him. Fede's in the middle of telling her his grand plans to own his own bagni someday when I slip out the door, making sure it doesn't slam behind me.

I stand in the cool sea air, leaning against the railing of the passeggiata and looking up at the terraces. Back to the beginning, I guess. And that's when I see it—a passing flicker somewhere in the vicinity of the villa. At first I don't believe it, and I have to redraw the contours of the hill to make sure that it's not a jet or a satellite or a figment of my imagination. But there's no doubt. The windows are lit. Three or four of them. I start running toward them up the hill, my legs pumping like pistons, all my muscles clicking into place. It seems to take no time at all before I'm standing in front of the iron gate.

It wasn't a mirage. The lights in the villa are burning brightly. I fix my hair, look into the security camera, and press the button.

Another light comes on in the second floor. I buzz again.

"Etto, is that you?"

Shit.

"Etto, what are you doing here?" It's the voice of Signora Malaspina's niece.

"Sorry. I thought the Ukrainians were here."

"They've been gone for three weeks. Don't you even read the tabloids?"

"I thought they might be back."

"To San Benedetto? No, no. They're in Genoa now. You want to come in, Etto?"

"No, thanks."

"Hey, maybe I'll have a party up here next weekend. Would you come, Etto?"

"Maybe."

"Tell everybody, okay?"

"Okay."

The intercom goes dead. Shit. Very funny, God. Is that what you do all day, just sit up there laughing at us?

My phone lights up.

HEY, WHERE'D YOU GO?

DON'T WORRY ABOUT IT.

I imagine him down there, chatting with Camilla, both of them grateful that I've left them alone. It's only a matter of time now before Fede goes the way of Casella, and we start having bullshit conversations.

Maybe the four of them will start to double-date, and Casella and Fede will eventually become brothers-in-law. Maybe in sixty years this whole town will be filled with ghosts and people I used to be close to. I light a cigarette, my head a thick fog as I stumble toward the field. The losses multiply inside me, opening holes like rat-a-tat-tat guns, the darkness spreading like a thick puddle.

For some reason, I don't think as much about the night Luca died as I do the morning Mamma came into my room. There was something definitive and final about Luca's death. That was how he always was. He never waffled, never maybed himself to death like I do. If he wanted a girl, he went after her. If he kicked a ball, he followed through. If he jumped off the molo, he did the biggest cannonball anyone had ever seen.

But with Mamma, it seems if I just keep thinking about it, I can still save her. So I constantly replay the same few minutes, fast-forwarding and rewinding, stopping at crucial places and zooming in. I try to see the shadow of the weight belt around her waist. I wonder if she had the hook already or did she go downstairs afterward to get it? Why didn't I hear her rummaging in the shop? Why didn't I see anything in her face or feel anything strange in the way she ruffled my hair? Why couldn't I see it? Why couldn't Papà? Maybe we were all blind in those days. Maybe Mamma wasn't consciously choosing between death and life or between Luca and me. Maybe after Luca, she was just stumbling around in disbelief like the rest of us. Maybe she just had her eyes closed.

"Lucky bastard," I tell Luca. "You don't have to go through any of these mind games anymore. Any of this earthly bullshit."

I pick up the ball from his grave. It's lost some air in only the past couple of weeks. I set it up on the penalty spot, drop back, and kick it as hard as I can. Thump. Swish. Gol. I chase it, set it up again, drop back, and kick. Thump. Swish. Gol.

"Mwah-ha-ha-ha-ha." I hear Fede's voice before I see the flashlight through the foliage. He does his fake sinister laugh, crashing through the brush like fottuto King Kong.

"Etto, are you up here?"

"No."

I keep kicking, my foot and my heart hardening into stone. Fede breaks through the line of cypresses. "There you are. Why'd you run off like that? You got a hot date with a sheep up here or something?"

"Baaaa," I say, and I drop the ball on the ground and keep kicking. Thump. Swish. Gol. Thump. Swish. Gol. An entire season's worth of penalty shots, and yet it seems like it's never enough. I ignore Fede, and he watches me for a while.

"I don't get it," he finally says. "If you're so upset, why don't you go after her?"

"What makes you think I'm upset?"

"It's pretty obvious. Ask anyone. You haven't been the same at all since the Ukrainians left. The nonne are worried sick about you."

"Oh, so everybody's talking about me now, eh?" Thump. Swish. Gol. "Cazzo, what I wouldn't give to live someplace normal, where everyone would just stay out of my business and leave me the fuck alone."

"Go live in some high-rise in Milan then if you want."

"Maybe I will."

"Might as well dig yourself a spot next to Luca while you're at it."

I stop and back off the ball. "What did you say?"

"You heard me."

"Vaffanculo, Fede. That was over the line."

"It was a metaphor, Etto. A metaphor."

Thump. Swish. Gol. "Ah, so now you know about metaphors, eh? Where'd they teach you that—hotel school?"

I run after the ball and set it up again. Fede only stares at me, not saying a word. Maybe I've insulted him enough to make him go away. Thump. This time, the ball goes sailing over the goal.

"Shit."

I run after it and set it up again. I back off it to make another shot, and do you know what that stronzo does? He snatches the ball off the ground and holds it above his head.

"Give me the ball," I say.

"Not until you talk to me."

"Give me the ball, Fede."

"No." He's got about ten centimeters on me. "Not until you tell me why you always have to expect the worst from people."

"You don't think after all that's happened I'm entitled to expect the worst?"

"Come on. You were already like that a long time before Luca died. Do you know how much it bothered him how jealous you were of him?"

"I was never jealous of him."

"Yes you were. It really hurt him, you know."

"How do you know?"

"He was my best friend for fifteen years, Etto. You seem to block that out. Like you're the only one who misses him."

"Oh, yeah? And what else can you tell me about my brother? My *twin* brother. Go ahead, Fede, enlighten me."

"That he cared about you a lot. That he was always asking me to look out for you. It was the last thing he said every time he went back to the academy. Cazzo, it was the last thing he said." I make a grab for the ball, but Fede is too quick.

"Well, I'm a big boy now, Fede. You don't have to hang out with me out of obligation anymore."

"That's not what I was saying."

"Or out of guilt over loaning him the motorcycle." It's a low blow. I know.

I make a grab for the ball, but Fede hides it behind his back. "You know what, Etto? You're an asshole. And I'm not telling you this to hurt you. I'm telling you this as a friend. A complete asshole. For the past two years, you've had the whole fucking town looking out for you, and in return, you've been nothing but an asshole to them. And you see it. I know you see it. But you pretend you don't."

"Right, Fede, please tell me what I do and don't see."

"I will. You pretend you don't see it because then you can pretend you don't owe them anything."

"What am I supposed to owe them?"

"Yourself, maybe. A little empathy. A little openness. But that scares the shit out of you, doesn't it?"

"Right, Fede. *You're* lecturing me about relationships."

"That's a cheap shot and you know it."

"It's a true shot."

"You know what, Etto? I'm only going to tell you this once, so you better listen up. Other people care about you. And if you want to ignore it or pretend you're too smart for them, or be cool and emo and sulk and tell yourself that you're all alone in the world, well, go ahead. Go ahead and lock yourself up and bolt the door and refuse to ever love anyone back. Go ahead and let Zhuki get away and be bitter for the rest of your life. But I want you to remember one thing. It's your fucking choice. It's your. Fucking. Choice."

He makes a motion to chuck the ball high into the terraces, but he stops himself and sets it on the ground instead. He walks away, his hands in his pockets, then turns around and tosses something at my feet.

"Bocca's keys," he says, and he disappears between the cypresses.

I dig the key out of the grass and rub the smooth plastic of the fob between my fingers. I hate it when someone walks away at the end of an argument like that. I hate it when somebody presumes to tell you what's inside your own head.

Most of all, I hate it when they're right.

Fede's right. That deficiente is right. I do see it. Martina and her dinners. Silvio trying to negotiate truces every time Papà and I don't see eye to eye. Even Fede and all his pestering to get me to go out. I do see it. But it's like my joints are frozen, my actions locked in place.

I lie on the field for a while, staring up at the moon and the mess of stars, my thoughts pecking at me from head to feet. Charon used to tell us that this is what hell is really like. It isn't black smoke and eternal fire. It's not rolling a fottuto boulder up the hill or being torn limb from limb by nine-headed monsters with pointy teeth. No. That hell is for children. Real hell, he said, is a state of perfect consciousness when you realize just what a stronzo you are, to other people and yourself. Real hell is when everything you've ever said or done rises to the surface in brilliant Technicolor. If you think about it, that's a hundred times worse than any of the medieval stuff.

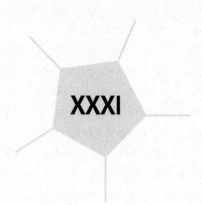

XXXI

*I*f you ever fall in love, try not to fall in love with someone from Genoa because there's no place to park a hulking white American truck, and you'll end up down by the docks bargaining with some guys loading and unloading container ships at midnight. If you ever fall in love, try not to fall in love with someone from Genoa because you'll walk farther than you ever thought you could, through warrens of vias and vicos, vicolos and viales, through the city plans of the Greeks, the Etruscans, the Phoenicians, the Ostrogoths, the Byzantines, the Spanish, and the French, hitting dead end after dead end, private courtyard after private door, growing frustrated and tired but no less determined. And when you finally arrive at a real house after hours of staring at an address printed neatly on the corner of an envelope, you will wonder why the cazzo you ever thought this was a good idea.

The house is at the end of a street named after a saint and guarded by a phalanx of motorinos and recycling bins. A stone griffin perches over the pedestrian gate, and I wonder if Yuri had it installed or if it has always been there. The shutters are closed for the night, but I can see the light seeping through two of them on the second floor. I check my phone. It's almost two in the fottuto morning. I'm officially a stalker.

I try to calculate how long I might have to wait here until they leave the villa of their own accord, and I realize that with a villa this size, it could be days. At least until the morning, and I will surely die of anxiety by the morning. Is it better to die of rejection or anxiety? Better to have the blade fall right on your neck or be pricked to death by a second hand on a clock? Maybe she's awake anyway. Maybe the lights are hers. Maybe like me, she hasn't been able to sleep since Ferragosto.

I open my phone and stare at the screen. Oh, humble cell phone, controller of the world, mover of continents, creator and destroyer of love, please tell me what to do.

But it doesn't even blink.

So I look up at the faint light striping the shutters and try to channel the great Chuck Norris. I try to imagine my cells compacting and coating themselves in steel courage, superhuman strength, and lightning-fast competence. I examine the intercom and imagine it's a nunchuck or a lead pipe, and that I am about to make a perfectly executed ninja move. But my hands are shaking.

Chuck Norris's hands shake. In fear of Chuck Norris.

I buzz and wait. After what feels like a lifetime, I finally hear the click and gasp of the button.

"Chi è?" The vowels are heavy, weighing down the words. Ihor.

"It's Etto." I smile sheepishly into the security camera and imagine my bulbous head in the fish-eye lens.

"Etto!" He mumbles something in Ukrainian, then, "Vieni! Vieni!"

The gate opens, and I walk into a lush garden invisible from the street, filled with knobby old trees and flowering bushes. I hear the locks bang in the ancient door, and I hold my breath as it creaks open.

"Ihor?"

Silence.

"Is anybody there?"

I peer into the dark shadows of the entryway, and Ihor jumps out at me from behind the door. "Aah!"

"Aaaaaaaaah!"

He laughs, steps into the doorway, and puts me in some kind of python-wrestling hold that I think might be a hug. "Etto! Surprise," he says in Italian. "Why you here?"

"I'm sorry it's so late. I really need to talk to Zhuki. I mean, only if she wants to see me."

Ihor looks confused. He motions me into the cool, dark hall and shuts the door behind me. "I no understand."

"Is Zhuki here?"

He shakes his head. "America. Chicago." And with his hand he makes a slow, swooping arc over an imaginary ocean.

"Oh. So what are you still doing here?"

"Eh?"

"Why are you here? You." I point at his chest. "You. Here. Why." I imagine Bocca and his caveman face.

"Aha," Ihor says. "Bodyguard no so important in Chicago. I go . . . September . . . no. October. October I go America. Now I watch villa." He spreads his arms wide, and the dark entryway begins to take form, with frescoes of angels on the ceiling and stone griffins and gargoyles peeking out into the hallway ahead.

Ihor furrows his eyebrows, big as hairbrushes. "Why you go Genoa? Very far, no? Why you no telephone she?"

"We had a fight." I knock the knuckles of my fists together.

"You fight? You? With Zhuki?" He scowls and knocks his fists together, only when he does it, it seems like a threat.

"No, no, no. I didn't *hit* her. We had an argument." And I turn my hands into puppets, talking back and forth. "Argument." Shit, this is humiliating. "I want to apologize. I want to say I am sorry."

"Only sorry?" Ihor cocks his head.

"Sorry's not enough?"

"Say me, Etto. You love she?"

"I don't know, Ihor, that's a really hard question to ask a man, you know. How does somebody know if they're in love? And who knows exactly what love is anyway?"

Ihor furrows his brow. "I no understand. You love she? Yes or no?"
And he looks down at me with the same tenderness as he did at the guitar
onstage at the festa.

"Yes."

Ihor grins in relief, as if this is a question that's kept him up at night,
and it releases a flurry of words. "She love you also. I know. She love you.
I see she cry. I know she love." He points to his forehead, and I imagine
him as a Ukrainian Cyclops, the tiny body parts of Ulysses's crew dangling
from his mouth.

"You telephone she," he says again. "You say she."

It seems so clear when Ihor says it with his ten-word vocabulary, but as
soon as I'm back out in the maze of darkened streets, my mind tangles
up again. I walk around for an hour or two, and end up sitting on a bench
down by the old harbor, watching the cranes load the container ships and
the planes landing and taking off from Christopher Columbus Airport.
I think about what would happen if I hopped the next plane to Chicago.
What Papà would do. Most likely, he would hire an apprentice to help
him, and the guy would turn out to be a paragon of hard work and responsibility. He and Papà would develop their own private routines and jokes,
and the space between us would only grow wider, our lumpy Pangaea drifting apart until one of us becomes Africa and the other South America, and
we can't even understand the simplest command like "Go."

We're okay, right? he said, but how far does *okay* reach? Not as far as
good or *close*.

Then I imagine it the other way. Going back to San Benedetto and
waiting for another girl like Zhuki who never comes, letting my heart
slowly shrivel up until it fossilizes in the middle of a beat and I have to
pluck the useless thing out of my chest, heave it over the terraces, and
watch it sink to the bottom of the sea. Maybe I should just move to an
anonymous high-rise in Milan. All that concrete and steel to protect and
insulate me. I used to believe it was the fear of death that kept me out of
the water, but maybe I have the same disease Mamma had. Maybe I'm terri-
fied of life creeping back in, and with it, the guilt of living.

You telephone she, I hear Ihor say in my head.

No afraid, no afraid, Yuri says.

Open your eyes! Papà shouts.

It's your fucking choice, Fede adds.

I hear the steady ringtone of America, a mechanical voice asking me to leave a message, and finally a beep.

"Hi . . . Zhuki? It's Etto. From San Benedetto. Well, I'm in Genoa, actually. I was just at your house. I know that sounds a little . . . well, like a stalker. I didn't mean it like that. Unless you want it to be like that." Shit. I pull the phone away from my ear and look at it, like there is some button that will make me sound like a rational human being. "Anyway, I talked to Ihor, and he said to call you. I mean, I wanted to call you . . . I've wanted to call you since you left. I'm sorry. That's what I'm really trying to say. I'm sorry and I miss you. And I'm kind of worried I'm going to say something stupid, or even more stupid, so I'm going to hang up now. But I miss you."

I hit *end*, and I imagine the message splintering into gigabytes and zooming through the air, dodging through the cybertraffic like a bicycle messenger and weaving through the clouds of early morning SMS-es leaving the EU—feathery cirrus clouds floating over proper France and thicker cumulous ones over those perpetually awake Spaniards. There it goes, soaring like an eagle, zigzagging through the tiny puffs over the islands in the Atlantic, plunging through the thick smog of night traders in New York, and hovering above Chicago until it spies the house or the high-rise where they live now. There it goes again, zooming down like on Google Earth, finally coming to rest on her nightstand with a soft buzz, like a butterfly landing and adjusting its wings.

I find Bocca's truck and squeeze through the narrow city streets until they release me onto Via Aurelia. The sea fans out to my left, the granulated dawn revealing the black wicks of the cypresses, the rounded silhouettes of olive and lemon trees, and the maritime pines arching toward the water. I remember coming back this way from Luca's matches in La Spezia or Rome or wherever he happened to be playing, Mamma and Papà in the front seat chatting softly as I drifted peacefully in and out of sleep. I remember the steady vibrations of the road beneath me and the certainty of heading toward a fixed pin on the map, of knowing that however long the ride was, when we got there, we would be home.

I take a deep breath and think about Zhuki. There's nothing more to do. Whatever happens next, at least I've done something. And as I speed down the coast through tunnels and across terraces, I have the sensation that I'm throwing off weight, that it's bouncing on the road behind me and careening over the cliff. I open the windows to breathe in the sea air and hear the pounding of the waves, and I feel so light, it's hard to believe I can keep the truck pinned to the curves.

It's about five thirty when I roll down Via Londra. The passeggiata is abandoned, and as soon as I park the truck, I head straight for the molo. I walk all the way out, past the warning signs and the benches. My skin pinches into gooseflesh as I strip down to my underwear and climb over the railing. I hang my toes off the edge and play with the spring and the slack in my arms as I bounce my back gently against the railing. I still feel the old fear, but I don't even bother trying to summon up any courage or to think about what Chuck Norris or Yuri Fil or any of the rest of them would do. I'm scared. But there are some things more important than fear.

Pronti . . . attenti . . .

Pronti . . . attenti . . .

Pronti . . . attenti . . .

Via!

I take a deep breath and jump. Shit. I go down and down, falling to the bottom, the sea closing over me, thick like gelatin. I can feel my hair trailing behind me like speed lines, my body slowly losing momentum until I stop, nothing under my feet. I open my eyes and see the dark shapes of the pylons and the remains of Signor Cato's fishing boat. This is the last thing Mamma saw. My muscles relax. My heart stops. My lungs prick.

At first I think I'm dying because I start to see Mamma and Luca. But instead of the clips of their last moments, my mind starts to flood with good memories. The summers on the beach. The winter breaks we spent skiing. The smell of pancakes on the weekends. The trip to America. I feel the air inside my lungs buoying me up and the water brushing against me in the other direction. I pick up momentum as I rise, the color through my eyelids changing from gray to pink to bright white as my head bursts through the surface of the water. I gasp for air and blink hard. The water clears from my ears, and I hear the gulls crying again, and the gentle waves unfurling on the shore like lace. I tread water for a minute, turning my body in a slow 360, seeing it all like a tourist in my own town. It's all here. The molo. The horizon. The hump of Laigueglia. Our apartment. Our shop. Martina's bar. I swim toward the stairs, buried under the tide. I feel for the edges of the concrete with my toes, lift my dripping weight out of the water, and climb.

If you ever fall in love, don't fall in love with someone from Genoa because it will make you dare to hope. And once you open the door to hope, my friend, it's all over. You can try all you want to slam it shut and pretend you don't care. You can try to go back to your cynical self, expecting the worst, and living your low, groveling life day by day. But once the door is open, all the possibilities of the world will come flooding into your veins, and you will feel your heart accelerating, trying to keep up with your feet as you run down the molo, chasing the blue light of a fottuto cell phone.

CALL ME TOMORROW, ETTO.

Now, I know that maybe compared to you, I'm a very young man with myopic thoughts and small experience, living in a tiny town clinging to a coast very far away from the chair or the bed where you sit right now.

So who am I to tell you anything?

But if you'll listen, please let me tell you just this one thing: you have never felt such warmth as putting on dry clothes and walking into your own house as the sun is rising, of tiptoeing past your father's bedroom, where he is sleeping like a stone, of twirling a piece of fishing net around your wrist into infinity, of slipping under the covers of your brother's bed.

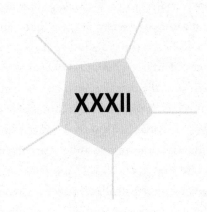

XXXII

*O*ne of the last comics Casella and I drew together was about a bunch of Japanese tourists from Hiroshima who fanned out over the world with their cameras around their necks, seeking retribution. They would smile and nod. They would compliment their subject's beauty and politely ask to take a picture. But when they clicked the shutters of their cameras, everyone in the frame disintegrated into a heap of ashes and dust. I drew four full-page panels of the news being broadcast throughout the world, the dust storms and panic spreading through the Champs-Élysées, the Taj Mahal, the Vatican, and Times Square. People tried to save themselves by flooding into places like Bishkek and Nome, Alaska—wherever there were no five-star hotels or three-star restaurants—but the Japanese tourists found them anyway, and they were no match for Japanese courtesy and flattery. In the end, only the Amish survived.

That's what it feels like in San Benedetto at the end of the summer when the tourists leave. No matter how long I live here, I will never be used to it, this sudden exodus and the complete stillness that follows. In one day, the beach is cleared of cabanas, gates, boardwalks, chaises, and umbrellas, the carts rumbling back and forth to the storage spaces under the passeggiata. The restaurant and shop owners pile their chairs and tables and racks onto the sidewalk and give everything a good scrub. The vicos fill with long shadows, and the voices of my neighbors echo against the stone walls. San Benedetto is ours again, and the intimacy will last all winter long.

In the shop, there's less work, and we're not open at all in the afternoons, so after lunch with Papà, I go up to work on the aula. The seventh panel becomes Mamma scooping and pushing apart the water and the land, and I give Luca the one next to hers, the one with the planets, only the planets morph into giant soccer balls, Luca's feet cocked under him, his leg muscles rippling as he goes to kick the sun. I start filling in the ancestors and prophets over the windows, and I draw Nonno and his lemon tree.

On Tuesday mornings, he still comes by and works the banco while Papà and I do the butchering, and sometimes we stop our work to listen to him joking with the nonne about things that happened fifty years ago, or telling Regina's kids that the calf's head is really the chupacabra, caught in the light of the last full moon.

They scream with delight.

"Now, who would like some chicken feet?"

"Me! Me!"

Papà and I watch through the beaded curtain as Nonno hands each of them a chicken foot, toes up, and the kids wave them in each other's faces, making lightsaber noises as they swish through the air.

This is the way I remember the shop when Luca and I stopped by on our way home from school—full of life, Nonna or Mamma chatting with the customers, keeping Papà and Nonno in the loop of gossip as they worked in the back room.

Sometime in October, I break down my first vitello. The cuts are not the clean, preschool shapes that come from Papà's hands, and a few of them are so ugly they will have to be ground up. But Papà and Nonno seem proud. One day I come in to find Yuri's jersey moved to the back, and my portrait hanging at the end of the line. And even though my days look pretty much the same as they ever were, I find out that there is a difference between turning on the lights of your father's shop and turning on the lights of your own. As Yuri would say, I'm not playing the catenaccio anymore. As Fede would say, it's my fucking choice.

Martina's is finished by the time the cold weather comes. At first Papà and Silvio insisted on waiting for her to come back and host the grand reopening, but the postcards kept coming from every corner of the world. Besides, it seemed a shame to let the new flat-screen stay dark while the calcio season was already under way. So they all started taking turns opening and closing the bar, and as a result, there are probably ten sets of keys to Martina's new door. Papà makes me an eleventh, so at least a few times a week, I can let myself into the bar at midnight, sit in the glow of the computer, and find Zhuki waiting on the other end, the parallelogram of afternoon sunlight on the wall behind her shifting slightly each day.

One thing they never tell you when someone close to you dies is that it will change every relationship you have. Even with the person you're mourning. Since you will be different, you will see them differently, and what you had together will morph into something new. The same goes for the living. I thought I'd gotten to know Papà over the months of working side by side at the back table, breaking down the meat, or watching him play calcio or become friends with Yuri off the field. But it turns out the way I really get to know him is in those late nights talking to Zhuki, when I discover how Papà must have felt in Vigo so many years ago. I start to see the man who would try to drive a Vespa all the way to Piedmont. The man who had so much love for a woman, it was enough to stretch to another continent, and even another realm.

What do Zhuki and I talk about? We talk about the future sometimes, but mostly we squander our time on stupidaggini. Because once you see a tomorrow and a next week and a next year, you can afford to. We talk about Yuri and Papà, Little Yuri and Principessa, and all the people in San Benedetto who ask about them. We laugh about Yuri's old dream of melting right into the American pot and walking the streets unrecognized. Instead, he went on one talk show and instantly became a star. The Americans, they love his footwork and his jokes, his Scottish-Ukrainian-Italian English, his single-father pathos, and his philosophizing about calcio. He's invited to all the talk shows, fund-raisers, and red carpets, there are several sponsorship deals in the works, and even rumors of television and movie roles. Yuri has clearly won the breakup. Vanni Fucci moved on from Tatiana to steal another teammate's girlfriend, and by Christmas, Tatiana has skulked back into the kick line with the other blond, scandalized former WAGs.

It is the comedy of life, no?

XXXIII

e are near the end now, and I know there are many of you who call it soccer and not calcio, who—like I once did—will still try to argue that calcio is not a real sport. How it takes more skill to play baseball or more courage to play American football or how basketball's high scores and ticking clock are so much more exciting. You complain about the tie games and the vagueness of injury time. You compare the Italians dropping on the field in agony to opera, and laugh about how all the Europeans make it seem as if calcio is a matter of life and death.

It isn't, of course. It's much more important than that. It's a matter of hope.

People dedicate themselves to calcio, season after season, for the same reason they keep getting married even though they're tripping over their friends' divorces wherever they go. For the same reason Regina Salveggio is pregnant again with another brat even though she can't handle the first two. For the same reason the tourists come to San Benedetto every summer even though they go straight back to the same sweaty offices and boring jobs. Because the rim of a calcio stadium, the railing of a baby's crib, and the line between sky and sea are the few places on earth where the firmament cracks open and shows the hope of the world.

Or maybe just the deep longing for it.

Either way.

Maybe this is why I keep going on the aula even though I know I will never finish. As it turns out, all those annoying thirteen-year-olds who've been hanging around are going to be entering high school next year, and enough of them aren't screwups so that the liceo can reopen. Father Marco says Charon heard the news and can't wait to get back from Rome and whip them into shape. I would just like to be there for the moment when he walks into his aula for the first time. Will his mouth gape open? Will he finally be speechless? He'll probably have Pete the Comb Man paint over it immediately. Then again, maybe he won't.

Papà's hope is the San Benedetto Calcio League. Papà and I play on the same team now, the San Benedetto Fire, named after Yuri's team in Chicago, and on Saturday afternoons, I help Papà coach the five-year-olds on our developmental team, as he likes to call it. The San Benedetto Sparks. For three hours a week, he clutches his forehead as he watches them run around the field in a cluster, kicking the ball with their cleats like they're hacking away at a block of ice.

"Play your position! Play your position! Where are my defenders? Where did my defenders go? That's it, pass it! Pass it! No, no . . . the other way! The other way!" He shouts with as much passion as when he watches the matches at Martina's, but whether they win or lose, he buys them ice cream and tells them that one day they will be stars in Serie A. And as assistant coach, I try to pass on all the things Yuri, Mykola, Ihor, and Zhuki taught me. Look up. Keep an eye on your teammates. Don't be afraid. Shut off your brain once in a while. And for God's sake, stop playing the catenaccio, this silly game of defense.

Maybe twenty years from now, they'll know what I mean.

In June, almost a year from the day I first set eyes on the Ukrainians, the world stops spinning, and six and a half billion people on every continent but America sit paralyzed in front of television sets, watching the World

Cup finals. Whatever poverty, disease, war, scandal, or terrorism plagues their country, it is all forgotten for a few weeks. Because calcio is the panacea, the pill, the tincture, the balm for every ill. In fact, maybe this is why the Americans don't understand it. Because they already live in the promised land, where hard work is rewarded, people fall in love in sixty minutes minus commercials, and scandals, if they happen at all, are roundly denounced and swiftly punished.

By mid-June, Italy is again mired in them. Match fixing, steroids, illegal recruiting, affairs—all of it this time.

"A bunch of stronzos they are, these Azzurri."

"If they lose the World Cup this time, they deserve it."

"All they care about is their bonuses anyway."

This is what I hear all June as the tourists start to fill the streets. It's a smaller crowd this year because many of the Germans have decided to stay in their own country to watch the action, either in the stadiums or at the fan fests.

WHEN ARE YOU COMING OVER?

I TOLD FEDE I'D WATCH THE PREGAME AT CAMILLA'S.

IT'S ALREADY PACKED OVER HERE.

SAVE ME A SEAT.

The Ukrainians came for Christmas. I mounted an all-out campaign. Everyone in town was in on it, trying to make me look good. I knew I'd made great progress when Yuri, Mykola, and Ihor sat me down and told me if I broke Zhuki's heart they would come after me and the police wouldn't be able to find the pieces.

At the end of January, she was back with all her things, and they put her in charge of Martina's.

I know. It's a miracle. And do you know how when you see something once, you get the pattern in your eye and you start to see it all over? That's exactly what happens, and I realize the world is full of miracles.

Like Fede not talking about any girl but Camilla for ten months and counting.

Like Signor Cato going out to the molo to fish again.

Like Nello walking into Martina's distraught because Pia finally left him.

Like Guido and Nicola Nicolini inviting their parents over for dinner, and their parents accepting.

Like the multiplying photos of the four of us around the apartment, at least as many as the years we were together.

Like Yuri getting tickets to the World Cup for Papà and Silvio, and both of them flying to Germany for two weeks.

Like Ukraine—*Ukraine*, for God's sake—making it to the final eight teams, and the Azzurri *finally* throwing away the catenaccio.

"How can you tell?" I ask Zhuki.

"See the backs? They're usually well behind the line."

"Which ones are the backs?"

"See . . . right . . ." Her index finger floats in front of the screen, but her voice trails off. Unbelievably, the rounds have worked out so Ukraine is playing the Azzurri in the quarterfinals tonight. Zhuki's blazing yellow shirt is bobbing in a sea of azure, and I imagine Papà in the stadium in Germany, his hands clasped to his mouth, barely breathing as he sorts out his loyalties.

At Martina's, the tables have been stacked at the edges of the room, and rows of chairs are lined up in front of the flat-screen. For the past three weeks, there has been a strict seating hierarchy, the regulars and the old guys up front, the overflow sent to Camilla's, any perceived violations sorted out by Mino.

A cheer goes up on all sides. Zhuki hunches on her elbows, sputtering jagged consonants and raggedy vowels. Mamma was the same. She loved speaking Italian, but whenever she was upset or moved or passionately arguing about something, she would revert back to English, and not just English, but an almost incomprehensible stream of California slang.

By the fifth minute, I stop asking for explanations. Zhuki and Nonno and everyone else are caught in the same trance, their concentration never wavering, even when Vanni Fucci heads it into the goal in the sixth minute, even when Luca Toni scores the second and third goals in quick succession. The bar explodes. Signor Cato stands up, spreads his arms wide and kisses the screen.

"I love you, Luca Toni! I want to make love to you!"

"Come on, Yuri," I hear Nonno whisper on my left. "Let's at least make it a real contest."

But Cannavaro has been clinging to Yuri like a barnacle, and he's been unable to get a pass, much less score a goal. Zhuki's neck and shoulders soften, and as the minutes line up and the massacre continues, she sinks lower on her elbows. Behind us, the crowd is calling for blood.

"Get those sonofawhores, get them!"

"No mercy!"

"Kill them!"

But there's a close-up of Yuri, and suddenly the shouting is muffled, the cursing tamped down to half of what it was. Out of respect. Not for the Yuri who's running around the field in a yellow jersey, making a run at our own Gigi Buffon, but for the Yuri who ran up and down the field at the liceo, the Yuri who passed the ball even to the weaker players, the Yuri who would politely wave whenever he scored a goal, but shout at the top of his lungs when anyone else did.

The match runs into injury time, and it's clear that the Ukrainians are done for. It's then that I hear it start in the back, a low, quiet rumbling. One voice, then two, then five.

"Yu-ri. Yu-ri. Yu-ri. Yu-ri."

It spreads across the rows and fills the room.

"Yu-ri. Yu-ri. Yu-ri. Yu-ri."

Zhuki finally hears it through her trance. She picks her elbows up off her knees, turns around, and smiles at the rest of the room.

"Thank you," she says.

The injury time evaporates, and the stadium erupts in cheers and flares. The Azzurri jump on each other and run around the field, shouting and pointing to the heavens or their children at home in their pajamas. They start to peel off their wet jerseys and exchange them with the Ukrainians, along with a pat on the culo or the back, or even a caress of the head. There's a close-up of Vanni Fucci throwing figs in the air, and another one of Yuri, alone in the middle of the field. He's on his knees, his hands grabbing fistfuls of grass, his forehead pressed to the ground like a Muslim praying. The bar goes silent.

"Tell your brother sorry, Zhuki."

Signor Cato is the first to offer his condolences, but pretty soon, they are filing past her like at a funeral, shaking her hand and patting her on the back like she's one of the men.

"Next time."

"2010."

"South Africa."

"Tell your brother he played a good game."

Zhuki and I end up sitting on the rocks, leaning into each other, the water washing around us.

"That was his last big match," Zhuki says. "He's going to finish the season for the Fire, and then he's done."

"Isn't he too young to retire?"

"He wants to end his career while he still has his legs. Now he feels like the scandal and the divorce are behind him, and he has made Ukraine proud."

"When does the season end in Chicago?"

"In October. Nearly the opposite of here."

"And what's he going to do then?"

"He says he wants to go back to Ukraine, get a house in the country, and start a training institute with Mykola and Ihor. He wants to raise Little Yuri and Principessa near their grandmother."

"I can't believe she finally left that guy."

"I can't tell when I talk to her whether she left him or he left her. Doesn't matter, I suppose."

"And what about Yuri's Hollywood career?"

"Ach. Yuri says he is too old to fall in love with another country."

"And you?"

She grins. "I am younger than he is."

The next day, Yuri makes his retirement announcement a thousand kilometers away, and it's like a single tree falling in the Bavarian forest, a quiet bump among the crashing fortunes in Serie A that are strewn like postapocalyptic telephone poles across *Gazzetta dello Sport* and Sky News every morning. But this is part of the beauty and mystery of calcio—the inexplicable rise and fall of men and fortunes, and the surprises of fate.

We watch the rest of the quarterfinals. It's a blood bath, the referees thinning out the teams with red cards. When I ask Nonno who he wants to win each match, he says simply: "Whoever can beat France." And then for the next ten minutes he mumbles like someone mentally deranged about the 1998 World Cup in France and the cheating-bastard French that stole the quarterfinal from us.

Portugal beats England.

France beats Portugal.

We beat Germany.

"I can't believe it!" Nonno shouts. "I can't believe it! We're in the finals with those rotten-bastard French again. Has there ever been a people so vain as the French?"

I'm sure the French are laughing at us across the border, too. Déjà vu, they say, hunh-hunh-hunh. A replay of the 1998 quarterfinals, of the 2000 Euro Cup, both of which the French won. To make it worse, the final is played in the foreground of the crescendoing investigations in Rome, which will decide the destiny of thirteen of the Azzurri and their teams back home.

It's a clear July evening in Berlin when the two teams walk out of the tunnel and line up on the field, clutching the hands of children, a show of peace before the bloodletting. "La Marseillaise" and "Fratelli d'Italia" echo across the world. Shakira shakes her hips, and the whole world stares, eyes cast upward, mouths slightly gaped, faces frozen. The human equivalent of a stopped clock.

From the first minute, the match rages. Some of the French players are from the '98 team, a little slower and a little older, with a little less hair. Zidane was always Luca's favorite even though he played for Juventus and even though Nonno spent hours trying to convince him not to admire a Frenchman. When the second half starts, the sky turns dark, and I imagine all the people watching across the world, basking in the glow of flat-screens in trendy bars or velvet-choked pubs, huddled in living rooms and church basements, or crouched around a screen as big as a hand, taking turns cranking the generator.

It comes down to a shoot-out, just like in '98. Man vs. Keeper. Man vs. Himself. The goalkeepers, Gigi for the Azzurri and Barthez for the French, have both been here before, and they embrace each other before the firing squad begins.

Pirlo. Gol.

Wiltord. Gol.

Materazzi. Gol.

Trezeguet. Miss.

De Rossi. Gol.

Abidal. Gol.

Del Piero. Gol.

Sagnol. Gol.

Grosso. Gol.

And it's Grosso who wins it this time, or rather, Trezeguet who muffs it. Trezeguet, hero of the last time, who now takes his turn in the tragedy.

And it's Gigi spreading his Mickey Mouse hands wide as he streaks across the field, and Barthez, the French keeper, sitting against the post, paralyzed from the loss.

And it's Zidane sitting in the clubhouse missing it all. Zidane, who came in a hero of France and a gentleman foreigner of the Italian leagues, who goes out a head-butting rogue. And Materazzi, who comes in a rogue and goes out a hero for saying whatever it is the lip-readers say he said to Zidane, forcing the French to play with ten men.

I know that you who call it soccer instead of calcio will have trouble keeping track of these unfamiliar names, so go back now, and substitute the name of anyone you know. Maybe even your own.

The Azzurri leap across the field and lie on the ground in piles of disbelief. Clean-cut gray-haired men in suits jump up and down like little boys. French players stand around in a daze, stroking their chins as fireworks light up the Berlin sky. A snowstorm of ticker tape and toilet tissue covers the field, the white blotting out everything but the Rai announcer's voice.

"It is finished! It is finished! It is finished! It is finished!"

Everyone at Martina's is shouting and hugging and jumping up and down, and I imagine the vibrations shaking the foundation of the building clear down to the center of the earth, to the cavern where they say the devil sleeps, his muscles shifting and twitching under his matted fur, the tremors from hundreds of millions of reconstituted hearts disturbing his sleep.

Outside, fireworks and flares whistle and boom over the sea. People are already flooding the streets, jumping into their cars and blaring horns, running down the passeggiata chanting, singing, and waving flags. The Band emerges one instrument at a time, adding notes to the cacophony.

The rest of the summer will be more chaos. Martina will be reunited with her postcards and be so moved by the reconstruction of the bar that she and Zhuki will start serving food. Zhuki will travel back and forth from San Benedetto to Chicago to Strilky. The German tourists will return for the second half of the summer. All of Italy will be engulfed by the demotions, penalty points, and fines drifting down the boot like a poisonous gas. Juventus will be stripped of the Scudetto, Milan, Fiorentina, and Lazio cowed.

There will be a hundred hopeless endings, and these will be written clearly across the expressions of the suited men who fill the flat-screen every night. Even though they try to set their jaws and fix their stares, I can see the shadows of resignation and regret. They know what I know now, that it is impossible to go back to the beginning. You can't go back to the big bang or the primordial swamp any more than our family can go back to the nosebleed seats of Estadio Balaídos in Vigo, or these scandalized players can go back to being little boys running through dusty streets, kicking a peeling calcio ball.

Instead, you have to cobble together your own beginnings where you can, out of imperfect clay. Messy synthesis instead of clean separation this time around. The sky cleaving to the earth, the sea lapping up on the land,

323

the light infiltrating the darkness. And God is up there doing his part, too, throwing down terraces for us to train on and people to wander into our crooked paths—Ukrainians and French, calcio players and soccer players, little boys with dreams they will never accomplish and old men with foggy memories of the past. Paparazzi, showgirls, fathers, mothers, brothers, sons. And nonne. Lots and lots of nonne.

Zhuki and I, we escape to the end of the molo. We watch the steady streams of headlights and cell phone screens, the explosions of sparklers and sprays of fireworks in the sky. I think about Papà and Yuri and Silvio in Berlin, and I pull the fishing line into an orbit around my wrist. I imagine that it connects me not only to Mamma but Papà and Luca, too, and that we can all feel each other's gentle tugging as we move around the universe.

Nonno has brought the 2CV of course, and he leads the procession down the passeggiata, the griffin finally rearing up in victory on the hood. Nonno is behind the wheel, sitting tall like a Roman emperor, and Nonna is by his side, her white hair blown into messiness, her arm leaning out the passenger window.

"Viva l'Italia! Viva l'Italia!" Nonno shouts at the top of his lungs as he blares the horn. "And death to France!"

Young guys leap onto the running boards and cling to the sides so that the little 2CV looks like a monster sprouting heads. I spot a few girls from the class below me holding the screens of their cell phones high in the air, their faces striped with red, white, and green, and flags trailing off their shoulders like the capes of superheroes. I watch the faces going by and they all look familiar, even the tourists who've been swept up into the crowd.

Zhuki and I sit out on the molo the whole night, watching the celebrations. Midnight comes and morning follows.

The next day.

And the next.

And the one after that.

And I look around, and I see that it is good.

Acknowledgments

I first went to Italy in 1992 at the behest of Christina Hieber, the same friend who dragged me to Poland for the first time. I was so taken with the country that I taught myself Italian and spent the next twenty years traveling to Italy whenever I could. The most significant of these trips was the summer I spent in Alassio as an au pair to the Gazzolo-Ienca family. It was there that I was first introduced to both daily life on the Riviera and the international congregation of calcio. Laura, Massimo, Pietro, and Carlo, thank you sincerely for all of your kindnesses then and since. I would also like to take this opportunity to publicly apologize for teaching Pietro and Carlo to chant "U.S.A." during the 1998 World Cup; at the time, I didn't realize how serious an offense this was.

Thank you to the rest of the Ienca, Gazzolo and Bonora families, especially Chicca, Sandro, Camilla and Carolina, as well as Susan Scott Hettleman and Stefania Bucci, who both showed me the magic of their own personal Italys. Thanks to Danielle Bonneau for initial research and Annie Hawes for her book chronicling her and her sister's adventures in Liguria. For suggesting, checking and rechecking all things Italian, thank you to Camilla Bonora of Alassio, Charlene Floreani of Chicago, and Daniele Minisini of Bologna and Austin, Texas.

I have read several books on SO-chair in the past few years, but Paddy

Acknowledgments

Agnew's *Forza Italia* and Joe McGinniss's *The Miracle of Castel di Sangro* were my favorites and the most informative for my purposes. Thank you also to Phil Imm and Michael Borisov for initial research, as well as to the Chicago Fire for access to practice fields and locker rooms. I owe an especially great debt of gratitude to my colleagues, Ian McCarthy and Emily Steffen, who used their calcio expertise and sensitivity to language in reading final drafts. Also, this book would not have been as much fun to write if it weren't for all the calcio fans out there meticulously chronicling the minutes of matches, the miraculous goals, the fan club chants and the funniest segments of *Have You Heard The Latest About Totti?* I realize now that these are all labors of love and celebrations of life.

For my education in butchering, I am eternally grateful to Antonello Valdora and his parents, proprietors of Macelleria Valdora in Alassio, Italy, for patiently answering all of my questions and allowing me to take photographs of every inch of their shop. Thanks also to Bill Buford and Julie Powell, whose meticulous written descriptions of butchering saved me the time and grist of doing my own apprenticeship.

Dante is, of course, a major influence on this novel. San Benedetto is populated largely with versions of his characters, and I have incorporated some of his imagery as well. I still would not call myself a "Dantista" by any stretch, but for the knowledge of Dante I do have, I am most indebted to Anthony Esolen. His translation of the *Divine Comedy* inspired me and kept me going, and his annotations and explanations were as constant a guide as Virgil was to Dante. I was also fortunate to come across the writings and podcasts of Robert Barron. Without the wisdom of both of these men, Dante's words wouldn't have made much sense in either my life or my work.

The creation of this book has itself been a winding plot. Thank you to the students and faculty at the Ukrainian Catholic University in L'viv. It was because of them that in the summer of 2007, I ended up in a pasture in rural Ukraine, where I began to write this book in longhand. Thanks especially to Romcik and The Prince for dumpster-diving and recovering the first five chapters, which were inadvertently thrown away, and to Yuri Fil for inspiring the first chapter and for loaning out his name. The nickname

Acknowledgments

Zhuki was also borrowed from a young woman I met there but have since lost track of.

From the first word of this book to the last, I have continued to teach at Whitney M. Young Magnet High School in Chicago, and I am grateful for their continued support as well as the support of the community at St. Clement Church. Thank you to my first readers, Lisa Cloitre, Lizz Graf, and the Petersburg Pig Cooperative, and to JP Fanning for a key detail.

The Hemingway Foundation, the PEN Foundation, and the UCross Foundation gave me the space, time, and courage to fight through the murkiness in the middle of the process, and I can't thank them—the organizations and the individuals—enough.

Thank you to my friend and agent, Wendy Sherman, who, with her grace and integrity, has helped me navigate this new world intact. Thanks to Anjali Singh, who has without a doubt made me a better writer, and to Millicent Bennett, Wendy Sheanin, Anne Tate, Nina Pajak, and Julia Glass, for showing me their passion for books and being such strong advocates of this book in particular.

I am, as ever, grateful to my family and friends and especially my husband, Will, for his love and understanding, and for being the sturdy molo that I can both dive off and swim back to.

Finally, I would like to remember three of my classmates at Dartmouth—Gary, Dan and Mark—who left this world far too soon. Many times as I was writing this book, I heard each one's vox clamantis in deserto.

About the Author

BRIGID PASULKA spent the summer of 1998 as an au pair for a family in Alassio, Italy, where she was first introduced to small-town Riviera life, the Italian obsession with soccer, and the butcher shop that features in her second novel, *The Sun and Other Stars*. Her debut novel, *A Long, Long Time Ago and Essentially True*, won the 2010 Hemingway Foundation/PEN Award and was a Barnes & Noble Discover Great New Writers selection. Brigid currently lives in Chicago with her husband and runs the writing center at a public high school. Visit her website at brigidpasulka.com.